Willie

A Romance

HEATHER ROBERTSON

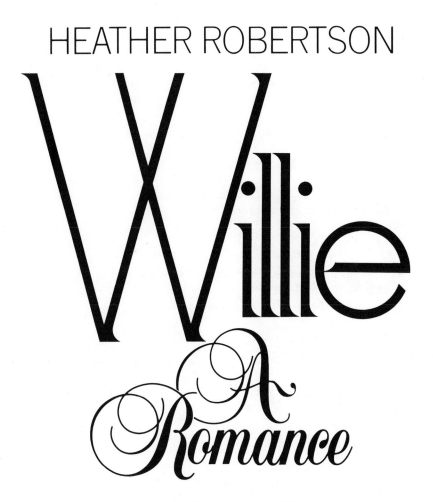

Willie

A Romance

VOLUME 1 OF THE KING YEARS

James Lorimer & Company, Publishers
Toronto 1983

ISBN 0-88862-671-1 cloth

Design: Don Fernley
Jacket photo: Arnaud Maggs

Canadian Cataloguing in Publication Data
Robertson, Heather, 1942-
    Willie: a romance

1. King, William Lyon Mackenzie, 1874-1950 — Fiction.
2. Canada — History — 1867-1914 — Fiction. 3. Canada —
History — 1914-1945 — Fiction. I. Title.

PS8585.023W54 1983   C813′.54   C83-098849-1
PR9199.3.R6285W54 1983

James Lorimer & Company, Publishers
Egerton Ryerson Memorial Building
35 Britain Street
Toronto, Ontario M5A 1R7

Printed and bound in Canada
6 5 4 3 2 1   83 84 85 86 87 88

Acknowledgements

Research for this book was undertaken with the assistance of a Canada Council Explorations grant.

The fictionalized portrait of William Lyon Mackenzie King is based on King's personal diary and other papers in the Public Archives of Canada. The medical report on pages 236-7 and the diary entries on pages 255-9 and 277-8 are taken directly from the King papers, with some editing and adaptation.

The letters of Talbot Papineau are in the Public Archives of Canada. They have been abridged and adapted for the purposes of this book. Helen Paulin of Toronto kindly allowed me to read letters from Talbot Papineau to his law partner, Andrew McMaster.

I am indebted also to the essay "The King of Clubs: A Psychobiography of William Lyon Mackenzie King, 1893-1900" by Lynn McIntyre and Dr. Joel Jeffries of the Clarke Institute of Psychiatry in Toronto.

Without the assistance of my editor, Roy MacSkimming, I could not have brought King out of chaos.

This novel is based on real people and events but the story, the dialogue and the characterizations are completely fictional.

H.R.
Toronto, April 1983

PROLOGUE

Meach Lake, Quebec
Saturday, July 22, 1950

"The old bugger's dead at last!"

Charlie calls down the news just before 10 p.m. I'd guessed it when I heard the sudden break in the music, then silence, the murmur of the announcer's voice. Charlie's excited steps, the bang of the screen door. She turns the radio up full blast when the announcement ends. Guy Lombardo goes back to "Chattanooga Choo-Choo." I can hear Charlie laughing as she dances.

I lie on my back in the black lake, my heavy, sulphur-coloured legs sinking slowly, my tits keeping me up like twin zeppelins, watching the stars. Which star are you, Willie? Or have you had time to make it to Heaven yet? Trust you to die on a starry summer night and spoil everyone's weekend.

I will have to go back to Ottawa tomorrow and print up my pictures. I have, by luck, the last photographs of Canada's late prime minister, the Rt. Hon. William Lyon Mackenzie King, taken last Tuesday at Kingsmere, four days before his death. They will be worth something. At least, Willie, you left me this.

I didn't really want to go to Kingsmere. Nobody wanted another photograph of Mackenzie King. The press had bushel baskets of them and Willie hadn't been news since he'd retired from politics two years ago. He was an old man, sick — senile, people said. I didn't want to see him. But McGregor's voice on the telephone was imploring. Then Willie came on the line himself. He sounded hoarse, far-away. They were naming a bridge after him, he said, and he wanted to have a photograph in case he couldn't attend the ceremonies, although he was quite recovered from his heart attack. I would come for lunch, a quiet talk. He'd send the car.

It was a warm, sweet morning when we turned up the driveway past the stone wall I'd watched him build — how long? thirty? thirty-four years ago? — and pulled up in front of the old farmhouse, a pretty stone house all gussied up with pillars and porticos and pagodas now, mute evidence of Willie's unerring instinct for the banal. I wondered, as I went in, whether he still got his flowers free from the Experimental Farm the way he used to.

The house smelled of medicine. And dog. I was introduced to Pat III, a big, rough terrier who jumped on me and tore my stockings. I told McGregor I would not take any more dog pictures. "No, no!" he said and rubbed his eyes. He looked very tired.

Willie was in the cool shadows of the sitting room, bent over a desk, scribbling with his stumpy little pencil, his nose, with the old wire-rimmed glasses sliding down, nearly touching the paper. How little that pose had changed in the years since he and I had shared a room, those long summer days filled with the scratching of his pencil and the clatter of my typewriter, writing, always writing, editing, revising, rewriting, surrounded by cardboard boxes full of unopened books and unanswered letters and the thick, thumbed notebooks of the diary. Always the diary. I would have liked to photograph him this way, at his desk, but he would never stand for it. He hated to be taken by surprise, in private. He liked to confront the camera head-on, remove his glasses, straighten his back and put on his jack-o'-lantern grin. He never understood why he looked so silly.

He tried to rise when he saw me but shook like a leaf and sank back into his chair. "Please don't bother," I said. I was shocked by how dry and brittle his hand was. And his face, gaunt and shrunken, the skin stretched over his cheekbones and hanging in loose folds around his throat. I had never seen Willie thin before. His eyes were pale, watery, his skin grey, and beads of sweat stood out on his forehead. He was bundled up in a heavy tweed suit and a scarf.

"My memoirs," he said, fluttering his hand over the stacks of papers on his desk. "I am trying to get the groundwork laid. I had hoped to find someone competent to carry out this task but as usual the only thing is to do everything myself."

He breathed in short, sucking gasps. I suggested perhaps another time, when he was better.

"I am quite well!" he snapped. "You see, my appetite is coming back!" He pointed to the remains of a boiled egg and slice of toast on a tray by the desk and smiled triumphantly at me in his shy, childlike, captivating way.

I suggested we take the pictures on the lawn by the sundial. He rang a little bell and a nurse materialized, clucking and scolding and squawking and soothing, followed by faithful McGregor. They each took an arm and Willie shuffled slowly towards the door.

"A little fresh air and an invigorating walk will set me up in no time," he rasped. He shrugged away McGregor and the nurse as we came out the front door, and he and I made our way across the grass alone. He gripped my arm in a vise.

"Have you seen Mother?" he whispered.

"No," I answered, glancing around. "Not in a long time."

"They have taken my little table away, Cookie. My tapping table. They say it excites me too much."

His faded eyes were quick with fear.

"The spirits have left me," he said. "I've lost them!" His grip tightened, trembled, his eyes brimmed with tears. "I am surrounded by evil influences."

He glanced back. McGregor and the nurse were standing by the door, watching.

"I haven't slept more than one hour in the last two nights," he hissed. "Not one hour! Not one of the people looking after me thinks of anything but their own comfort! They bring me wet nightgowns in the middle of the night, and cold tea, and nobody will tell me what's wrong with me! They make me take whisky and opium — to make me sleep, they tell me, but I don't sleep! Don't they see I must have calm, I must have rest? No man in my position is as badly cared for as I am! Well, I have refused the whisky at least."

We reached the sundial. The old stump it used to sit on had been replaced by a marble pedestal.

"I took your mother's picture here, remember?"

"Yes."

"She must be nearby."

"I saw a doe the other day. I thought for a moment she might be Mother. But she ran away."

Noon. The sun was hot. A cicada shrilled in the pines.

"I have decided to destroy all my papers of a personal nature," Willie said. "Such things are easily misunderstood. I have a number of letters."

"Yes?"

"You would like me to return yours?"

"If you like."

"In exchange for my own?"

"Of course."

He sighed, his shoulders hunched, his eyes averted — fixed on the sundial.

"Nothing will be said then, about our little secret?"

"Not as long as I live."

He raised his head and smiled again. The sweat was standing in drops on his cheeks and running down his neck. He mopped the top of his skull slowly with a damp handkerchief. His weight on my arm was almost insupportable. I waved towards the house. The chauffeur rushed up and practically carried Willie back to the house. A heavy wooden chair was produced and Willie was propped up in it. An engraved brass plate was affixed to the chair, just behind Willie's head.

"This chair," said McGregor reverently, "is from the Presbyterian manse in Scotland where Mr. King's father was born."

Balls. Willie and I bought that chair in the Byward Market. I was willing to pay $2 for it but Willie had screwed the poor fellow down to $1, or Jewed, as he would have said, had the shoe been on the other foot. The junk dealer said it had belonged to Robbie Burns. It was just as ugly as ever.

The nurse handed Willie a glass of water and a pill. He swallowed as meekly as a bird. I took my pictures. He smiled. As I was setting up my last shot his head suddenly slid to one side, and he fell into a deep, serene sleep.

"I'll be in to check the proofs," said McGregor, walking me to the car.

So now Willie is dead and I still have his letters. Who has mine?

Ottawa
Sunday, July 23, 1950

The bells of the carillon are driving me nuts. Must be the fifteenth time around for "Abide With Me." All Willie's favourite hymns chiming out from the Peace Tower in endless succession. There is no escape.

Ottawa
Monday, July 24, 1950

The radio is giving a head count of the number of people who've filed past Willie's coffin in the Hall of Fame — 18,553. Francis Twillersly (one of the Young Liberals, as the courtiers are now called) has a man keeping count. He wants to break Sir Wilfrid Laurier's 1919 record of 30,000 mourners. The Liberal Party is busing them in from Toronto and Trois Rivières. Twillersly's flunkies hover around the Hill, urging the long, shuffling line a little faster, a quick peek at the simian cadaver in the shabby black suit, then zip, zip, out the door. "We'll beat it easy," Twillersly said this afternoon. "City's full of tourists. Yanks love this sort of thing."

I took pictures of Willie lying in state, so small, a shrunken stranger. His shirt was frayed at the collar and cuffs. A champion of poverty to the end. He looked as though he'd suffered. Well he might. A bad conscience. A hard death. His cheek felt cold and stiff. Poor Willie. I feel sorry, now.

Retouched my photos tonight to eliminate the six-foot cross of red and white roses at the head of Willie's coffin. J.D. Rockefeller Jr. sent it. Mr. Rockefeller has been invited to the funeral. He has declined. A snub. Willie was used to snubs. He seemed to thrive on them. Dignity has eluded him in death as in life.

Ottawa
Tuesday, July 25, 1950

The will has been opened. Willie has left a fortune: almost a million dollars, counting Kingsmere and Laurier House, which have been left to the nation. All Ottawa is agog. His closest friends, with hardly any money at all, were giving him little presents up to the end, out of pity. Even his Buick was a gift from Sam McLaughlin. Why on earth didn't he spend it? people ask me. He was constipated, I explain.

He has left me $3,000. I didn't expect it. I didn't expect an invitation to the funeral either, but it came this morning. I shall wear white. Willie loved white. White dresses, white hair, white roses. Stupid Joan Patteson has ordered red roses for the hearse. She will wear black.

The *Citizen* called today asking for an interview about Willie. I said I was too upset. *I'm* not going to lie. People who've hated Willie for years are singing his praises. His cunning is wisdom, his lies are prudence, his selfishness is strength, his superstition is faith. Sanctification proceeds.

The body count is only 29,276. Twillersly will have to hustle. Maybe he'll run them through twice.

Ottawa
Wednesday, July 26, 1950

Sunny and warm, a good day for a funeral. Willie's luck. All the government offices and shops were closed and thousands of tourists turned out, so there was a good crowd. Willie would have been pleased. The final count was 34,093 according to Twillersly, so Willie got his record. The difference was that the 30,000 people who followed Laurier to his grave were weeping.

The service was short, full of the romantic scripture Willie loved and the lies he accepted as truth, his consideration and thoughtfulness, the countless acts of kindness and of love, as if it wasn't plain to all that love was the one thing Willie was incapable of. The preacher got going about life after death and I got nervous, but he came out of it all right without talking about the seances.

I had a seat in the front row with Willie's other girlfriends: three old flames all in a row, Mathilde, his first love, on my right, a bent old lady, eighty-five at least, then Julia, Princess Cantacuzene, daughter of Ulysses S. Grant, a gaunt old bird but tough as rawhide. I am the youngest by more than twenty years, but fifty-six is fifty-six and it was laughable to think that even Willie would find anything seductive in our flabby flesh. Did he have a sense of humour after all? The chief concubine, Mrs. Patteson, was blubbering behind, next to Mr. Patteson, still rosy and robust at eighty-one, the immovable impediment to her happiness, so she thought. We all shook hands after the service, smiled, and talked about the weather. What was there to say, except that we had outlived him? A triumph, given Willie's rapacious nature, and revenge enough.

I walked to the station behind the hearse, alone in a crowd of morning coats and pinstripes, stepping to the beat of a single muffled drum. It was a civilian funeral, thank God, no guns or soldiers, Willie riding, as usual, in the comfort of a black Cadillac limousine. I half expected to see the door open and Willie step out, smiling in that shy way of his and tipping his hat to the crowd, a political Lazarus once more. How he hated to lose!

We waited in the station while the coffin was loaded onto the baggage car for the trip to Toronto — not Kingsmere, as he'd once hoped, beneath the ruins, a shrine for the faithful, but Mount Pleasant Cemetery, next to Mother. Hers to the end. The engine gave two toots and the train slowly pulled away. I glanced at the clock. Its face was blurred through my tears but I could see that the hands were in a straight line. Exactly 6 p.m. Ah Willie, you are with me yet.

We will go to war in Korea this week. The cabinet is unanimous. The announcement would have been made last week, Twillersly said, except Willie balked. He told the Duke of Windsor over tea that Korea was a Yankee plot to annex Canada, Australia and New Zealand. The Duke told the Duchess and the Duchess, of course, told everyone. "The Old Man must have been slipping," Twillersly said. "He was the best damn friend the Yanks ever had."

Is that what killed you, Willie? An attack of heart?

Ottawa
Sunday, October 22, 1950

Twillersly returned my letters today. They were tied with a yellowed satin ribbon and smelled of rose petals. It gave me a chill, thinking of all those students from the University of Toronto truffling through the kitchen midden of Willie's career, their curious, callous eyes searching for tidbits to be passed around and smacked over. Have they found the crystal ball yet, the plaster cast of Abe Lincoln's hand, the trunks full of Christmas cards and dinner invitations, the false teeth and eyeglasses, the signed photograph of Adolf Hitler in a silver frame that Willie reluctantly removed from his mantlepiece the day Canada declared war against Nazi Germany? Have they found the notebooks where he listed the bribes he'd taken, persuading himself they were gifts from generous friends, or the transcripts he kept of his talks with St. Luke, through the medium of the tapping table? Have they dug up the hundreds of photographs of Mother, her wedding ring and lock of hair, or the pictures of Willie I took over nearly forty years, each embossed with a fleur-de-lis, Photo by Lily, Photographer to the Prime Minister? It was a painful and unrewarding relationship, since no one wanted pictures of Willie except Willie himself and he wanted them posed, retouched, faked and framed. Willie was hypnotized by the camera, unlike most unphotogenic people, and eternally optimistic that the next shot, the very next snap would reveal some miraculous hidden beauty. I tried, but nothing worked. Often, after he became famous, we would sneak into the Regent or the Capitol after the lights went down, sitting through Mickey Mouse until the newsreel, and there he'd be, waddling down Parliament Hill in his raccoon coat grinning like a manic snowman, or on the terrace at Quebec, sandwiched between Churchill and Roosevelt, stiff, black, an anxious chaperone between two flamboyant courtesans, his puzzled face turning first to one, then the other, ignored. And then we would sneak out again and sometimes, in the back of the limousine, Willie would weep. It was one of his disconcerting characteristics, this childish tendency to bawl, and it aroused pity, which some women mistook for love. Pity has never been my strong suit.

"The diary will be burned," said Twillersly.

"It seems a shame."

"He left no instructions."

"He often read from it aloud. It was his Testament, you know."

"The Word."

"He thought that when things were written, they were true. Life imitated art."

"Nobody can read it. The Old Man wrote like a mouse with muddy feet."

"It's not so hard."

"You've read it?"

"A little. I used to type for Mr. King, when I was young."

"Well, it would be a help. The personal stuff, people go for that, nothing dicey, add a little colour, don't have to worry about Dawson, the historian, he's safe.... You could read it into a dictaphone, McGregor type it up, save time, hell of a lot of it, fifty-seven years almost, hard to know what the Old Man found to write about."

"I'm not sure...."

"Money's no problem. Rockefeller's paying the shot. Oodles of boodle."

"Well, I've got my work, and the Legion poppy drive coming up, and the civic election, and I promised Charlotte Whitton I'd help with her campaign...."

"You're not tied up with that crazy bat are you?"

"She's a friend. We grew up together in Renfrew."

"She's a raving Tory."

"I am told that some of your young history students are not perfectly, how shall I put it, reliable?"

"Who?"

I didn't give any names. He'll find out. Some pimply heads will roll, I'm afraid.

Strange I should feel protective towards Willie now. I am getting cautious in my old age, comfortable, a Rockcliffe matron like all the other Rockcliffe matrons, mink and pearls, an old Ottawa girl: Miss Lily Coolican, Liberal, life member of the Royal Canadian Legion, past-president of the Women's Canadian Club, the capital's leading portrait photographer, a handsome woman for my age, well-to-do, known to drink a little too much, an old friend of Mr. King's, if you know what I mean, too bad we never married, there was another man, I recall, killed in the war, no not the last war, the first. Broke my heart, so sad.

Am I afraid? Yes, not ashamed, but afraid. I have spent too long in the shadows under the black hood, to want to be exposed now, imprinted by accident on Willie's historical monument, a station of the cross on his pilgrimage to immortality. He used me enough in life.

It was good of Twillersly to return my letters. Has he read them? I'll have to be nice to him.

Ottawa

Sunday, December 17, 1950

Willie's birthday. He would have been seventy-six. I took champagne to Laurier House. Everyone else had forgotten. We sat in Willie's study on the third floor and drank a toast.

"To the virgin King," said Twillersly.

We have scarcely made a dent in the diary. It may take as long to read as it did to write. I have taken the liberty of checking the important dates, those that concern me, and found what I had suspected: the diary is a work of fiction, a political pilgrim's progress, justifying the ways of Willie to man, or at least to Willie, and those of us fortunate enough to be among the Good need fear no blame. The crucial pages are blank or excised with a razor blade, Willie acting, true to form, as his own mythologist. The content, for the most part, is predictable enough: meetings and conversations, illnesses, fears, trivial sins confessed, terrible sins left unconfessed or blamed on others, gossip, guilt and greed, a lust for power so overwhelming it moves all before it, a world of intrigue glimpsed through a politician's jaundiced eye. It's Willie's voice that's disconcerting. Not his familiar public voice, that strong, high-pitched, querulous voice of a small, spoiled boy, but a private voice, a voice I knew long ago, soft and seductive, a tantalyzing, confidential voice singing a love song of pain and paranoia, a hymn to hatred, the long, pitiable lament of a passionate man unable to love.

No wonder he was unable to destroy the diary. It was his first love, wife and mother, the magic mirror to which, at the end of every day, he put the fateful question and received the same reassuring reply: every banality a profundity, every truism a parable, a temple of words as false as the fake ruins he constructed out of stolen stones at Kingsmere, a masterpiece of delusion. He started it in 1893, the year I was born. Knowing Willie's savage, superstitious mind, I wouldn't be surprised if he had courted me for that connection alone, finding in me a convenient symbol for a masturbatory fantasy infinitely more erotic than feminine flesh could offer.

"I am not a psychiatrist," cried Dawson the historian. "What am I to do?"

"Better queer than crazy," said Twillersly.

After a hot debate on the historical relevance of sex, it has been decided to present only Willie's public face to the world, the plain, homely face he presented in life. What a masterpiece of disguise! How well Willie knew that had he been tall and commanding, he would never have lasted — how long? — twenty-six years as prime minister of Canada, thirty as leader of the Liberal Party, an Empire record, his single triumph. So instead of the mad Merlin of Kingsmere he gave us a fat little fussbudget with ill-fitting teeth and ill-fitting suits: William Lyon Mackenzie King, Knight Commander of St. Michael and St. George, grandson of William Lyon Mackenzie, the heroic rebel who brought Responsible Government to Canada, friend of Rockefeller, confidant of Churchill, a lonely bachelor selflessly devoted to the nation, a simple Christian, champion of peace, friend of the poor, temperate in habits, moral in outlook, cautious by nature, a true Canadian, drab perhaps, boring some people said, a man of compromise and conciliation, not two-faced but even-handed, secretive, yes, and smug, stubborn too, but a good man whose chronic hypocrisy could be taken as evidence of political genius, a humble man who summed up his political creed on the eve of the Second World War with the phrase: "I may not have accomplished much, but think what I have prevented!"

How well he rehearsed that litany. He chanted it over and over in countless speeches, a song of myself for fifteen million voices, his lackeys piping the chorus, until Willie, and Canada, came to believe it true.

Anything that contradicts this portrait will be omitted. I will be omitted.

So I sit here writing. Willie wasn't the only one to keep a diary. Mine isn't as big, and parts of it are missing, but it's a habit, a vice we shared (among others), although mine, unlike his, was never intended for publication. I was always shocked when he read from his aloud, after dinner, to his guests, oblivious to the social blunder of entertaining present company with an account of the foibles of those who were absent. Willie often made a fool of himself because he never realized he was being foolish. It's an endearing quality in politicians. Prime ministers must have started out as court jesters. Is democracy only a revolt of the fools?

I shall keep my promise, and my secrets, forever, if Willie's diary is destroyed; if not, until my death, although I'll be sorry to miss the fun.

SELF
PORTRAIT

I began my diary when I was twelve, the year I won my Brownie. The Kodak company had a slogan that year, "So Simple Even a Child Can Use It!" with advertisements showing a little girl in ringlets taking her father's picture. Mr. Sims, the photographer in Renfrew, offered three Brownies as prizes in the school spelling bee. I won mine with "ecstatic." Mum threatened to confiscate it, being a Hornerite Methodist and fierce about graven images, but Granny Coolican said it was an act of God, coming that way, and Bishop Ralph Horner volunteered to sit for his portrait right away. Besides, Mum had a weakness for spelling bees. She coached me day and night out of *Pilgrim's Progress* and took such pride in my victory that she prayed on her knees for foregiveness for a week afterwards.

Mr. Sims showed me how to use it, which wasn't so simple after all because I was small, and cut off people's heads or photographed their knees. He told me to buy a notebook and keep a record of every picture I took, its subject, location and lighting, so I would learn how to correct my mistakes. "It will teach you how to see," he said, which sounded peculiar at the time, but it did teach me how different my snapshots were from what was in my mind's eye, and how important it was to watch the light.

I practised on the corpses. Granny took me around to wakes, and it was still popular, at least among the Irish, to have the body photographed either alone or with the family standing around. Most of the people were too poor to have a portrait taken while they were living, or too superstitious. But it was reasonable to assume that if a camera stole your soul in life, it might return it in death, and the relatives hovered hopefully around, half expecting the dead to rise when the shutter clicked. I liked the corpses, so still and white, like shells, and they had such serene expressions on their faces. Besides, they didn't move, and the candlelight reflected on the white shroud gave a wonderful effect.

The dead were the only people, if you could call them that, I was allowed to photograph for money, since Mum couldn't say it was vanity. I photographed all the local kids for free, because they were small, and not afraid. Mr. Sims taught me how to develop and print my pictures, although I never showed them to anyone. Sometimes I'd take them out of their box and shuffle them like cards. I'd lay them out on the table face down, the way the gypsies did, telling stories around the faces that I turned up. I kept the studio clean and helped Mr. Sims paint a canvas backdrop of Venice, but there wasn't much call for Venetian portraits in the Ottawa Valley. Mr. Sims was also the carpenter and made more money building coffins that I ever made from taking pictures of the bodies in them.

I had no ambitions for a career, not like Charlie Whitton, who wanted to be a boy. "Boys have all the fun," she always complained. "They do things. We sit." It was true that the boys drank and beat each other up and went away to strange places, out West, or to the Boer War, or to Toronto, or just into the bush, but fighting or cutting down trees never struck me as much fun, even though Papa was a shantyman and had gone with Wolseley up the Nile to rescue General Gordon from Fuzzy-Wuzzies. Being a boy seemed like a lot of work unless you could be a hockey player. My brother Jack played left wing. He scored the winning goal for the Cobalt Silver Kings in 1910, the year they beat Renfrew, the Stanley Cup champions. When he came back to the dressing room his boots were stuffed with $100 bills.

That was the year Jack blew the fingers off his left hand with a dynamite cap. They took him to the miners' hospital in Cobalt. I went to see him at six o'clock the next morning. He was all alone in a big, bare room, unconscious, his arm hanging over the edge of his iron cot, a big pool of blood on the floor. I tied his arm up to the bedpost. Mum said I had a calling to be a nurse — like Miss Nightingale, who'd died the week before — but I was frightened by the smell of them, and the crackle of their white dresses, like wings.

I couldn't see spending my life helping people die, the way Gramp had died the summer before in the typhoid epidemic. They dragged him out of his little cabin by the lake, a helpless old man, and shot his beloved dogs, George and Bertie and Prince and Rex, named after the Kings, and carried him off to the big white tent on the hill because the hospital was overcrowded. He died up there, alone. Everyone died who went to the white tent on the hill. At sunset we were taken to a gully back of town where a pit had been dug and the dead tossed in, every which way, and the priest and Methodist preacher read prayers through their little white masks and Jack and Papa helped cover the grave with clay and lime. That night there was a dance in the miners' hall and I saw the nurses going in and heard their laughter over the fiddles.

All I wanted was to fall in love and live happily ever after, preferably with a hockey player, although by the time I was eighteen I realized that happiness and hockey players were mutually exclusive. They were mostly married anyway, although you'd never know. They didn't take me seriously either. I was just Silver Coolican's kid sister, although I was only ten minutes younger, skinny, shy, a stick-boy in a skirt. Charlie and I always got good seats, right behind the players' bench. We went to all the games, if you could call them games, free-for-alls really, blood all over the ice, everybody screaming blue murder and throwing eggs. The games were fun but I loved the practices, the slanting sun turning the ice the colour of pearls, the sharp *scrape*, *scrape* of the skates, the shouts and the slap of the sticks and the lovely echoing boom the puck made when it hit the boards, the players swooping and darting like swallows, hair flying, scarred faces stiff, ecstatic, oblivious to fear or pain. They were proud, and vain, and clamoured to have their pictures taken, but they were clumsy as ducks off the ice and I could never capture the magic that held me there — those sudden, perfect moments when a skater would break away and seem to rise off the ice, flying towards the goal with serene and effortless grace. All I got was a blur.

Nobody suggested I marry a prime minister, and the idea didn't occur to me at the time. But the only girls who worked were old maids with dismal jobs at the Renfrew Creamery or the Renfrew Steam Laundry or the Renfrew Knitting Mill or the Renfrew Hotel, not counting the hoors who came to town every spring when the drive came down the river — like the swallows returning to Capistrano, Mum said. Nobody looked on sex as work because the hoors sat around all day in silk dresses painting their nails and blowing kisses to men in the street and you could tell from the way they laughed that they really enjoyed what they were doing. I gave a lot of thought to being a hoor, like Grace, who lived over the oyster bar where a black man played ragtime all night and Grace danced, so they said, with no clothes on.

"You have a nose like the Divine Bernhardt," Grace said the first time I met her.

"It was broken."

"All the better."

"It has a bump."

"So distinctive."

I loved her from that moment. She ordered two big glasses of Coca-Cola, with ice, from downstairs, and eclairs, the first I'd ever tasted, and she showed me her scrapbook from when she'd been an actress in New York and London and Chicago, with all the famous people, her picture in the newspapers too.

"Bernhardt is ugly," she said. "But she behaves as if she is beautiful. It is not hard."

She taught me how to walk and sit and curtsy, pivoting my whole body in a single fluid motion, and how to hold my head and arms so I didn't scrabble about like a raccoon. She brushed my hair with her heavy silver brush until I purred and allowed me to try on her beautiful dresses, like jewels, violet and aquamarine and crimson, satin and velvet, trimmed with lace, real lace, and made me walk back and forth in front of her looking-glass until I wasn't afraid any more. Mum had broken all our mirrors before I could remember, when she got religion, and the only glimpse I had of myself was a fleeting one, from shop windows and rain puddles. I came to think of myself as transparent, a negative image of Jack. I don't know if we were born opposites, or grew that way because people expected it, but it seemed to me we were a single person split in two and only together would we be whole.

Jack sold me to Harry Oakes for $1, as a joke, because Harry was broke and I wasn't going to put out on credit, and Harry told him to come back with a "real" woman. I put the evil eye on Harry as hard as I could but it didn't have any effect because he and Jack struck gold the next winter. Being a witch was a dying trade too, Granny said, with people switching their faith to doctors, although all *they* did was saw you up like a side of mutton and call her in when it was too late so she'd take the blame. She'd wash the corpse and lay it out with pennies on the eyes and Gramp would come with a gallon or two of wine and his tin flute to help speed the soul on its way. Granny had her successes too. She could clear up poison ivy and stop a cut from bleeding and cure almost anything with mouldy bread. Even at worst I doubt she did more harm that Lydia Pinkham. She had hundreds and hundreds of bottles filled with powders and roots and leaves and little twigs and mushrooms and bits of bark. They weren't labelled, because Granny couldn't read, but she knew from memory which each was and what it did and some, like wintergreen, you could tell by the smell. She'd make up soups and teas for people who were sick and they'd drink it down and they'd get better, or die, but nobody except Granny knew what they were drinking. It took faith, because if she made a mistake she could kill you. Granny said that faith was a big part of getting well. Mostly she was a midwife. She took me along to a childbirth once when I was twelve, to show me what it was all about, but I threw up, and swore I'd never be a midwife, or a mother either, if I could help it. The dogans whispered that Granny could stop babies as well as bring them. That was no magic, she said.

"Why do you think all them fairy tale princesses used to sit in tubs of milk? I can tell you, girl, it wasn't to get clean, or white." It was a lot simpler, she said, to stick a dill pickle up two or three times before sex. I kept that in mind, but it got me into a big fight, years later, with Red Emma Goldman, who thought I was poking fun.

Sex didn't count for much in the Valley. I don't think one of us was a virgin, whatever that means, after the age of ten. It just happened. If a girl didn't have a Methodist Mum to scare the men away, she'd be knocked up by sixteen. I envied them, in a way. Later, in Ottawa, where people thought that sex before marriage made your hair fall out, being "from the Valley" carried a certain cachet. It gave me a "reputation," although I was too young and innocent to appreciate it at the time.

Mum was a Hornerite, a Roller, literally. Some nights, when it was wet, she'd come home from meeting covered with mud from head to toe. People said that women who rolled around in the bushes half the night were up to no good. Who knows? But I'll never forget the joy on her face. Bishop Ralph Horner took the Scripture very literally. If the Bible said "Rejoice in the Lord," Bishop Ralph rejoiced. The Methodists expelled him from church for being too cheerful. They said you could hear the laughing and singing halfway down the Valley. He started the Holiness Movement Church in Ottawa but every spring he'd come up the Valley with a flaming tent revival, starting in May, at Pentecost, and travelling all summer until the harvest was in and the ground too frozen to take a peg.

Mum always took me to the tent meetings when I was small. Ralph Horner was God to me, his voice thundering high over the boom of the wind in the canvas, the tent flaps cracking like the Devil's tail, Horner standing with his arms raised to Heaven, invoking the power of the Lord. He loved stormy nights. "We want to hear the sound from Heaven and feel the rushing, mighty wind!" he'd cry as the thunder crashed around. "Let the wind howl and the lightning flash! Let's have a cyclone! A cyclone of salvation! Hallelujah!" He always stood on a chair at the front, his white face lit by a kerosene lamp swinging from the tent pole, passing from light to shadow to light like the moon behind scudding clouds, shouting, pleading, commanding sinners to come forward, leave their sins behind in the dark, come into the light of holiness, be washed white in the blood of the Lamb. "I have the power!" he'd cry. "I have the living flame of fire which cannot be quenched! I have the Holy Fire resting on my soul. It is burning all through me! My soul is a living flaming fire! Do you want the power? Are you hungry for it? You can *have* it! God can save you. He can save you now! Get to your feet! Come to the Lord Jesus! Come to the fountain of God's love. Come and wash in the purple flood and be cleansed of sin. Won't you come brother? Won't you come sister? Weep your way to the feet of Jesus and plunge into the fountain of the Saviour's blood. Hallelujah! Bless His Name! Bless Him! Oh, Glory Halle-lujah! Let us drop on our knees. Let us weep and groan for God's blessing! Let everyone cry to God for it! Oh, Glory! Bless His name!" His voice would rise and fall in incantation and he'd lean out, sweeping people forward with motions of his big, rough hands, his eyes transfixing the lost sheep one by one as if by sheer force of will he could compel them to rise from their benches and shuffle on to salvation, Mum kneeling in the dirt at my side, her head in her hands, crying out, swaying and rocking, all around me a sea of people kneeling, some rolling on the ground, raising their arms and shouting "Hallelujah!" then bending again, all rocking and swaying and praying together, voice answering voice with hypnotic rhythm.

I'd close my eyes and clutch my wooden bench with both hands, pretending I was on a ship at sea in a storm, a small wooden ship like the one Gramp had come to Canada on. The tent pole was the mast and the canvas was the sails and Bishop Ralph was the captain trying to save us, but no matter how hard we prayed we were drowning, swallowed by the sea as black as night outside the tent. I'd imagine I was being sucked down into the black water, tasting the salt, picturing my hair and skirt floating out around me, my hands and face ghostly white and I'd hold my breath as long as I could, down, down, feeling slimy fish brush against my skin, watching the huge shapes of sharks and whales passing by. Once I held my breath so long I fainted. Mum declared I had been touched by the Holy Spirit. All I remember is coming to at the front, feeling very fuzzy and sleepy, and Bishop Ralph picking me up under the arms and holding me up to the crowd. I had been saved.

I was six that time, and I was saved a lot of times after that, but it never seemed to help. My sins multiplied. Mum said my problem was a rebellious heart. Whatever it was, no matter how hard I tried I could never *feel* the waves of glory Brother Ralph said I was supposed to feel. By the time I was twelve, I'd decided I was damned and figured I should try to make the best of it.

Mum was a Grit by tradition and temper but she was really a theocratic socialist: vice, she believed, increased in direct proportion to worldly wealth. No crime was too vile, no vice too obscene for the rich, and among the rich the artistocrats were the worst, and within this nest of thieves and fornicators the greatest sinners were beyond doubt the Royal Family. Mum's frequently expressed opinion, that Queen Victoria was the Whore of Babylon, and her head should be chopped off, did not endear her to the Orange Lodge or the Anglican pastor, although it won her support among the Irish Catholics, whom she abhorred. When Jack and I started school she forebade us to sing "God Save the Queen" because it was blasphemous. There was a terrible row, and we would have been expelled except that the truant officer said it was illegal, so we compromised by arriving five minutes late and leaving five minutes early, although nobody minded if we didn't show up at all. Mum had taught us both to read before we were five. The first word I learned was printed on a flour sack in the kitchen, and for more than a year I thought "flour" was spelled "Booth."

Papa was a Booth man, like Gramp, and a Tory. All the Booth men were Tories, or, more accurately, the Tories were Booth men. J.R. Booth owned most of Ontario, including the Conservative Party, and everyone talked about him, in a respectful way, as the Lumber King. I was so disappointed when he came to our house one Christmas. I'd expected someone fat, like Henry VIII, with a sword and a sceptre and an ermine cape and a gold crown, and here was this little old man with long, white hair and a big red nose, dressed in shantymen's clothes and smelling of drink and tobacco just like Gramp. I burst into tears. When he gave me a gold turtle with emerald eyes on a chain I decided he was a king in disguise, like in a fairy tale, and resolved to be more careful in future about kings.

Booth was benevolent, as kings went, visiting from shanty to shanty all winter in his railway car, inquiring after the men's health, sharing their beans and bread, dancing as good a jig at eighty-five as a boy of nineteen. No one coveted Booth's money, or hated him for it, or saw himself in Booth's shoes. Good fortune was a matter of luck. You had it or you didn't. If you didn't, it was a good idea to stick close to someone who did, in the hope that a little would rub off. You didn't step on his toes or spit in his eye. It made sense to me. "Someone's got to be boss," was all Papa would say. He was loyal to Booth ahead of God or country and would have died for Booth, as many men did, expecting nothing but a rough cross on the riverbank where their caulk boots dangled until they rotted. Papa always showed them to us when we went into the bush in the fall and told us each man's story. He'd been a riverman too, but when he hurt his leg Booth made him a cook, *le chef*, second only to the foreman, because he was a silent man, and strong. We'd camp out for two weeks while the men built the shanty, Jack and I splitting wood and hauling water and greasing pans, Papa making thousands of biscuits and broiling schools of pickerel on a bedspring. They'd eat it all up in ten minutes and we'd start again. In the winter Papa had a Chinaman helper. The men took one look at my long, black pigtail and I was "Cookee" Coolican from then on. Jack called me Chink.

It was just as well Papa was away all winter. And when he was home in the summertime Mum was usually off at a camp meeting praying for his sins, so they didn't see too much of each other. When they were together Papa would sit silent as a stone, letting the torrent of Mum's exhortations pour over him like the Blood of the Lamb. Once in a while he'd say "Umph" and go on smoking or whittling or darning or shuffling cards. It drove Mum nuts. Papa would have made a good politician and Mr. Booth tried to persuade him to stand, but he preferred the bush. At election times he helped deliver the vote, driving Mr. Booth from shanty to shanty where Mr. Booth would stand on a wagon load of whisky and tell the men they'd all be out of work if the Grits got in because he'd shut down the mill. Papa would pass the whisky jug with the ballots and make sure the men put their 'X' in the right place with their blue pencils. His polling stations often had a hundred votes for the Tory out of a population of thirty, but nobody complained because the Grits did the same thing. People gave Mr. Booth credit for beating Laurier in the Reciprocity election, but Mr. Booth said it was the whisky and besides, even the Grits hate Yankees.

I came to Ottawa the year I turned twenty, the winter after our house burned down. Papa was killed and Mum was taken away. They said she killed Papa and burned the house down. The flames were so hot men carrying buckets up from Smith's Creek couldn't get close to throw the water, and by the time the fire engine came tearing up, the horses snorting, half-harnessed, the bell clanging louder and louder, all they could do was hose down the trees to keep the whole town from going up. The logs were dry and every few minutes a fountain of sparks would shoot up into the sky and clouds of black smoke would billow out as the fire exploded inside. A great crowd of people stood around in a circle, shielding their eyes against the heat, their faces orange in the glare, watching the chinks between the logs glow crimson, then yellow, and the glass in the windows burst into a thousand slivers, groaning "ooohhh" and "aaahhh" as the roof fell in, Mum's white leghorns running everywhere underfoot *cluck cluck cluck* and high on the fire engine Papa's big red game cock, The Macnab, crowing with all his might, thinking it was dawn, and right in the middle of the circle, kneeling in the grass, her hair flying and her hands clasped, my mother, rocking, writhing, shouting out "Glory to God! Hallelujah!" Her wild, keening cries rose over the roar of the flames. No one dared go near her. Not even me. It was Granny Whitton who went up to her and spoke to her and put her arm around her and Mr. Whitton, Charlie's dad, who picked her up and carried her away into the darkness.

They found Papa the next day, at least they found his spectacles and the brace he wore on his gimpy leg. Mr. Whitton asked me if I wanted a funeral, they'd pass the hat, but I said no, Papa wasn't much for religion. In the afternoon I wrapped the spectacles in a handkerchief and buried them in the ashes and put a big bunch of tiger lilies on top. Isaac Pedlow came with his pipes and marched around the black circle playing "The Green Fields of Canada" while Mr. Whitton and Barney McDermott and a lot of Papa's friends stood there in their best clothes with their heads bowed. Then they all went back to Pedlow's store and got drunk.

Out loud everyone said it was an accident. They whispered different things. They whispered about Papa's money. Papa kept a lot of money for shantymen who were afraid they'd lose it in the bank or spend it themselves. They'd come for it in the middle of the night sometimes, dead drunk, banging on the door, but Papa never gave in and they were grateful the next day. He'd buy them a train ticket home, and give their purse to the conductor so they only got it when they got off the train and their wives were there to meet them. He loaned money too, to men he trusted, interest-free. He hated usury. Money that didn't come from honest work was theft, he said. He hated banks. He kept his money in a tin tea chest behind two loose stones in the cellar wall and he'd mark the debts on the two-by-fours, the man's initials and a notch for every ten dollars. He never loaned less than $10 or more than $100. At lot of it wasn't real money, but "Booth bills," chits that the Booth company issued to the men to buy things from the company storehouse, one chit for a plug of tobacco, two chits for a pair of socks, ten chits for an axe, but the men gambled with them and traded them around like real money. Even the storekeepers would take them in trade. Every September before he went into the bush Papa would take me down to the cellar and show me the two-by-fours and the tea chest. "Just in case I don't come back," he'd say.

They whispered about Papa's homebrew too. He made it up in Algonquin Park every summer at one of Booth's supply depots near Joe Lake. Ignace Delorme looked after the still for him after Gramp died. Ignace's wife, Old Suzanne, kept cows and shipped milk once a week to the Renfrew Creamery, so they'd fill some of the cans with milk, and some with whisky and Papa would pick them up at the station. The whisky cans were marked "MM" for moose milk. Papa never got caught because he gave it away, whole crocks sometimes, or he'd cut it with hot water and maple syrup and pass it around at poker games, just enough to loosen tongues and make faces red, not so much anyone puked or fell asleep. It was a secret recipe of Gramp's from Galway, dried apples and raisins and yeast and beans, but mostly molasses. Barney McDermott the policeman said it was the best high wine in the whole Valley and he should know because he'd sampled it all. Barney only gave us his blind eye, but all winter long men would come to the door with barrels of apples and potatoes and turnips and a side of beef, and a pig in November from Johnny Moran, and a turkey or two at Christmas and crocks of butter and pickles and jam, and Mum would write the man's name in a ledger with the donation and the note "in exchange." We even got free candy at the drugstore and Mr. Pedlow never sent a bill for all our boots and skates and scarves and coats. Mr. Pedlow had a terrible thirst. Papa said it was best this way because when Mum got her hands on a cent she gave it to the Hornerites.

It was the C of E parson, Canon Quartremaine, who started people blaming Mum. "We all know the Hornerites have incendiary tendencies," he whispered. Canon Quartremaine hated the Hornerites because they'd taken away half his congregation. Almost nobody in the valley was C of E except the remittance men, old soldiers who'd come over after the Crimean War, drunkards most of them, Gramp said, nothing more than horse grooms or batmen, lording it over us because they were Imperials, with pensions and a free homestead and ribbons on their dirty jackets, living in squalor on a pile of stones they called a farm. To hear them talk, Gramp said, you'd think they'd led the Light Brigade and banged old Florence Nightingale herself. Canon Quartremaine was English too, with no chin, and he flapped around like a starved crow in a long black cassock and a funny squashed hat. Mum called him a baby snatcher. If he thought a woman was dirty, or drunk, or promiscuous, he'd take her children away and farm them out to other families and after a while they'd be sent away, nobody knew where, not even the mother, who'd have another baby the next year to make it up. Gramp said the children were pickled and fed to the British army.

Mum did act very strange. She didn't speak or eat but just sat rocking in the Whittons' parlour humming hymns. She didn't seem to hear or see anything and she had a strange smile. Dr. Murphy said she'd be safer in hospital than in jail, so he took her down to the Queen Street lunatic asylum in Toronto the next day.

I knew she didn't do it because she didn't have Papa's tea chest, and the tea chest was gone. The stairs to the cellar had burned out, but I would get in through the back door dug into the bank of the creek. I saw the hole in the wall right away. Some of Papa's things were scattered on the ground, a carved wooden gum box still smelling of spruce, two photographs of the last log raft down the Ottawa River, a pink satin boot stitched with yellow glass beads a gypsy tinker had given him, a broken pipe. I picked them up. Tucked into the pipe bowl I found the little gold turtle Mr. Booth had given me. It would bring me long life and good fortune, he said. I'd worn it under my dress, but Mum caught me one day and tore it off. I still have the scar where it cut my neck. I thought she'd given it to the Hornerites. "I can wear it now," I thought and put it in my pocket with the other things. I placed the two stones back over the empty hole.

I became public property, passed around from hand to hand like a bruised tomato. Lily should marry. Who? Lily should work. Where?

"You should have a career," Charlie said, waving an advertisement in the Renfrew *Mercury*.

"Learn to type in two weeks," it said. "Good jobs. High wages."

The Pennefather Business College, temporarily located in a dreary, dusty room over the Sons of Temperance Hall, was a fly-by-night affair run by Mr. Ambrose Pennefather of Chicago, who travelled the backwoods with a single typewriter. The five of us took turns using it while the others practised on pieces of cardboard with raised letters. "Faster! Faster!" Mr. Pennefather would shout, taking snuff and sneezing and banging his cane by our knuckles when we dared to peek down.

I was banging away at about thirty words a minute when Mr. Booth sent for me, just before Christmas. He had broken his hip that summer and needed someone to fetch and carry. I would have room and board and a Christian home.

"A Christian home!" squawked Charlie. "It's a christly castle!"

I had never been to Ottawa, even though it was only two hours by train. There was no reason to go there. Everyone said it was a terrible place. It seemed wonderfully wicked to me, a den of thieves and grafters, murderers, adulterers and white slavers who pursued decent girls with pins on the streetcars, a Babylon of vice where wild men bit off each other's ears and the streets ran with blood on Saturday nights. Nebuchadnezzar, in the Word according to Mum, was the Duke of Connaught, third son of the Great Whore and Canada's Governor-General, who looked, to me at least, more like the Walrus about to devour the Oysters. And everyone knew the Duchess' face from the $2 bill, very common in the spring, being the going price for a hoor.

"Arriving tomorrow," I wired.

My triumphant departure created something of a stir in Renfrew. People who had never spoken to me stopped me on the road to ask if it were true. Some of them even wished me luck and one old man took off his cap, as if he were in the presence of the Lumber King himself, and bobbed a little bow. Isaac Pedlow, unwilling to see me leave in Charlie's homespun hand-me-downs, beckoned me into his store, and with a sweep of his generous hand, told me to help myself.

And so the very next day at 3:45 p.m., I was standing in the snow in front of Mr. Booth's brick fortress on Metcalfe Street, wearing Pedlow's black serge coat, Pedlow's black wool dress, Pedlow's black boots, with a suitcase full of Pedlow's black stockings, wondering whether I should ring the front bell or the back.

The old man came to the door himself.

He stared at me a long time.

"I thought y'were a *wee* girl."

"I was, I mean, I used to be. Before."

He squinted at me. My feet were cold and I missed Charlie's warm kitchen.

"When the good Lord scrimps on a girl's looks, he usually gives her a brain," he said at last. "My own girls got neither. They got money, which is worse. In with ye."

Mr. Booth's house was panelled in golden pine carved like a honeycomb, but he kept it cold and dark to save money and we camped out in the kitchen with Old Martha, the cook. Mr. Booth rocketed around like a fire engine in his wheelchair so it wasn't long before I was put to work typing letters at the mill. We drove there together every morning before sunrise, past the Parliament Buildings rising on the bluff like a stand of pine, the pale moon in the clock tower with its hands at 5:45, the runners of the sleigh squeaking over the newfallen snow. "My clock," Mr. Booth would say, pointing with his whip. "My building." And he'd tell me again the story of how he had won the contract, nearly sixty years before, and made his fortune.

The Booth mill was on the Ottawa River at the Chaudière Falls, right across from the E.B. Eddy mill, so close you could spit, which Mr. Booth often did, although old Eddy was long dead. The rotten stench from the Eddy pulp mill hung over the city like a curse. And if there was any vice in Ottawa, it must have been on the Eddy side, in Hull, because I never saw it. Ottawa was just like Renfrew, only bigger. The rich lived in big, brick houses with trees and lawns, the poor in shacks with chickens and sometimes a cow, and nobody spoke to you until you'd been introduced, nobody except Alice Millar, my only friend, who spoke to me one day after church and asked me to tea at the Shadow.

I had a very clear picture of the Shadow in my mind, a large cave lighted by candles full of happy people in evening dress dancing and eating eclairs, and I had looked for it surreptitiously for weeks, afraid to ask.

"It's not far," Alice said. "We'll walk." I'll never forget how my heart pounded with excitement as we headed towards the Union Station, or the look on Alice's face when I leaned against a pillar in the lobby of the Chateau Laurier, babbling helplessly, "It's a hotel! It's a hotel!"

Alice was never fooled. She was from Alberta. She was only a year older than I, but already she was private secretary to Mr. R.B. Bennett, the Conservative Member of Parliament from Calgary West and a member of the cabinet of Sir Robert Borden, although precisely what Mr. Bennett did, other than make money, was none too clear, even to Mr. Bennett, said Alice.

"Can I trust you?" she asked long after she knew she could. "Sir Robert is going to the country this autumn. He will see the Governor-General in August as soon as His Royal Highness returns from his vacation in Banff."

She paused for a moment, looking across the room.

"Banff is in Mr. Bennett's constituency."

She stopped again, smoothing the tablecloth with her fingers, trying to straighten things out.

"A successful Royal visit will mean certain re-election. An unsuccessful Royal visit will mean...."

Alice gave me a hard look and drew her finger across her throat.

"Princess Pat is a trouper. His Royal Highness is a dear, although he has never quite grasped the concept of parliamentary democracy. The Duchess...."

Alice's voice trailed off and she peered into her tea leaves.

"Difficult?"

"Uncommunicative," smiled Alice, pleased at finding, as always, the politic word. "Arbee, Mr. Bennett, has proposed a Canadian secretary, a capable young women of discretion who will...."

She smoothed her fingers against the tablecloth again and looked up sharply.

"Can you type?"

I could, by the spring of 1914, type as fast as Mr. Booth could bellow, at the same time translating his toothless slang into English. Some nights I came home from the mill so tired I went to bed without eating, my head still buzzing with the scream of the saws.

Any illusions I might have had about becoming chatelaine of the Booth mansion had been immediately dispelled by Mr. Booth's eldest daughter, Gertrude — Mrs. Fleck — an enormous, ugly woman of sixty or so with a fishy eye and a hooked nose that nearly met her chin. Gertrude had married an ironmonger and become a pillar of St. Andrew's Presbyterian Church. On my first Sunday in Ottawa, when I would have liked to have gone walking in the snow, she propelled me along Wellington Street to pay a call at the Home for Friendless Women, to offer my services, voluntarily, on the Presbyterian grounds that it took one to help one.

The Home was a ramshackle old frame house, painted brown, with an inscription on a white board over the door: "Repent! Ye Must Be Born Again!" The parlour smelled of grease and onions and boiled sheets. In the cellar clouds of steam billowed out of an immense laundry where red, sweating women with their sleeves rolled up stirred cauldrons or churned mangles. Beyond it was the drying room with sheets hanging from racks and old ladies on chairs bent over scraps of clothing, patiently mending, or just staring ahead at the wall, dreaming. Girls were ironing at long tables in the centre. At each girl's feet, under the table, was a laundry basket, and in each basket, a baby.

As we inspected the dormitories upstairs I had a sudden dread that Mum would be here, behind a locked door, manacled and gibbering, but the rows of iron cots were empty — lifeless, except for the pathetic array of trinkets on each white enamel table, a tortoiseshell comb, a photograph, a pink baby's bonnet. We were shown around by the matron, a fussy old woman in a nanny's blue dress, who had raised the five children of a prominent Ottawa family and been dismissed, the day after the youngest was married, without a pension or a reference.

"It is good, clean work and a Christian service," said Mrs. Fleck. "The Friendless Women do the laundry for the Home for Incurables and the Protestant Orphans' Home as well as several smaller charities. If there is no husband in sight, and if the unfortunate girl sincerely repents of her sins, a place is found for her in a respectable family home. The baby is placed in the Orphans' Home. The attractive ones are adopted quite quickly."

My duty, she said, in my weekly Sunday visits to the Friendless Women, would be to set a shining example of the Christian life open to young girls in reduced circumstances.

"Let us pray, Miss Coolican," she said. "that you will never be in need of *public* charity."

"The wage is $20 a week," said Alice.

"Yes!" I said.

Part I

LILY

1

Rideau Hall, Ottawa
Monday, July 20, 1914

I was taken into the Duchess at nine o'clock this morning. She was in bed,
propped up on pillows, an Oriental-looking woman with yellow skin and
slanty eyes and tiny, tiny hands covered with beautiful rings. Her hair was the
same colour as her skin, very thin, and pulled back tightly except for a puff of
curls on her forehead. I did my best curtsy and stood very still and straight.
She stared at me a long time, silent, her blue eyes quite startling in that sallow
face, almost daring me to speak, but I took a deep breath and held it. It made
me dizzy, or maybe it was the stuffy room and the strange sweet smell, not
flowers, although the room was full of orchids. A tiny black dog poked its
head out of the covers, bared its teeth and growled at me. The Duchess finally
made a twirling motion with her finger. I turned around full circle.

"Papist?" she said.

"No, ma'am. Praise the Lord."

"Methodist."

"Yes, ma'am. More or less."

"Less?"

"Yes, ma'am."

"You are an orphan?"

"No, ma'am. Not exactly."

"Exactly?"

"Mum... my mother is in... in the hospital, ma'am."

"We are sorry."

I looked around at Miss Yorke, the lady-in-waiting, who was standing next to me pinching my arm, but *she* sure didn't look sorry. The Duchess slowly unfolded a letter with her brittle, crab-like hands. Blue paper, blue ink.

"Your teacher at the Renfrew Collegiate, Miss Eady, says you are a clever girl but inclined to wool-gather. You did well in science and won every prize for spelling and penmanship."

"Yes, ma'am."

"Miss Eady says as well that you show ability at athletics and elocution, although she points out 'there is unfortunately not much future for women in hockey.'"

Miss Yorke brayed and covered her mouth with a handkerchief.

"That will be all, Dorothy," the Duchess said, and Miss Yorke scuttled out the door backwards.

"What position do you play?"

"Goal. Ma'am."

"And what do you recite?"

Oh, Jesus! I hadn't spoken a single word in public for years, not since the last school concert. What did I do then? My brain was as blank as an egg.

"'Cry From an Indian Wife,' ma'am."

"Proceed."

I shut my eyes. I could see Gramp's beaming anxious face in the dark right there in the front row of the Temperance Hall and smell the smokey aroma of my buckskin shirt that Old Suzanne had made for me and beaded with real porcupine quills. I had long braids down my back laced with ribbons and duck feathers I'd picked up along the river and a paddle in my hand and everyone said I was a dead ringer for Pauline Johnson even though I was nine years old and Irish.

"My Forest Brave, my Red-skin love...."

I spoke it quietly the way Pauline had done, yet ringing the rafters of the Lyric Opera hall with the resonance of her musical voice until we all shivered with the loveliness of it and clapped until our hands were sore. I was always disappointed when she changed into a satin gown at intermission. She looked just like an ordinary white woman. I wasn't allowed to see her the last time she came to Renfrew. She was living in sin, Mum said, with her partner, Walter McRaye, who did Drummond's habitant poems on the same bill, but I saw her on the station platform all the same, wearing a crimson velvet coat trimmed with fur, her face thin and lined and her hair white beneath her crimson velvet hat.

The Duchess was crying when I finished.

"Poor Pauline," she said. "We shall have a cigarette now, if you will be so kind."

She pointed a trembling finger at a small table next to the bed. It was littered with little knick-knacks. I guessed at the silver case worn smooth with the rub of fingers and handed it to her. There was a little box of Eddy matches next to it (how Mr. Booth hates the sight of Eddy matchboxes!) so I struck one and held it out.

"*Danke schoen.* You smoke?"

"Sometimes. Ma'am."

She held the case out, blowing smoke through her nose. I was wild for a cigarette! They were dark brown and long, like cigars, only thin, with beautiful gold paper at the tip, Egyptian, she said, and oh, the smell — frankincense and myrrh and a thousand and one delights.

"You are not the little Puritan you seem," she said, pointing me to a chair. "We shall get along if you are diligent and follow instructions. We do not intend to repeat them."

My instructions: to clip every story about the Connaughts out of the papers and paste it in a scrapbook; to make two extra copies of *every* photograph, one for Princess Patricia's album and one for the Duchess. The duchess has two albums, an official one and one she calls the "Bogey Book," all the photographs that make them look silly or hideous. There are a lot of them and they are awful, heads and legs cut off, mouths open, hats askew, overexposed, upside down, double exposures, out of focus. Miss Yorke, it seems, is responsible for most of them. She sneaks up on people from behind and shoots them when they turn around in surprise. The result is a big rump and a vacant look and a blur of waving arms. Princess Patricia is also a photographer but, as the Duchess points out, "One can't take pictures and be in them at the same time."

I am to take no photographs of the Duchess unless it is unavoidable and on no condition am I to submit a photograph of her to be published in a newspaper.

"We do not submit," she said, "to having our face thrown in the gutter and tramped upon, or used to wipe up spilled whisky in a filthy tavern. It is an indignity to any woman and a debasement of the Royal Family."

"It's no worse than money," I said, thinking of the two-dollar bills, then realized I should have kept my mouth shut.

She closed her eyes and made an awful face. "Democracy," she said, "will be the death of us all."

I am to arrange no interviews with the press, nor divulge any information of a personal nature. I am to make copies of all announcements and submit them for approval. I am sworn not to reveal anything I may see or hear during the period of my employment for ever and ever amen.

"Mummy is a little old-fashioned," Patsy said at lunch. (Everyone calls her Patsy. They don't seem to have a last name. The Duchess is Louisechen. Even the Duke is simply Arthur, as if he were the only Arthur in the world.) Lunch was a very small bowl of cold cucumber soup and sandwiches made of some green stuff I think was watercress. My stomach is still rumbling. No wonder Patsy is so thin, just a long drink of water, as Gramp would say. She's nearly six feet tall in her shoes (she has very big feet) but graceful with a perfect heart-shaped face and light, curly hair she wears up but loose like her clothes, which are simple and flowing so you can't tell if she's wearing a corset. She showed me her studio where she paints every morning, flowers mostly, and landscapes. There's a door to the roof where she can sit and look across the river to Point Gatineau and when the flies aren't too bad she goes down to the riverbank and paints the view upstream towards the Parliament Buildings. Her pictures are bright and sort of blurry. I asked if she had ever sold a painting.

"My God, no!" she said, looking at me as if I'd said something rude. Perhaps she's just embarrassed because they aren't very good.

I met the Duke at tea. He's deaf as a post. Patsy says it doesn't really matter because people all say the same things, so he simply varies the noises in his throat like a Victrola to indicate approval or interest. He drank a great deal of whisky, which he had a curious way of rinsing through his false teeth. I screwed up my courage and shouted, "My grandfather came from Connaught."

"Connaught?" he said, swallowing suddenly. "No good ever came from Connaught! To Hell or Connaught! Damn Godforsaken place they tell me. Never been there myself."

And all this time I thought he was Irish!

After dinner Herr Ribbentrop, the wine merchant, came with his violin for a little concert. He is just as handsome as everyone says, very tall and straight and sunburned with blond hair combed straight back in the European style. He even kissed my hand! I love that. He spoke German with the Duchess but his English is very good, just that funny hissing *ssss* and w's that sound like v's but it's very elegant. He played German music, I think, slow and boring, and he hit quite a few bad notes. Afterwards we had champagne! My first. I was a little nervous about it. When I looked into the glass I could see Bishop Ralph's stern face and my ears rang with his awful voice thundering imprecations against the Devil's piss. Ribbentrop smiled at me. "It won't poison you." I drank it. And another. Oh, I was floating on a dazzling golden cloud with angel choirs singing Hallelujah. Heavenly bliss. Herr Ribbentrop has invited me to a movie tomorrow afternoon, he calls it the "cinema," followed by ice cream at Page and Shaw's. Patsy says he's a "pet" but a bit of a "Lothario."

What's a Lothario?

Rideau Hall
Tuesday, July 21, 1914

We leave for the west on Thursday. Imagine, two whole weeks in the Banff Springs Hotel! I can hardly wait! Patsy says I'll be disappointed in the cowboys. They're all short and smelly with bow legs and bad teeth. I don't believe a word of it. She's just sour because she's twenty-seven and an old maid.

I have a title now, "Private Secretary to Their Royal Highnesses, the Duchess of Connaught and the Princess Patricia," and a small office in the servants' wing. It's like a hotel here with dozens of footmen and gardeners and maids and aides all jumping out at me when I don't expect it. The Duchess calls the place "the barracks," which is true but doesn't make her popular. That's why I'm here. The Duchess is so unpopular, Sir Robert Borden is afraid she'll be booed in the streets of Banff. No one can speak to her unless she speaks first and she speaks only to people of royal blood, which leaves out everyone except Members of Parliament, who raised a fuss, so now she receives them once a year at a banquet in the ballroom where they have to eat standing up, facing the Duke and Duchess who are seated on thrones on a dais. When she demanded the *whole* Banff Springs Hotel, at government expense, for a private holiday, Sir Robert blew up and said that if the Connaughts didn't make some effort to show the flag and meet the people in the west he wouldn't give a fig for the Empire or the monarchy either. The Duchess said she wouldn't be dragged through the streets like a side of beef. Sir Robert said he wouldn't pay for the hotel. After a terrible row they agreed on a semi-private tour, two floors of the Banff Springs Hotel, and me.

"The Royals have to be boomed," said Alice Millar. Arbee made his money, Alice said, by booming.

"Think of a farm," Alice said. "It's got alkaline sloughs and scrub and tumbleweed on it, but if you can persuade people there's oil underneath, or a city's going to be built there, they'll go crazy for it."

"But that's lying."

"Imagination."

"Why don't *you* do it?"

"We need pictures."

She showed me a telegram from Mr. Bennett's friend, Sir Max Aitken, who owns the *Daily Express* in London.

"PAT PRETTY STOP PLASTER PRINCESS PAGE ONE"

"But it's Babylon, Alice."

"Beats the Booth mill, doesn't it?"

So here I am with my typewriter, borrowed from Alice, ribbons, carbon, two cameras, rolls and rolls of film, tank, pans, developer, a ton of stuff to drag around but I've been promised a darkroom on the train so I can print up the pictures in time for the next day's newspapers. Alice says to get Mr. Bennett in as much as possible because of the election coming. Alice knows everything. She talks about the tariff and the Naval Bill and suffrage and things I haven't the faintest notion about. She wants to be a lawyer, although Mr. Bennett says women will never be admitted to the bar, their minds aren't suited for the law, but she studies on her own, and reads *Hansard*, and pretty much looks after Mr. Bennett's constituency singlehanded because he's busy booming. She shares a house on Cooper Street with four other secretaries and an old widow as chaperone. They buy her a bottle of sherry every week so she nods off to sleep at nine o'clock, not that they'd ever have men in the house, but they often work all night when the House is sitting and most landladies spread rumours, especially since Mr. Bennett is the most eligible bachelor in Canada. Alice does very well out of his girlfriends, little gifts of silk stockings and chocolates and perfume and gloves so she'll put in a good word for them, but she says Arbee is secretly in love with Eddy's widow and would marry her except the old man put a clause in his will disinheriting her if she married again. I think Alice is sweet on him herself although I can't see why. He's old, forty at least, with red hair and freckles and hardly any chin.

I can hear the frogs down by the river and, very faintly, the saws at the mill. If I listen hard I can almost tell their separate voices the way I could tell the drones of Papa's cronies coming up the stovepipe from the kitchen on rainy nights when the oven was open for the heat.

Sleepy now. Scared.

R.H.
Wednesday, July 22, 1914

Alice telephoned this morning all in a flap to say there wasn't a word in the Ottawa papers about the tour and we had better do something. I spent two hours typing up an intinerary in triplicate. I went in to the *Journal* first, since it's the Tory paper, and asked to see Mr. Ross, the editor. Mr. Ross was in conference, I was told, and I knew I'd come at a bad time because everyone was running around shouting and waving sheaves of paper and nobody gave a fig whether I was there or not. I was sent over to a dirty little man in shirtsleeves who snapped "Social" without even looking up. "Social" turned out to be Mrs. Ross, who seemed to be all dressed up for a garden party. She was typing with white gloves on. They were clean too. "Why, you're much too late and this is much too long!" she cried. "Calgary! My dear, what possible interest can this be to us? This is Ottawa!"

Miss Chadwick at the *Citizen* was ruder. "What is the Princess wearing?" she said. "Who's made her wardrobe?"

"I don't know."

"And how is her 'affaire' with Captain Ramsay coming? Has old Daddy given in yet? She's getting a little over the hill, you know, can't wait too long."

"I'm sorry. I don't know what you mean."

"There! You see! You won't tell us any of the juicy things, and you expect us to print all the boring things! Well to be perfectly frank, your Royals are simply not news." And she threw my itinerary in the waste basket.

I got back just in time to change, still mad enough to spit nails. I put on my best dress but I felt terrible; it was so plain and ugly I could have dropped through the ground when Joachim Ribbentrop drove up in his big white touring car, the "Ottawa Dairy Mobile" people call it, wearing *a white suit* and a yellow shirt with a daisy in the buttonhole, then driving down Sparks Street through the crowds with heads swivelling and fingers pointing and little boys whistling, and when we got to the theatre and sat down the manager came up and said "I'm sorry sir, it's our policy that gentlemen must wear jackets," and Joachim stood up very stiff and said "If you use your eyes, sir, you vill see zat ziss *iss* a jacket," and sat down again. Well thank God the lights went down and the picture started. It was a western with Lillian Gish and I liked it and then I had an enormous raspberry sundae and a Coca-Cola at Page and Shaw's. It's hard to believe Joachim is exactly my age. He makes me feel such a baby. He's been all over Canada and seems to know everyone. Lord So-and-So, Sir Somebody, His Excellency Such-and-Such. He came over four years ago for his health, he says (I've never seen anyone look healthier in my life), and now he imports Henckel champagne "as a favour to friends." He really should be in the army, like his father, but "I am in love with Canadian girls," he says.

"Meine jungfräuliche Lilichen," he calls me. He says I should study photography in Germany. The best photographers in the world are in Munich. I could apprentice in a studio there. He will write to friends to arrange it. He will get me a German camera. They're the best, he says. "Zee camera was inwented in Chermany," he says. I didn't know that. I feel very stupid, especially when he stares at me and shows his white teeth, and he has a way of touching, very lightly, my arm or the small of my back, that sends shivers up my spine. He bought me a bunch of lillies. My first bouquet.

Somewhere
Friday, July 24, 1914

Rain. Two days on the train. Trees and lakes. Lakes and trees. I had no idea Canada was so big.

Made a list of the clothes Patsy and the Duchess will wear for the next week. They change three times a day, sometimes four, so it was a big job but I love it. Everything is from Paris and so beautiful I could cry. I love to roll the French words around on my tongue. *"Crêpe charmant, la couleur de bois et marron glacé, avec la dentelle Guipère."* Oh, I would love to be a real lady and wear a white linen suit like Patsy's, piped with navy, with a matching straw boater trimmed with white ribbons, and kid leather shoes with the tinest Louis heels. She laughs at me and says that people can see for themselves, they don't have to read about it, but Alice says that's *exactly* what people want to read about. Besides, I'm not allowed to say anything about important things, like Captain

Ramsay, her fiancé. It's so sad and romantic. They fell in love three years ago when he came to Canada as naval attaché but the Duke forbade the marriage because Ramsay is a commoner even though his father is a Scotch, Scottish, earl, and Ramsay was shipped back to Britain. Patsy says she'll die an old maid if she can't have Alex. The Duke is furious. He has tried to marry her off to all the princes in Europe. The current suitor is Crown Prince Alfonso of Spain. Patsy calls him Count Dracula. She says if she marries Alex she is going to give up being a Princess.

"It's very boring, really."

"Trade?"

She just laughed.

You never think of a princess having a broken heart.

Kenora tomorrow. Regatta and picnic. I have typed up a little statement saying the "HRH, the Duchess of Connaught, is looking forward to a restful and informal visit to the beautiful Lake of the Woods." HRH loathes regattas. HRH abominates picnics.

Can't sleep.

Kenora, Ontario
Saturday, July 25, 1914

Nearly drowned. Launch sprang a leak in the middle of the lake and we were over our ankles in water before we were rescued. The Duke and Duchess stood on the seats while the band in the next launch played "Rule Britannia" and all the little boats scurried around blowing their horns and flapping their sails. Col. Farquhar, the Duke's military secretary, said it was sabotage and wanted to call in the Mounted Police, but the Duchess said she hadn't had such fun in years. I had to run around to the reporters asking them please not to mention the "incident" as it would mortify their Highnesses and embarrass the hosts who had been *so* kind. They all promised.

At sunset the Duke went out to the station platform in his kilt and played "Loch Lomond" on the bagpipes. A huge crowd gathered around cheering and waving and the Duke shook hands all round to show there were no hard feelings. We are all quite sunburned. Washed my photos in the lake and went for a swim with the aides-de-camp. They ignored me. I was just as glad. They call me the "Kodak kid" in a sneering sort of way and say rude things in French, thinking I don't understand. They do nothing that I can see except polish their boots.

We have been presented with a horrible stuffed trout mounted on a board. Patsy has christened it "Sir Robert."

Regina, Saskatchewan
Sunday, July 26, 1914

Tried to read the book Joachim gave me, *Foundations of the Nineteenth Century*, by the Englishman who's married to Wagner's daughter. I thought it might be about music but it seems to be religious. Can't get into it.

"It proves Jesus wasn't a Jew," Patsy says.

"Does it matter?" I said.

Hot. Flat. No cowboys yet.

Calgary, Alberta
Monday, July 27, 1914

Went to Senator Lougheed's house to get the guest list for tomorrow's banquet and the details of the ladies' gowns. It was a very grand stone house but the lawns were all brown and there wasn't a tree in sight. Lougheed owns most of Calgary, Alice says, at least the part Arbee doesn't own. He is another great boomer.

The door was opened by a tiny woman in a shapeless brown smock, her lank, dark hair hanging straight to her shoulders. She grinned from ear to ear, her round, brown face crinkling into wreaths of wrinkles, a gold tooth gleaming in the sunshine. I was flabbergasted to think that a millionaire would hire a squaw as a housemaid, but then this was the wild west, after all.

"May I see Mrs. Lougheed?" I asked, wondering if she understood English.

"I am Mrs. Lougheed," she said with a perfect British accent. "Please come in."

Well Jesus I truly felt a fool and kicked myself as she led me across the vestibule, her moccasins making a nice *slip-swish, slip-swish* noise on the marble floor. The house was all green marble that looks like rotted cheese and black wood and great palm trees blocking out the light and red Oriental rugs the colour of dried blood.

She showed me her gown, white satin embroidered with seed pearls with a small tiara of pearls and diamonds. Did I think it too elaborate? No, I lied. The Senator, she said, likes to put on the dog, but it only causes criticism because so many people in the west are poor, especially "my people," she said. She stroked the heavy satin with her large, sinewy hand.

"Some people here think that 'breeds have no business with fine things," she said, "so sometimes I dress up and have a party. They accept my invitations." She looked at me with eyes like two brown stones.

Tonight everyone is buzzing about the war in Europe. "Serve the wogs right," the Duke said. He tried to send a wire to the King but the station agent had gone home to bed. Where is Serbia? What's a wog?

Calgary, Alberta
Tuesday, July 28, 1914

I held my first "press conference" this morning while the Connaughts were off
downtown christening the new fire engine. It was Sir Max's idea too and Alice
arranged everything. A lot of ladies came, not just from Calgary, but from
Edmonton and Red Deer and High River and Okotoks. They're all British
here, Alice said, and nuts about royalty. They were all dressed to the nines,
flounces and bows and immense hats stacked with feathers and fruit and
wound around with chiffon like storks' nests. The lady from Okotoks was
wearing a whole nesting partridge on her head. She shot it herself, she said.

We had tea in the dining car, which is just like a real dining room with a
crystal chandelier and they *ooohed* and *aaahed* and took notes like mad, then
Trudy, the Duchess's personal maid, brought out the dresses for the Lougheed's dinner, Patsy's lovely blue silk chiffon with silver lace and the Duchess's
peacock blue brocade embroidered in gold, with her pearl choker, tiara and
diamond earrings as big and blue as robin's eggs. I wasn't sure what to do
about the judge's wife and the bishop's wife who were wearing identical black
dresses so I gave the judge's wife a little lace and an extra bow. The reporters
were all very polite and grateful. I guess they're just housewives mostly, like
Mrs. Maloney in Renfrew who wrote up the church teas for the *Mercury* and
didn't put your name in if you weren't nice to her. I was afraid they'd ask if the
Duchess had cancer or whether the Duke wore a corset (it's one of the
Duchess's with the bust cut off, and it pushes his stomach up from his belt
buckle to his chest) but they didn't.

At noon we were supposed to drive to Okotoks to see an oil well owned by
Senator Lougheed and Mr. Bennett but when they brought out all the scarves
and goggles and dusters the Duchess put her foot down and said we'd take the
train. Mr. Bennett got very red, then very white, and swelled up, and ran
around like a chicken with his head off. I explained that hundreds of people
had driven in miles from their ranches and were waiting by the roadside and
they'd be terribly disappointed, but the Duchess said, "they won't see anything of me in that get-up anyway," and you have to admit the dust in Calgary
is terrible.

Half of Calgary scrambled on the train before anyone could stop them,
even the aisles were crowded like it was a Sunday picnic. Some of the men had
pocket flasks and were quite drunk by the time we arrived. The oil well was a
disappointment, just a rough shed with a big pump in the ground and all that
came out was gasoline! Just as well though, because if it had been oil we would
have been black from head to foot. The gasoline spouted up about twelve feet
and refracted the sunlight into a dazzling rainbow and I got some lovely
pictures of everyone standing around. "Isn't it pretty!" Patsy said, which was

the right thing, since we were all feeling sick and dizzy and we reeked of gasoline for the rest of the day.

A picnic lunch had been set out in two big tents but almost a hundred people showed up instead of thirty and the food ran out so a lot of us had nothing to eat and somebody poured gin into the mint punch and we all got very drunk, even the women from the Women's Christian Temperance Union — with their little white bows pinned to their dresses — and Mr. Bennett, who's a Methodist and never touched liquor in his life (he says). Coming back in the train he told Patsy off-colour stories about some crazy newspaperman called Eye-Opener Bob until he fell asleep with his head on her shoulder. (He pumped me later about what he'd said but I just told him he'd been very amusing, which was true, for a change.) Mr. Bennett even talks in his sleep! He stuck to Patsy all day like a burr. I asked Alice if he had designs on her but she said he just wanted to get into the photographs. This morning he turned up at the train an hour early, pacing up and down the platform all decked out in striped pants and tailcoat like a man who's been to a party and not gone to bed. He kept pulling out a great gold watch and pecking lint from his coat and smoothing down his thin red hair and wiping sweat from his forehead, patting and stroking himself with his long white hands as if he were a batch of bread dough, which is what he looks like, all soft and flabby and white under his freckles. Patsy says he started talking the moment she stepped off the train and didn't stop for breath for the rest of the day, *yakketty yak yak yak* in a loud, booming voice that could be heard a dozen feet away, all about Calgary, the oil business (he tried to sell her some stock), his millions, Oliver Cromwell, Napoleon, the King, concrete, electricity, his mother, the evils of tobacco and how he expected to succeed Sir Robert as prime minister. The worst thing, she said, was the way he kept pulling on his eyebrows.

When the train is pulling out for Okotoks Patsy grabs my arm and hisses "Help!" in my ear so I sit opposite them, still carrying the book of poetry the partridge lady has given me for Patsy, poems about the "real" Canada they're supposed to be. It's called *England Overseas*. "Aha!" cries Mr. Bennett snatching it from my hand. "I've often thought of turning my talents to poetry. Nothing so elevates the human spirit or provides inspiration for the daily tasks, a few sacred moments of reflection in the strife and turmoil of our lives." He leafs through it, still talking. Sweat stands in drops on his head. I watch them roll down his cheeks into the folds of flesh under his little chin and disappear into his wing collar. He mops his face with a white handkerchief rolled into a damp glob. It smells of lavender. His hands are damp. His hair is damp. Even his monocle is steamed up.

"Splendid," he says, pulling his right eyebrow. "'Spring Madness.'" He clears his throat. I watch his wet mouth open and close like a pink mollusk, his voice deep, deafening, as if he were speaking to a thousand people in a hall. . . .

I stoop and tear the sandals from my feet
While the green fires glimmer in the gloom.
The hot roar of madness
Swells my veins with gladness.
I smell the rotting woodstuff
And the drift of willow bloom.
And the moon's wet face
Lifts above the place....

I glance at Patsy. Her face is perfectly blank, expressionless, only her blue eyes get rounder and rounder.

She sent for me tonight, just after eleven, when they got back from Lougheed's dinner. "I want to show Mummy Mr. Bennett reading 'Spring Madness' as interpreted by Isadora Duncan," she said. "You do Mr. Bennett." So I tucked my chin down into my chest and read in my deepest, most ponderous voice and pulled my eyebrows and Patsy wrapped herself in a tablecloth and let her hair down and leaped about the car, tossing her shoes in the air and snuffling the wind like a dog that's scented a bear. We all laughed until we were weak.

Poor Mr. Bennett. Such an Imperialist too! He's a hard man to feel sorry for. Still I feel a little guilty all the same. He reminds me a little of Mum, talking all the time, tugging at her nose, people making fun behind her back. Maybe it runs in Methodists. Or maybe he's crazy too.

Banff Springs Hotel
Wednesday, July 29, 1914

Sunny, cool. Arrived this morning. Huge crowd at the station and all along the route. They stayed there for hours watching the luggage go past. The wagons made a continuous snake between the station and the hotel, just like a parade. The whole town is jammed with people who've come to stare. They fill the courtyard and stand in the hall and even jostle around the doors to the dining room. Every time I open a door I look into a shimmering jelly of faces that oozes and undulates in front of me like frogs' eggs, sucking back and forth to make a path, closing behind, murmuring, gasping, clapping, pointing, their little Brownies snapping like black flies. I snap back at them. You can feel their eyes touching, stroking, poking. The Duchess says that at the end of the day her very soul feels soiled. Maybe that's why they change their clothes so often.

When they went to the sulphur springs this afternoon the *whole* baths were cleared of people for an hour while they swam. They have a whole floor to themselves, even a dining room, so they don't have to go downstairs for meals, and a separate dining room for the staff. I eat in the public dining room with Capt. Boscawen, the junior aide. He says we're sacrifices to equality, but it's grand enough for me. Our table is marked with a little flag and people come up to us with calling cards and invitations and little gifts and lots of questions, curtsying to *me* of all things. Boscawen is very friendly and takes their names and talks with them. It's his job, he says, to pick up interesting people and local gossip and tidbits about historical events and curious sights so the Duke can delight everyone with his astonishing knowledge of wherever he happens to be. It must be strange travelling around the world but never really *meeting* anyone or making friends, just like staying at home except the scenery changes. Maybe they're not snobbish but afraid.

With Miss Yorke it's just snobbishness. She mimicks the way I say "aboot" and "eh?" and "that's for sure" and a lot of other things until I'm scared to open my mouth even though she brays through her nose like a donkey. She says my pictures make Patsy look too tall and the Duchess too tired and the Duke too fat but it's just envy because she's so ugly. Everyone dislikes her. Boscawen says he and Alex Ramsay found a huge stuffed bear in the attic at Rideau Hall last year and carried it down in the middle of the night to Miss Yorke's room and stood it up by the side of her bed so it was the first thing she saw when she woke up. You could hear her screams over in Hull.

Brought the scrapbook up to date. Made the front page of the Calgary *Herald*!

Banff
Thursday, July 30, 1914

Went up Tunnel Mountain this morning on horseback. I would have preferred to walk but the horse was placid enough. Four Japanese bellhops carried Patsy's sketching things out of the hotel in solemn procession, single file, one with the easel, one with the stool, one with the sketch book and one with the paintbox, then they stood around grinning and bowing. I took their picture and they all demanded a tip! I took a picture of Patsy on her horse but she looked so frightened it will be one for the bogey book.

The view was glorious, looking west with Sulphur Mountain on the left and Norquay on the right and the sun on the snow of the Sundance range in the distance and the shadows blue in the gorges and valleys, but I didn't even try to photograph them. They seemed too big, too distant, too difficult to reduce to a piece of paper. You'd have to do mountains and nothing else, I think, and devote your life to them to get them right. So I just sat there feeling like I was flying, the air is so light and fresh and delicious, not hot and musky like the smell of the pines at home but sharp with spruce and balsam and cedar, and mossy, with the mysterious smells of water and rock and snow. At noon Brewster, our guide, brought up lunch from the hotel, smoked salmon and strawberries and chilled wine complete with silver dishes and a linen tablecloth!

We are all in love with Brewster. He's not dark, like the Cisco Kid, but lean and leathery with crinkly little lines around his eyes. He smells wonderfully of sweat and smoke and he wears a battered old stetson and a neckerchief just like cowboys in the movies. He's a bit bowlegged and slouches, but when he moves his whole body ripples in a single motion from his shoulders through his behind to his boots. He has a sly smile as if he's laughing at us and he talks very quietly, which makes everything he says sound important. He tried to scare us with stories about bears but we only saw one tiny black cub and it ran away as fast as it could. I bet they've all been shot and skinned and laid on the floor of the Banff Springs Hotel just like the deer and elk that stare down at us with glassy eyes in the dining room. Brewster says that when cowboys sleep out at night they put a lariat of horsehair in a circle around them to keep the rattlesnakes away because the rattlesnakes won't cross the prickles. You can kill a rattlesnake by making a circle of burrs around it while it's asleep. It will starve to death rather than touch a burr. Sounds like Gramp's blarney about how the giant Joe Mufferaw dropped his pack and made the Ottawa Valley or how Coolican is just short for Cuchulain, the Irish king who fought with the waves of the sea.

I took a picture of Brewster standing beside his horse. He stood very still and easy, looking right at the camera. How is it that a cowboy can have the sort of grace that draws your eye, while Their Highnesses, who are paid immense amounts of money to look graceful, are so hopelessly stiff? Is it his hat? Without his hat Brewster is quite ordinary. His forehead is white all the way down to his eyebrows and when he smiles you notice that his teeth are yellow.

We came back early to see if war had started but the Duke had gone fishing. He drove up to the hotel at six with thirty-five fish and the game warden. "I am under arrest!" he boomed. "A common poacher! This young pup has caught me red-handed with hot fish!" He guffawed and slapped the game warden on the back. The game warden looked like he could die. "Fifteen fish per angler per day, he tells me," the Duke bellowed. "I said, 'Per angler, per day, perdition,' my good man. What, I ask you, is the sense of my being governor of this wide-spread, far-flung sea-unto-sea Dominion if I cannot catch all the fish I have a mind to? Eh?" He thwacked the game warden again good-naturedly and they posed for a picture with the string of fish between them, then disappeared upstairs for a shot of whisky.

Fish for supper. Too many bones.

Banff
Friday, July 31, 1914

Sunny. Cool. Golf this morning. Duchess at sulphur baths. Lunch with Alice Millar and her parents. Bought postcards.

This afternoon the Duke was made a chief of the Stony tribe, a grand ceremony, a great crowd of Indians on their ponies in the hotel courtyard, all decked out in paint and feathers, some of them half-naked except for buckskin breeches, strange bits of skin and ribbons and hairy things that looked like scalps dangling from their spears. The Duke sat crosslegged on the cobblestones with the chiefs, and they passed the peace pipe around the circle very solemnly while the warriors danced and played the tom-toms, grinning from ear to ear like it was a big joke. They gave the Duke a wonderful headdress of eagle feathers that reaches right down to the ground and a suit of white deerskin embroidered all over with red and blue beads and named him Great Mountain Chief — *Teenchaka Eevake Oonka* is the way it sounds in Stony. The Duke put on the suit and headdress right away and posed for a dozen pictures with the Stony chief, Walking Buffalo, who really does look like a buffalo because he wears a buffalo scalp, with horns, on top of his head and has a broad, brown face and big flat nose sort of pushed in, squat, and is broadshouldered but dignified and gentle. He had two or three silver medals around his neck amoung the bits of bone and fur and he carried a medicine rattle so he made a curious tinkling noise when he walked. He said nothing at all until Patsy asked him in to tea and made a low bow and said "Thank you, Princess, I shall be honoured."

The *Herald* today says that world war is inevitable. No one really believes it. It is just a summer storm, the Duke says, a family squabble. Willy is a bully and Nicky is a brat. The King will knock some sense into their heads. "*Zwei dummkopfs,*" he said, rapping his knuckles against his skull.

Somewhere in the west
Saturday, August 1, 1914
10 a.m.

Awake since midnight. Terrible dream. There is a bonfire in the hotel courtyard and Bishop Ralph Horner is there wearing his black suit and dog collar but all smeared with war paint and he is shouting at me that I will be burned unless I can remember the words to a certain psalm but I can't remember even what psalm it is because there is so much whooping and shouting. I woke up and there *is* whooping and shouting in the courtyard right underneath my window and the sound of horses' hooves and neighing. I look out. A cowboy is bucking his horse right there in front of the steps, waving his right arm in the air and cursing at the top of his lungs. The doorman shouts at the Jap bellhops. They stand in a perfect dark circle against the wall. Not one moves. I can't quite make out what the cowboy is shouting between his whoops and ya-hoos. It sounds like "dook," "gimme dook," then "England" and "King" and a wild whoop and a sort of *pop-pop* sound. The glass on one of the lamps shatters and the light goes out. The doorman waves his arms and takes a couple of steps towards the bucking horse. The cowboy points his gun at the doorman's feet and two little puffs of dirt fly up. Then I see Brewster's hat. He takes a flying leap at the horse, grabs the reins and rolls the cowboy into the dirt. The Japs run up and form a little procession, one with the gun, one with the cowboy's hat, and follow solemnly as Brewster drags the man into the hotel.

I wrap myself in a blanket and run downstairs. Mob of people in the hall. The cowboy is sitting on the floor, hands tied, singing "Rool Britannyuh, Britannyuh roolsh shuh wash. . ." I go upstairs with Brewster. All the lights are on and the aides are running around opening and closing doors. Col. Farquhar meets us in the hall waving his pistol. "Have you seen His Highness? Has he been abducted?"

Patsy and the Duchess are in the drawing room quietly smoking. Brewster stands on one foot, then the other, wringing his hat in his hands. Unfortunate. Drunk. Payday. Excitement. A veteran. Boer War. Come to offer services. Meant well. Hard luck. Apologies. Brewster wipes the sweat from his face with his sleeve. He shuffles and looks at the floor.

"One cannot rule out the possibility of assassination," Col. Farquhar says.

The hall door opens and the Duke stands framed in the doorway, still in his headdress and white deerskins, half-profile, left hand on hip, right hand holding a piece of yellow paper.

"*Wir werden Krieg haben*," he says quietly. "England will fight. God save the King!"

So we're going home, most of us. Miss Yorke refused to leave. "We've just arrived!" she kept saying. "We've just *arrived*!" So she will stay to pack the bags. We've brought only what we can carry. The German chef has disappeared and there's not a crust of bread on the train.

Today Brewster was going to take me on a trail ride up Mount Norquay. Alone.

Moose Jaw, Saskatchewan
8 p.m.

We stopped for water at a little place just before one o'clock, hardly more than a few shacks and a station, and I could swear I smelled ham and eggs cooking, so I jumped out and ran down the track. Sure enough, in the baggage shed there was a man cracking eggs into a frying pan on the little potbelly stove.

"Excuse me, sir," I said, "Do you know where I might find some more?"

He wheeled around and glared at me through a pince-nez.

"I am *Miss* Cora Hind, of the *Manitoba Free Press*," he said, sticking out her (his?) bosom and looking me up and down. "You might try the Chinaman but you're sure to be poisoned."

"We can cook ourselves," I said, "on the train."

"Train!" she said. "I have been waiting *three hours* for a train. The CPR refuses to tell me why it is late or when it will arrive. Censorship, they say. Censorship! Horsefeathers! When I get back to Winnipeg I shall teach them the meaning of a free press!"

"It's us," I said. "The royal train. We have the right of way. An emergency. We're starving."

Miss Hind wiped her hands on her breeks and strode over to the doorway.

"Mercy!" she said and darted down the platform to the agent's office. By the time I got there she was cranking the telephone and it wasn't five minutes before people began running towards the station carrying bags of eggs and homemade bread and sides of bacon and butter and fresh vegetables and they stood there shyly squinting into the sun and grinning and bowing while the Duke shook hands with them all. Then Miss Hind hopped aboard with her valise and her frying pan and we cooked up a wonderful feast. She always carries "rations," she says, because she never knows when she'll spend the night in a haystack. She is "agricultural analyst" for the whole west and she wears men's clothes because they're the only thing that makes sense for gallivanting through wheat fields. A war will be a godsend for the farmers, she says.

Stopped for coal. We are near the stockyards and there is a cattle car across from me. The cows moo so sadly. Terrible stink.

Moving again. Red clouds, blue sky, no not blue, what's the word, *cerulean*, a cerulean Saskatchewan sky.

What will become of me?

Kenora, again
Sunday, August 2, 1914

Bought a basket of blueberries from a squaw at the station. At first she wouldn't take money for them, pointing at me and saying "For Queen! For Queen!" but she happily accepted a sovereign with the Queen's face on it. I've gobbled the whole thing like a bear. Nobody else would touch them. I'm not picky. My hair is stiff with cinders and my dress is filthy. At least black doesn't show the dirt. We are all hungry and grumpy and seasick from the pitching of the train and stiff from the hard plush seats and fed up with the *clickety-clack, clickety-clack* and the endless scenery.

"Scenery is bloody, isn't it?" Patsy said.

She is teaching me bridge. Every once in a while we whiz past a station with a white board saying the town's name and a knot of people on the platform, their clothes bleached white by the sun, brown faces turned up expectantly as if we carried some message. They wave all at once as we go by. At Portage la Prairie, the Hon. Arthur Meighen's town, the band turned out in full regalia and played "God Save the King." The Duke shook hands with Mr. Meighen and the mayor and made a little speech and Patsy accepted a bouquet of wild flowers from the Imperial Order of the Daughters of the Empire. There were a lot of flags and cheering and some men were wearing bits of old uniforms, going back to Riel I think, and one man was proudly wearing a row of medals on his overalls. I noticed that the country people stood back towards the end of the platform among the wagons and the cream cans, shading their eyes with their hands, their faces serious and strained, the women with their arms folded tight across their faded cotton dresses. A row of tall, tow-haired farm boys leaned against the station chewing grass, staring, curious, big and bony and strong as horses. The Duke saw them too. "Look!" he said, pointing them out to Col. Farquhar. "What material!"

We have no army, only the Governor-General's Foot Guards, and Capt. Boscawen says they're only good for show. I always thought that armies were sort of *there*, only invisible, and when war came they suddenly appeared out of nowhere in their red coats and white belts and shiny boots and marched off to fight, like General Wolfe or Isaac Brock at Queenston Heights. But armies are just people after all. I have tried all day to imagine those sunburned kids in red coats and I can't.

Sudbury, Ontario
Monday, August 3, 1914

Germany has given an ultimatum to France and Russia. The Duke is in the station telegraphing the Kaiser and Sir Robert Borden, who is golfing somewhere in Muskoka. The only politician in Ottawa is Col. Sam Hughes, the Minister of Militia. Col. Hughes has called out twenty thousand volunteers and says he will lead them into battle himself. "Over my dead body!" says the Duke, who is Commander-in-Chief of the Canadian armed forces. I was angry when he called Sam Hughes a "bloody nincompoop." Papa always said that Sam Hughes was the best soldier Canada ever produced. He just never got a chance. Sam's pretty old now to be fighting, he must be sixty anyway I'd guess. But the Duke is sixty-four. You could fire a cannon in his ear and he wouldn't hear a thing.

Huge crowd. Singing and cheering. The Methodist ladies gave us a lovely dinner in the station, pickerel fillets and fresh biscuits and pickles. As she was clearing away the Duke's plate one lady carefully removed his fork and set it on the tablecloth. "Keep your fork, Dook," she said, "we're havin' pie." My heart was in my mouth but the Duke said "Thank you madam" very politely and then his moustache started to twitch and his eyes twinkled and his face turned very red and his shoulders shook and he took out his handkerchief and *harrooomphed* very loudly into it and wiped his eyes. There is such a *feeling* in the air, excitement, like electricity, fun and recklessness and good will. All the stuffiness has gone. Everyone laughs and jokes and presses around, and the Connaughts wave and smile and chatter away like they've all been friends for years. It's just like a wedding!

The pie was blueberry. The Duke had two pieces. Home tomorrow.

Rideau Hall, Ottawa
Tuesday, August 4, 1914

Arrived 8 a.m. Joachim Ribbentrop at the station with flowers. He is going home to Germany, he says, to join the army. Tonight. He borrowed $10. He will repay me after the war, he says, when I come to Germany. He kissed me.

The news that war was declared came at 8:45 tonight. Capt. Boscawen and Capt. Rivers-Buckley, the comptroller, are leaving for England tomorrow. The Connaughts may go this week too. No one knows what to expect. I feel like the world is flat and I've come to the edge of it.

R.H.
Saturday, August 8, 1914

I am conscripted. Bandage-maker, third class. They gave me the bandages to roll because I am so hopeless at sewing and knitting. Mum thought sewing was servitude. It was the only thing we ever agreed about, I think. The Duchess would win every prize at the Renfrew fair. She is knitting something called "cholera belts," which are just long strips of wool as far as I can see, and I don't know what they have to do with cholera or how a soldier would wear one but I am too embarrassed to ask. "Generals are remembered for knitting long after their battles are forgotten," the Duchess said, which is just as well in the case of Lord Cardigan who ordered the charge of the Light Brigade, and "Raglan" to me means the main street in Renfrew. Then there's Wellington boots and Napoleon hats and a chewing tobacco called "Bobs" after Lord Roberts.

Patsy has had a regiment named for her: Princess Patricia's Canadian Light

Infantry. It sounds so grand! Not that she leads it but she is a sort of patron. It is being raised by Mr. Hamilton Gault of Montreal who had hoped to command it himself, but Col. Farquhar has taken over and Mr. Gault is a major. Patsy is embroidering a regimental "colour," which is a kind of flag soldiers carry into battle. It is stretched out on a frame in the blue sitting room, a piece of crimson silk about three feet by four feet. She designed the emblem herself. I suggested shamrocks, but she said they wouldn't go well with the red, and decided on a cluster of white marguerites against a blue background in a gold border, with a crown on top. Major Gault's wife is named Marguerite. It will look very pretty. Patsy works at it day and night. "Stitch, stitch, stitch in poverty, hunger and dirt," I chanted at her yesterday the way Mum used to when she was mending shirts. Patsy had never heard of the poem. She made me say it right through, at last as much as I could remember. It makes you think, she said. Rideau Hall *is* pretty dirty, especially now that the German maids have left, and at night I can hear the mice in the walls.

We have given up smoking for the war effort.

R.H.
Sunday, August 9, 1914

Hot. Muggy. I am to stay on here "for the duration." It may be a week, it may be a year. The social events are all cancelled but everyone is clamouring for news about the "Pats," and Mrs. Gooderham, the president of the IODE, has asked the Duchess to be patron of a campaign to raise money for a hospital ship, so there will be a lot of bookkeeping and typing.

I have been given Col. Farquhar's office. He is camping out with the regiment in Lansdowne Park. It smells of stale tobacco. It's quite large with a nice carpet and two leather chairs and a folding cot so I might move in altogether. I found a flask of whisky in his desk drawer. If he doesn't claim it in a day or two I'll hide it away. Sam Hughes says there's to be no liquor in camp, and I can use it more than Col. Farquhar. The champagne has disappeared with Herr Ribbentrop. So has the Ottawa Dairy Mobile. He still owes $200 on it, Alice says. He left debts all over town. His older brother Lothar came to see Mr. Bennett yesterday. He hadn't eaten in three days. He is sick with tuberculosis and Joachim left him without a cent. Alice says Lothar will be arrested as an "enemy alien" and sent to a concentration camp. Everyone says that Joachim was a spy.

Tomorrow there will be a meeting of women in the ballroom to launch the hospital ship campaign. I put a notice in the paper today. An open meeting, no invitations. No tea. Mrs. Ross at the *Journal* was shocked. You'll get all the riff-raff! she said. All the better, said the Duchess, if they are prepared to contribute. (Besides, the Gooderhams are only distillers and poteen is poteen whether it's licenced or not, if you ask me.)

Alice says the Duchess is turning socialist. No, I said, she's a born general. She seems to thrive on the war, up and dressed every morning by eight, making lists, issuing orders, ransacking the closets for old linen. She's even making a speech tomorrow, her first in Canada. She's very nervous. We have done six drafts and it's not right yet. She is afraid of her accent, I think, so I have secretly racked my brains for words that will hide it. I have even taken out the word "war." Miss Eady would be proud of me.

R.H.
Monday, August 10, 1914

We set out four hundred chairs in the ballroom and by two o'clock every seat was taken and hundreds more women came in and stood. Lady Borden and Mrs. Gooderham were with the Duchess at a table at the front and Miss Yorke and I had a small table to one side with a very large silver bowl and a ledger to take down the names of donors to be published in the press.

Lady Laurier was directly opposite me in the front row. She is the ugliest woman I have ever seen, very old and immensely fat with a long, witch's nose and tiers of chins and a face that looks like rice pudding. Her white hair was done up in little ringlets, like a girl's and she was decked out in a birthday cake pink gown, all lace and ruffles and tiny pink bows and a spun-sugar hat to match with bluebirds in it. I couldn't take my eyes off her and felt rude but she is almost blind, her eyes covered with a white film like a pair of oysters. She tilts her head in the direction of sounds and gropes with her fingers like a prehistoric creature waving its antennae. Everyone says it's too bad, Sir Wilfrid is still such a handsome man and his English is perfect.

The Duchess' voice shook and she spoke in a whisper so almost no one heard her, but they clapped — it didn't sound like much with gloves on — and then Lady Borden whispered a few things and Mrs. Adam Shortt, the archivist's wife, read a long speech in a very loud voice. Mrs. Shortt is a medical doctor and a feminist and everyone is afraid of her. Her speech was about how we should give up ball gowns and bonbons because other women were sacrificing their sons and husbands. I couldn't get down half of it but Mrs. Shortt gave out copies to the press herself. Then Mrs. Gooderham announced that Ottawa's goal was $20,000 out of a total of $100,000 for all Canada.

The room buzzes like a beehive, handkerchiefs fanning like wings. Then the Duchess stands up.

"I shall lead off the campaign with a personal donation," she says in a clear, loud voice. She marches over to our silver bowl and drops in a crisp bill. It's

blue. The King goggles up at me from the bowl. A $1,000 bill. I suck in my
breath and dutifully enter it in the ledger.

"Her Highness has donated one thousand dollars," Miss Yorke calls out.

A sucking sound goes round the room. Squawks and shuffling. Whispering. The ladies fiddle with their parasols and dab at their foreheads with bits of
lace. They sit still, eyes shifting from floor to windows to ceiling to windows to
floor. At last a tiny woman rises at the very back of the room and starts to
make her way across the knees and over the feet, riding the sea of silk like a
small, plump ship in a storm. In the hush I can hear her "Excuse me" and "So
sorry" as she struggles through the waves, disappearing from sight in the
crowded aisle, arriving flushed and breathless at the silver bowl.

"I will give $250," she says apologetically. "It is so little." She puts a cheque
in the bowl and spells her name for me, Mrs. F-r-e-i-man, freeman, you know
the department store on Rideau Street. Mrs. Freiman seems very young and
she has the most beautiful brown eyes, round and bright and soft as a doe's.

I look out expectantly. Not a ripple. The women sit as if turned to stone,
their faces stiff and blank, eyes wide, glassy. My stomach's in a knot. I know
this look. I have seen it before a thousand times on the faces around Papa's
poker table when the stakes got high. They have no money.

The silence is broken by Mrs. Herridge, the wife of the preacher at St.
Andrew's.

"Perhaps many of us came here today with the idea of *pledging* a contribution to be collected at *a later date*," she says in a high, anxious voice. Everyone
smiles and claps. Handkerchiefs fan happily. Mrs. Herridge takes a deep
breath.

"My *personal* feeling is that I should like my donation to remain *anonymous*." Applause and cheers. "I do not wish to seek personal reward from this
tragic situation, nor do I wish to *embarrass* those less fortunate women who
are able to contribute only a few pennies. I believe that now is the time to sink
our selfish identities in a large and noble cause."

Mrs. Herridge sits down to a storm of applause. A committee is formed to
organize a public collection. Mrs. Herridge is elected chairman. We sing "God
Save the King" and the ladies herd to the door.

Miss Yorke picks the two pieces of paper out of the silver bowl. "Isn't it
curious," she says, "that the Canadian hospital ship should be launched by a
Prussian and a Jew?"

R.H.
Tuesday, August 11, 1914

Went to the *Journal* and *Citizen* first thing with the Duchess' speech.

"It looks like your ship's torpedoed!" Miss Chadwick cawed. "That's what
comes of letting the Jews in."

Her story was quite complimentary, even gushy, praise the, thank goodness. A short list of donations was printed at the end. Mrs. Herridge's name was first. One hundred dollars. Mrs. Freiman's name was not mentioned in the story or in the list. I clipped two copies for the Duchess' scrapbook. "What iss ziss?" bellowed the Duke. "Page nine? Page *nine*! Is the Royal Family not good enough for page one, eh?" Alice says the Duke is taking his role as commander-in-chief rather seriously. He wants the police to lock up all the enemy aliens in Canada. Alice says there are four hundred thousand of them and most of them are Liberal. Sam Hughes says they should start with the Prussian bitch at Rideau Hall.

R.H.
Friday, August 14, 1914

Hot. Sticky. I am so tired my fingers miss the keys and the words float around on the page. The telephone rings constantly. What is the Princess wearing to the opening of the House? Black? How fashionable! Will she go overseas with her regiment? Will she wear khaki? Is it true she has broken her engagement to a German officer? Bushels of letters every day. People sending socks and bandages and toothbrushes and snapshots of fair, grinning boys in gardens. My son. He is only seventeen but big for his age and strong. Can you take him? Coins are taped to the paper to pay for return postage to Guelph or Montreal or Saskatoon. There are letters from mothers trying to get their sons into the Pats and letters from mothers trying to get their sons out of the Pats, women sending money and asking for money, women volunteering for nursing service and women asking Patsy to address the Equal Suffrage Association or the Canadian Women's Press Club in Vancouver. I file them all and reply. The answer is always the same, "Her Royal Highness regrets. . . ." but the letter has to be graciously written all the same and typed up neatly on Government House stationery with the royal crest, so whoever sent it will have a little souvenir for their grandchildren. So many women so excited! What can I do? What can I do? What on earth did they all do two weeks ago before the war? What did I do two weeks ago?

R.H.
Saturday, August 15, 1914

Had a bit of a scare tonight. Went for a walk down to the little wooden footbridge over the Rideau River. There was a breeze off the water although it was damp and smelled. The river is low this year with the drought and full of reeds and garbage. You can hardly hear the Rideau Falls, just a trickle. It was about 10 o'clock, still a little light in the western sky, and the nighthawks were screeching. I lit a cigarette I'd snitched from the soldiers' supply and leaned against the railing looking upriver towards Porter's Island, where the pest house used to be. Gramp's first wife died there of cholera. "So they say," he shrugged. "Never found a grave. She might be walkin' around yet, lookin' fer me. Maybe she took up with somebody better."

I got nervous when I heard the footsteps, *trip-trap, trip-trap*, quick and light but definitely a man's. Ottawa is full of men trying to get into uniform. They get drunk a lot and rowdy. Some of them are too poor to get a hotel room so they camp out in the parks, covered with newspapers, hardly more than bums, and beg on the streets. But the steps didn't sound like a drunk and from his shadow I could see he was well-dressed, a dark suit, a straw boater, a cane. I could see its silver tip as he swung it. He was heavy-set, with short legs, a banker probably or a businessman, working late, going home. He slowed down when he saw me and stopped. I stared at the river praying he'd go on.

"Lovely evening." He tipped his hat.

"Yes."

"Do you come here often?"

"No."

"It is out of the way."

He leaned against the railing, his shoulder brushing mine. I edged away. Miss Eady had warned me about strange men who stuck girls with needles and carried them off. The worst, she said, were decent-looking men, and women too, who pretended to be friendly to lure you into a life of sin.

"Do you know, today is the most important day of my life," he said, watching me, his eyes bright. "Today I begin my life's work. I have dedicated myself to the fight for peace."

"Which regiment have you joined?"

He started, and twiddled his cane, as if he'd been thinking of something else.

"I have offered my services to Sir Robert, and to Sir Wilfrid, to use as best they see fit in this tragic conflict," he said quickly. "However, I shall be at the same time a soldier on a more important battlefield, the battlefield of Ludlow, Colorado in the struggle for industrial peace."

I couldn't for the life of me understand what Ludlow had to do with Belgium or the Rockefeller coal mines with the Empire so I said nothing, but he didn't seem to notice and went right on talking anyway. He seemed very excited, fiddling with his cane, rhythmically caressing the silver tip with the fingers of his right hand. There was something slightly familiar about him, the square head, heavy jaw, broad cheekbones, something to do with religion. Maybe he was a preacher.

"This war is only the bursting of an abscess," he said, fixing me with a glittery eye. "It is the draining of the festering sore, the disgorging of the bile and corruption of a wicked civilization. In that way it is beneficial. Militarism will be crushed. Britain and Germany will destroy each other. The Empire will crumble. The United States will emerge as the first power in the world, the champion of a brave new order of mankind."

My God, I thought, he's a Yankee spy! Everyone says Ottawa is full of spies. Just last night a man was shot on a railway bridge. Sam Hughes says he was trying to blow it up. The Duke says he was a French-Canadian who didn't understand what the sentry was yelling at him. The Toronto home guard has been called out in case the Germans invade across Lake Ontario the way the Fenians did. "If the Yanks aren't with us they're agin us," Sam Hughes, says. "They've been agin us since 1776 and the war ain't over yet." Guards have been posted at the waterworks and the power plants and the bridges. Except this one.

"Do you know who I am?" he asked suddenly.

I shook my head.

"What will you call me then?" he grinned in a leering sort of way.

"Billy," I said, thinking that his footsteps on the wood planks reminded me of Billy Goat Gruff. He gave me a hard look. I was wondering whether he had a sword in his cane, or a gun.

"And what shall I call you?"

"Cookee," I said, giving my old nickname. Nobody in Ottawa knows it.

"Sugar?" he winked, "or molasses?"

"Oatmeal," I said, figuring I'd better get out of there pretty fast. He grabbed my elbow as I turned.

"May I see you home?"

It was only three blocks up to the gate to Rideau Hall and I prayed a guard would be on duty. Some of the houses had lamps lit. He pointed out a brick house where he said his brother used to live. His brother is dying of tuberculosis in Denver. I relaxed a little when we came to the shops on Thomas Street although there wan't a soul in sight. I offered him a cigarette, hoping he'd let go of my elbow, but he said no, he didn't smoke. I should give up cigarettes, he said. A vicious habit. Yes, I said. He talked about the pitfalls facing young girls in the city, poor wages, unhealthy conditions, corrupt employers, they fell into vice out of their innocence and poverty, he said. I agreed about the poor wages.

"If you'll let me help you I can find you a decent job with a respectable, Christian family," he said, looking at me earnestly. "A warm, happy home. I'm sure Mrs. Herridge. . . ."

"Thank you," I said, stopping at the gate. "I shall be safe now." I darted through the iron bars and ran full tilt up the driveway.

"You look like you've seen a ghost," Patsy said.

I showed her the red mark on my elbow. "He was either a spy or a white slaver."

The guards searched the grounds and the streets nearby but no trace of the man was found.

R.H.
Sunday, August 16, 1914

Slept in. Connaughts went to church at St. Bartholomew's down the way. Big crowd. The Duke wears his uniform all the time now, khaki, very dull I think. It's supposed to be practical because it looks like dirt. Papa would be furious. When he went up the Nile to rescue General Gordon he said the British soldiers rowed in their shirt sleeves but they always put their red coats and white helmets on before a battle even though they stood out like drops of blood on the sand. It was psychological, he said, to scare the enemy by showing you were not afraid, but the Mahdi's niggers were much scarier whirling around in their war paint and white sheets with the most blood-curdling screams. They murdered Gordon too, and stuck his head on a pike, and sacked Khartoum so there was nothing left when the British got there but rotting corpses. The voyageurs never got there. Papa was always angry about that. You bust your ass for six months hauling barges up rapids in the blazing sun so you can get the bloody British army to Khartoum and they won't give you a peek before you have to turn around and haul them down again. War, he said, is just work. They didn't even get medals. But Papa was a hero in the Valley, "Khartoum" Coolican, although he'd been called "Tom" for Thomas D'Arcy McGee. Poor Papa. He gave Mum a string of beautiful turquoise beads from a Pharaoh's tomb but she never wore them.

Miss Yorke came up after lunch with a package. Did I know of anyone on staff named Cooke? It was a small square package, wrapped in expensive paper and addressed in a tiny hand to "Miss Cooke." I said I'd ask around. I opened it gingerly. It was a book, bound in red leather, with gold lettering, *The Secret of Heroism*, with a note attached. Apologies. An unfortunate misunderstanding. Princess a friend. Noble and beautiful soul. Remarks should not be construed as disloyalty to the Crown. Devoted servant.

I haven't dared to tell anyone that the spy was Mr. William Lyon Mackenzie King, former Minister of Labour. Of course that's where I've seen him, at St. Andrew's Presbyterian Church, although we went very seldom, Mr. Booth tending to nod off and snore during Dr. Herridge's sermon. He says Dr. Herridge is a fool and a cuckold anyway, but then Mr. Booth shocks everyone with his language.

"Oh, you have an admirer!" Patsy crowed when I showed her Mr. King's book, saying he'd given it to me at church. "He gives one to every girl he has his eye on! He must have six dozen in the attic! He even gave me one once. We had him up to lunch and he called every day afterwards for six weeks! He even sent me his photograph. It was rather pathetic. He's proposed to all the eligible women in Ottawa, at least those who have a fortune. Of course he's out of office now and poor as a church mouse, or court mouse, we call him because he's always around to fill up an extra chair at official things. Mummy calls him '*der Lueckenbuesser*,' the stop-gap. He asked me once to call him 'Rex.' I declined but Daddy called him 'Sexy Rexy' once at a smoker when they'd all had too much port and he seemed quite flattered."

We looked up the photo in the album. A stiff, ungainly face, closed and almost defiant, with an odd cowlick of fair hair falling over the forehead, a righteous nose and a wide, fleshy mouth, lips thick and bowed like a girl's, beautifully carved, like the Negro piano player in Grace's brothel.

"He probably wants an invitation to dinner," Patsy said, giving me an appraising look. "Well, we are supposed to be kind to Liberals, for the war effort, as long as he doesn't bring his dreadful mother. Imagine anyone being proud that her father was a traitor with a price on his head! He should have been hanged! And he would have been too if he hadn't scampered away to New York in a woman's dress. The last time I saw Mr. King he told me how much I looked like his mother! Such a compliment! Thinking she had died, I said rather lightly that I believed in reincarnation, so we had a long heart-to-heart talk about death over the chocolate creme. He was surprised, he said, to find a girl of my wealth and position so natural, so intelligent, so *unaffected*. He was so pleased that I didn't smoke. Women who smoked were vulgar, so indecent. Then of course Mummy pulled out a cigar and lit up!"

I must have had a funny look on my face because Patsy stopped laughing and patted my hand.

"He's a strange bird," she said, tapping her forehead, "a real bookworm, has a dozen degrees, but he does *try*, and you have to admire his perserverance. He has a thick hide. People say he will go far. He'd be a good catch, Lily, for you."

Wrote a note to Mr. King thanking him for the book. Patsy says it's something to do with Sir Galahad. She hasn't read it. She reads very little except romances and the serials in the newspapers. Herr Ribbentrop used to smuggle in German magazines and chocolates and opium cigarettes for the Duchess in his violin case but of course that's all gone now. I went looking for a dictionary today and I realized that there isn't a single book in Rideau Hall. Patsy's colour is half-done. Very pretty.

R.H.
Monday, August 17, 1914

Telephoned the *Citizen* and *Journal* with the latest donations for the hospital ship. It's going very badly, hardly more than $200 in a week. The wealthiest women give almost nothing. Mrs. Harriss, who entertains at lavish musicales at least once a week, gave $15, and Mrs. Lorne MacDougall, who owns most of Renfrew county, gave $10. Mrs. Eddy has given nothing, neither has Mrs.

Fleck, who is worth millions. Most of the money comes from little donations of one dollar or less. Miss Chadwick says most of the ladies drop more during an afternoon's bridge, but then they pay in jewellery or tea cups so it's not quite so crass. Miss Chadwick won an opal ring from Lady Borden by running up the tab.

I told her that Patsy would be presenting the colour to the regiment at church parade on Sunday. I described it on condition that she not breath a word until Monday's paper.

"Marguerites?" she said. "My dear child, *everybody* knows that Marguerite Gault *bought* the regiment for Hammy to get rid of him! They simple detest each other! She's sending him to France to kill him off!"

Patsy is ripping out the design. She thinks it's just wicked gossip but if the stories about Mrs. Gault's *affaires* are true the regiment will be laughed off the field. I didn't tell her the rumour that chief among Marguerite Gault's many secret lovers is His Royal Highness, the Duke of Connaught.

It all seems so silly! I've never thought of war as stupid before, or funny, depending how you look at it. Everything has changed, but nothing happens! There is fighting in Belgium and the British seem to be winning, but the Germans aren't losing and the despatches are so contradictory they're no better than rumours. People telephone me because they think I have special information but I don't really so I just say it's "classified."

Princess Patricia's Canadian Light
Infantry
Lansdowne Park
Ottawa, Ontario
Tuesday, August 18, 1914

Mrs. L.J. Papineau,
Manor House,
Montebello, Quebec.

Dearest Mother:

Here I am under canvas at last and reasonably comfortable, with bed, chair, table and soap box. Blatchford, my batman, seems very capable. He brought everything out from town this morning and has bought several little things for me which I had neglected such as sponge, pillow, mirror, hooks etc. I need some needles and thread, a fountain pen, soap, towels and a pair of canvas shoes.

I am on my feet a great deal. I was up at 6 this morning and must report tomorrow at 7. I am very worried as to whether I can properly perform my duties. They are numerous and far more difficult than I ever imagined. We have a splendid lot of veterans — I am more afraid of them than the enemy as yet.

I have had such nice letters from "my girls," Beatrice especially. She will call to see you as soon as you are in town. Poor Miss Macpherson seems frightfully disappointed at not seeing me. She says she came up here again in the hope of finding out she *wasn't* in love with me! Entre nous, of course –

There might be a chance of my being dropped at the last moment as some good men have applied for commissions but I would build no hope on that idea if I were you.

Cheer up dear old mother, this won't last long.

Very lovingly,
Talbot

Please send my safety razor here at once. Address me now as Lieutenant Talbot Papineau, Company 3, Princess Patricia's Canadian Light Infantry.

R.H.
Tuesday, August 18, 1914

I have found a bicycle! Was searching in the attic for rummage for Belgian Relief and found it in a corner behind a canoe with a tear in the canvas and a stuffed goose. I guess all the awful things governors-general are given end up in the attic, like Geordie the bear, which the moths have got at, and the sheep's horn the Connaughts were given in Calgary. It's an old bicycle but the tires are good and I bought a pair of bloomers and a middy at Freiman's department store and now I can get downtown in less than fifteen minutes. The Duke approves of women exercising, so as long as Mr. Booth doesn't see me I'm fine. I get a lot of whistles and cat calls from the crowds of men in front of the Russell Hotel. I smile and even flirt a little. They're all very young and handsome and sunburned, country boys, and I find myself searching the faces for one from home. They seem a little lost, and very shy. They make rude noises behind my back but when I turn around and look them in the eye they go all red and stare at their feet. Hundreds come in on the trains every day heading for the military camp at Valcartier near Quebec City. They sleep in the station or even on Parliament Hill and there are great long line-ups in front of all the recruiting offices. The ladies are in a terrific tizzy about it. Lady Borden refuses to go downtown alone for fear of being "molested" and they all whisper behind their hands about "indecencies" and "crude language," especially the ugly ones.

I love the noise and the liveliness and the cool, beery gusts of laughter that float out the door of the Russell saloon as I push my way along the sidewalk. There's nothing to be afraid of. Just watch your step, like in Renfrew, when we kids always made a big circuit into the road in front of Wright's Hotel so we didn't step in the tobacco juice with our bare feet. The war is just like Renfrew in the spring, when the drives came down the Bonnechere and hundreds of men suddenly came out of the woods. How mysterious they were, those wild bush men with their long, stringy hair and great bushy beards, unshaven for six months, their pale little eyes peering out like small animals from the shrubbery. They'd stand patiently in long lines in the cold mud outside Gramp's bathhouse, laughing and drinking and waiting their turn in the big steamy barrels, each one holding a neat, wrapped package of new clothes from Pedlow's or Fraser's. How they'd yell when they hit the hot water! Then yell again in the cold shower that Gramp piped in from Smith's Creek. Gramp threw their old clothes out the window into a big pile in the yard and Papa would pour kerosene on and put a match to them. The men in line would make bets on the number of greybacks they could see running away. Shanty-man's pets they were called. Gramps always said that Joe Mufferaw had lice as big as grizzly bears and twice as fierce. In about fifteen minutes the man would come out in his new shirt and trousers, face shining, hair dripping, and Papa would sit him down on a chair in the middle of the yard and zip, off would come the hair and beard, a mountain of damp, curly hair big enough to stuff a mattress growing up around the chair, the man coming out like a shorn lamb, his shaven skin soft and white against his windburned nose and frost-bitten cheeks, scars livid from the steam, a gold earring gleaming against the black hair on his neck.

Then they'd all go off together and drink. Two days, three days, some of them were still around weeks later, broke, filthy, begging odd jobs to earn enough to get home. They said the Renfrew hotels sold more whisky in one week in the spring than during the rest of the year. You could see the old wooden buildings shake when a fight got going. Once in a while Barney McDermott would peddle up on his bicycle, brass knuckles on his hand, Sam, his yellow Great Dane at his heels, glowering out of his one good eye as he pushed open the barroom door, emerging a few minutes later dragging a bleeding body too drunk to know what had hit him. Barney would usually leave the man in the gutter to sober up. "Jails just make work for honest men," he said. Barney never carried a gun. Nobody ever got shot except by accident in the hunting season. The men fought with their fists and feet. They said it was fairer, gave the little guys a chance. A little Frenchman, no bigger than a minute, could drop-kick a big Swede or a Polack in the blink of an eye. You saw a lot of men with scars and a few with tiny holes all over their faces where they'd been kicked or stomped with caulked boots.

I saw a man killed once — well, I didn't see the fight because we girls were kept in, but I saw the body lying on the road. His throat had been cut. Everyone figured it was an Indian. The loggers were scared of knives. Their hands were too callused and thick from swinging an axe, Papa said. They didn't have the touch. And their knives were always dull from whittling. Papa always kept his knives razor sharp and hung them in a slotted wooden rack against the wall.

Saw a parade of soldiers marching along the streetcar tracks all out of step, only scraps of uniforms, a cap here, a jacket there, no rifles. It seems the rifles aren't made yet.

> P.P.C.L.I.
> Lansdowne Park
> Ottawa, Ontario
> Wednesday, August 19, 1914

Mrs. L.J. Papineau,
Manor House,
Montebello, Quebec.

Dearest Mother,

Your note and my razor just received with thanks.

We are busy learning the business. We have our first parade parade at 7, breakfast at 8 and at 9 o'clock we carry out manoeuvers. An imaginary enemy line is selected and we advance precisely as though we were actually engaged. At the end we fix bayonets and charge, shouting, officers with drawn swords. We march home and have luncheon and do the same thing from 2 til 4:30.

My uniform will be ready on Friday. It feels strange to be running around a football field in short pants as if I were a boy at McGill again but infinitely better than sweating over dull papers in my stuffy office, don't you think? We are all in good spirits. In spite of your protests, I doubt that I shall be missed by my friends, since most of them are here with me, or by the Liberal Party, which seems in no hurray to have me.

Keep up your courage, dearest mother. I am sure it will all turn out well in the long run.

> Yours very lovingly,
> Talbot.

R.H.
Wednesday, August 19, 1914

Patsy has made a new design for the colour. It's her initials, "VP" for Victoria Patricia, in a scroll script. Very stupid, she says, but it can't be helped since she has only three days to finish. It was too late to call back the badge, which has already gone into manufacture, so the Pats will wear marguerites on their sleeves after all.

Mr. King came to supper, very informal, "just family." We seem to be almost camping here anyway. Even the footmen have enlisted. The food was terrible. Mr. King was very nice. He seems to have changed his ideas about the war. He said he thought the war was in the nature of a crusade, and that peace when it came would be all the more beautiful. He said he thought that the sacrifice would have an ennobling effect, would help purify the world. He quoted Sir Galahad's words, "If I lose myself, I save myself." He said he wasn't actually moving to New York but would do most of his work in Ottawa, that he wasn't cut out for military affairs, being nearly forty, but would offer his services on the home front. We talked about a dream he'd had, that he'd been in a war, and tried to imagine what it was like to be suddenly swept out of existence, and Patsy mentioned Conan Doyle, who has given up Sherlock Holmes for spiritualism and swears he has actually spoken to people living beyond the grave, and that it was paradise just as it had been described in the Bible. Mr. King said the scientific proof of an afterlife would be the greatest breakthrough since Isaac Newton.

The Duke offered Mr. King a cigarette and he took it, placing it gingerly between his lips like a firecracker, and the Duke lit it from his own, and Mr. King took a couple of puffs, puff, puff, hardly taking the smoke into his mouth, then put the cigarette into an ashtray and didn't touch it again even when it turned into a long column of white ash. He has a certain nerve. They talked about the election rumours. Mr. King said he thought Sir Robert would go to the country and the Tories would sweep in on war fever. The Duke said there were many in the party who wanted that, like Sam Hughes and his ranting about the fiery cross, but he wouldn't hear of it and would resign if an election were called at this time.

After supper I sang "Londonderry Air" and recited Drummond's "Habitant." Everyone said I got the accent just right. I loaned Mr. King Chamberlain's *Foundations*. We're going to Kingsmere for tea tomorrow, then he goes to New York for a week. He is not working for the Standard Oil Company, he said, but for the Rockefeller Foundation, which is a charity.

Rolled bandages until midnight. Tired.

R.H.
Thursday, August 20, 1914

Took the train to Kingsmere. We were just out of the station, crossing the bridge, when Willie leaned over and pointed down river.

"That's where poor Bert drowned. Dear Bert. So loyal and true. No man ever had such a faithful friend. Such happy times we spent together. Good old Bert."

I opened my mouth to ask what kind of dog he was, but Willie kept right on talking.

"I'll never forget how he used to lie in front of the fire in our apartment while I real aloud 'The Idylls of the King.' That's where I got the idea for the statue on Wellington Street. I couldn't very well erect a statue of Bert Harper. Nobody knew who he was. It would have no significance. So I hit on Sir Galahad as a symbol of courage and purity, the ideals for which poor Bert so nobly gave his life."

I leaned back and closed my eyes.

"But of course you know Bert from my book," he said.

Book? Book? Oh Jesus! *The Secret of Heroism.* It was in my drawer, unopened. I'd completely forgotten.

"Yes. It's very beautiful."

He flushed and rubbed his hands together.

He tells me about his cottage at Kingsmere, how he and Bert bought the property thirteen years ago, just the summer before Bert was killed, a small lot on the lake, the cottage very small too, a bachelor's den, but he's going to buy more land as it becomes available and add on to the cottage, clear the underbrush and put in flower beds, a driveway with a stone wall, a dock of course and a boathouse. He draws a little map on his knee showing me where everything is, even the sundial that he'd been lucky enough to pick up at Schenkman's junk yard for one dollar, and how big it is and who built it and how much he paid for it. He's so pleased with these things, like a little boy with a pocket full of frogs, that it's quite touching, and I feel a little flattered that he's chosen me to show them off to.

We get off at Old Chelsea and take a buggy the rest of the way. He points out the Booth cottage, a dark old house on a hill, the house where May Belle, the Booths' youngest daughter, died of tuberculosis, the year I was born. She was only twenty-three, a fair, pretty, spoiled-looking girl. Mr. Booth used to sometimes call me by her nickname, "Chum," when he was tired. He never goes there now.

The lake is hardly more than a puddle, shallow and swampy with reeds in the water that make me think of leeches. I'm glad I didn't bring my bathing dress. The cottage is tiny and painted an awful yellow. A very tall, old man with a white beard and red cheeks is rocking on the porch.

"Is that you, Billy?" he shrills, turning his head to the sound of our footsteps on the path. "Where on earth have you been? You have left us completely helpless here!"

"I . . . I'm sorry, Father."

"That dreadful Frenchwoman you hired to cook came to me this morning and demanded money! I refused of course. Well she simply left us to starve! The man has not come to chop wood or bring water. You know, Billy, your mother is simply not up to this sort of rough life!"

The place is a mess, clothes strewn all over, the table in the single room covered with dirty dishes, tracks of dirt across the floor, flies buzzing over the

dried food. The sound of coughing and a terrific banging comes from the
kitchen. A woman in an apron is trying to stuff a log into the stove. Smoke is
billowing out. The woman is weeping and rubbing her eyes. She must be
Willie's mother. Her hair is quite grey. I have never in my life seen anyone so
thin. Her arms are like sticks, twigs, her eyes are sunken and the skin on her
face shrivelled back to show her teeth.

"My sister, Bella," Willie says.

I open the draft but it doesn't help. The ash box is full. Willie takes it out to
dump it. I send Bella for some newspaper and look around for kindling. The
kitchen smells of grease and sour milk. Even the slop pail is full. Not a stick. I
find a dirty apron and go out to collect some branches. The ground looks as
though it's been swept. I catch a glimpse of white through the trees. Someone
is coming down the path towards the cottage, running, a woman, a woman in
a billowing white dress, an old woman, her long white hair flying out behind
her, a daisy chain around her neck and another on her head. Her face is ashen.
Her feet are bare. Oh Lord save me, it's the Queen of the Faeries!

"Mother!" Willie cries. He scoops her up like a snowflake and carries her to
a chair. She is laughing wildly.

"We're saved!" she gasps. "Marjorie is bringing us a picnic! Won't that be
fun? You see, God does provide!"

Marjorie is Mrs. Herridge, who is bustling down the path followed by her
son, Bill, a sleek, sauntering young man with a head shaped like a bullet, and
calculating brown eyes. They each carry a picnic basket. Roast beef and
biscuits and lettuce and cake and ice-tea and lemonade and even plates and a
tablecloth. She has forgotten the knives and forks.

"Never mind!" cries Mrs. King. "We shall eat with our fingers. Won't it be
fun?"

The food is laid out on a cardtable on the porch. Mrs. King begins to snatch
at it like a starving sparrow. She feeds her husband, selecting radishes and
buns and bits of meat and putting them on his plate. He eats silently, not
looking at the food or asking what it is. I watch his hands. He is blind.

"Why, when I was a little girl," Mrs. King carols, "we were so poor we had
only six knives and forks to share among the eight of us so we had to pass them
around! And here I am, after all these years, with a husband and a son who are
even more improvident that dear old Papa!" She laughs and wipes her eyes
with a rolled-up handkerchief.

I glance over at Willie. His face is flushed and he looks at his plate. He sits
very still, like a large pink egg.

"A Rockefeller connection is hardly improvident, Belle," Mr. King says. "I
have always said it's not what you know, it's who you know. A man of
reputation and means is in a position to set a young fellow's feet along the
right paths in life. One can do worse than to cultivate the great."

"It's a great chance to do good, Mother," Willie says.

"I shall tend the home fires, Willie," his father says. "A note to Sir Wilfrid now and then wouldn't be amiss. We need to keep your seat warm. Can't be too long before an election."

"Laurier has chosen Billy as his successor, did you know?" Mrs. King beams at me. "He'll be the next prime minister!"

"Mother!"

"Well, it's true! You told me yourself!"

I take a glass of lemonade and a slice of cake not to seem rude.

"Are they looking for nurses?" Bella asks, turning her skeletal face towards me. "I haven't practised for some years but I trained in...."

"Bella!" Mrs. King cries. "Don't be a fool! I'm sure they're looking for pretty young girls to cheer the boys up, not an old maid like you! You'd scare them half to death!"

"You have two invalids here at home, Bella," her father says sharply, "and your own health is not good."

"If I went to war, I'd go with the guns!" cries Mrs. King, "and ride on a cannon!" She gallops across the porch waving her arm like a flag.

Mrs. Herridge makes clucking noises in her throat. She rocks and knits, knits and rocks. *Click click creak. Click click creak.* Socks. For the Red Cross. Her tenth pair this week. She smiles serenely.

"War is just like having a baby, isn't it?"

Willie apologizes for Mrs. Herridge's coarseness while I'm setting up the camera to take his mother's picture. He has insisted I bring a tripod and a flash. Even the great W.H. Topley has failed to capture Mother's especial beauty. Her features were too sharp. He had to pay $100 for three sittings and sent all the proofs back.

"Isn't she lovely?" he asks. "Just as pure and sweet as a young girl."

"She has beautiful hair."

Mrs. King is sitting in a wicker chair while Bella brushes her hair. It is long and curly and snow white but her face is withered and ravaged, the face of a seventy-year-old woman. I would like to take her in the chair, relaxed (wicker always gives good texture), but Willie wants a woodland scene — something as simple and natural as she is herself, he says.

We decide on a full-length portrait by the sundial, her lace dress against a background of evergreens. The dappled light will make strange shadows but it will break the glare of her white dress. She offers me her profile.

"Billy says this brings out my character best."

Her nose is sharp and slightly hooked, a tiny beak. Willie demands something "contemplative" and insists she look down at the sundial. He barks out orders like a circus master. I take two. Then I whistle. She looks up, smiles and turns her head slightly towards me. I get what I want. I take two more of her sitting on the grass and some of her with Willie. Willie insists on taking a picture of me. "So we'll all be together in one place." Nobody suggests I take a photo of Bella or Mr. King. Bella has disappeared but Mr. King is flattered. He is a handsome man with a soldier's bearing, a Confederate general.

Mr. King goes off to take a nap. Bill Herridge goes swimming. Willie's mother nods off in her chair. Mrs. Herridge suggests Willie read aloud something inspirational. I dread a bout of *Pilgrim's Progress.*

He reads *Maud.* It's about how capitalism leads to war, he says. Miss Eady always said it was about sex. She forbade us to read it but we did anyway. It was disappointing, all that mush about lilies and roses, but I liked the part about the flying gold of the ruined woodlands, which was just like the Valley in October.

Willie reads surprisingly well, his voice strong with a hard edge. The words spill out like jewels. He looks up at me every time he reads "lilies." It is very bloody. I had forgotten. Mrs. Herridge is knitting very fast. Her hands are shaking. When we get to my favorite part, "Dead, long dead, Long dead!" she gets up suddenly and goes into the kitchen. Willie keeps reading to the end, "the blood-red blossom of war."

I find the outhouse, glad of the sun. When I come out Bill Herridge is standing by the back door, his bathing suit dripping down below his knees.

"Can you get me by the medics?" he whispers.

"What's the matter?"

"Bad back. Accident. Nothing important."

He looks at me pleadingly.

"I could be an officer. They don't have heavy work to do."

A woman's voice drifts through the screen door. She is speaking softly but the tone is tense, angry. Mrs. Herridge. I catch a word here and there:

"Unfeeling. Our poem. Your daughter."

Willie's voice, low, hard:

"Selfish. Ruining my happiness."

"Rex!" she cries. "How can you be so cruel?"

Bill bounds up the steps and bangs through the door.

"Hey mum, what's to eat?"

They spring apart like scalded cats.

Willie is pleased I have enjoyed myself. I must get to know Mother, he says. She has had an unhappy life, born in exile, the thirteenth child, bearing the burden of poverty and the ignominy of ostracism. I say that my Mum is unhappy too but he doesn't seem to hear. He prefers to talk about his own family. I don't mind. At least he doesn't talk about last week's horse race or yesterday's golf score and he doesn't treat me as if I were a ninny. He knows about a lot of things, like capitalism, and he's met just about everyone, and he doesn't seem to mind if I listen or not, although I usually do. There is a sort of energy about him that cheers me up too, a buoyant optimism, so sometimes when I listen to him I feel like I'm floating along in a tiny basket underneath a big, bright, hot-air balloon.

Read *The Secret of Heroism* after dinner. I don't see what all the fuss was about. A girl falls through the ice and instead of doing something sensible like holding out a stick Bert jumps right in after her, skates and all, saying, "What more can I do?" and drags her under. Poor Bert couldn't swim a stroke.

"That's the heroism of it!" Willie says.

2

New York City, Friday, August 21, 1914

His hand shakes so hard he has to rest his arm against the sink. It won't do to meet the richest man in the world half-shaved or covered with plasters like a prize fighter. Why do the rich never have razor nicks? Or body odor? Or bad teeth? Not that he envies them! Oh no! He, William Lyon Mackenzie King, has dedicated his life to the cause of the poor, the working classes, and he's not going to turn on them now. He's not afraid of John D. Rockefeller Jr. and his millions. He'll turn the offer down flat if it means any dirty work or a betrayal of the working man. On the other hand, if he can persuade the greatest capitalist in the world to take the lead towards reform, think what they can accomplish together!

Ever since the telegram from the Rockefeller Foundation arrived William Lyon Mackenzie King has been distraught with nervous apprehension, oppressed by the certainty that his whole career, his whole life, is hanging in the balance, to be tipped irrevocably by this one decision: to work for the Rockefellers as an advisor on industrial relations, or to refuse. To accept might mean moving to New York, giving up his political career (already Tory jingos in Ottawa are whispering malevolently that he has sold out to Standard Oil), severing all those connections with Sir Wilfrid and the Liberal Party that he has so labouriously built over the last twenty years, yet to refuse will be to abandon an opportunity to transform the industrial life of the whole English-speaking world, to leave a mark on history as large as Toynbee or Marx, to be revered for generations as the father of industrial peace. William Lyon

Mackenzie King is not insensible to the appeal of fame, and, to be perfectly honest with himself, he desperately needs the money.

He had not paid much attention to the violence in the coal fields at Ludlow, Colorado, last April. He had been shocked and revolted, like everyone, by the murder of women and children, suffocated in a cave beneath their burning tent, but the striking miners had been armed too, and a number of militia had been killed. He found violence repugnant. He had no use for the rough and irresponsible element among the working classes, and the United Mine Workers was notorious as a union of Socialists and Anarchists. Besides, this sort of incident would not happen in Canada, where he had brought in the Industrial Disputes Investigation Act to prevent conflict while he was Minister of Labour.

In fact he has been so depressed lately, so obsessed with his own troubles, he has paid very little attention to anything outside his own faltering career. Except for the hack work of editing the *Liberal Monthly*, he has been out of work since his defeat in the election of 1911. From cabinet minister to party flunky in one swift, cruel blow. It had been a terrible shock. He'd been in politics only three years and a cabinet minister all the time, a *wunderkind*, not yet forty, a coming man, a scholar and an intellectual with a degree from Harvard. Surely Sir Wilfrid would find him a safe Liberal seat somewhere as he'd found for others, a position where he could still make his voice heard in the House and be part of the inner circle around Laurier. But Laurier had not found him a safe seat. Laurier had snubbed him on the street. He, William Lyon Mackenzie King, was left to flounder in the muck of partisan politics, begging, dealing, trading, lying, his high ideals soiled forever by the petty sordidness he had entered politics to abolish.

He had struggled on through the slough of despond, seeing it as a God-given test of his humility, a trial of strength and patience, taking comfort in the Book of Job in the face of the private disasters that followed on his political defeat. Yet no matter how manfully he tried to be humble and patient, no matter how silently he suffered, he could not help feeling a certain resentment, not just against the stupid voters, who had rejected him, but against his family, who had failed him. His father's blindness would not have been such a tragedy had he been provident, and laid aside a comfortable fortune for his old age, rather than a pile of debts and mortgages for his son to pay off, and a weight of worry for poor Mother that undermined her health and drove her to flights of hysterial fantasies, and made poor Belle thin and frail from overwork. And his brother Max, dying of tuberculosis, imagine, a medical doctor, helpless to cure himself! Not that he, William Lyon Mackenzie King, blamed his brother, or blamed himself, but surely with a little more care and foresight all of this could have been prevented. God had chosen him, he was certain, for some great social purpose, as yet undisclosed, and he was impatient to get on with it, resentful of the delays and intrusions and distractions with which others strewed his path, critical of his own faults and errors, which had impeded his progress. No, he was not selfish, that wasn't fair — on the contrary, his motive was an entirely unselfish one, a desire to be of service to mankind.

Into this agony of anxiety the Rockefeller telegram had come like a Heaven-sent deliverance: a totally unexpected, fortuitous act of God fraught with fatal significance. William Lyon Mackenzie King is not a gambling man and he brooded for a long time over the odds. Would the Rockefeller wealth boost him to the highest rungs of political power? Or would he be hopelessly blackened by the mud that clings to the Rockefeller name? In spite of all the advice he has sought from Sir Wilfrid (reject) and his American friends (accept), he has been unable to make up his mind. Today he must. If there is one thing that he, William Lyon Mackenzie King, hates above all others, it is having to make a decision.

He shaves his upper lip, wipes the lather from the corners of his nose, wets his comb and plasters down the tuft of hair across his forehead. He is going bald in the most peculiar way, as if his head had been shaved in a tonsure, like a monk. He wonders at times if this isn't a sign, although he is Presbyterian, that he has been ordained for a bachelor life. He might have welcomed that in his youth, assuming that the flames of passion, so hard to control then, would subside with age; but he has recently discovered, to his alarm, that his lust burns as hot as ever, and his imagination runs wild with lascivious fantasies that wake him up in the night in a sweat and force him to resort to the solitary vice, which he abhors, to get some peace. He would rather die than inflict his gross desires on a wife. But if he doesn't marry, William Lyon Mackenzie King is afraid he might go mad, and harm someone, or humiliate himself. Twice now, while speaking on public platforms, he has experienced an urgent and irresistible erection, hidden only by the lectern, and been forced to end his speech early and sit down, holding his notes on his lap, until it subsided. As Minister of Labour in His Majesty's Government and later, as editor of the *Liberal Monthly*, he has walked the banks of the Rideau Canal, and prowled the Lovers' Walk behind Parliament Hill night after night, resisting the importunities of the girls until he has been able to hold back no longer and, beneath a bridge or behind some bushes, succumbed. Even now, a blob of shaving lather on the mirror seems to take the shape of a woman's breast, soft and round and white, with a nipple standing out as if it had been sucked, a shape that makes him think about Miss Coolican's breasts, not that he's seen them, but he has dreamed about nothing else for two weeks.

He is puzzled by this nocturnal obsession. It is not love, as he has imagined it, quite the reverse in fact, and his waking hours are tinged with shame at the imaginary indecencies he has performed with Miss Coolican in his sleep. He does not care for dark women. (She does not look at all like Mother. Mother always teases him how his "flames" resemble her. ("You might as well give up, Billy," she said laughingly once, "and marry me.") He does not care for tall women either, and she's nearly as tall as he is, in her shoes, ah, dear God, her exquisite, soft, kid shoes the colour of peppermints that match her stockings, her ankles the colour of raspberry sherbet or lemon ice, slim and hard as those sweet candies he loves to suck. Her skirts are much too short, he can see almost to her knees when the wind blows ("It's an economy measure," she says, "because of the war") and she wears her dresses cut in a deep V at the neck with lace collars and a tiny gold chain around her throat, and when she leans forward the little turtle at the end of the chain hovers in the dark cleft at the bottom of the V. At Kingsmere, last Sunday, he couldn't take his eyes off her. He blushed to the roots of his hair when she caught him staring, helpless, not just because her breasts were large, and lovely, but because every time she raised her arm, or shifted in her chair, they moved, quite independently, as if they had a life of their own. He had never seen a woman's breasts move before. And as he watched, and pondered this phenomenon, it struck him that she was not wearing a corset, and there was nothing, absolutely nothing, between him and her naked body but a single layer of silk and a petticoat. He had never been aware of seeing a woman without a corset before, except Mother, in her nightgown, and he contrived, as they were boarding the train for Ottawa, to place his hand on Miss Coolican's waist, just to make sure. The warmth and softness of her flesh startled him. The touch of her delicate ribs beneath his fingers, the ripple of her muscle as she raised her foot to the step, passed through him like an electric shock, so he snatched his hand away. It was too late.

William Lyon Mackenzie King is in trouble.

He leaves the Harvard Club at nine-fifteen, wondering, as he makes his way up Fifth Avenue, whether the clock's hands, in a straight horizontal line, might symbolize the border between Canada and the United States. But the exact implications of this he has not been able to divine by the time he gives his name to the doorman at the Rockefeller mansion. His attention is distracted by the revolver on the doorman's hip.

He is shown into a large, pale anteroom that contains nothing, absolutely nothing, not a book or a magazine or a newspaper or an ashtray or a potted plant, except six spindly chairs around a spindly table and on the table, open on a reading stand, a large, illuminated Bible. It is open at St. Luke. He rests his hand lightly on the page, closes his eyes and prays.

Aside from the Bible, and its almost antiseptic austerity, the room yields no clue about the personality or appearance of John D. Rockefeller Jr.

William Lyon Mackenzie King prides himself on his ability to judge people at first glance, even from a photograph. (What better example could there be than dear Mother, whose sweetness and honesty shine from her face?) But his judgements are in fact based, thanks to his scholarly habits, on exhaustive research, conducted through the medium of gossip on the social grapevine. His information about Mr. Rockefeller has come from the press, namely the Toronto *Star*, and the mental image he has formed as a result is of a large, coarse, hairy man, reeking of whisky and cigars, who talks loudly about money, tells obscene stories in mixed company and whose long, bloody fangs are embedded in the neck of the working man, an image strongly reinforced by his own considerable acquaintance with the wealthy capitalists whose money he, William Lyon Mackenzie King, humbly solicits on behalf of the Liberal Party of Canada, and himself.

"Nobody must be able to say that Rockefeller bought you, and you will speak with his voice in the future," wrote his friend, Violet Markham, from England. "I am sure this can't be so as you would not have considered the offer and been the first to turn from it in disgust. . . ." He fingers the letter in his pocket as he waits. By the time the butler leads him down an interminable hallway to the library, he is determined to stand fast by the cause of labour, nail his colours to the mast, not yield one jot of his independence no matter how great the personal sacrifice. He feels quite calm now, even exhilarated, championing once more the cause of the poor and downtrodden in the very lair of the most brutal, heartless monster of them all.

"Mr. King, sir," the butler drones, silently opening a heavy, padded door.

"G-g-good m-m-m-morning," says a fair, slim young man, coming towards him with hand outstretched. "G-g-glad to m-m-meet you." The hand is soft, delicate, the man himself is tiny, hardly bigger than a boy, with a boy's shy, diffident stance and open, beaming face. It is not until they are seated side-by-side on the sofa, with the boy's sky-blue eyes fixed intently on his face, and the boy's tiny hands clasped eagerly on his knee, that William Lyon Mackenzie King realizes that this anxious elf, this charming, twinkling little person is not a secretary, nor a son, but John D. Rockefeller Jr. himself. ("Imagine expecting Frankenstein," he will write home to Mother that night, "and meeting Peter Pan!")

He is pleased that Mr. Rockefeller does not mention Ludlow, or Colorado, or Standard Oil. He is pleased that Mr. Rockefeller does not mention money. In fact Mr. Rockefeller says very little except to ask questions, and seems content to listen to his own theories of industrial relations, nodding happily "Yes, yes" when William Lyon Mackenzie King speaks about the nobility of the working man, his honesty and strength of character, his right to a fair wage and decent living conditions ("Quite so, exactly!"), his constitutional right to freedom of assembly ("Liberty, yes, the Declaration of Independence") the necessity of collective bargaining in modern industry for the sake of efficiency ("Efficiency. Excellent!"), the terrible tragedy of strikes. . . .

"T-t-tragedy! There, you've g-g-got it! How can we abolish strikes? That is the k-k-key, right there!"

"I believe that any strike can be prevented," says William Lyon Mackenzie King, flushed now with excitement at having such a ready, receptive ear. "My experience of almost twenty years with the mines and railways and sweatshops of Canada has led me to the inescapable conclusion that strikes are not caused by unions, or by management, or by abuses or grievances or socialist agitators, nor by greed or rhetoric or political differences. No, no, the root cause is simply personal antagonism, the bitterness and hatred, the wounded pride and animal fury that possess men when they fight. But why are they fighting? Are not labour and management on the same side, working towards the same end of a better life for all? Cannot men of character and good will, rich and poor, sit down together, in a conciliatory manner, before feelings are inflamed, and settle their differences in a fair and reasonable way? We are all men, sir, and industrial relations are, like everything else, relations between human beings."

"Human beings!" exclaims Mr. Rockefeller, clapping his hands. "That is it. That's what we m-m-must remember! They are *human beings!*"

He takes a little notebook from his pocket and writes in it with a silver pencil, "Human Beings," underlining it several times.

At lunch, before the meal is served, Mr. Rockefeller reads from St. Luke about the Good Samaritan, glancing significantly at William Lyon Mackenzie King. Lunch with the Rockefellers is a plain lamb chop accompanied by ice water.

"We live very s-s-simply, as you can s-s-see," says Mr. Rockefeller, poking at his chop. "Our lives revolve around our ch-church and our ch-children. My business, as chairman of the Rockefeller Foundation, is not m-m-making m-m-money, but g-g-giving it away. You will s-s-see in the course of your association with us, how difficult it is to try to do g-g-good."

"The people do not appreciate Junior's great burden of responsibility," says Mrs. Rockefeller. "He derives no pleasure from his wealth. Neither of us believes in privilege, nor do we like to be treated as people entitled to it. As Christians, we believe in only one measure of value, and that is the spiritual."

Abby Rockefeller, with her sharp nose and fair, curly hair, bears such a startling resemblance to Mother that William Lyon Mackenzie King is prompted to show her Mother's photograph, in his wallet, and she remarks on the likeness, although Mother is older of course, and prettier, and she comments too on another extraordinary coincidence: his own resemblance to Junior, in build and colouring and age too, both having been born in the same year. William Lyon Mackenzie King mentions how his mother had been born in New York, in poverty, when her father was suffering exile as a champion of the common people. And now here he is, in New York, championing the cause of the common people before a man enough like himself to be his brother, a man endowed with all the riches of the world, whose own home life is so true, so natural, it reminds him of the sweet, sacred family circle in which he was raised.

"You will find working for the Rockefellers much like b-b-becoming a member of a family," smiles Junior.

"Have you no family of your own, Mr. King?"

He squirms in his chair, in spite of himself.

"Not yet, I'm afraid."

"We'll fix that, won't we Junior? I know dozens of lovely girls. I may assume, then, may I Mr. King, that you are, how shall I put it, available?"

Abby Rockefeller winks. William Lyon Mackenzie King blushes right up to the top of his balding head.

"Why, y-y-yes," he stammers, "certainly. Available? Oh, yes."

He looks at his plate, ashamed of the mean, uncharitable prejudice he has harboured in his heart towards John D. Rockefeller Jr. What a stroke of luck, to have this chance to meet face-to-face! Why, surely this is one of the truly noble men of the world! A man beset by deadly temptations who puts them boldly aside, who dedicates his life to Christian charity and receives for it nothing but abuse and vilification! Why, his courage and integrity shine from his face! His modesty and Christian zeal are apparent in every gesture. How terrible that he should be a virtual prisoner of his wealth, the helpless victim of unscrupulous agitators and muckraking journalists!

"Your words this morning, Mr. King, about b-b-bitterness and hatred and strife, cut close to my heart," says Junior quietly, almost as if he were reading his thoughts. "Had it been in my p-p-power to stop the b-b-bloodshed in Colorado, I would have done so. I am, however, only a member of the board. I trusted in our superintendents. Yet it is I whom am blamed for the m-m-murders. The name 'R-R-Rockefeller' has become a byword for everything that is cruel and w-w-wicked and vile about f-f-free enterprise. We are the victims of a terrible prejudice."

John D. Rockefeller Jr. puts his head in his hands.

"I will do anything, Mr. King, to help clear the Rockefeller name, and to show our m-m-motives in their true and faithful light. You will have complete independence to pursue your studies as you wish. M-m-money is no object. I am not asking you to b-b-bail me out, or cover up my faults, but simply to advise me how to assist the working classes and advance the cause of industrial peace."

William Lyon Mackenzie King bows his head. He is conscious of a clock ticking. When he looks up, the clock's hands are in a straight horizontal line. Two forty-five. The longest undefended border in the world. One hundred years of peace. Peace between nations. Peace between classes. Peace on earth.

A familiar fragment from Isaiah passes silently across his lips: "And the government shall be upon his shoulder: and his name shall be called Wonderful, Counsellor, the Mighty God, the Everlasting Father, the Prince of Peace." His call has come. He hears it as clearly as the voice he hears sometimes in his dreams, the clear, small voice that says 'Willie, Willie! Light! Light!"

John D. Rockefeller Jr. raises his head from his hands. Their blue eyes meet and John D. Rockefeller Jr. smiles the most beautiful, trusting smile William Lyon Mackenzie King has ever seen. He smiles in return, then laughs, and they grin like a couple of schoolboys, hands clasped across the table.

"Perhaps I have found the b-b-brother I always wanted, and never had," says John D. Rockefeller Jr.

William Lyon Mackenzie King blushes to the roots of his hair.

He twirls his silver-headed walking stick all the way down Fifth Avenue, stopping in a drugstore to buy a postcard showing the Rockefeller mansion. A lucky omen. Wait until the world hears the news! Mr. John D. Rockefeller Jr. isn't an ogre at all but a perfectly capital fellow! He, William Lyon Mackenzie King, has shaken his hand and looked him in the eye and seen the truth! He could shout it from the rooftops!

He writes the glad tidings to Mother, seated at a small table in the lounge of the Harvard Club, her photograph before him (as it is every night), next to the envelope with the handsome cheque from Mr. Rockefeller, for his inconvenience. He kisses Mother's photograph twice (as he does every night) and returns it to his wallet, next to the cheque.

William Lyon Mackenzie King is in love.

3

R.H.
Friday, August 21, 1914

Smoke in the air. Forest fires in the north. When the wind blows down the Valley a brown haze hangs over Ottawa. Mr. Booth's depot at Montreal River has burned and he's lost almost half his timber limits. No rain for weeks. I can almost see the pines exploding into balls of flame, fire licking up their trunks, kindling them into torches, whoosh, a puff of black smoke, sparks racing ahead on the wind, touching the granite cliffs with bursts of flame, the whole land blackened as far as the eye can see, even the soil burnt, the rock standing out strangely white. No work in the woods this winter.

Bicycled down to Mr. Bennett's office with a huge box of maple fudge sent to the Duke by Mr. Ganong, a candy maker, who has donated five thousand pounds of candy to the troops. He wants to put the Duke's picture on the box but the Duke detests maple fudge. Alice says Arbee eats as much as a pound a day. He used to be so skinny in Calgary that he ate three breakfasts and two dinners every day to put on weight so he'd look more "distinguished." I said I didn't see anything distinguished about looking like a pear.

There's a great crush of men at the door and a line three deep stretching all the way up the stairs. They are in a surly mood, shoving and cursing, and a lot of them are drunk. They all seem very dirty and I wonder for a minute if I haven't gotten stuck in the Sally Ann soup-kitchen line. I fight my way upstairs. The office door is open and the room jammed with men. Alice is barricaded behind her desk in a corner. She has a big smudge of carbon on her face and her pale hair is hanging down in wisps.

"Lily!" she says. "Thank God!" And she bursts into tears. The men seem alarmed at this and quieten down a little.

"These gentlemen are trying to enlist," Alice says, blowing her nose. "They have been rejected for various reasons." She looks pointedly across the desk at a grizzled old coot whose left arm is missing below the elbow. "Many of them are veterans and I am sure their service record is perfectly fine but some time has passed since the last war and we simply aren't taking men over forty-five. Somehow the rumour has got around that Mr. Bennett can 'fix' things with Col. Hughes. I keep explaining that we are only in charge of supplies. But then some of them are constituents. . . ."

"Where is Arbee?"

"He is trying to find five thousand pairs of woollen socks. And underwear. Everything is supposed to be in the armouries, but when we went to look, there wasn't a scrap. Col. Hughes has no idea where it's gone. I have tried the Ottawa stores but they have no winter things yet and the prices they ask are triple the value. We can have it made up but that will take at least two weeks and there are twenty thousand men at Valcartier already and more arriving every day with nothing but the clothes on their backs and we can't send the army overseas naked!"

There is an upheaval in the crowd and a rolled umbrella appears like a mast over the heads, followed by a derby hat and a monkey the size of a man.

"Hiho!" the monkey says, kissing Alice on the cheek. "I've come to win the war. Dickie in?"

He darts off towards a heavy oak door on the far wall.

"Mr. Bennett is not *available*, Sir Max," Alice cries.

"Available?" the monkey turns. "Am I to get the brush-off when I've come five thousand miles with priceless information about the collapse of the German front?"

"Hear, hear!" the men cry and break into applause. "Give it to the buggers!" "Kill the Kaiser!"

"These gentlemen have been waiting to see Mr. Bennett for *some time*," Alice shouts. The monkey looks at the mob with a bright eye and grins from ear to ear.

"Soldiers!" He jumps on the desk and holds his umbrella like a sword. You could hear a pin drop. "My name is Sir Max Aitken. You may have heard of me. I have just come from London!" Wild cheers and applause. He waves for silence.

"Lord Kitchener. . . ."

Cheers and whistles.

"Lord Kitchener has appointed me his personal envoy to the Canadian government. Just this moment I have come from Col. Sam Hughes. . . ." Boos and catcalls. "Col. Hughes tells me he can take another two thousand men.

First come, first served. He's at his office now drawing up the notice. East Block, room 105. Right across the street."

The stampede down the stairs makes the windows rattle. Not a soul remains. "Okay, Dickie!" Sir Max calls. "You can come out now!"

The heavy oak door opens slowly and Mr. Bennett peeps out.

"Bless you, Max," he says. "You're a rascal."

"Poor Col. Hughes," I say to Alice, who is shaking and making whuffing noises into her handkerchief.

"Don't worry," she giggles. "It's not his office."

The clock on Parliament Hill is striking twelve when I come out onto Wellington Street. We don't really need a clock in Ottawa. We set our time by the sawmills. They start to screech at six in the morning and stop at six at night, unless there's an emergency or a big contract like when they built the Parliament buildings in 1860 and the sawmills ran day and night. The noon sirens go all at once, each with its own voice, and in the silence that comes after the fading whine you can hear the tiny boom of the cannon on Nepean Point left over from the days when this was a military garrison. Ottawa is just a lumber town really. Everyone thought Queen Victoria had lost her wits when she named it the capital of Canada. "Mummy was duped," the Duke says. "'It's a long way from the Americans,' they told her. Indeed, I say, it's a long way from everywhere."

I take the streetcar to Booth St. and walk down towards the mill through the piles of drying lumber. The piles are as big as houses, bigger, as big as office buildings, and they stretch away in all directions as far as the eye can see, acres and acres, a forest lying sideways. Some of the boards are still white and smell sweet and some are pale brown and others are already silver with age, and the sun makes crazy shadows shining through. Train tracks run everywhere through the maze and trucks tootle around beeping their horns and the workmen sit in patches of shade eating their lunches out of paper bags made from trees. It's a whole city in here — the inhabitants are two thousand men, brown as scarecrows with sawdust. When photographers take panoramas from the top of the clock tower they always face west towards the lumber yards. When the light is hazy and the focus not too sharp Ottawa looks twice as big.

Mr. Booth is scrambling around on a flume twenty feet over the boiling rapids, so close to the rocks the spray wets his trousers to the knees. His leg is still stiff where he broke it last year but it doesn't seem to slow him down. If you want something done right, do it yourself, he says, and he does, although everybody thinks an eighty-six-year-old man is crazy to be skipping around over the Chaudière Falls like a trapeze artist. The Booth mill is built right out into the rapids on a series of rock ledges so the rushing water powers the saws. The Eddy mill is built out from the other shore, and the main chasm of the river flows between in a series of rocky steps, the tea-brown water whirling and foaming and steaming like a witch's cauldron. The French explorers called it the Kettle, la Chaudière, and they said you could hear the roar of the rapids two miles downstream. Even when the saws are silent you have to shout at the top of your lungs. In the spring, at the height of the run-off, Mr. Booth and I would come here on Sundays and we'd sit on the ledge high over the whirlpools with our feet dangling and watch the water foam and hiss over the rocks. If I closed my eyes I felt I would fall in, but I wasn't afraid, and I could understand why people often jumped off the bridge. Before we left Mr. Booth always threw a pinch of tobacco into the water to appease the river spirit, the way the Indians did. The spirit takes its due all the same, five or six men a year who slip or lose their balance or get crushed by runaway logs, not counting those mangled and killed by the giant saws, an arm or a finger suddenly lying on the ground, the man not even feeling it, looking surprised at the blood.

Mr. Booth shoves his bag lunch toward me. A wedge of cheese, two raw onions, hardtack, a carrot. No, thanks.

"This damn war's gotta be stopped!" he shouts at me, waving an onion. "All them damn fools offerin' any two-bit bum three squares a day and $1.10 *includin'* Sundays! And here we are tryin' to make ends meet payin' loggers $1 a day on a six-day week. And what are we gonna be left with, eh? I'll tell, ya! Cripples! And I gotta feed 'em at army prices too, pork's up already almost double, flour's up. It'll be the death of business in this country. Socialism! Well I'm goin' to shut 'er down! Shut 'er all down. Sell out to the goddamn Yanks. Let Eddy have it."

"Socks!" I shout back at him. "Soldiers need socks. You won't be wanting them."

Mr. Booth gnaws on a biscuit. He squints at the warehouse and then at me. We did the inventory last June: there's enough beans and flour and salt pork and molasses and boots and longjohns and flannel shirts and mittens and socks in that warehouse to keep four thousand men in the bush for six months.

"Whadda they eat?" he says.

"Who?"

"Soldiers."

"I don't know."

"Beans. Nothin' wrong with beans. Blackstrap molasses. Hair on their chests."

He shakes the crumbs out of his paper bag, folds it neatly and puts it in the pocket of his homespun jacket.

"Remember, this ain't a donation," he says. "It's a sale."

He peels a greasy twenty dollar bill off the top of an enormous roll and tucks it in my hand.

"You're a good lass," he says.

R.H.
Saturday, August 22, 1914

Wrote a little speech for Patsy to give at the colour ceremony. She can't memorize so I've printed it in block letters. We cut a small tree in the park to make a staff and found some gold fringe on a pair of old curtains to trim the edges. "It won't look so gaudy when it gets shot up a little," she says.

The *Citizen* is telling women to forbid their husbands to enlist. Sam Hughes has threatened to horsewhip the publisher, Mr. Southam. Alice says that the Southams aren't really subversive, they're Christian Science, and besides, it's stupid because the men will enlist anyway and just lie about having wives and no wives get no money.

The election is off for this year. The Grits have been saying everywhere that the Duke won't permit it. Sir Robert has accused the Duke of blackmail. They had a terrible row. Did I know how it leaked out? It wasn't me, I said.

Postcard from Mr. King. A photograph of the Rockefeller mansion. Willie says the Rockefellers live very simply. He certainly looks at things in a strange way.

In the afternoon I went shopping. I was standing in front of the Russell Theatre reading the poster for Ideal, the Lady Diver, trying to figure out how people could see anything when she was swimming around in a tank of water, when somebody pinched me right through my petticoat. I yelled and turned around. It was Jack. I hardly knew him, his face was burnt so black from the sun.

"What the hell are you doing here," we said together, and grinned.

"Where did you get those *teeth*?" I said next. In the empty spaces where his two front teeth had been knocked out years ago there were two big, shiny gold nuggets.

"Dug 'em up," he said, spitting them out into his hand. "Almost pure gold. Had the dentist file 'em down a bit, made a bridge, safest place for 'em. Worth a fortune. Lots more where they come from."

I looked at his faded plaid shirt, all out at the elbows, and his stained work pants with patched knees.

"You don't *look* rich."

"Shhh!" he hissed, looking around at the men crowding by on the street.

We went up to his room in the Russell Hotel. He took off his shirt and unfastened a leather pouch tied around his waist. He loosened the drawstring and turned the pouch upside down over the bedspread. Gold nuggets as big as aggies tumbled out. I picked one up.

"Bite it," he said.

My teeth left tiny dents in the gold surface.

"Keep it. It's yours."

"I don't believe it."

"Lookit, there's a vein as big as my arm, pure gold, right on the surface, on that piece of land Harry Oakes and me staked out in the snow, just east of Swastika. Found it this spring. There I was, sittin' havin' a smoke after diggin' a trench down to bedrock and comin' up empty, and I rubs my butt on the rock, with my heel, like this, makin' sure there's no sparks, and my toe kicks up a piece of moss, and right there, right under this piece of moss, clean and bright as a whistle, there's this trickle of gold in the rock. Well, I starts rippin' up the moss like a crazy man and the vein gets wider and wider and disappears under a tree so I get my axe and cut down the tree, you never seen a tree go down so fast, and I push over the stump and the vein's still there, so I'm whooping and hollerin' for Harry and diggin' at the dirt with my bare hands. Well, you should of seen Harry! He comes up and takes a look, the eyes just poppin' out of his head and then he gets down on the ground, right flat on his belly, and he kisses that vein, kisses 'er over and over until his mouth's all black and then he just lies there and bawls! I never knew old Harry had a tear in that horny old heart of his."

He rummaged in his wallet and held out some pieces of paper. They had "Rainbow Mine" printed on them in a blue border, and "One Share."

"Only forty cents a piece," Jack said. "I'll sell you as many as you like. You'll be rich."

"I don't have any money."

"I thought you were bunkin' in with old man Booth."

"I'm donated to the war effort."

"Jesus."

He stuffed the papers back into his pocket and put the nuggets into the pouch.

"I'll go see the old bugger myself. He'll be good for fifty, sixty grand right off. We'll get ourselves some machinery, and a few guys with strong backs, and we'll be away. It ain't gonna be no hole-'n'-bucket operation. You gotta spend money to make money, Harry says."

"I've never noticed Harry making any."

"Aw, come on. He's not so bad. It was his idea, stakin' this land. He only cut me in because he had no dough for the licence fee."

We came back downstairs and walked out past a recruiting desk in the lobby. "Hey soldier!" an officer at the desk called at Jack. He didn't miss a step but raised his left hand, with the stump where his fingers had been, in salute, and grinned his golden grin. "Tough luck," the officer said, and turned away.

Jack walked with me as far as Sparks Street, hands in his pockets, whistling "Tipperary" and ogling the girls.

"Lookit," he said, as we turned down Metcalfe, "can you let me have a little loan? Just a couple a bucks to tide me over?"

"I don't *have* any...."

"Hey, come on. I'll pay you back. You gonna let me starve?"

I gave him the $20 bill. Came home broke, with a handful of shares in the Rainbow Mine and a fool's gold nugget.

Sunday, August 23, 1914

Jack keeps his eyes closed against the sun and shifts painfully on the hard seat. The rocking motion of the coach makes him want to puke. Good old Timiskaming and Northern Ontario Railway must've built their tracks out of corrugated iron. He opens an eye cautiously and squints out. They're past New Liskeard now. Not too much farther to Swastika. He could use a beer or two to clear his head.

Jack feels for the pouch at his waist. He'd made more than $200 shooting craps in the back of the Russell Hotel but it was peanuts compared to what he needed. Harry'll be mad, him coming back almost emptyhanded. He'd picked up a couple of grand around the hotel, but the guys with the really big bucks had let him down. "How do we know where you got these?" they said when he showed them the nuggets. "Come back when you've got some real results." How the hell do you get real results without real money?

He'd gone to see old man Booth and offered him fifty percent. "You know what a gold mine is?" the old buzzard cackled. "A hole in the ground with a liar on top of it!" Jack had damn near punched him out. Shit, you offer a guy a gold mine and he treats you like a thief. Shit. Shit. Shit. What kind of country is this? Shit. Well, they'll keep on digging. They're down almost ten feet now, taking turns on the hammer and steel, driving through solid porphyry, scooping out the rock after the dynamite blast with their bare hands. Hand. Shit.

Jack remembers, as the train slows for Swastika, that he still owes Chink her $20. Hell, she's doing okay. She'll catch herself a rich husband, an English lord somebodyorother, some dink who talks with a clothespeg on his nose. Woods are full of them. Harry at least ain't a dink.

He half expects Harry to meet him at the station with the wagon. No such luck. It's nearly dark by the time Jack tramps the three miles over the bush road to Kirkland Lake and the Rainbow mine. As he comes around the last bend he listens for the sound of Harry digging. Harry is always digging, long before sunrise, long after dark, by moonlight. Harry is a strange bird all right, but most of the old timers are strange, not that Harry's so old, not even forty, but he's been kicking around for years, Alaska, Australia, California, though nobody really believes the stories he tells. Harry's tough, though, with a mean hard look around his mouth, and dirty. Hell, who isn't dirty? Cheap too.

"One-Treat Harry." Jesus, one treat out of Harry Oakes is a fucking feast! He's always bumming. Well, there are a lot of bums in the north.

No, it's something else about Harry that people dislike, aside from him being a Yank. He's a liar. It's hard to put your finger on, but for one thing, with all the moaning Harry does about being broke, he always has money. He'll be living in flophouses, begging his outfit on credit, eating out of garbage cans, then the next thing you know he's off to Toronto for a few days, to the mining office, saying he's bumming the ride, but a conductor once told Jack Harry'd paid in cash. So a man's entitled to his secrets. The bragging's worse. About how he knows more geology than all the professors, can tell gold-bearing rock at a hundred yards, yammer yammer about quartz outcrops and seist, when the truth is that Harry does most of his prospecting in the records office, reading up geologists' reports, then waiting for a claim to open in a likely spot and running in to stake it before the next man gets there. If Harry's staked one bum claim, he's staked a thousand.

They struck it lucky with the Rainbow. It had come open at midnight, January 7, and they'd snowshoed in at forty below just two hours ahead of Bill Wright, who already had a mine in the Porcupine. So Jack's not sorry he staked Harry Oakes to the licence fee. They're in it fifty-fifty.

The mine is silent and deserted when he arrives. The tent's there, and the gear, but there's no sign of Harry or supper. Jack walks down to Charlie Chow's cafe by the lake.

"Where's Harry?"

Charlie points his spoon towards the far end of the lake.

Jack follows the rutted trail through the swamp and up on to a granite bluff at the western end of the lake. There's Harry, bent over a shovel, digging at the topsoil.

"What the hell are you doing?"

"Diggin'."

"Yeah. For what?"

Harry doesn't answer.

"Look, you asshole, our mine is over *there*."

"This is mine."

"Your what."

"My mine. Property of Harry Oakes. Staked 'er last night. Came open."

Jack hits him hard across the face, then in the gut. He doesn't remember much about the fight except his hand across Harry's throat and Harry's bloody face saying "Okay, okay, fifty-fifty." He lets Harry get up, then pushes him off the rock into the lake.

Harry writes up the deal on one of Charlie Chow's trestle tables. Fifty-fifty. They sign it. Charlie marks his 'X' and puts it in his strongbox where he keeps wills and birth certificates and odds and ends of prospectors' valuables.

"I admire a fighting man," says Harry, sticking out his hand. "Shake."

"Let's eat," says Jack, digging for the $20 bill. "Hey Charlie, the grub's on me!"

> P.P.C.L.I.
> Lansdowne Park
> Sunday, August 23

Mrs. L.J. Papineau
Manor House,
Montebello, Quebec

Dearest Mother,

We woke up with it raining torrents and drilling is called off. It is raining still and promises to continue. A fine spray is always dropping on everything and it is none too warm. Otherwise I am very comfortable. I spend as much time as possible reading my manuals. There is a great deal to learn. The other day I tied my platoon all up and had an awful time getting it straightened out. I seem to get along well with the men but I make a good many mistakes in drill, which is most annoying.

I am growing a moustache. A very poor thing yet but growing rapidly. I do not consider it very becoming, however it is the Colonel's wish that we should grow them.

We are to be officially "blessed" at church parade this morning and receive our regimental colour from the Princess herself on the playing field here. Perfectly awful day.

> Love to all and all
> love to you,
> Talbot

R.H.
Sunday, August 23, 1914

Rain. Windy, very cold. Woke up dreaming of Papa. He was sitting in the old kitchen at home, knitting, the way he often did, his spectacles perched half-way down his nose, but he was wearing a British soldier's red coat with the crossed white belts because the fire in the stove had gone out. I tried to ask him what he was knitting but he didn't seem to know I was there. A year ago today Papa was killed.

Patsy presented the colour this morning at Lansdowne Park. The poor thing was soaked and hung around the staff like a limp rag. We had to stand out in the middle of a football field for an eternity while some awful parson droned on and on and the Edmonton pipe band played "Abide With Me," that dreary dirge, all out of tune because their pipes were wet. The rain filled the brim of Patsy's hat like a birdbath and ran in a stream down her back when she tilted her head. The rain blurred my printing so she had to improvise, whispering in a tiny voice that carried no farther than her feet. The Pats were lined up at attention, more than a thousand strong, but they looked pitifully few in that great green field, and small, like rows of wet mice. The men had no coats so the Duke removed his, and all the staff officers followed suit, so they were all wet to the skin while the spectators in the grandstand who'd brought slickers and umbrellas and rubber boots were quite dry.

Afterwards the men were marched off to their billets in the Cow Palace and the Connaughts went to have lunch with the officers. No one seemed to care what became of the rest of us, especially when we were miles from downtown and the streetcars ran only on the half-hour, so I started to walk, tottering along like a wretched coolie in my new hobble skirt listening to my shoes go squelch, squelch in the mud. I was really in the sticks, every house with a pump and a privy and a big vegetable garden and most of them had chickens scratching around in the yard. I came up to a little red brick church just as the congregation was coming out. I glanced up at the big white sign, "The Holiness Movement Church. Enter and Be Saved!" Jesus! And sure enough there he was, shaking hands at the door, Bishop Ralph Horner, in the same rusty black suit, his pale, bald head glistening in the rain. I could hear the rumble of his voice. I tucked my head down into my macintosh and walked as fast as I could, waiting for the voice to find me.

"Lily!"

I stopped dead. Bishop Ralph was running towards me through the mud.

"Lily! Is it really you? The Lord be praised!"

He grabbed me with his powerful hand and wrapped a bear-like arm around my shoulders, his plain, Irish face wreathed in smiles.

"Rejoice with me, for I have found my sheep which was lost!" he cried, propelling me into the church. "Hallelujah! Praise the Lord!"

Half of me wanted to run and half of me was glad of a warm place, glad for someone glad to see me, so I allowed myself to be led meekly through the church. Bishop Ralph proclaimed "Hallelujah!" to the empty pews, until we came to a small room at the back. A wood stove, a boiling kettle. Tea. Bishop Ralph pulls up a chair for me and wraps me in a heavy black coat. I'd love to take off my wet shoes and toast my feet but I'm afraid. I might still want to run. I keep them on.

"He shall feed his flock like the shepherd!" Bishop Ralph cries, getting out biscuits and jam. "'He shall gather the lambs with his arm, and carry them in his bosom, and shall gently lead those that are with young.' Isaiah, 40:11."

It's hard to get used to the way Bishop Ralph talks. He knows the whole Bible pretty much by heart, and the words of the prophets come easier than his own, so you sort of get the feeling you're talking to God. "The Good Book was my first book and my last book," he always says. Mum taught him to read from the Bible. She was nineteen. Ralph Horner was twenty-five and he'd never been to school a day in his life. She taught him to read in two weeks, starting with Genesis, and he finished high school two years later. Mum taught Papa the same year. He was twenty, and it was Ralph Horner who gave him the courage to come, two big, husky men in a class of giggling children. Papa learned from the primers. He had no truck with the Bible.

"Consider the lilies, how they grow," Bishop Ralph beams, scanning me with those x-ray eyes, probing for the slightest blemish, the faintest spot of sin. I feel black with spots and I shrink into my macintosh, afraid he'll see my dress, a violet jersey Patsy'd had cut down for me, with lace collar and cuffs. Bishop Ralph always said that plain dress did not mean holiness, but satin, velvet, silk, feathers, flowers, lace, corsets, gathers, tucks and beads were sure signs of carnal lust, and only depraved women wore gold jewellery or bright colours. Bishop Ralph was never content with the seven deadly sins, but added a whole host of others, evil-speaking, whining, rebelliousness, doubt, the lust of the eye and of the mind, jesting and frivolity, so that you could hardly turn around without sinning. It was good business, Papa said, because it kept the sinners' benches full, and as far as Bishop Ralph was concerned, no matter how often you'd been saved, you could always be saved some more. He was entirely sanctified.

"The Lord has turned your steps back to the fold today," Bishop Ralph says, leaning over me. "He is speaking to you, Lily. He is asking you to repent, to soften you heart. 'Except ye repent, ye shall all likewise perish.' Luke 13:3. Don't you know there is joy in Heaven over one sinner who repenteth? They are pleased in Heaven to see you here! Hallelujah to the Lord God Almighty! Make your heart tender towards the Lord, Lily, pour out your sins! Humble yourself before the Lord God. He will hear you! He will shower blessings upon you! He will bless your going out and your coming in. He will bless you everywhere. You will never lack. His grace will flow through you in waves of glory. Hallelujah! Hallelujah to God! Praise the Lord!"

"I've quit smoking, pretty much," I say brightly.

"Bless you, it's a beginning," says Bishop Ralph. "Praise God for it!"

He pours the tea and spreads jam on the biscuits. It's raspberry. Home-made. I have three, and two spoons of sugar in my tea. It's strong and black, like home, tea you could walk on, without sanctification, and it's scalding hot too. Bishop Ralph never got snooty like most preachers. He was always simple and plain-spoken and homely. That's what scared people as much as

anything, the way he'd come up to them on the main street and accuse them
of lying or fornicating right out in public, shaking his big fist under their
noses, and he was so tough even the bullies were afraid to punch him out. It
worked too. One summer he called down the wrath of God on the Orange
Lodge the night before the Glorious Twelfth, and if it didn't happen the next
day, in the middle of the parade, a bolt of lightning struck King Billy and
threw him from his horse and killed the piper and the Grand Master. They
were carried across the street to Dr. Connolly, the RC doctor, who was
closest, and Mrs. Connolly let them in, but she wouldn't let the doctor touch
them until Dr. Murphy, the Protestant doctor, had arrived. "I did what I
could," she said later, "but I knew it would be as bad for the county to have
these poor fellows leave the earth in our dispensary, as it would be for their
relations to think of them dying, their sashes on them, before the picture of
Pope Leo."

Bishop Ralph smiles, holding my hands. "I have seen your mother. She is
happy."

Happy? Jesus, who could be happy in the looney bin?

"She is doing the Lord's work. She has brought many of those tortured
souls to Jesus. Praise the Lord!"

"Is she going to jail?"

He shakes his head.

"And you? Are you happy?"

"Yes," I say, and burst into tears.

R.H.
Wednesday, August 26, 1914

Captain Boscawen has been killed in Belgium. I didn't know him very well.
Still, it's a shock. He was only at the front two days.

The Princess Pats leave for England on Saturday. Tomorrow we are
having all the officers for dinner. It was supposed to be a stag, but Patsy said
if she was the bloody Colonel-in-Chief she would bloody be there, so now we
all get to go, me and Alice and Ena MacAdam, Sam Hughes' secretary. Just
us and thirty men!

Flora Denison, the dressmaker, has made a wonderful gown for me out of
a sari. It's saffron silk shot with gold, the colour of a sunrise, cut very low
with a handkerchief hem and matching satin shoes. It seems a shame to walk
in them. Flora Denison is the only woman in Ottawa with an ounce of style,
Patsy says, although you'd never guess to look at her, she's so plain and stout
and wears the most hideous mud-coloured smocks she calls "earth dresses,"
which are supposed to be good for you, and bare feet, or moccasins, even in
winter, and she eats nothing but vegetables, and claims to be psychic and

have visions. Some people say she murdered her husband, she's such a fierce feminist. Everyone's a little afraid of Flora. She likes that, I think.

I promised Bishop Ralph I'd go to prayer meeting tonight but I won't. I am sick of sin. To hell with Hell.

R.H.
Thursday, August 27, 1914
6 p.m.

Thunder in the air.

I am dressed. I hardly know myself. Patsy has dabbed me with rouge and dusted me with violet powder and sprayed me with scent and blackened my eyelids and twisted my hair into a double chignon with a "bang" on my forehead. What a funny word. She says I have a pre-Raphaelite profile and she wants to paint me this summer against a background of bullrushes. A moment ago she came in with pearl-drop earrings, like tears, and an enormous string of pale peach pearls with an emerald clasp. I was afraid to touch them, they looked so alive.

"The Nizam of Hyderabad would be offended," she said. I am wearing the Great Whore's kid gloves too. It will be hard to eat with gloves on, especially with all those men, and me half-naked.

What if I spill? What is pre-Raphaelite?

P.P.C.L.I.
Lansdowne Park
Thursday, August 27

Mrs. L.J. Papineau
Manor House
Montebello, Quebec

Dearest Mother,

Just a line to let you know we go to Montreal tomorrow. I shall be able to dine with you. Tonight the Connaughts are giving us a send-off dinner so we shall go as fatted calves.

I had luncheon yesterday in private with Sir Wilfrid — very interesting. There will be no election until the war is won so it is better I am here than in Montreal, worrying about where to run and if I'll get elected. In the evening we gave a dinner for Colonel Farquhar at the Rideau Club. I made a long speech and was much congratulated. Some men said I should be Premier some day!

Regret nothing. I am entirely resigned to what may occur. There is no value in repeated expressions of sorrow. The whole experience will be of incalculable advantage to me in every way. Of my own feelings I am indifferent. I am only sorry for you, Mother. You have by far the hardest part to play. However, we may not get into the firing line at all. So keep up the good cheer. The war in any case will be short and.…

"Nineteen hundred hours, sir. Have to hurry, sir."

Blatchford, his Cockney batman, is holding out Talbot's jacket.

Reluctantly Talbot signs and seals the letter, annoyed at being fussed over this way, constantly brushed and polished and reminded of the time and asked if he'd like tea. He'd prefer to be alone and polish his own things. He must play the game. God, that phrase! Does Colonel Farquhar really think that war is a cricket match, or is it camping here, on a playing field, creeping about with imaginary rifles, that makes them talk like school boys? Talbot finds himself instinctively waiting for the whistle to blow, when they all will take off their sweaty uniforms and put on clean shirts and pack up their things in dunnage bags and head home on the streetcar. Sometimes, when it's five o'clock — damn, seventeen hundred hours — and they're dying of thirst on the parade ground, he has to bite his tongue not to say to his men, "Okay, that's it for today," and invite them all across the road to the Rowing Club for a cold drink.

His men. His platoon. He is still appalled by those forty blank faces staring at him, waiting. His men. His orders. His responsibility. What if he makes a mistake? Talbot has never given an order in his life before, much less obeyed one, and he finds the necessity of pulling rank as embarrassing as the indignity of suffering it. His men are all old sweats, veterans of India and South Africa with rows of ribbons on their chests, while his own tunic is as bare as a sparrow's breast. The only thing he can beat them at is marching. He can do twenty miles with a full pack and hardly feel it, while they're all puffing and groaning. Hardly enough to earn his pips.

"Thank you, Blatchford. You're very prompt."

"Can't keep a princess waiting, sir."

"Do you think she'll kiss me, Blatchford?"

"Oh no, sir!"

Talbot hasn't kissed, or been kissed, since he left Montreal. He is out of love at the moment and the army seems to offer little in the way of opportunities. He is beginning to feel deprived. Love and war, are they not the two great events in a man's life? And here he is at war, but not in love. It would be glorious to be in love, wildly, madly in love, consumed by a grand passion wrought to a perfect pitch of desire by his courtship of death. Think of the letters he could write!

"I am an idiot, Blatchford."

"Not at all, sir."

R.H.
Friday, August 28, 1914
2 a.m.

He is standing directly in front of me when I walk into the drawing room, alone, slightly apart from the knots of men, in front of the tall windows, his neck and shoulders silouetted in the golden light from the setting sun. His face is tanned, freckled, with a white strip over the ears where his hair has been cropped short. The sun shining on his fair, curly hair makes a halo around his head. He raises his glass of wine to his lips and it splinters into a rainbow full of rubies.

It's an angel, I say to myself, and hold my breath. Granny always said they come unexpectedly, in disguise, and carry a sword, like Gabriel. I stand stock-still, staring into the sun for what seems like hours but must be only a split second. He meets my eyes and smiles. He has come for me, with a message, a matter of life and death, and he will tell me at the proper time.

A shadow at my side, a damp hand, a whiff of peppermint and Arbee is complimenting me on my dress, all the time mopping his face and peering over my shoulder wigwagging at friends, mumbling greetings, carrying on three conversations at once, listening to none. The room smells of leather and shaving soap and wet wool and horses and sweat. The officers stand in little circles, heads together, bums out, flicking their riding crops against their boots as if they're swatting flies.

He has gone. Where is he?

The officers all look alike to me, brown, like hens, and I realize too late that I can't tell a colonel from a captain. What do you say to an officer? Are you enjoying the war?

Where is he?

I am standing by the door afraid to move when there is a great thudding of boots and barking of orders. Colonel Sam Hughes sweeps in, cape flying, spurs clanking in the sudden silence. He makes a tour of the room, *clank, clank*, riding crop tucked under his left elbow, right arm folded across his back, chest out, head cocked, black eyes darting, tense, alert, strutting, each step arched, deliberate, tailfeathers up, a fat old fighting cock inspecting his harem. The Macnab.

Ena MacAdam is carrying her shovel.

"Greatest invention since the catapult!" thunders Colonel Hughes, waving it around. He has ordered twelve thousand to be shipped to the front. The shovel has a folding handle and a blade with a hole in it and it weighs fifteen pounds. I don't understand how it works. If you dig, won't the dirt run through the hole? How can you aim a rifle through the hole if you can't see what you're shooting at? Ena is very proud. I am jealous.

Where is he?

The Edmonton Pipe Band strikes up "God Save the King" and we all take our places around a horseshoe-shaped table, Patsy in the centre, Britannia in silver lamé and diamonds, the Duchess in gold with Nigger, her lap dog, under her arm, the Duke stuck with medals like a pommander, Alice and I down at the ends, two stoppers to keep the luck from running out. On my left is Captain George Bennett, Arbee's kid brother, and *he* is on my right. Lieutenant Talbot Papineau, the placecard says. He doesn't look at all French. He is short and fair, with an elfin sort of face, a dimpled chin and a turned-up nose that doesn't seem to go with his long arms and broad, calloused hands, a riverman's hands, but his touch is light and sure and he knows which fork to use without even looking.

"Have you been in the army long?" I ask, swallowing hard.

"Two weeks."

He grins at me as if we shared a secret joke. His eyes are the colour of honey with amber flecks and little crinkles at the corners when he smiles.

"I'm not a soldier. I'm not a cowpuncher or a prize fighter or a hero of Ladysmith. I'm a lawyer. I got in through pull, and my willingness to atone for the indiscretions of my rebellious ancestor. I am the token Frog."

"I'm a bank clerk, Regina," says Captain Bennett. "Dickie felt one of the family should be in on it. As paymaster I'll be pretty well out of the action. Just as well. Never fired a gun in my life."

We are served squab. The officers poke hopelessly at them except for Lieutenant Papineau, who separates the stringy meat from the tiny bones with surgical deftness.

"I was afraid we might be served pork and beans again," he smiles. "Colonel Farquhar says it's good for morale. I don't see how we can fight a war with half our men in the latrine."

"They were a gift..."

"Ah."

"...from Mr. Booth."

"And the red longjohns?"

"Yes."

"And the socks? They all have 'B' woven into the heel."

"Yes."

"I thought the 'B' stood for Bennett," says Captain Bennett. "Dickie told me he rustled them up."

"Is that why we have no rifles?" says Lieutenant Papineau. "Are we meant to rush the Boche in our red underwear loaded up with beans and blast them back to Berlin? It might work."

His bluntness shocks me a little. His voice is low and musical but there is a mocking, bitter edge to it.

"I am called a traitor in Quebec for fighting an English war," he says.

"What shall I do? Dress in priest's skirts and hide in the church? They are still fighting General Wolfe, the French. They are not cowards, but they have learned to cringe, as Papineau cringed, *le grand seigneur, le martyr*. They adore him. So you see, I carry this albatross of a name around my neck."

"It's better than Coolican," I say.

We are all quite drunk and giddy by the time the speeches start. We sing "For She's a Jolly Good Fellow" and "Tipperary" and we cheer and clap so much when Arbee is speaking that he has to sit down. I am surprised when Lieutenant Papineau jumps up to make a speech. He talks about civilization and liberty and British justice. It sounds wonderful and makes me quite weepy. I concentrate on his left ear, which is small and beautifully curled, and on the golden hairs on his wrist above his watch. The watch is big and silver and it says 10:04. I can hear it ticking.

He is beginning to speak in French when Nigger rockets out of the Duchess' lap, streaks across the table smashing glass and disappears underneath. The tablecloth billows out as he scampers down between the chairs yapping furiously. There's another sound too, a deep *woof woof woof* and snarling and the crash of chairs being knocked over as the officers jump up and peer under the table. Nigger shoots out past my legs, pursued by a yellow dog the size of a wolf. They shriek around the room while Miss Yorke screams and flaps her arms and the officers all whistle and shout, "Here boy! Here Bob! Come here boy!" Nigger streaks for the door, the yellow dog's jaws almost around his neck. The Duchess storms out in pursuit. We ladies follow. The door closes behind us and the men burst into great guffaws.

We comb the house for Nigger. He is not to be found. Nor is the yellow dog, Bob. I don't much care. Nigger was a hateful little beast. He peed everywhere and chewed the hem of your skirt when you weren't looking. I am furious that the door is closed and the men are on the other side laughing and drinking and singing and having a wonderful time and I will never, never see Lieutenant Talbot Papineau again as long as I live.

I go downstairs to the kitchen. Madame Pacquette, the cook, is scraping plates. A huge man in a checked shirt is sitting at the table shovelling forkfuls of chicken pie into his mouth.

"'Dis is Jacques Munro, d'heavyweight champion of d'world, 'cept for Jacques Johnson," beams Madame Pacquette, heaping his plate with dumplings. "'E's going to beat up d'ole British Army!"

"They figure I'll win the British Army championship," says Jack Munro, holding up two big fists as thick and red as hams. "Dunno. Got KO'd last time out. Ain't no spring chicken no more."

"But why are you here, in the kitchen?"

"Oh, I ain't no officer!" He gives me a big, cauliflower grin. "They ain't even got a uniform big enough to fit me. I'm only here on accounta Bob. Bob's the mascot. Brought him with me, signed him up. We'll probably be sacked now, on accounta the trouble. He's probably chewed that little runt t'bits."

He looks down at his dumplings as if they hold the answer to his fate.

"*Maudeezanglais*," snorts Madame Pacquette, rattling the stove lids. "*Cochons*. I trow out d'ole damn bunch 'cept for d' Frenchman out dere on d'step."

Talbot is sitting on the back steps stroking Bob. I get a bowl of scraps and take them out. Bob wolfs down the remains of forty pigeons. I ask Talbot about Munro. He says I shouldn't worry, the army is not like real life. Everything is inside-out. You get ahead in the army by doing the opposite of what makes sense. If it makes sense to shoot Bob, they won't.

A bugle sounds from the front of the house.

"Retreat!" shouts Munro and shoots out the door like a rabbit, Talbot and Bob and me galloping after him through the rose garden. Talbot and Bob and the men tumble into their cars and roar off to "Tipperary." That song doesn't make sense either.

My dress is covered with grease spots and dog hairs. My shoes are smeared with mud.

I must learn to throw away beautiful things, and not regret.

I am trying to imagine myself at Lansdowne Park rolled up in a grey blanket on hard earth listening to the crickets. Does he sleep in his clothes? Does he sleep?

R.H.
Friday, August 28, 1914
10:20 p.m.

I wake up dreaming I am home and Jack is throwing pebbles at my window to let me know Mum has gone to a meeting and the coast is clear. There is the soft crunch of steps on the gravel driveway under my window and the smell of fresh-cut grass. It's the convicts, I think at first, come to tend the garden, and I am afraid for a moment that Jack is down there with his head shaved and his legs in irons. I wait for the sound of the mowers and clippers but it is perfectly quiet except for a single pair of feet walking slowly, stopping, walking again.

Talbot is right underneath my window staring intently at the ground. I hardly know him. He is in white flannels and a red-and-white striped jersey that shows off the muscles in his brown arms. Holy Jesus! And I look a perfect fright! Well, it's not to be helped. I throw on a dress, pin up my braid, stick on a straw hat to hide the mess, fly down the stairs and saunter out the front door trying to look astonished.

He blushes.

"I'm sorry, Did I disturb you?"

"Oh no!"

"I lost my glasses last night, I thought I might find them without creating a fuss. The trouble is I'm quite blind without them."

We poke through the geraniums and trace our steps back through the rose garden. The lawn is silver with dew. It's a perfect still cloudless morning, not a soul stirring, only the robins and the bees buzzing around the roses. Talbot picks a red one and tucks it in my hatband. He has a day's leave, until six, he says. Would I be free for lunch? Would I!

"Thank you. That would be lovely."

Regimental rolls, P.P.C.L.I.: Papineau, Talbot Mercer; born March 23, 1883, Montebello, P.Q. Enlisted P.P.C.L.I. August 8, 1914. Rank: Lieutenant. Marital status: Single.

Yippee!

He comes for me at noon in a pearl-grey roadster with red leather upholstery. The seat is hot from the sun, like flesh, and smells of soap. He is wearing a pearl-grey suit and a matching fedora tilted over one eye. And his glasses.

"I left them back in the tent, with my kit," he grins.

He doesn't tell me that lunch is with Sir Wilfrid and Lady Laurier until we are turning into the driveway.

"I don't speak French."

"Never mind. Nobody in Ottawa speaks French. Not even the French. Play bridge?"

"A little. Not well."

"Good. Zoé likes to win."

That monstrous old woman with the marble eyes. Talbot smiles as if he'd read my mind.

"She sees better than she lets on."

We are going up the walk when the front door opens and Willie King comes out, pushing a bowler hat onto his round white head like a cap on an acorn. He looks as startled to see me as I am to see him, and his eyes dart between us, full of questions. He says nothing but smiles, nods and tips his hat as he hurries by, clapping his gloves nervously against his leg. We both glance around at the same time. Willie turns away quickly, *trip-trap, trip-trap.* He pulls the brim of his bowler down and tilts it slightly over one eye.

"Mr. Mackenzie King is a busy man," says Talbot. He is frowning and the muscles on his jaw stand out.

Sir Wilfrid opens the door himself and kisses my hand. His hands are thin and paper white with big veins. He waves them around like a magician's scarf when he talks, slowly and deliberately. He moves the same way, or prowls, an old lion with his mane of white hair and long, thick, aristocratic nose, his face folded into furrows so deep that his eyes are just dark slits in two pouches of dry, leathery skin, and his mouth a narrow crevasse.

He wears powder and scent, like the Duke, and a diamond pin in his cravat, and his trousers are cut very tight. I'd guess he was queer except everybody says he's got a bastard son in Montreal.

We climb the stairs. The carpet is worn right through in places and there are balls of dust in the corners. The wallpaper has brown stains where water has come in, and here and there the plaster is falling away in scabby patches. The curtains are drawn. The whole house smells of dirt and mold and stale food and old age. A poor house. A blind house.

"It saddens me to hear that our dear Connaughts are returning to England," Sir Wilfrid says in a voice so soft I have to lean to hear.

"Oh no," I say. "They have been instructed to remain...."

Jesus, I could pull my tongue out by the roots. He's foxed me out of a secret no politician in Ottawa knows yet. I could kick him. Or myself.

Lady Laurier is in the morning room by the window, Marie Antoinette in a white lace cap, her jewelled fingers playing with a deck of cards on a lacquered table beside her. She raises her white face expectantly toward us. Talbot hugs her and she kisses him on both cheeks.

"Come here where an old woman can see you!" she says to me. Her voice is deep, strong, almost harsh. She pats the sofa beside her. It is a white brocade sofa embroidered with pink cherubs carrying nosegays. The room is full of cherubs, cherubs on the chairs, cherubs holding up the lamps, cherubs on the vases and the vases full of nosegays. Some of the flowers are dying and the carpet is strewn with petals.

"You will call me Zoé," she says. "You see I am fond of flowers."

The room smells of sweet peas. The curtains have a pattern of leaves on them. The wallpaper is cabbage roses. The carpet is mint green with a darker green design like vines. It's like sitting in a garden, a late summer garden overgrown and gone to seed, but warm and lazy and sinful.

Her fingertips flutter over my face and she stares at me with those pale, unfocussed eyes. I force myself to stare back.

"You are dark. Good. I was myself. Long ago. I was pretty then, on my wedding day. It is hard to believe now, eh? That was long ago. I was not yet twenty. It is a good age for marriage, twenty, eh?"

I wish she wouldn't talk so loudly.

A canary sings. The windows are full of gilt cages and the cages are full of birds, canaries, parakeets, and under them are the cats, cats asleep in the sun on the sill, on the carpet, on the chairs, among the bric-a-brac on the tables. White cats, orange cats, striped cats, fat cats. She rattles off their names, stroking them as they come to her, Chouchou and Mimi and Pierre and Louis and Fifi.

"My children," she says. 'My menagerie. How do you say in English? Zoo? They are all quite gentle except for this one," she laughs, pointing at Sir Wilfrid. "This one is my most ferocious beast!"

Miss Coutu, a woman with a harelip, serves lunch, cold chicken, potatoes, green beans, chilled wine and peach pie. The cats purr around my ankles like the little waves when I used to sit with me feet in the river. Sir Wilfrid talks about Quebec and the war.

"I am glad I have no sons!" Zoé says suddenly. "A terrible thing to say, eh? I would not let them be soldiers. Never! That would make trouble, eh?"

"They would all be generals," Talbot smiles.

"And stay at home," says Sir Wilfrid.

"Pfft!" says Zoé. "I am not a coward. I do not mind them getting killed. But I am a patriot. They should get killed here, for Canada, not for England, not for France. *C'est mon pays, ici!*"

The slap of her hand on the table makes the glasses jump.

We leave in time to drive Sir Wilfrid to the House of Commons.

"You must not let this one get away!" she whispers at the door. "He is a jewel, one in a million. I will tell you some day how I caught Laurier. But then you may not want to end up like me."

She kisses me on both cheeks, lightly, like a moth.

"Come for bridge, Tuesdays."

I hesitate.

"Ah," she says. "You prefer poker?"

"Yes."

She claps her hands like a tickled baby.

"You saw my little table, eh? It is my favourite too. You must come then and, how do you say, clean me out!"

"She likes you," Talbot says after we leave Sir Wilfrid at his office on Parliament Hill.

"I like her."

"She has been trying to marry me off since I was in knee pants. I am unmarriageable."

We drive out to the Rowing Club and hire a silly little flat-bottomed punt. The river is dotted with them like gumdrops. Ours is grey.

The Rideau is calm and scummy. It smells of dead leaves and the end of summer. They found a corpse here yesterday. We head upstream, making our own breeze. Talbot rows strongly, *scree, grunk, scree, grunk*. He rowed for McGill and for Oxford. He prefers to paddle. I feel like a sack of flour in the stern holding my parasol.

"I feel like Cleopatra."

"Cleopatra was old. And ugly."

Why do compliments embarrass me? Other girls thrive on them. I look down at the brown water and the reeds drifting with the current like a woman's hair. We both begin the poem with the same breath:

> *On either side the river lie*
> *Long fields of barley and of rye,*

That clothe the wold and meet the sky
And thro' the field the road runs by....

We're shouting with laughter when we finish it, all four parts, word perfect, in unison. They must have heard our "Shalott!" in Hull. People on the riverbank stare.

"I'll show you Camelot one day," he says. "I live there."

Montebello isn't far, he says, only about forty miles down the Ottawa River, towards Montreal. The seigneury belonged to Bishop Laval originally. Talbot's great-great-grandfather took it from the Church as a legal fee.

"They were glad to be rid of it. It produces nothing but bush and babies. We've had to sell most of it. We may have to sell the rest. Even the manor house. Louis-Joseph Papineau built it after he came back from exile. Montebello was his Elba. Nothing was too good or too grand or too expensive for Le grand Seigneur. He bankrupted the seigneury to play emperor. Still, it is beautiful, and I love it. I shall miss Montebello."

"You don't look like him." In the history books Papineau looked more like Sam Hughes, stern jaw, black eyes and a white forelock standing straight up in the air like a baby's curl. Talbot smiles.

"I am three-quarters American, one-quarter French and one hundred per cent republican."

"What are you doing in the British army, then?"

He misses a stroke. We drift for a moment. He shrugs. "*Je suis canadien*, I guess."

We talk very little. There seems no need. What is there to ask? We have no future. I don't want to know about his past. I hate all the other women he has loved, or loves. I am jealous of every second he has lived beyond the range of my imagination. I feel as if I've known him all my life. He has opened a secret door in my memory and walked in. Time has stopped and we will float forever on a hot, pale August afternoon, our feet slightly touching, lulled by the noise of the oars and the pull of the current and the high faraway cries of little boys in sailor suits playing on the lawn and the stray, incomprehensible words from passing boats.

We stop at Page and Shaw's for Coca-Cola and sundaes. I have butterscotch, he has chocolate. The ice cream reminds me of Joachim.

"Ribbentrop and I worked together, you know," Talbot says. "It was his first summer in Canada. We were laying track for the Grand Trunk Railway in Saskatchewan, north of Moose Jaw, a lark really, chance to see the country, at least I was laying track. Ribbentrop had a clerk's job, timekeeper I think, making sure the rest of us didn't slack off. He was just a kid. Hays, the president, took a fancy to him, but Hays went down on the Titanic and Ribbentrop disappeared."

Everything in Page and Shaw's looks like ice-cream, vanilla tables, a lemon ceiling, butterscotch floor, cherry and strawberry and pistachio cushions on the chocolate chairs, a big ceiling fan stirring the air like a paddle in a butter churn. And, sitting in the window, a gingerbread gypsy in a marzipan skirt and peppermint scarf reading palms. She has a crystal ball too, and a pack of cards, just in case.

"Flora! What are you doing here?"

"It's for the Soldiers' Wives Fund. A benefit."

"Come on," says Talbot, nudging me towards her.

"No."

"Superstitious?"

"Yes."

I draw back and pull my gloves on.

Talbot puts a dollar in the bowl and holds out his broad palm. The oar has made a blister at the base of his ring finger. Flora bends over it, tracing the lines with the tips of her fingers.

"Ah," she says, "you have had much success. You will have more. I see good luck. Trouble. Fighting. You desire fame. Fame will come. You are going on a voyage soon. Tomorrow. I see trees, many trees. White trees. You will die where you were born."

"That's good news," Talbot says, tucking my hand under his arm. "The white trees are the birches at Montebello. I was born at Montebello, on Easter Day. My mother considered it an omen."

Damn her, she didn't see me in his future.

"Will you knit for me?" he smiles.

"You'll be the only soldier in the army with holes in his socks before you put them on."

"Send me pictures, then. Yours to start with. I'll tack you over my bunk between my mother and Mary Pickford."

I will him to kiss me. He squeezes my hand.

I hate Mary Pickford.

R.H.
Saturday, August 29, 1914

He's gone. It was a wonderful parade. The regiment came marching up Metcalfe on the double, the pipe band going full blast, every man in uniform, even Jack Munro, who was at the very front holding Bob on a leash, all grinning from ear to ear — even Talbot, who was trying to look serious. Everybody cheered and threw flowers and waved little flags. Now and then a woman ran out and gave a soldier a big kiss and the crowd roared with delight.

I found a perfect spot on the funny little statue on Wellington Street, a sort of an angel, as far as I could tell, with a sword and a cloak and one of those curly hairdos, although why anyone would put an angel on Wellington Street was beyond me. Two workmen gave me a boost up. They were very disappointed Patsy wasn't in the parade. They pictured her on a great black horse galloping along in a plumed hat and a scarlet cape. It did sound wonderful. I didn't tell them how perfectly terrified she looks on a horse, ready to topple off at the first whinny.

I was snapping away as fast as I could when there was a tug at my skirt and a loud angry voice.

"Miss! Miss! You are standing on Sir Galahad!"

Jesus, police. I looked down into a round, furious face beneath a round, black hat.

"I'm sorry, Mr. King, I have to, I have to see over the heads!"

I turned back, angry at missing so many shots, afraid of losing my balance. The last of the soldiers were turning onto Wellington.

"Let the lady be," the workmen were shouting. "She ain't doin' nothin'."

"Miss Coolican!" cried Mr. King in his high voice. "You are desecrating poor Bert!"

Well damn Bert. The damage was done anyway. The last of the men had turned the corner and I had to get to the station before the train left. My workmen lifted me down and I retrieved my shoes from their pockets.

"I'm very sorry, Mr. King, I didn't realize."

There were tears in his blue eyes.

The soldiers were all aboard when I got there, leaning out the windows, reaching down towards women holding up letters or parcels or babies or just their hands. Some of the women just stood there, mute, stiff in that painful moment that comes when everything has been said and nothing is to be done. I searched the rows of faces, so alike, so hard to find a single face. What would I say? Goodbye. Have a nice time. It was too dark in the station for pictures, so I just stood there like a dodo until the train pulled out.

Mr. King has sent an immense bouquet and a long letter, all apologies. He has invited me to church tomorrow but I think I will print my pictures. I'll send one to Talbot if they come out.

Patsy has come to take back her pearls.

R.H.
Sunday, August 30, 1914

Found Nigger this morning in the fruit cellar. One ear and a lot of fur missing.

R.H.
Thursday, September 3, 1914

Mrs. Frieman has taken over the hospital ship campaign. We've raised only $4,000. Mrs. Herridge was gracious about resigning. The Jews have a natural talent for making money, she said. Mrs. Herridge is taking up Belgian relief. The *Citizen* is going to collect the money and publish the names of the donors. That's a weight off my back. Miss Yorke is upset because Mrs. Freiman has organized teams of women to go from door to door collecting. "You can tell her father was a pedlar," she sneered.

Everyone is talking about the German atrocities. It must have something to do with sex because when I asked Lady Borden exactly what the Huns did she just rolled her eyes and covered her mouth and said it wasn't for unmarried girls to know. It's so annoying. She looked as if she would enjoy being atrocitied.

R.H.
Friday, September 4, 1914

Mrs. Freiman telephoned this morning at half-past eight. "Your name has been accidentally omitted from the list of contributors to the hospital ship," she said, a whisper of shock in her silvery voice. "An unforgivable oversight. I am putting you down immediately for $50. It will be in the *Citizen* tonight."

"Yes," I said. "Thank you."

I couldn't decide whether to kick myself or strangle Mrs. Freiman. How did she know I had exactly $50? She didn't even ask for it, she just took it!

My name was on the front page, large as life. All the other donors were Jews. They gave $250 each. I couldn't believe it! Their husbands are all junk dealers!

Am I just being selfish?

R.H.
Wednesday, September 9, 1914

The hospital ship fund is nearly $14,000! The Duchess is pleased. Everyone else is scandalized over Mrs. Freiman's "tactics." She arrived at Fleck's on Sunday afternoon, uninvited, and asked for $500. Mrs. Fleck said they gave it to her just to get rid of her. It's indecent, she said, to be soliciting money on the Sabbath. Moreover, Mrs. Freiman has guaranteed the *Citizen* a column of advertising for every column of news about the fund and she runs about selling the ads herself. I don't see anything wrong with that but what do I say to all the women who demand that the Duchess "do something" about Mrs. Freiman?

"Ask them why they send their sons to war," said the Duchess, "yet begrudge the money to save their lives. Do they not love their children? Why then are they not generous? Why is it necessary to squeeze them for a few paltry dollars? Are they not ashamed? Tell them I have contempt for their greed. Tell them I will 'do something' about Mrs. Freiman. I will give her a medal. They will learn, these Canada *Streckruebe*. It hurts to bleed, yes. The hurt is only beginning. They will get used to it. Soon they will be jumping all over themselves to see who can bleed the most. You will see."

I told Mrs. Fleck not to breath a word to a soul but the King was considering a special medal for women who made an outstanding contribution to the war effort, something along the lines of a Florence Nightingale cross. May God strike me dead if I lied.

R.H.
Saturday, September 12, 1914

Red Cross bazaar at Rae's department store. Patsy was patron. Five cents of every dollar's worth of goods sold is to go to the Red Cross. "It's nothing but a sale!" Patsy said. "In a shop!" She hadn't been in a shop since she's been in Canada. I buy her stockings and things, usually at Ogilvy's, the rich people's store, at the other end of Rideau Street, although I get my own things at Freiman's on credit. I was surprised to see that Mrs. Freiman had volunteered to sell men's wear at Rae's for the bazaar. Rae's is Freiman's biggest competition.

"I won't be a, what do you call it, a loss leader!" Patsy said.

"It's for the Red Cross," I said. "Think of the regiment."

She put on her plainest dark gabardine suit and a fierce hat and a muff so she wouldn't have to shake hands. She was mobbed as she got out of the car but she set her lips and stalked into the store looking neither to right nor left. She headed straight for the men's wear department with Lady Borden and Mr. A.E. Rae bobbing in her wake.

Mrs. Freiman was all alone in men's wear. I guess her friends stayed home out of sympathy. Patsy ordered $100 worth of shirts, mufflers and socks, for the soldiers, she said loudly, and we left. We weren't there more than ten minutes.

Lady Borden telephoned tonight to say that the Red Cross had netted $1,759.31. How lovely, I said, Mr. Rae must be pleased. Oh yes, said Lady Borden, he'll be pleased to let us have his store any time, *any time*, for a charitable purpose.

The *Citizen* tonight says that the women of Renfrew have donated a carload of oats to the Canadian Expeditionary Force. Wouldn't you know.

R.H.
Tuesday, September 15, 1914

Hospital fund over $17,500. On Sunday we go to Valcartier to inspect the troops before they leave for England. I am counting the minutes!

R.H.
Friday, September 18, 1914

Nigger died this morning. Buried him in the rose garden, full honours.

4

Valcartier, Quebec; Saturday, September 19, 1914

"Lieutenant Papineau!"

"Yes sir!"

"I have been informed that on Thursday, September 17 at zero six hours your platoon failed to report to the rifle range for target practice."

"Yes, sir."

"Do you have an explanation, Lieutenant?"

"It was dark, sir. I thought...."

"You thought."

"I thought there had been a mistake, sir."

"You thought?"

"We couldn't see anything, sir."

"Let us assume, Lieutenant, that a German patrol was lying in ambush at the rifle range..."

"That wasn't the information, sir."

"...the whole damn regiment could have been wiped out!"

"But...."

"You do a great deal of thinking, Lieutenant."

"I'm sorry, sir."

"Junior officers in the British Army do not think, Lieutenant. Is that quite clear?"

"Yes, sir."

"That will be all."

That was yesterday, his second dressing-down in as many weeks. One more and he'll be out on his ear, even court martialled. He was right too, it was a mistake, the order paper was meant to read 16:00 hours, but Colonel Farquhar never admitted it. Truth, in the British Army, is the perquisite of rank, and of all the things he dislikes about army life, Talbot dislikes that the most.

He's almost decided to resign his commission. Better to quit than be dismissed in disgrace. He's never failed at anything in his life before, but — it was stupid, parachuting in as an officer simply because he was a friend of Hammy Gault's. He could go with the French-Canadian regiment as a private, one of the great brute mob, ignorant, unthinking, herded here and there like cattle, ours not to reason why, he can take the punishment. But his soul shrinks from the communal life, the lack of privacy, the deadening routine, the blind obedience, the bare, primitive existence without the few comforts, simple as they are, that so far have made military life bearable: a hot bath, his own tent and the excellent Scotch at the officers' mess.

What is he doing in this monastery? He is a rational man, not religious, not even Christian. He has cultivated the classic virtues, wisdom, justice, courage, to the best of his ability, his mood fluctuating between stoicism and epicureanism: epicurean when falling in love, stoic when falling out. It's epicurean at the moment. He has always had a passionate weakness for beauty, for pictures and pearls and pretty girls, although he liked Lily better without the pearls, in her plain pink dress with the parasol. And he is sensitive to wealth, never having quite enough, but not greedy, having little desire to possess, only to enjoy, to immerse himself wholly in the excitement of discovery and then to pass on when the feeling fades. It has kept him out of debt, but in trouble with women, who like being taken up and appreciated, but resent being put down again. He has not been deliberately unkind, since the feeling was real enough at the time, and his disappointment at the outcome as great as theirs, but it has made him wary, at thirty-one, of impressionable young girls.

He would never dream of inviting a girl he hardly knows to Montebello for his last leave, except that it is his last leave. The war seems to have swept away all conventional constraints, leaving possibilities as broad and bright as the Valcartier plain, where tomorrow, with a little luck, he will see Lily again at the march past, and speak to her, and decide, possibly for the last time, to resist or succumb.

"Major Gault wants you, sir. PDQ."

What the hell is it now? The end? So sorry, Papineau, just not up to snuff, tough break old man. Why on earth did he enlist in the first place? Talbot has always been opposed to imperialism, militarism, and the war has brought out all those characteristics of the British jingo that he, more French Canadian than he cares to admit, finds most repulsive. Yet here he is, one of a handful of colonials in an overwhelmingly British regiment, subjected continually to the condescending arrogance that so enraged him at Oxford. He had gone from McGill, a Rhodes scholar, to study constitutional law, dreaming of a career at the British bar and hopefully Westminster, the diplomatic service if not the House, only to find himself frozen out, all doors closed, relegated to the company of black Africans and Indians simply because he was from another of those far-flung outposts of Empire. A fuzzy-wuzzy with a funny name, not rich enough to be cultivated, not exotic enough to be amusing, a dull, drab, disappointing Canadian.

He came home fiercely Canadian, a passionate nationalist, committed heart and soul to liberating Canada from the last vestiges of the Imperial yoke, only to find himself suspect, because of the Oxford connection, as an anglophile, a jingo and an intellectual — of which vices, to the Liberal mind, the last was certainly the worst. You are young, Laurier had said. Wait. Build a practice, put money aside, marry. The time will come. But time passed, and Laurier fell, the Liberals in retreat, the nationalist mantle picked up by his cousin, Bourassa, not Laurier's mantle — the dream of liberty, equality and fraternity in a united Canada — but a narrow, sectarian nationalism founded on two superstitions, race and Rome, which Talbot abhors. Bourassa has inherited Le Grand Siegneur's talent for demagoguery, his ability to excite people's emotions, arouse them to revolution; Talbot has inherited his respect for reason and the rule of law.

There is not much room for either of them in the Liberal Party, all the space being occupied by heelers and time servers, grafters and fools whose sole function is to grease the wheels of the political machine. They are bored by young men's ideas, jealous of their talents. Laurier is old, tired. Wait, he says, wait. Wait! God, he is over thirty, he is old! How much longer? When he is too old to care? Too old to do anything? He is ambitious, yes. He is smart, yes, and energetic. Why hide it? Why not make use of it?

He volunteered on impulse, the day the regiment was formed, because it seemed something wonderful to *do*, an opportunity, a clear straightforward way to express his love for his country and his joy in adventure, and it has only occurred to him now, at Valcartier, that he might have acted out of boredom, or romantic illusion, too naive to realize that of all the books he'd read about Frontenac and Montcalm and Napoleon and Wellington at Waterloo, not one was written from a junior lieutenant's point of view, too obtuse to see that all his talents, so unappreciated by the Liberal Party, would be even less appreciated in the army.

He has voluntarily entered an utterly strange and unfamiliar world, a babe in arms, ignorant of the customs and inarticulate in the language, a world without contemplation, without literature, without civilization, in which his power to analyze, question, debate is the exact reverse of what is wanted. It is a world of more grinding tedium, more maddening frustration, more limited horizons than the one he left. It is a world without freedom, and Talbot cherishes freedom above all else.

"Hammy, I'm submitting my resignation."

"Don't be an asshole."

"The Colonel says...."

"The Colonel says you have great potential. You use your head."

"Do you want me to stay on?"

"Buck up. You're not an idiot, like Niven, or a drunk, like Stewart. Now shut up and sit down. This is personal. I have a letter from your mother."

Oh dear God.

"It's her third. I threw the first two away thinking she'd take the hint. She's stubborn. This one went to the Colonel. He's asked me to deal with it. You're not supposed to know about it."

Gault slides the letter across the table and runs his big, bony finger under the paragraph at the top of the second page.

"...in recognition of Talbot's exceptional qualities and the brilliant future that lies before him in public life, I ask you to consider that he made his decision in haste, without due reflection, and I most sincerely request that you release him from his commission and any further obligation to the regiment...."

"She can't touch you, Talbot. You're a grown man. Hell, you're getting gray, no wife, no dependents."

"She's a widow."

"Sure, but she's not poor, is she? Or sick? You've got three brothers, two married. What makes you so bloody priceless?"

He's been trying to answer that question all his life. Why he should be the favoured one, focus of his mother's cares and fears, object of her hopes, subject of her dreams, crucible of her ambitions, a flattered Fauntleroy so secure in self-esteem (a snob, some say) that it comes as a shock even now to find that he is not universally considered indispensable? He enlisted without telling his mother, assuming she would agree, but she flew into a fury, and insisted he back out. The more she railed the harder he dug in his heels, but he never, never suspected she would secretly shame him like this. His face flames.

"If you want out," Gault says, "you're free to go. It's up to you."

So that's it. They think he put her up to it. Mama's boy. A coward. A familiar door opens at the back of Talbot's mind and he looks out into a forest, the birch wood at Montebello, in winter, and a dark figure in a monk's robe is running through the snow, the hood pulled up to conceal a hunted face, a face with a square jaw and a baby's curl, a frightened face, a black figure fleeing through the trees, running, running, running from the Redcoats, running from the hangman's noose, running from death.

"No, sir."

"Good man! I knew you weren't a pansy. I'll get the Colonel to call the old lady off. Women are a son-of-a-bitch, aren't they?"

For the first time Talbot is grateful for the numbing chores, the endless drill, the exhaustion that brings deep dreamless sleep. The last of the many things he had not known about war was that the first casualty would be his mother.

Valcartier, Quebec
Sunday, September 20, 1914

It's getting light. I'm freezing. My breath rises in a cloud over my head. A crow caws. I drag my wool bloomers and thick stockings under the covers and pull them on, then a heavy sweater and Patsy's old macintosh, which is two sizes too big but warm. I put on my thickest boots and creep up to the front of the coach. Our engine is gone. I look out at a wilderness of trees and track. There's a shack with a board that says *Valcartier* and rows of red boxcars. Our train is parked on a siding. There is only one house in sight, about half a mile away, on a little knoll. Sam Hughes said we'd be more comfortable here, on the camp site, because St. Joseph, the nearest village, is full of sightseers and all the hotels are full. It must have been one of Sam's jokes. All night long the troop trains came in, whistles tooting, cars clanging, men shouting and cursing and the bloody bagpipes bleating, and after the men had marched away the horses came off neighing and kicking and after the horses the guns or trucks or cannons rumbled off reeking of gasoline and backfiring like rifle shots.

It's quiet now, not a soul to be seen except our sentry, who's curled up on the ground like a big shaggy dog sound asleep. I tiptoe around him. Curtains of mist billow between the trees but the sky overhead is blue and the rising sun reddens the tips of the tall spruces. Most of the trees have been cut down. A field of stumps stretches between the station and the house on the knoll. I follow a little path along the river toward a bluff, hoping to get a view of the camp. The bush is dense here and clouds of mist roll up from the gorge. I come out suddenly in a clearing. Neat white crosses are planted in two rows in the underbrush, a mound of fresh-turned earth at the base of each. Nine. The paint is fresh and the names are lettered on the crossbars in black.

The bluff drops away suddenly into a valley white with fallen clouds. The faint, clear notes of a bugle rise out of the cloud, far away, then another, answering, calling one another like tiny golden birds. The sun breaks over the distant hills and the mist turns to rose petals, an ocean of petals neatly laid out in rows, like waves, curling into tents! Tents! The mist is a sea of tents, round, white bell tents stretching row on row as far as the eye can see, and between the rows the smoke of campfires rising and tiny figures running and the crisp, metallic sound of voices calling. I stand and wait for the tents to take shape in the sun. I take three pictures, trying to place each so they will form a panorama when placed side by side.

Something whizzes past my right ear. A bird? A bee? Another whine and a white scar appears in the bark of a tree beside me.

"Hey you! Getchyer hands up!"

A soldier is coming towards me. At least I think he's a soldier. He's wearing overalls with a khaki jacket. His rifle is real and he holds it at the ready. The bayonet shines in the sun.

"Whatcha doin' here?"

His voice cracks. He is tall but very young. A farm boy's sunburned face and big, knuckled hands. The rifle is trembling a little but I'll bet he can hit a ground hog in the eye at fifty yards. I stand very still. The bayonet is sharp and very shiny.

"Walking."

"Whatsa password?"

"I don't know. I'm not in the army."

He squints at me. His eyes are fixed on my camera.

"Whatcha doin' here?"

"Walking."

"I'll hafta turn you in," he says, pointing with the bayonet to the path. We walk single file through the scrub for what seems like miles. The sound of voices and the smell of horses get closer. We come out suddenly beside a row of tents. A half-dozen men in undershirts and suspenders are sitting around a fire. The smell of bacon is overpowering. I'm starved.

"Hey!" my soldier calls. "I caught one! I caught one! Come 'ere!"

The men jump up and run towards us, still chewing, wiping their greasy lips with their hands and their hands on their pants. They stand around in a semi-circle, whistling and grinning.

"Hey, *parlez-vous français, cherie?*"

"Prob'ly jist a local cunt. Lookit them boots."

"Spreckenzeedoitch?"

"Not even a Kraut'd wear that get-up."

"She sez she's chums with Princess Pat!" shouts my sentry. "Ain't that a good one!"

A crowd of men gathers around. The sun is in my eyes, hot. I shiver. My sentry stands beside me, rifle cocked, jealous of his prize. I notice he has two dead rabbits hanging from his belt loop.

An officer pushes his way through the circle, cap askew, jacket unbuttoned. He is strapping on his revolver. He is a thin, pale young man with sloping shoulders, like a yellow wax bean. A toothpick protrudes from beneath a pale, fuzzy moustache. He picks his teeth while I tell my story. Then he looks me up and down, slowly, from head to foot. Chew. Chew. The men snicker. He nods at my camera and holds out his hand. I hand it over. He turns it around, looks through the viewfinder, shakes it.

"Loaded?"

"Yes."

He picks at the back with a penknife. I reach over to show him how to spring the catch. He yanks it away. He digs away with the penknife, shakes it, bangs it against his boot.

"Shit!" he says.

He throws the camera hard against the ground and grinds it under his foot. He pulls the roll of film out of the shattered mess and unwinds it against the sun.

"Maybe we should search 'er, sir," my sentry winks. "She might have more, uh, concealed on her person, sir."

I estimate the distance between my knee and the officer's crotch, too mad to care about the consequences, but he's more interested in my handbag. He paws through it, tossing combs and hankies on the ground. He pulls out the envelope of money I carry for Patsy's tips and little souvenirs for the soldiers. We counted it last night. One hundred two-dollar bills. He runs his thumb over the bills, closes the envelope and tucks it into his shirt.

"Better take her to Sam," he says.

"Yes, sir! Captain Dempster!" says my sentry.

I am placed in the back of an open car between the two dead rabbits and Capt. Dempster. The sun is high now. Clouds of dust rise in our wake as we roar through the rows of tents towards the little house on the knoll. It's an old white frame farmhouse with a porch on three sides. A wooden platform has been built on the roof with a railing all around and a flagpole in the middle, like a lookout on a ship's mast. The platform is lined with men in uniform peering through binoculars.

We go into the parlour. The room is full of men, men in uniform, men in soiled blue suits, men in overalls reeking of horses and chewing tobacco. They are sitting on the tables, on the window ledges, on the stiff horsehair chairs. They all stand at once as I come in with my escort. I smile graciously and nod. I have my pick of seats. I take one next to the window beside the cleanest-looking man, a thin man with a yellow, horsey face.

We wait. The men stare at me furtively and look away. No one speaks. No one moves. The air is hot and sweaty and blue with smoke. We are all listening to the one voice in the room, a rough, raucous bellow coming quite clearly through the closed door at the far end of the room. The voice belongs unmistakably to the Minister of Militia, Commander-in-Chief of Camp Valcartier, Colonel Sam Hughes.

"...snivelling cocksuckers! Arse from a hole in the ground...."

A second voice. *Mumble, mumble.*

"Who's on the rug?" whispers Capt. Dempster to the man with the yellow face.

"The Bishop of Montreal," he says. "Col. Hughes has dismissed the Anglican padres from the Expeditionary Force. He is determined to take only Salvation Army men."

"The Bishop wants his cut, like the rest'a us," grins one of the men in overalls.

"Shhh!" hisses someone behind me.

Sam's shout startles us into silence.

"Forget 'em! Shove 'em in a hole. Dead men don't win wars! No point in snivellin' over 'em. Gimme a padre who'll get his hands dirty. Clean latrines. Make himself useful. Sally Ann boys'll do that. Get right down there in the dirt, by Jesus. You won't find 'em ten miles back whinin' for their tea."

The door bangs open and a little man with a purple shirt and a purple face flaps out.

"You can complain to the Lord God Almighty," Sam hollers after him. "I don't give a sweet goddamn. No pansies are sailing with my outfit!"

He turns his scowling, scarlet face towards us like a beacon.

"Okay you buggers, take off! That's it for today. I got company comin'."

"Excuse me, sir!" The man with the yellow face is on his feet waving a piece of paper. "Campbell, here. Toronto. I have an appointment."

"You'll have to wait your turn," Sam snaps, waving his hand.

"I've been waiting two days, sir!"

"Can't be very important then."

"It's a matter of life and death, Colonel Hughes! The death of innocent beasts. I represent the Toronto Humane Society, Colonel Hughes. We have received a complaint, sir, that horses have been kept here at Valcartier in barbed-wire pens without food and water, sir, and that many have died, and that on the 29th of last month an officer, an officer sir, was seen to light a fire underneath a horse that balked and I wish to tell you Colonel Hughes...."

"Who squealed?" snaps Sam.

"Pardon?"

"I said who fed you all this crap?"

"I am not at liberty to divulge the names of our informants...."

"Because it's lies! Damned lies! Only a scoundrel skulks around behind his commander's back. Let's bring him out in the open and expose the truth!"

"We suggest a full inquiry, sir...."

"We'll inquire right now. And we'll start with the evidence, Mr. Campbell. I want some evidence. I tour this camp every day, Mr. Campbell, I have not seen a dead horse or a sick horse or a horse on fire, sir."

"The officer who lighted the fire is Major Sharpe, of the Fourth Battalion, I am told, Colonel...."

"I have known Major Sharpe for more than twenty years. There is no finer officer in Canada. He would never do such a thing. Who is spreading these slanders?"

"I cannot say."

"But you can come here and publicly blacken the name of an honourable soldier! You puking bleeding hearts! You're worse than the most spavined, sway-backed toothless old nag that ever drew breath! I wouldn't send a man like you to the front! You are not worth sending. You are not worth keeping. I wouldn't even feed you."

The men in the room nudge and wink at each other.

"If you are not prepared to divulge to me the name of this scandalmonger, Mr. Campbell, I shall be forced to conclude that you invented these vile stories yourself with malicious intent to blacken my reputation and the reputation of the Canadian Expeditionary Force and I shall instruct Major Sharpe to take action against you, personally, for slander, and I shall advise him to push it to the very limit of the law with the full support of the Canadian armed forces and the government of Canada."

"The complaint is that the officer *ordered* the fire to be lighted," squeaks Mr. Campbell. "No one alleged that the officer *himself* set the fire."

"Ah! Now you deny it! You are a liar, a damned liar! Get out!"

The front door opens as if by magic and Mr. Campbell is swept away on the gust of Sam's rage.

"Who the hell are you?" Sam says, looking at me.

"Spy, sir," says Capt. Dempster, saluting. "Picked up this morning at zero eight hours."

He holds out my draggled roll of film.

"May be armed, sir. Should be searched, sir."

The men shift and move in closer. Captain Dempster's hand pulls on the sleeve of my macintosh.

"Hands off the prisoner!" Sam roars. He squints at me. "Now who the hell are you, girlie, and why are you here?"

"I'm Tommy Coolican's daughter, from Renfrew, General Hughes, you know my...."

"Khartoum's lassie? Not Khartoum Coolican's wee girl? You are too! A chip off the old block! Why there never was a sweeter man or a finer soldier! I loved the man like a brother. Where is he? Is he here? Hell, I'll give him a battalion! An army!"

"He's dead, sir."

"Dead? Ah." Tears well out of Sam's eyes and run down down his cheeks. He pulls a white handkerchief from his pocket, mops his face and blows his nose.

"What can I do for you, girl?" He puts a great paw around my shoulders and squeezes me until I nearly cry out.

"I was hoping to take a photograph of yourself, sir, but Captain Dempster destroyed my camera."

"It came apart, sir, under examination." Dempster wets his lips.

"And I'd like my money back, General Hughes, please."

Captain Dempster pats his pockets. He fumbles at his buttons. Coughs.

"It's in my moneybelt, sir. For safekeeping."

"Get it out!"

Captain Dempster fumbles at his gun belt. It drops to the floor. He unbuttons his jacket, slips off his suspenders. It's so quiet I can hear the flies buzzing on the window sill. Shirt off. Undershirt. He unfastens a leather pouch around his waist, pulls out my roll of bills and places it in Hughes' outstretched hand.

Sam counts the bills.

"Is that correct, girl?"

"Yes, sir. Thank you."

Sam turns and cracks the back of his hand across Captain Dempster's face.

"Now get out of here, you syphilitic son of a hoor! If I spot your ugly face around this camp again I'll have you shot and I'll dig your grave all the way to Hell, you miserable slug."

Captain Dempster bends to retrieve his clothes. Sam kicks them away and spits on them.

"Get out! You defile a uniform!"

Captain Dempster scuttles for the door, suspenders dragging, clutching his pants in his hands. My sentry with the rabbits stands still as death against the wall.

"You!" Sam points. "See that this lovely lady gets home. God bless you, girl."

I invent a dozen excuses on the way back to the train but I needn't have bothered. My absence is of no account compared to the absence of water on board. A company of men has been despatched to the river with pails. Miss Yorke says it's a plot by Sam Hughes to besmirch the dignity of the King. Moreover, she says, Lady Borden is throwing up, having been too enthusiastic about the port last night, and Sir Robert is trying to calm a man called Campbell who came in with an incredible story about an officer being burned alive, and the Duke is being shouted at by the Bishop of Montreal.

We leave for the march-past an hour late. The reviewing stand is a rickety wooden platform with hard folding chairs. Behind us and on either side dozens of touring cars drawn up in rows are full of people waving flags and eating lunches out of picnic baskets. Some the women snap at us with Kodaks. The sun is high and hot. The reviewing stand faces south, into the wind, looking down an enormous flat plain pounded hard and dry by weeks of manoeuvers. The troops are massed at the far end, a mile away and more, marching thirty thousand strong under a cloud of dust that the wind drives towards us in whirlpools of sand. The Duke gallops out to take the salute, medals twinkling on his chest, the royal pennant flying in the breeze. Picnickers cheer and wave their chicken legs. He reins in suddenly in front of the stand. The horse rears, bucks, and His Highness sails through the air into the horse buns. The Duchess covers her eyes. When she looks up her eyes are wet and twinkling but the rest of her face says, "This is ghastly but I'm doing it for the Empire." "Arthur's accidents" are a stock joke around the dinner table. He scarcely gets through a meal without knocking something off the table or lighting the wrong end of a cigar and he says himself they'd never let him into battle because he has no sense of direction. He blames it on the time he fell out of a window in Buckingham Palace and landed on his head. "No harm done," he says. And there's no harm done now, except to his uniform, and he soldiers on.

The Pats go by first and Patsy takes the salute. My heart skips a beat when I pick out Talbot, at the end, leading his platoon. When he's gone I pretty much lose interest, although it *is* a sight, a whole division in motion with the pipers and horses and guns, all looking so brave and proud even if they are a little out-of-step and it's hard to see much for the dust.

"That's it!" cries Lady Borden. "I know what I've been trying to remember. Troy! It's Troy, isn't it Robert? You know that wonderful line, 'Far on the ringing plains of windy Troy,' Homer."

"Tennyson," rumbles Sir Robert. "Ulysses."

"Yes, Ulysses! Colonel Hughes is Ulysses, isn't he, the aged warrior about to take his men across the sea, and His Highness is the brave Achilles!"

"Whom we knew," rumbles Sir Robert.

"Indeed," says the Duchess.

"Splendid day for golf," says Sir Robert, squinting into the sun.

"Quite," says the Duchess.

By three o'clock we're crabby and black with grime. Patsy looks at me and begins to hum "Swanee" very softly. We take it up one by one, in harmony, Sir Robert singing bass, and in a minute we're all grinning like coons.

The men are taken away for beer, and Miss McAdam takes us ladies on a tour of the kitchen facilities and the sanitary arrangements. Valcartier has more miles of water pipe than any army camp in the world. The men have cold showers every morning. The shower we inspect is nothing but a lattice of pipes in the middle of a field surrounded by a canvas screen. The canvas was put up only last week because women were driving out from the village at dawn and spying on the men through binoculars. Same with the latrines. The men still think it's a joke to cut the ropes when a buggy full of ladies is driving by. Miss McAdam says I am not to write that in the newspapers. Security, she says. Jesus, the CPR is running daily excursions from Ottawa, $6 round trip. The Kaiser himself could come for a peek. But I am forbidden to describe the camp, or the soldiers, or to give anyone's name except Col. Hughes'. He's worried, I think, that news of the riot will leak out. It happened last week. The men burned down the YMCA tent because it was showing the same movie for the third time in a row. They wrecked the canteen, and stole all the cigarettes and candy. Ena McAdam says they were drunk. Liquor's not allowed in camp but bootleggers get it off the trains and women sneak it through in their handbags. We drive past the place where it happened, a big charred circle with a lot of waste paper still blowing around.

So now I have to write about water pipes and latrines. What do you say about a ten-holer?

"It's very clean," says Lady Borden.

"It ought to be," Ena whispers to me. "It was dug an hour ago by two nice chaplains from the Church of England."

Montebello, Quebec; Tuesday, September 22, 1914

Armand meets them at the station with the buggy. He grins and touches his cap with the whip when he sees Talbot. Talbot hugs him and kisses him on both cheeks. A little circle is gathered around the buggy, familiar faces raised to him like sunflowers. He makes his way around as usual, shaking hands, waving bonjour, but the people hang back and duck their heads, blushing and shuffling their feet. It's his uniform. *Un maudit soldat,* their beloved Papineau. He's worn it on purpose, to face up to it, no backing down now, he is going to fight, for Canada, and he is not ashamed.

In his excitement to be home he's forgotten Lily and he turns, anxious. She is standing alone by the buggy, watching, waiting in that expectant way she has, as if there's something he's supposed to say and has forgotten, and she is waiting, patient, for him to remember. What can it be? He is disconcerted by her calm, her silence. He has never before known a girl with no small talk, a single girl who worked, for that matter, except school teachers, and she is the exact opposite of the hairy-lipped harridan he would have expected. He had made a little joke, the morning they were looking for his glasses, about how it must be a picnic working for a princess, and she had said "Picnics are the worst," and given him a proud, quizzical look, as if to say, "What a fatuous fool! What do you know?" And it was true, he'd felt, that in spite of his scholarships and degrees, in spite of the books he'd read and the concerts he'd attended, in spite of his winters in London and vacations in Rome, in spite of the girls he'd known and the hearts he'd broken, he didn't know a damn thing that mattered, at least he didn't know how to impress this girl, and that's what suddenly mattered. He'd found himself chattering away like a schoolboy, trying to close the space between them, to sound her soul, but talking instead about himself, his law practice, politics, friends, the regiment, his ambitions and dreams, personal things, selfish, not the conventional chatter of court-ship: something deeper, compulsive, a confession.

What is happening to him?

"*Et maman?*" he asks Armand as the buggy rolls past the great stone church, the church Papineau built, for his people, but refused to cross the threshold, as *he* refuses his Church now, and his people. They are always the same, poor, their good-natured faces beaming: whitewashed cabins, flowers in the gardens, washing on the lines, urchins staring from the ditches, thumbs in their mouths. Armand hunches his shoulders around his ears and shakes his head.

So it will be unpleasant then. *Tant pis.*

They are whirling through the wood now, his wood, sacred, silent, subterranean, branches arching high overhead, sunlight flickering greengold through the canopy of leaves, leaves fallen thick on the path ahead, red and gold, as if the sky had fallen and they are riding on the sunset. She is smiling. Her eyes are not black, as he'd assumed, but the colour of the shadows under the firs, and he has a sudden wild impulse to ask her to marry him, right now, in the village, so he can come home today a married man and spend tonight, his last night, and tomorrow, his last day at Montebello, making love. The shock of it makes him speechless. By the time he is able to think again, and breathe, the moment has passed and they are out of the wood, turning the bend by the paddock and stables, the river ahead, broad and blue. Then up the hill and there it is, four grey walls and four grey towers overlook a space of flowers. They spin past the round tower, thick with ivy like Rapunzel's hair, under the little bridge that joins the square tower to the house and around to the front door. His mother is standing on the veranda, small and straight, in black silk, with her best jewels, dressed for combat.

"How do you do, Madame Papineau," Lily says, extending her hand.

"Mrs.," his mother hisses. "I do not speak French." She ignores the hand.

No prisoners, then.

He carries his bag up to his room. It is the same as always, the narrow bed with the bright *habitant* quilt, the books neatly arranged on the shelves, his old *Chums* and the Henty books, Stevenson and Haggard, his old friends on the cold winter nights, his .22 on the wall, and the paddle he won the Two Hundred Mile Canoe Race with. Even his old clothes are hanging in the closet, his tennis whites and McGill jersey with holes in it, the same pictures on the walls, small boys playing soccer, boys with a trophy, the trophy itself on his bureau, next to it a picture of himself at two, a mound of scarves in the snow, his brothers beside him and behind, a man, tall and thin as a tree, black coat, black beard, a shadow on the snow, his father. It's the only photograph of his father that his mother has not mutilated or destroyed and he is always surprised, when he comes home, to find it still here.

The jersey is tight. He's heavier now, stronger. It's a boy's sweater, a stranger's, something that belonged to a child he knew once and has almost forgotten. Why doesn't his mother put these things away? Even the school room is the same, the long oak table and straight chairs, the Neilson map with the red Empire (let her blame that), the mysterious passageway that leads to the great stone tower where Le Grand Seigneur stored his four thousand books, beautiful books that froze solid in the winter and had to be thawed before they could be read, weighty books that served, in summer, as missiles to drop on the Iroquois when he played Dollard at the Long Sault.

Had he been happy? He'd thought so. His mother had said she lived for his happiness, and he'd believed her, and had been happy, to make her happy, to the best of his ability. But it had never quite come off. No matter how hard he tried or how well he succeeded, and he always succeeded, there was a higher fence to jump, a more difficult obstacle to conquer, a greater state of perfection to attain, and he'd been seventeen, at McGill, before he realized how perfectly miserable he was. He had never questioned his role as loyal lieutenant in his mother's Napoleonic campaign to restore the Papineau fortunes, but it came to him in that wretched year that her enemy was not, as he'd supposed, his dissolute father, but himself. She would hound him, hunt him until he was beaten, broken by her love. The knowledge made him fearless, and he changed from a shy diffident boy into a reckless daredevil whose athletic skills soon matched his scholarship and charm, a paragon, a prisoner.

"Your uniform is hideous," she says from the door. "You look very handsome in it."

"Thank you."

"I had hoped we'd be alone."

Her eyes are red, swollen. Tears. He can handle that.

"She is absurdly young. Is she rich?"

"I have no idea, Maman."

"No?"

"It doesn't matter."

"Does Montebello not matter?"

Montebello, the one thing she knows he loves more than life itself.

"If you go overseas," she says, "I shall sell it."

"And where will you live?"

"Me? Does it matter?"

He looks away, out the window, the familiar view across the lawn towards the river, a river of molten brass now in the afternoon sun, flowing to the sea. The white gazebo still perches on the edge of the bluff and to the left, Lily, looking downriver, her arms outstretched to the wind like a bird, the way he always stood as a child, hoping the wind would catch him up and carry him across the sea to France. He turns back, grieving for his mother's grief, but otherwise unfeeling, remote. It is as if Montebello is already a memory, part of a long-ago past, beautiful, beloved, but better put behind.

"I have already left, Mother."

Montebello
Tuesday, September 22, 1914

Midnight.

Talbot and his mother are fighting. It's so still the voices carry a long way. I can't make out what they're saying, only the anger. A while ago I tiptoed out to the veranda and sat on the fire escape underneath her tower. They seemed to be arguing about money. His mother was crying. I caught "sacrifice" and "gratitude," then Talbot's voice, very low, furious. It frightened me. I had the feeling they'd fought over this ground many times, it was an old fight, nothing to do with me, yet I was part of it somehow. Audience? Mum always liked an audience. Whatever it was, I couldn't do anything about it, and I decided I didn't want to hear any more.

His mother doesn't like me. I have offended her. I don't know how. Well, I don't like her either. She's very snooty, for a Yankee, considering they're nearly ruined, Talbot says, and may have to sell the seigneury to pay the debts. "All the Papineaus have an exceptional talent for spending money, and none at all for making it," he said. "I'm the worst of the lot. Mother wants to marry me off to an heiress. She finds me a fresh one every year."

The house is very beautiful, drawing rooms opening one into the other like puzzles, all blue and gold, gilt ceilings and gilded woodwork and gold fleurs-de-lis on indigo wallpaper, glittering chandeliers and gleaming floors and daffodil draperies, all washed in a yellow light from the river and reflected two, three times in giant gilded mirrors, so the rooms seem to repeat themselves on and on forever.

"It's Versailles! I thought you were republican," I said.

"Republicans aren't necessarily puritans."

Everything is very old, scrounged from ruined aristocrats and brought back from France when Papineau was pardoned. "Louis' leftovers," Talbot calls it. He smiles, as if it's a joke, but it's not.

"He died, the great republican, at a ripe old age, just before I was born. He lived here in feudal splendor, wearing black. He was in mourning, he said, for his martyred friends, the *Patriotes* he had armed with pitchforks and staves against English guns, the followers he had deserted to be shot and hanged and burned alive, the people he'd abandoned to be turned out into the snow, their villages razed to the ground, while he fled, before a shot was fired, in a priest's skirts, for the safety of Washington and the celebrity of Paris."

He takes me to see Papineau's crypt in a little wooded hollow behind the house.

"The church of St. Louis-Joseph Papineau," he says, gesturing towards a tiny stone building with a steeple set in a lawn among the maples. "It's probably the only church in the world dedicated to an atheist. My father and grandfather are here too. The women are across the tracks, safe in holy ground."

The chapel is cool and plain. A small altar and a handful of chairs. A simple, tattered flag hangs from a beam, three horizontal stripes, red, white and brown, and on each stripe, a crude, handpainted letter "P.L.H."

"*Patrie, Liberté et Humanité*," he says, following my eyes. "The *Patriote* flag. The old humbug is buried beneath it. He liked to call this place the Tomb of Liberty."

"Are you an atheist?"

"I had a Jesuit tutor as a child. God knows why. I hated the priests. A lot of crows waiting for innocent people to die so they could grab another soul for Heaven. Added them up in little ledgers. Six dead savages for the Blessed Jesus! Hail Mary! Praise the Blessed Martyrs! To hell with the martyrs. I always cheered for the Iroquois. My priest told my father I was an agent of the devil. My father came after me with a hunting knife one night. I believed in the devil after that. God has never made any sense to me at all."

"Me neither."

"Are you a communist then? They go together, in the public mind."

A communist? What on earth was a communist? I must have left school before we came to communists.

"Are you?"

"I don't believe in paradise."

It seems a silly thing to say in that lovely hollow, leaves fluttering around us like scarlet birds, walking on the flaming floor of Heaven itself.

"I do."

I have such a strange feeling about this place. I feel that I have been here before, lived here, that it's somehow my house, my wood, my river, my place, everything is so familiar, as if I'm remembering something I've forgotten. I feel so at home, as if Talbot has been there, only invisible, and I only had to open my eyes to see him. And now he's going away, tomorrow. Is this all the happiness I deserve?

Talbot walks down the path to the river, guided only by habit and the tobacco plants winking like fallen stars. He will sit on the warm boards of the dock and let the waves lap away his wounds.

His mother had lain in ambush for him, as he'd expected, waiting until he was happy, sitting with Lily in the sun room drinking cognac, watching the river turn from blue to violet to black. He would have been perfectly happy to sit there all night with the stars and the fireflies, holding Lily's hand, but his mother had come with a candle and said to her, "You must be tired," and Lily had gone to bed.

"I expect you'll be getting married now, without telling me," his mother had said, reading his heart, and they had gone on from there, over the same old ground, his mother weeping as if he'd already been killed.

"Do you *wish* me dead?" he'd said at last and slammed the door.

He's startled to see a pale shape, a shimmer of jade and silver, huddled by the boathouse, her knees tucked up under a long Chinese coat. She hands him her cigarette, guessing his need.

"I'm sorry. We disturbed you."

"It's the ghosts."

"That's Grampa Amédée. He was very fond of young girls. He married one at eighty-one and died four years later, in your room. Happy, I think."

"He smells of hair oil."

"Yes. That's him. Vain, but benign, not like some of the others. My father died out there, on the island, raving mad. We used to live in terror that he would escape somehow and murder us all."

"Why didn't you go away?"

"I don't know. It was never considered."

"She must have loved him."

"Yes. She must. I never thought of that before."

"And you."

"Yes. She lived for us."

"And you're going away."

"Yes. She wants me to go to the States, like Mr. King, or find a job in politics with Laurier. I can't make her see that the war *is* politics. The enemy has changed, but the cause is the same. *Patrie. Liberté. Humanité.* I will fight."

"Are you afraid?"

"I am not afraid of death. I don't want to be old. I worry more about killing. I abhor violence."

"It's not that hard."

I have to think for a moment to remember her name. Margaret. Margaret McFadden. She was in my class at Renfrew Collegiate, a prissy girl who pursed her lips with disapproval every time she saw me, and thumbed her nose if she could get away with it. I ignored her but she seemed to lay in wait for me, in Pedlow's, in the cloakroom, not to speak to me but to sneer, or hiss, as if her dislike were a kind of devotion. I hadn't even noticed her the day it happened. We were practising archery. It was the latest of Miss Eady's physical culture schemes. We'd already been through the dumbells and medicine balls and Swedish rhythmics, Miss Eady standing out there skinny as a rail in her bloomers clapping and shouting: "That's it, girls! Stretch and down, two, three, stretch, let's reach for the sky, one, two, legs straight, tummies in, three, four!" Miss Eady was very keen on posture. Archery was to strengthen our shoulders and backs. "Straight and tall! Straight and tall!" she'd call, running her hands down our backs, patting our tummies, our bums, while our arms trembled with the effort of pulling the bowstring.

I was standing there, feet planted, eyes fixed on the target, bowstring beside my ear, when Miss Eady's bony hand suddenly flattened my stomach. "Muscles firm, but relaxed!" she cried. I let go at exactly the moment Margaret McFadden decided to run in front of the target. The arrow got her right through the chest.

"Well, that's it for archery," I thought. I didn't faint, I didn't cry. I felt nothing, absolutely nothing at all.

"But it was an accident," Talbot says.

"Yes, I guess so."

He takes my hand in his warm, broad one, fingers thick, hard, calloused, kisses the palm and holds it against his cheek. I could slip my arm around his neck. I could kiss him. He could kiss me. He could put his arms around me and carry me up to bed and kiss me kiss me kiss me kiss me now now now now now now now.

Her hand lies very still in his, small and bare, like her feet — two curved white shells beneath the silk, waiting. Her face is turned towards him, still, watching. He wants to kiss her but he's too bruised, too hurt, to be able to stop there, he cares too much to want it this way, quick and crude, and afraid, not of tomorrow, but of forging a bond he must break, too strong to offer himself as hostage to a time that is past. She turns her head away and rests her cheek on her arm and sighs.

"It's late," he says. "You're shivering."

We walk up the path through the fallen stars.

"It would be a cruel joke, wouldn't it," he says, "to fall in love now."

She takes the little charm from around her neck and presses it into his hand.

"For luck."

"I don't believe in luck." It's warm, and his fingers close around it.

So here I am, down here in Grampa Amédée's big cold bed, and there he is, up there in his little cold one, and we're both sad, and that's a waste of time, isn't it? He a worse puritan than I am. Can't he see that *there is no time*?

Montebello
Wednesday, September 23, 1914

Slept in. Cranky. Crabby. No water. No bath. No breakfast. Nobody around
the house. Where is he?

The big grey touring car is parked in the driveway. Are we going
somewhere?

Talbot is coming up the path from the stable leading a big red horse. There
is a girl beside him, small, fair, wearing a flowing blue skirt that hugs her legs
as she walks, and a pale blue blouse with two rows of brass buttons down the
front and perfectly starched collar and cuffs. She has a little starched cap on
her blond hair too, with a white veil, tucked back, and a red cross, and over her
shoulders she's wearing a long blue cloak with a scarlet lining. The cloak
matches her eyes. She looks like Mary Pickford.

Do I know Edith Macpherson? Talbot asks. She has motored up for the
day, from Ottawa, with her brother Jamie. Old friends. He doesn't look at me.

I have seen Edith Macpherson several times, at Rideau Hall, sorting piles of
Red Cross supplies. Edith Macpherson is May Queen, of the May Court, and
an heiress.

"We just popped in to say good-bye," she says, linking her arm through
Talbot's. "It won't be for long. I'm off to London next week. Marguerite
Gault has found places for six of us in the Red Cross. Isn't it thrilling?"

"Your uniform is stunning."

"Isn't it sweet? It may not be exactly right, you know. I had Mrs. Denison
run it up last week, from photographs, to get in the mood, you know."

The horse rolls back its lip and sticks its teeth out at me. It's named Sweet
Caroline, for his mother, Talbot says. The horse is going to England too.

Wild duck for lunch. "I guess I'll miss the hunting season this year," Talbot
says. There is a terrible silence. I spill tea on my striped silk dress. Jamie is
wearing a McGill jersey like Talbot's. He has blue eyes like his sister. They talk
about McGill, Montreal, tennis, horses, Oxford, London, places I've never
been, people I've never met. Talbot doesn't look at me. What have I done?

His mother smiles at me. Her eyes are like his, only lighter, almost yellow,
like her hair.

"Jamie is dreadfully disappointed at not getting a commission in the Pats,"
Mrs. Papineau says. "I am hoping Talbot will give Jamie his place."

Talbot looks out the window, his face tense, shut, ridges of muscle standing
out on his jaw and his lips tight, like his mother's. What has gone wrong?

"It's rather late," I blurt out, "there is quite a long waiting list for openings,
even in the ranks, perhaps some other regiment...."

"And go with Sam Hughes' circus?" Jamie sneers. "Those clowns'll be dead
in six months."

Bridge in the gazebo. Edith knits, slowly, carefully, her blond head bent over the needles, counting stitches.

"I've promised myself to do twenty rows a day," she says. "This is the twelfth, I think, although I lose track with all the ripping out. Well, it's something."

I win the bid on the first hand. Talbot is dummy. He sits with Edith. After that I pass. Three o'clock. Four. Talbot doesn't look at me. I begin to see Bishop Ralph's point about the evil of cards. I try to picture God up there in the scudding clouds and pray for a thunderbolt. The thunderbolt doesn't come. An hour until my train. That's the trouble with Bishop Ralph, the thunderbolts never come, not for me, not when I need them.

Talbot drives me to the station in Edith's car. The deer in the park flick their tails at me like handkerchiefs and bright dead leaves sift sadly into my lap as we pass the chapel under the maples.

"I don't want you to feel obliged to me, in any way, by coming here," he says, staring straight ahead. "I have been selfish. I have taken advantage of your kind heart. I wish you every happiness. I shall probably never marry."

"Me neither."

"I understand that you are to marry Mr. Booth."

"Mr. Booth? *Old* Mr. Booth?"

"Yes."

"But he's eighty-seven!"

"Edith told me...."

I picture myself lying beside Mr. Booth on his narrow cot, his teeth in a jar on the night table, his nightshirt yellow with tobacco juice, his hands rustling on my thighs like dried leaves. I laugh so hard Talbot has to lend me his handkerchief to wipe my eyes. I still have it. It has his initials embroidered on the corner.

"Aren't you going to marry Edith?"

"Edith! God, no!"

Talbot swerves so he barely misses the ditch and stops beside the cemetery wall. He takes the pins out of my hat, one by one, places the hat carefully on the back seat, cups my chin in his hands and kisses me softly, searchingly, for a very long time.

I leave my hat in the car. He runs after the train, waving it furiously. The conductor pulls the brake and Talbot tosses it in the window, backhand, and everyone claps.

"I'll write," he calls, and waves, and I lean out, looking back, until we turn a bend.

The Citadel, Quebec City
Tuesday, September 29, 1914

He sailed tonight. Didn't see him. Wouldn't have known him if I had, all the soldiers were so caked with mud, faces, hands, uniforms, everything, as if they'd rolled in it, and I guess they had. They were in wonderful spirits, though, half-wild with excitement, and marched everywhere roaring:

> We are Sam Hughes' Army,
> We are his infantry,
> We cannot shoot,
> We cannot fight,
> No bloody good are we!

They did seem more like a mob than an army. *Die Schweine*, the Duchess called them, and they swarmed everywhere like those squishy brown worms that crawl through the woods sometimes leaving everything bare and ugly, all the parks turned into quagmires, the streets running with horse turds and piss. It wasn't their fault. The orders got fouled up and the streets near the harbour are so steep and narrow that the wagons and the guns couldn't turn around, so they just sat there and set up camp, and not even Sam Hughes could get through on his horse, and all the streets behind clogged up, through the whole city, and the troops just sat down where they were and sang and shouted and slept and waited. Finally they were all loaded on the ships pellmell every which way, guns, men, horses, hay, hooting and hollering and honking and shrieking and clanging and tramping and the bloody bagpipes going day and night. I swear we were heard in New York.

Do you suppose the Huns are this disorganized? I always thought of war as happening in the summer, at sunrise, with everyone neat and bright, the uniforms standing out like jewels against the grass and the cannons making little popcorn puffs in the sky.

The silence woke me up in the night as if I'd been poked. Nothing. Then a faint *hoot, hoot* like an engine saying all aboard and when I looked out my window all the campfires on the Plains of Abraham had disappeared. The clouds had blown away and the wind was cold. I dressed and went out the front entrance. From Dufferin Terrace I could see the ships strung out down river, dark except for the glow of their smokestacks, a necklace of round red beads stretching down river, the last ship just pulling away from the wharf under a pall of red smoke, its thudding engines churning the water into silver foam.

The railing along the terrace was crowded with people, dark shapes shivering, huddled together for comfort. A few were waving, most silent, left behind, lost, helpless, our hearts sailing on those ships, wrenched out with every turn of the screw, the space between ship and wharf widening, widening, cold and black. I strained against the rail, searching for something familiar, someone, trying to close that space somehow, but the deck of the last ship seemed to be empty except for a sprinkling of little lights that flashed on and off at random. Signals?

There was a flash at my shoulder, a familiar face, walrus moustache, hands cupped around a match, the glitter of gold braid as he bent his head forward to catch the flame. A dozen flashes from the ship. Cigarettes! Soldiers! Why, the decks *were* black with men, hundreds, crowded as we were against the railings, warming their hands around tiny flames, as we were, watching the lights of Quebec grow smaller.

The Duke gave my shoulder a little pat. "*Gott mit uns bie*," he sighed. He touched his fingers to his cap in salute and stood, very straight, his eyes far away, on the river.

The ship gave a final *whoot, whoot*, cut its engines and turned silently into the current. We caught the singing on the wind.

"... od save ... King ... Heav ... en bless
    Ma ... pull ... eef ... for ... ever ...."
I stood on the terrace watching the lights until the last one disappeared. Cold.

5

Rideau Hall
Thursday, October 1, 1914

Cold.

Hospital ship fund closed today. $23,089.62. Big success. Mr. and Mrs. Freiman are being asked to lunch. It's the first time Hebrews have been invited to Government House so it's causing quite a stir. Miss Yorke says it wasn't Mrs. Freiman's doing at all. "You can credit the casualties," she said. Maybe we should have them up for lunch, I said. She called me a snip. I called her a snoot.

Do I speak better with a cold? Patsy says it cuts out the twang. I am supposed to speak in my throat so my vow-wells are row-wend.

R.H.
Monday, October 5, 1914

We have a knitting machine. The Duchess sits there all day now, *whirr, whirr, clackety, clackety*, her face as grey as the wool. One pair of socks a day is not enough. We must have ten, twenty, a hundred pairs, millions of socks, enough for the Germans too.

All the Red Cross things we had collected were left sitting on the wharf at Quebec. The boxes dissolved in the rain, the red from the crosses ran into the bandages and the bandages oozed all over the place. Alice says it looks like an enormous strawberry mousse. We start again. The ballroom has been turned into a storeroom. The carpets have been taken up. All the nice furniture is put away. We sit on hard chairs in bare rooms with trees in pots standing around the walls like waiters with nothing to do. Minimalism is the latest thing, Patsy says. Very *japonaise*. Raw fish next.

Oh to be in England.

R.H.
Tuesday, October 6, 1914

Went with Alice to an Equal Suffrage meeting, intending to join. We were told only married women are eligible! "It's a question of responsibility," said the lady at the desk. "Bullroar," said Alice.

Flora Denison made a speech saying that women have to get rid of the Christian Church before we'll be equal. What an uproar! She will probably be expelled. Of course she's divorced, and people say she reads obscene poetry, out loud, to men, at night. She lent me a poem last week, about lilacs and death. I like it. "God is okay, " she says. "It's that sadist, St. Paul."

R.H.
Friday, October 9, 1914

Another assassin scare. Reports of gun shots and blinking lights in the park last night. Police here all day. We all made long faces and scratched our heads. Who was going to confess it was Arthur shooting pheasants by flashlight? He got six. "Ottawa is not Balmoral," he said, "but a grouse is a grouse." He sent them over to Sir Robert, this morning, before the police arrived.

R.H.
Saturday, October 10, 1914

Ships have arrived in Plymouth. All safe. No letter.

Big row between General Hughes and Lord Kitchener. Kitchener said the Canadians would be dispersed among British regiments as reinforcements. "Like Hell!" Sam yelled and stormed off to Buckingham Palace to see the King. "Do you have an appointment, General?" the equerry asked. "Hell, no!" said Sam. "I'll wait." And he plunked down on a little gilt chair with his cap on his knee.

He told the King that if the Canadian Expeditionary Force were broken up, he, Sam Hughes, would personally guarantee that not another Canadian soldier set foot on British soil. "Quite," said the King. So Sam has his army after all, although it seems so small, thirty thousand, when you think that the Huns have four million and all the Canadian equipment, wagons, boots, mess tins, poor Ena's shovel, everything, has been scrapped by Kitchener as unfit for service.

Alice is keeping score: Sam Hughes — 1; British Army — 1. I am cheering for Hughes and the Canadians but I don't dare let on around here. Arthur is telling everyone Sam Hughes is off his nut. He ordered Sir Robert to dismiss him this morning. Sir Robert said the grouse were delicious.

Windy. Wet. The lawn outside my window is red with robins.

R.H.
Monday, October 26, 1914

Twenty-one today. I don't feel any different. You're not really grown up until you're married.

Alice gave me a silver teaspoon, for my trousseau, she said.

"From what I hear you'd better get started."

"Oh?"

"Everybody's saying you've got wee Willie King tugging on the line."

"What should I do? If he asks."

"Accept him of course, you ninny."

"I can't."

"Why not? He's not John Barrymore, but who is?"

"He's old. And fat. And I don't love him."

"He likes you. Don't scoff at that."

Alice looked away and tucked her lame leg under her skirt. No man wants a cripple, she says.

"I'm not getting married, Alice. I hate babies and cooking and sewing and bridge and tea parties and tittletattle and men. I hate men!"

"You're in love."

"I am not!"

"Yes you are! It's that lieutenant, the glamorous one with the brown eyes and the gorgeous deep voice, the one at the dinner, that you were sitting beside...."

"He is not glamorous!"

"But you're crazy about him."

"What am I going to do?"

"Where is he?"

"England. Then France or Belgium."

"Has he written?"

"No."

"Then forget him."

"How?"

Willie sent a photograph of himself with Mr. Rockefeller, taken in New York, and a copy of Tennyson's poems. It must have been given to him because the dedication to me was written over another that began "To Rex," and "Christmas." It was an old copy, he wrote, but would be useful because he had underlined all the significant lines and made notes in the margins. I wish he'd sent some of Mr. Rockefeller's money. How am I to get to England?

R.H.
Tuesday, November 3, 1914

Confined to barracks under guard. Rumours of a German invasion from New York. The Governor General's Foot Guard has surrounded the park. We have all been given hiding places in the cellar. Miss Chadwick telephoned to get "the inside story." She said the Home Guard has been called out and spies are being arrested every moment.
   "What do they look like?"
   "Who?"
   "The Germans."
   "How should I know?"
   "Hasn't anyone seen them?"
   "They're all in disguise, my dear."
   She wanted a quote from Patsy on the death of her cousin, Prince Maurice of Battenburg, on the German side. No comment, I said. Patsy is burning all her blue dresses. Prussian is her favorite colour. It matches her eyes.

R.H.
Wednesday, November 4, 1914

Inventoried Red Cross stuff. Ninety-eight and one-half pairs of socks. Some of them are pretty funny-looking. What can you do? Maybe some soldiers have funny-looking feet. I feel so sorry for the women who come to the door, girls, a lot of them younger than me, and most of them pregnant, so shabby and cold. They get only ten cents a pair for socks, twenty-five for a shirt, all made by hand because they don't have Singers, but if they had Singers they wouldn't be charity cases, would they? The Friendless Women won't take them because they're married.
   No invasion.

R.H.
Thursday, November 5, 1914

Packed galoshes for the Pats. It has rained every day they've been in England. Their boots have fallen apart. Paper mostly, it appears. They are wearing bits of automobile tires and biscuit tins strapped to their feet. Influenza very bad, meningitis too, although no one is allowed to breathe a word. Major Gault says the war has pretty much stopped for the winter. Both sides have dug trenches in the fields and are living underground, like badgers, shooting anyone who sticks his head up. Not very sporting, he said. Major Gault has written twice to Patsy. No letters for me.

Willie telephoned. He arrived by train from New York this morning. I asked if he'd seen any Germans. He said he'd slept all the way. He is speaking tonight at a meeting of the Patriotic Fund. Mr. Booth is honorary chairman. He's given $20,000. Sir Robert has given him a contract to build wooden barracks for the whole Canadian army.

I hope Willie doesn't go on and on about peace.

R.H.
Friday, November 6, 1914

The Guards have gone away. The invasion is off. A dozen members of the German Bund took out hunting licences in Buffalo and started a panic. It's a disappointment, in a way. Patsy and I haven't decided yet whether we prefer death or dishonour. She argues for death.

R.H.
Saturday, November 7, 1914

Jack's picture in the *Citizen* today with a notice that the famous Silver Coolican has signed to play with the Montreal Canadiens. He's not rich yet, I guess, but alive at least and I'll be able to see him when they come to play the Senators.

Willie says I shouldn't got to hockey games. It's "barbaric" and "unbecoming" for my position. I told him that the portrait of Lord Stanley, of the Stanley Cup, was hanging right there in Rideau Hall and hockey is every bit as becoming as watching Ruth St. Denis writhe around the stage half-naked pretending she's a snake. Ruth St. Denis is an artist, he said. So's Jack, I said, and he's my brother too.

I feel terrible, losing my temper and being rude, but just when I think I've seen the last of Willie he bounces back again, like a rubber ball, all sunshine and smiles, as if nothing has happened. What on earth does he see in me?

R.H.
Sunday, November 8, 1914

Lord Kitchener has decided he doesn't want our hospital ship. The money will go to ambulance cars or Lady Astor's hospital at Cliveden.

Kitchener – 1; Prussian bitch – 0.

R.H.
Wednesday, November 25, 1914

Patsy opened the May Court bazaar today. Willie bought her painting of Mount Rundle for $25. Made the *Citizen*, front page. Victory!

Me – 1; Miss Chadwick – 0.

R.H.
Tuesday, December 17, 1914

Willie's birthday today. He is forty. He says that he's glad, that people will take him more seriously now.

I gave him a photo of his mother, taken at Kingsmere last summer, in a silver frame. He didn't expect a gift, he said, but that was the nicest he could have wished for.

He had a little dinner party in the restaurant at the Roxborough Apartments, then we all went up to his rooms. They are very small and filled with books and bric-a-brac. We looked at the Christmas cards he had received and some bits of Egyptian glass a famous man in New York had given him, and a set of gold cufflinks that had belonged to Gladstone and several other things. I had no idea he knew so many famous people.

He showed me an album of family photographs. I felt embarrassed, not knowing he already had so many pictures of his mother, but he said none except mine was a true likeness. Actually I thought most of them quite flattering. She was a pretty woman when she was young, with her little nose and feathery hair and round cheeks and bright inquisitive eyes. We tried to guess what bird she reminded us of.

Wilfrid Campbell, the poet, read two of his poems aloud. He mumbled terribly and kept taking swigs out of a brown flask in his pocket to "loosen his throat." It got so loose he was almost incoherent, not that the poems made much sense anyway. Willie had to read the last one, "Lines on a Skeleton," while Mr. Campbell closed his eyes and let his head rest on his chest. I thought he was asleep but Willie said he was just in a trance. Poets do that apparently. I've never met a poet before. His hair was very long and looked as if it had been cut with sewing shears, and his tweed jacket looked as if he'd slept in it, not to mention eaten off it. He said absolutely nothing the whole evening. Willie says he's a genius. That's why he's peculiar. He's very spiritual.

Mr. Natchez, the Hungarian violinist, who everyone thinks is a spy, played some gypsy songs and I did my "Cry of an Indian Wife." It went very well. Everyone was weeping. Mrs. Harriss, the hostess, has invited me to recite at her next Wednesday musicale. She said I was the hit of the evening. "Willie King is a dear boy," she whispered, "but if I have to admire his hideous knick-knacks once more I shall scream. And imagine telling us how much he paid for them!"

We were all dying for a glass of wine or brandy but Willie has given up spirits for the war. He seems very happy. It was an inspiration, he said, to enter his fifth decade, to turn over a new leaf, "with such a distinguished and talented group of friends." He knows how to flatter, and he purrs when praised, like a cat being stroked, although it seems at times when he's talking to me that he's really talking to himself, and it doesn't matter if I'm there or not. He does feed me well.

It was snowing when we left. Big, soft flakes like cold kisses. The snow was a message, Willie said, from the Great Beyond, that he must strive for a life of greater purity in the new year. He is going to accept only one social engagement per week and devote himself to the poor.

Still snowing, black sky, white ground, the world a negative, back-to-front, inside-out.

She looks like a hawk.

OTTAWA NURSE A SUICIDE

New York, Dec. 18: Miss Edith Macpherson, a young nurse, of Ottawa, Canada, who took 30 grains of bichloride of mercury at the Grand Central Terminal on Monday, is dead today.

Miss Macpherson, who was intending to go to Great Britain to join the Red Cross, is believed to have swallowed the poison after a dispute with her mother, who had followed her to New York, with the intention of preventing her departure.

Miss Macpherson was Queen of the May Court club and one of the leading young ladies of Canada's capitol.

Red Cross Hospital,
Winchester,
December 18, 1914.

My dear Miss C.

I am sitting up before the fire feeling rather mournful and homesick. The regiment has already left for the front. I shall follow soon I hope. I do not believe they will be in action before I reach them. The bandages are all off my right hand. It is not a pretty sight but it is covered with a nice new skin. My face is quite healed and joy of joys my glasses have been found intact so I have been able to read easily. Writing is hard because I have to hold the sheet of paper with my elbow.

I have no heroic tale to tell, I'm afraid. It does not augur well for my military career, to be the first casualty, and an accidental one at that. You probably think me a fool and will toss this aside into the wastepaper bin. But it cheers me up to write and see your earnest face before me on the paper, so please indulge a poor soldier — I can work that poor soldier gag rather well — a slight diversion.

You have no doubt heard all about the fire. I have no idea how it started. I was sound asleep. Charlie Stewart came in about 11 o'clock. He smoked a cigarette and went to sleep. Since he and his side of the tent were more severely burned it is probable his cigarette or a candle started it. It was a very cold, stormy, windy night. I was strapped in my sleeping bag. My first recollection is standing up with sheets of flame all about me. I was only half awake and not a bit afraid or I might have come off better. My first impulse was to dart straight through the flames. I struck the side of the tent and was hurled back. I felt myself burn and I let out a scream like a trapped animal. There was no door. I was tightly fastened. Then I lost consciousness.

Suddenly I realized I was out in the cool evening. Someone was beating out the flames on my body. I could not move my hands. They flamed. My face throbbed. My pyjamas were soaking wet. I must have rolled in the mud or crawled out on my hands and knees. I don't remember leaving the tent. I recall the bugle going like mad. The whole regiment was turned out on the run. Somebody led us through the mud to the mess tent. I was trembling with the pain and the cold. I thought I should never be warm again. It was then about one o'clock. We were laid on benches and blankets piled on us. Five hot water bags were brought to us but still I shivered and shook. The ambulance was telephoned for and some orderly put oil and cotton on my burns. The back of my hand was a puddle of mud and big ridges of loosened skin. The pain I thought was the worst I'd ever had. They gave me morphine. I was so cold. Finally I was bundled up and put in a motor. I remember a glimpse of blackened ruins and a sentry standing guard with fixed bayonet. That night and the next day were pretty bad. They gave me hypodermic injections of morphine. Poor Stewart was in the next bed generally unconscious. The pain never ceased until yesterday when there was a sudden change for the better.

We have had splendid attention, day and night nurses all the time, everything we could wish for. I expect to be well enough to rejoin the regiment early in the new year. I hope, in exchange for my little scraps of news you will write me news of the political 'wars' at home, and who's been caught with his hand in the till and who is getting married to whom, in other words, all the gossip. I'd like to know that people somewhere are still dancing and squabbling and falling in love and doing all the ordinary living things that seem to have disappeared from the world I live in. This exile of mine is already too long.

Yours,
Talbot M. Papineau
PPCLI, 80th Brigade, 27th
Division, British Exped. Force.

Part II
TALBOT

1

On Active Service
Jan. 31, 1915.

My dear Miss C.

I crossed the Channel last night with a group of forty reinforcements for the regiment. We went to sleep, fully dressed of course, upon the seats of a very dirty railway carriage. Upon awaking we found ourselves in a tiny little village station. The air was cold and crisp, the water frozen and a light white covering to the earth. The sun came up but it remained cold. Our forty men had slept in two trucks. They had secured straw from somewhere and improvised braziers from their buckets and mess tins. I believe they sat up all night cooking tea and bully beef.

Off we went over miles and miles of cobblestones. There was a constant procession of men and motor cars, French and English guns and ammo wagons and various other things. We passed one long column of Red Cross carrying away the wounded and an aeroplane depot with five machines ready to go up at any moment. Now and then we passed through villages full of troops waiting their turn in the trenches. We saw many men limping along with their feet bandaged up injured by frost. We passed also several new graves with little wooden crosses. Eventually we reached a place just behind the firing lines. A big soldier with his gun slung across his shoulder presented himself with a note from the colonel stating that we were to join him that night for a tour of inspection. The messenger would show us the way. He left the high road and took what he called a short cut through some fields. It was already twilight. He said it would take less than twenty-five minutes to reach the colonel. An hour later we were still walking and our guide admitted he was lost. Big guns were barking away and there was constant firing. The whole place was honeycombed with exploded shells. We had to walk carefully to avoid falling into the pits. Every barn and house had been smashed to pieces. We were nervous and getting angry with our guide when we heard a word and ran into a column of men standing silent and ready. It turned out to be our own company.

The men crowded around and shook hands. There was old Cameron looking fat and well and DeBay, both veterans by this time. The colonel occupied a still undamaged portion of a wrecked house which we reached by a flooded passage. The room was full of our remaining officers, lit by a couple of candles and a wood fire. We sat talking for a long while. It was great to see all the fellows again although many were missing. Major Smith is accused of lying and cold feet and inventing a story to get back to England and Major McInery, a big, powerful, blustering man, lost his nerve and went to pieces and is back in England more or less crazy. He is not expected or wanted back. Stanley Jones was shot through the hand. Poor Fitzgerald has been killed. About three days ago. He practically committed suicide, so foolish was he. He leapt out of the trench to see a dead man that was lying out in front and was shot clean through the head. The same day Price was killed. His guide led him incorrectly into the trenches and he was shot through the chest and twice in the arm. Newton was killed by our own men. He went out of the trench at night to look for material to build a parapet, missed our trench, went towards the Germans, turned and came back to our lines. He was challenged but for some reason didn't answer. Cpl. Martin shot him through the stomach. He then called out 'Don't shoot again! I'm Captain Newton.' They sent out and brought him in. He lived for about twenty-four hours. Of the twenty-four officers who came to France I believe that nine are now available for active duties. The men have suffered also, not so much killed or wounded as sick with swollen or frozen feet. We only have about 500 effectives out of our previous 1,000. However there is a draft of about 500 coming to us shortly and what is left is mighty good.

We had a good feed in the colonel's den and started off. It was cloudy but the full moon left things pretty bright. You never saw such a scene of utter desolation and destruction. We passed a whole village smashed to ruins, church and all, only a stray cat or dog living. It was a curious walk, Col. Stewart ahead, then Buller and myself, the major carrying the colour, then a whole small bodyguard. Every now and then a bullet whistled over our heads. The Germans would throw up their famous lighting rockets and our whole party would throw ourselves down flat in the mud til the darkness came again. We visited the doctor in his quarters hidden among the ruins of a dismantled house, then Colquhoun stationed in a little den under a ruined stable. He is in charge of our sharp shooters. He is said to have accounted for 20 Germans in the last three days. We finally came to the colonel's new quarters in a cellar strewn with straw, in pitch darkness, people and smoke, a German prisoner, just given himself up, 18 years old, tired of fighting, says he loves the English and wouldn't go back even if we let him.

We may go in the trenches the day after tomorrow or next week. It is a curious war here. I cannot see how either side is to do anything for the rest of their lives but freeze in trenches and shoot at each other. It's a slow sort of murder.

It is snowing today. My earthly address is Captain Talbot M. Papineau, PPCLI, 80th Brigade, 27th Division, British Exped. Force, Eng. I should like to know if this reaches you. You may just say 'yes,' or you may abuse me, or you may write a folio, or you may have a fiance and say so, only don't ignore me!

Yours,
Talbot Papineau

On Active Service,
Feb. 5, 1915.

My dear Miss C.

I have been put in command of the regimental bomb throwers. We received instruction the other day and tonight we march into a little town for further practice. The bomb looks like a can of condensed milk. It weighs a couple pounds and it is full of shot somewhat smaller than shrapnel. Six seconds after I light the fuse it explodes. It is just time to transfer the bomb from my left hand to my right, draw back and throw it. The thrower must be under cover because the shot is as likely to fly back as forward.

I was in the front trenches last night. It was very dark most of the time with a heavy cold rain pouring down but about 10 p.m. the moon came up and we could see and be seen. I object particularly to the smells. The wind is tainted and the mud exhales gases of a most noxious kind. In one of the trenches there are several bodies buried and planks cover them but the gas bubbles up. We don't dare drink any water here. I haven't had a cold drink for a week — always tea and coffee. There is a big battery to our right shooting away. It makes me jump!

We got here last night covered with mud and hungry but not cold. I entirely enjoyed the experience. It's like a game, dodging and running and creeping and lying down. For a long time we lay silently waiting in a smashed up barn — roof gone and dead cattle lying about, lit now and then by a flare.

We go into new trenches tonight. As it grows dusk we meet our guides and in the dark, in single file, we are led silently across fields. All about is the sharp crack of rifle fire. We follow hedgerows and avoid the open. Then we creep up to the opening of the trench and one by one jump in. I wait until my men are all in and jump after. At the same time the men we are relieving creep out. These trenches have overhead covering as protection against shrapnel and we fire through peepholes.

I have not been badly frightened yet. That will come, I suppose. This is so much like a *fête de nuit*, a thunder storm and duck shooting, that I positively like it. Frozen feet and dysentery are the things most feared at present. Only one man killed and one wounded in the trench we occupy tonight. But you never can tell when the Germans will make an attack. I almost wish they would.

Goodbye.

Yours,
Talbot Papineau

On Active Service
Feb. 16, 1915.

My dear Miss C.

Once more safely out of the trenches and although very tired and sleepy none the worse for a hard experience. We went in Friday and were relieved last night, Monday. During all those days and nights I never once lay down. I never slept except to doze a few moments at a time in a sitting position. All the time it rained or snowed or hailed. There was a lot of heavy fighting. Four trenches immediately on my left were captured with heavy loss. A counter-attack was organized and by 5 a.m. the next morning the trenches were retaken but two of our brigades suffered severely. Of one company only eight men were left.   During the first two nights we constructed nearly thirty-five yards of new fire trench. To keep warm I laboured myself with shovel and sandbags but became exhausted. The want of sleep, the darkness, the wet, sticky mud, the poor food, the lack of water weaken one considerably. Also we work with all our accoutrements on and rifles with bayonets fixed close by. Every now and then a flare lights the scene and we cower down until darkness comes. If it was daylight and the Germans could see us every man would be killed at once. During the last twenty-four hours I ate nothing but a handful of oyster biscuits mixed with mud. Mud clings to everything.

Out of my famous platoon only fifteen men are left, though you need not say so. I censor all such remarks from the men's letters. Major Ward is back but I wonder how much more he can stand. I feel fine.

I have just examined No. 2 platoon, their feet, socks, rifles, ammunition, and emergency rations. It is pouring rain. We go into the trenches again tonight. It is said the Germans made another attack last night which was beaten off. There is a possibility we will make one ourselves tonight or tomorrow. I am ready. I don't seem to have nerves of any sort.

It is very nice when we come out of 'battle' to find letters waiting for us. We have a mail every day. Try to write frequently and I'll do my best to reply. I'd rather have your letter than a 'belted cholera band.' Don't wait for a reply. Just write again!

We have just got sudden orders to stand by ready to move at a moment's notice. Something doing! Goodbye.

Yours,
Talbot Papineau

On Active Service
March 3, 1915.

My dear Miss C.

We have made an attack at last and I have led it! The night we marched off to the trench it was pouring rain. We slopped along in the usual way. The colonel had informed me that an attempt would probably be made by us at 5 a.m. to capture and destroy the German trench, which had been brought up to within fifteen yards of our No. 21 trench. He said I should probably be required with my bomb throwers.

I first went into No. 22 trench with Major Ward. The night passed more or less uneventfully. About 3 a.m. I received orders to have three bomb throwers ready with two bombs each by 4:30 a.m. Then I went over to No. 21. It was the worst trench in the whole line. You walked across an open field and it was hard to avoid the skyline. On the way I passed two corpses and used the third as a bridge over the mud into the trench. There was no parados, only a lake of mud about ten feet wide in which lay any number of bodies. The parapet was only about three feet high and the fire over the top was incessant. The men lay huddled against the parapet, their feet in the water. I led the three bombers back to No. 22 and waited.

It had cleared and the moon was shining. Colquhoun came along and went out on his own between 21 and 22 to reconnoitre for the attack. About an hour later two of his snipers came and reported he had not returned. I told them to wait for another half an hour. He never returned. We have just learned that his body was found in a German trench with eight bullet wounds and a bayonet thrust. He was a big, brave, cheerful chap, strong as an ox, about 6'5". He was married in Quebec, just before we sailed.

His reconnaissance had failed but we decided to go ahead with the attack. The moon was well down but dawn was coming. Then I saw the attacking party coming along a bridge to my trench. The moonlight glinted on their fixed bayonets. When they reached my trench they lay down. The colonel was with them. The colonel said. 'There are six snipers that will go ahead of you, then you will go with three bomb throwers. Lt. Crabbe will be behind you with twenty-five men. Then there will be another party with shovels behind him. All right! Lead on!'

I was pretty scared! My stomach seemed hollow. I called on my men and we fell into line and began creeping forward flat on our bellies. I had a bomb ready in my hand. We lay for a moment exposed then suddenly we were all up and rushing forward. My legs caught in barbed wire but I stumbled through somehow. I set my fuse and hurled my bomb ahead of me. From that moment all hell broke loose. I never thought there could be such noise. I had my revolver out. A German was silhouetted and I saw the flash of his rifle. I dropped on my knees and fired point blank. He disappeared. I said to myself 'I have shot him.' I fired into the trench at whatever I thought was there. Then my revolver stopped. I lay flat and began to reload. I was against the German parapet. I looked behind me and could see only one man apparently wounded or dead near me. I though 'The attack has failed. I am alone. I will never get out.' A machine gun was going and the noise was awful.

Then I saw Crabbe coming. He knelt near me and fired over me with a rifle. I had got a cartridge home by this time and Crabbe and I went over the edge into the trench. It was deep and narrow, beautifully built, dried by a big pump, sides support by planks, looked like a mine shaft. A German was lying in front of me. I pushed his head down to see if he was dead. He wasn't. I told a man to watch him. Then I began to pull down some of the parapet and sandbags. Three or four men were there too with shovels. The German machine guns were going like mad. It was beginning to grow light.

Presently we were told to evacuate the trench. I passed the order then climbed out and made a run for No. 21. Another man and I went over head first. The man that came after me was shot through the lungs. The next man got it through the stomach. They fell on me in the mud. I could not budge. Then over on top of us all came a German! He held up his hands and a couple of our men took him away. Gault was there and he worked pulling the wounded men off each other. One or two men came piling over with fixed bayonets and almost put our eyes out. I was finally pulled out of the mud. It was not quite light. I had to get back to No. 22. I beat it across the open expecting to get it any minute. I was so exhausted I wobbled from side to side in the mud. However I reached home and dived for cover. I was tired but mostly glad to be back.

The stretcher bearers were carrying the wounded out past the back of my trench. The last party got half way then dropped their stretcher and ran. Gault crawled out to the man with a couple of volunteers and they dragged the stretcher into a ditch and then to a hedge. Gault was shot through the wrist. He will probably get a V.C.

The Germans were now back in the trench we had taken and they began throwing bombs into No. 21. It was awful. We could do nothing to help, just look on. Out of thirty-five men twenty-one were killed or wounded that day. At night I went over to the trench again to see them. I could find only one of my bombers. He had no more bombs so I sent him home. The night was very cold and very long. No sleep.

The next day No. 21 was bombed and we had shrapnel over ourselves. At a quarter to twelve a message came from Ward to help the artillery get range for the German trenches in front of No. 21. Great care had to be exercised. Ward was sitting next to me. He jumped up to look at No. 21 then sank back into my arms. He bled frightfully. He had been shot in the back of the head. I bound his head up as best I could. The brain matter was oozing out. I put on four field dressings and staunched the blood. I loved old Ward. He is one of the best fellows I know. It was terrible for me to see him like that so suddenly. I had to leave at once to direct the artillery. I did what I could to give them range but it was my first attempt. About four shells had been fired when our communications wire broke down. I could give them no more help. Fortunately I had sent word about Ward and asked for stretcher bearers as soon as it was dark.

I made Ward as comfortable as I could. He was now conscious and could recognize me although his mind wandered. He was in great pain and I gave him a good deal of morphine. He would hold my hand sometimes. He said 'Talbot, you're an angel.' He called for 'Alice, where's Alice?' A terrific snowstorm blew up. I never saw such darkness and such wind. Flocks of birds flew before it. It was bitterly cold. Later there was thunder and lightning. How long these hours were. It was not until 8:30 p.m. that the stretcher party came. Ward was still alive. The colonel came with him.

The colonel told me that No. 21 had been evacuated. This left me in a precarious position. No. 21 commands my rear and if the Germans occupied it they could fire straight into the back of No. 22. Fortunately we had built a pretty good parados of sandbags. I posted men along the rear. We were as in a fort. We stayed in the trench until about 10:30 p.m. when we were relieved. This was my third night without sleep. We were kept in dugouts as support while our attack was repeated by another regiment. There was a great loss of life. We were finally marched back and arrived in billets about 6 a.m.

We are able to rest here two or three days. I am feeling splendidly now. I have faith in your courage so I tell you what I am doing. Be sure not to let any letters be published in any form.

Yours,
Talbot Papineau

On Active Service
March 16, 1915.

My dear Miss C.

I have had no letters in some time. Perhaps it is only a few days but we live ages in a day in these times. I never know what day of the week it is.

I am told I have been mentioned in despatches for the bombing raid. I believe I am the first Canadian to be mentioned.

Yesterday I had another wonderful escape. By daylight we were massed behind the position we were expecting to attack but eventually we were ordered to withdraw. We had to cross the open to get to the shelter. The men behaved wonderfully. A number were killed or wounded, but no one ran. Charlie Stewart near me was hit clean through the lower part of his chest. With three other men I started carrying him in on rifles put through the sleeves of a coat. Then a machine gun opened on us. Charlie was hit again in the foot and one of the men at his shoulder was killed. We all fell down. A bullet passed over my shoulder and went between my fingers. We got him along over the mud. He is still living but there is little hope he will pull through. Colquhoun however has turned up alive, a prisoner of the Germans.

I am writing now in my blankets after a breakfast of three boiled eggs, bread and marmalade. For I am company commander now. Of course it is only temporary. We have no majors left and only two captains. DeBay and I are the only original officers left except the transport officers and the quartermaster. Tonight we go into the trenches for two days and three nights.

March 18: I have now all the duties of a major. I also have his horse and groom. I am a mounted officer if you please! I think they might give me a little holiday. I should like to be in the quiet peacefulness of Montebello. I should not permit any sudden noises or allow any target practice.

I wish the sun would shine here. It is always cloudy. I feel like a nighthawk. I long for the blue sky and the yellow sunlight in the late afternoons. How I shall enjoy every little bit of everything after this!

Yours,
Talbot Papineau

Rideau Hall
Easter Sunday, 1915.

Mr. W.L. McK. King
c/o Mr. J.D. Rockefeller Jr.
Pocantico Hills,
Tarrytown, New York, USA.

Dear Mr. King,

Your lovely bouquet of Easter lilies arrived yesterday as did your letter and the program from *Parsifal*. It was kind of you to remember me. I have the flowers in the window and they fill the room with their fragrance. Thank you.

Parsifal is a great favourite here. Patsy played a little on the paino after dinner but I am sure it doesn't sound nearly the same. It is beautiful. It is difficult to imagine that in New York people are still going to the opera. Here, if anyone sang in German he would be stoned. Mr. Bourassa, the Quebec nationalist who's so against the war, was nearly lynched in the Russell Theatre.

Did you go to the Easter Parade?

The spring offensive is expected soon and we are busy outfitting the regiment with cigarettes and things. They have been at the front since January. They have suffered very much but never complain. We are so proud of them!

The Canadian Expeditionary Force has arrived in France and great news is expected soon. I cannot tell you any more. We have to be very careful. I wish sometimes I didn't know so much. I feel so helpless. I cannot seem to work up a hate like the others. I keep expecting to wake up and find the war over. I am sure we will win soon.

I saw the first robin yesterday. It looked cold. It must be very brave. Don't you think it would be a shame to cut down the trees at Kingsmere? The Rockefellers must have a dozen gardeners to cut the lawns and keep the flowerbeds tidy. Wouldn't peacocks get eaten by the wolves?

Mr. Rockefeller seems very unhappy. However, the blackest sheep are often washed the whitest, don't you think?

Yours truly,
"C"

On Active Service
April 11, 1915.

My Dear Miss C.,

I have just been told that I am being given a Military Cross. Colquhoun and I will therefore be the first Canadians to receive it. I have my doubts that I deserve it but at any rate it is very pleasant to have. I have not seen the cross, but the ribbon which I can now wear is one of the prettiest, a certain shade of purple I believe.

I have been comfortable these last few days although very dirty. I suspect myself of even harbouring a flea, which can be expected when I sleep in a little dark hut on straw that has been used by troops for several months.

We are now situated in a blind wood thickly planted with young trees. The huts are made of the stems of trees chinked with earth and covered with boughs to protect against aeroplanes. It looks like a savage village in a jungle. We keep warm with a brazier of charcoal but I wake up several times a night with the cold.

There is a cool wind and the sun shines through the trees. There is almost a suggestion of spring in the air. Yesterday was much the same and we had a lunch party outside, a small table, one chair, one ammunition box, one biscuit box and a pile of pine boughs. We had turtle soup, then toast and potted grouse and cold tongue and there was a rice and raisin pudding which our servants had brought up to us with strawberry preserves and Devonshire cream. After lunch we played bridge.

Stray bullets whistle through the trees but do no harm. As I write a German battery is firing and shells are shrieking over. Our luncheon was twice interrupted by shells and we cut for cover. I am sitting at the door of my hut on a little rustic bench. The French have planted some flowers in a row to my right and there is one small purple bloom, so you see we have some compensations.

How interminable this war appears. I see no sign of it ending. How can it end? Our ranks have been replenished with fresh troops but what a different regiment we are. Of the 1,100 men we left Ottawa with, only about 150 remain. You probably know that anyway. Yesterday I was quite ill. Better today. We go into the trenches again in a few days.

Yours,
Talbot Papineau

On Active Service
April 23, 1915.

My dear Miss C.,

This has been our third day here and it has been a time of alternate peace and alarms. The situation is difficult and cloudy. I understand that the Canadians were used in some heavy fighting last night and there will soon be many sad hearts. Canadians do not yet know the price of empire or nationality but I believe we are ready to pay it.

The maple sugar has been a great treat. I have powdered it and used it on porridge and have sucked chunks. It was very delicious and gave me much pleasure. I gave a pound to the colonel.

April 25: I was suddenly interrupted by fresh trouble. We are going through most anxious times. The fighting all about us is terrific. Our own position has been rendered most dangerous. You may be reading something about it today. This is now six days constant alertness and we see no sign of relief. The terrific cannonade is trying.

April 26: Again interrupted. Things happen with lightning rapidity. We have only vague reports of what has occurred on our left. I should judge that the Canadians at great cost have made it possible for us to preserve these lines. Some reports of losses are appalling. I should feel dreadfully if they are true, yet what a glorious history they will have made for Canada. These may be the birth pangs of our nationality. Great moments are in progress.

My dinner was spoiled by a shell last night. It burst just above my head and a piece struck the roof sending a shower of earth into my dish. This is early morning. The dew is lifting and the sun will soon be bright and warm. I hope so.

Yours,
Talbot Papineau

On Active Service
May 6, 1915.

My dear Miss C.

How happy I was yesterday morning to receive five letters from you. Your letters are so cheery and encouraging. Even while I was reading there was an alarm. I rushed out of the hole in the ground to see the German gasses moving towards us like a fog. I began to cough, my eyes were sore and I felt sick about the stomach. The men had respirators which they soaked from their water bottles and I have one now, but then I had to use a field dressing which I tied tightly around my head. All the time I was pretty near panic. I was wondering how I could stand it and I was sure we would be forced to retire. This is the most barbarous thing imaginable. It will be a great war, won't it, when we're all poisoning ourselves like savages.

A shell has just killed two men and wounded seven. We sit with our backs to the inside of the trench wondering what will happen next. It will be worse tomorrow. We have to go back to the same trench where we suffered so heavily the day before yesterday. I will be out before you receive this.

It's a beautiful warm day and blossoms are out. When will the new armies come? Surely they are most needed now. We cannot keep this up indefinitely. However, by so much more will we enjoy peace when it comes. I cannot believe that such happiness will be for me. I will never know what I miss.

I am the only officer in the regiment who has been on the job now for over three months. I have not had my clothes off since the 19th. My rank is still the same. They never trouble about promotions now as you never know how long you may remain alive or well. Changes are too frequent.

Yours,
Talbot Papineau

On Active Service
May 26, 1915.

My dear Miss C.

For the moment I am unoccupied and I have only flies, rifles and the roar of distant cannon to listen to. I should sleep. I should have written more frequently of late but it has been impossible to do so. Even now I cannot hope to go over those awful days. The memory of them is confused and imperfect.

The worst day was the eighth of May. At one time I had the man on each side of me killed. We are only a remnant. They kept us in Ypres, which was being shelled, then we were put back in the trenches as a composite battalion with another regiment for three days.

The sun shines beautifully. I look up to the fringe of a wheat field filled with blood red poppies. Below the earth is brown and muddy. We are moles, and high explosives are searching to destroy us. Thousands of flies buzz around these underground homes where men have lived and died for seven months.

I am enclosing a little poem written by a Canadian medical officer during last month's engagement, which is now known as the Second Battle of Ypres. He was stationed quite near to us and the poem describes much better than I can how we all feel. I wonder if you can see that it is circulated around Ottawa? Perhaps you can include it in one of your "musicales" although it should probably be read by a man in uniform for greatest effect. The poet is from Ontario, I believe. His name is Dr. John McCrea.

I must sleep.

Yours,
Talbot Papineau

France, July 8, 1915.
My dear Miss C.

I am in a bad temper this evening and have tried in vain every other sort of amusement so I shall write to you. You are the victim of my mood. You may well ask why I do not inflict myself on some seasoned friend instead of your unoffending self. I suppose because the others can hold no surprises for me. They would not be shocked to get an erratic letter from me. While you, having been swept by curious chance across my orbit, present possibilities. I have picked up and thrown aside half a dozen books. I am sick to death of the life histories of imaginary people. I shall be interested only in my own, or in those of real people, and then only if they seem to influence or direct me.

We have ridden all afternoon. I am a little tired. We get so little exercise sitting in the trenches that an afternoon's ride is actually fatiguing. A few moments ago several shells whistled overhead and exploded down the street. A good bag, I understand, an old woman and a baby killed and a little girl of seven has lost the fingers of her right hand. Bobs, a little Belgian puppy that I take into the trenches with me whimpered and climbed into my lap, as he does every evening for a sleep. I doubt he will interfere with my penmanship. He seems inclined to wake up and play with the rapidly moving point.

More shells coming in. I don't like it. However, we give more than we take and the only way to finally stop these Germans is to keep killing them. But how I hate it! An explosion made the house shake just now. One may pop in at any moment. And this is supposed to be a rest in reserves! There goes another. Tomorrow we go back into the trenches.

I believe I have supplied a long list of soldiers' wants. I got the men to make their own suggestions. It's extraordinarily kind of you. I have only sent a long list so that items can be picked out.

Bobs is sound asleep in my lap. I am now tired of writing. This time last year I was at East Hampton, Long Island and I had a splendid time. I long for a holiday now. You are probably playing golf and learning some new dances. I envy you.

Talbot Papineau

France, July 15, 1915.

My dear Miss C.

I feel now quite triumphant. I have no victory over the Germans but I have succeeded in my venture to draw you into the vortex of my correspondence. It is novel and interesting to discover personalities from what is said on paper and from what is not said. I have no doubt you've subjected me to similar criticism. I probably find you more charming now than when we shall meet again. You have many faults that do not appear in writing. I have no illusions. I lost my capacity for them some years ago. You are absurdly young. I am 32 and with more luck I shall be 33 in March. You confess to a fondness for ice-cream sodas. My tongue is flannel at the thought. I sometimes enliven water with lime juice but usually slacken thirst with enormous quantities of indifferent tea in brimful canteens like tannery vats. Can I return to Sunday calls and the handling of delicate china and find aroma and not merely heat in tea?

I quite liked what you said about yourself and your art. You have vastly relieved me. I thought you might be wedded to it or else be the trailing green gown variety. I entirely approve of girls having some more knowledge than Mrs. Malaprop considered necessary, and where they can control talent without losing balance I favour its development. You sound natural. I should like to be able to admire a girl and be genuinely sincere. It would be such an agreeable relief and change. I know an old friend who has temperament and paints. She has a studio in London and is indulging in an orgy of artistic emotions. I find her pictures harrowing but I have to invent pleasant words. I like to be spontaneous. Then there was another girl I was almost in love with. I was in grave peril. But then I was trying to tie my tie before my mirror before dinner when I heard a voice raised in song or lamentation. I endured until the tie was tied, then I crept to the drawing room. It was she, alas my love was murdered! But she still has a coral pink cheek and the merriest laugh and I lied conscientiously about the singing.

Last night we marched four miles, dug trenches for four hours and marched back four miles. I feel asleep at 2 a.m. and was up at 7. But that's no hardship like dancing until 6 a.m. and pleading cases all day. We do the same tonight.

I have to go away. I'm sorry. If you really want to help me here, send me letters and let me write them. You shall be little bothered and despite your clover leaves I shall probably be hit one of these days, so in the meantime you may permit me to wander.

Talbot Papineau

August 5, 1915.

My dear Miss C.

This morning as I came up the steps of my dugout I saw a little green bunch of clover and I was reminded I had not thanked you for the four-leaved ones you sent me. I continued to think a letter and had to write one. I have the unfortunate quality of doing what I think of doing almost immediately.

Breakfast has just been eaten and our oilcloth table looks like a cheap boarding house board. We live in some luxury. I hardly like to tell you lest I lose the advantage of your pity. Even the morning paper will soon be here, only a day old. Perhaps it will have a sweet face instead of these unshaven, brown visages framed in soiled khaki! However, we have some daring ladies from the illustrated weeklies pinned on the walls, one balanced on a diving board in a diminutive bathing suit of flaming red and a winning smile, another examining a shoelace with a charming result, another with piled-up yellow hair plucking feathers from Cupid for her hat. These ladies are often the subject of comment. We discuss their characters. They are attractive but disturbing and create restless wishes for home or Piccadilly.

I was on duty until 12 last night and came on again at 6 a.m. We lost an officer wounded about 10 o'clock last night. Young Martin, a good footballer, from Victoria, shot through both thighs. Martin was just back from hospital. We are sorry to lose him again but we speak of him as "lucky" and the old timers would gladly change places. Another boy was less fortunate. He was hit through the chest and died in fifteen minutes. He was only about seventeen and fresh from college, the only son of a widow. It was his first night in the trenches.

Stewart and Grey went out in the early morning on patrol. Grey tells me he shot a German through the forehead. Stewart says he didn't. Personally I doubt Grey's sanity or his nerve. He will not be like the poor, I imagine. He will not be long with us. As for Stewart, I must write you some day a full account of him. We met in Ottawa when the regiment was forming and compared experiences in the far north. He has been a North West Mounted Policeman and fur trader and Yukon gold digger and was nearly killed several times. He was in South Africa. His father, a Colonel, was in the Crimea. His brother, a profligate rascal like himself, was a close friend of King Edward in his wilder moments. He has the vitality and appearance of Hercules but remains normal by constant undermining operations such as fifty cigarettes a day and the output of a whisky factory. On the 14th of March he was shot through the chest and we had to drag him in over the mud. He protested violently and made an awful noise about the pain. I promised to write to his various sweethearts and finally left him to die in the dressing station with the tears rolling down my face. The padre asked him if he wished him to pray. "Yes," Charlie said, "pray like Hell!" But he didn't die. He was taken to the Duchess of Westminster's hospital and raved so against what he called her "beauty chorus" and their open-work stockings and patent leather shoes that she had him transferred. She sent him in some hares which were stewed and served. Charlie had eaten nothing else for a couple of months when he was lost in the snow near Fort Churchill. When he discovered the dish he bellowed that he wouldn't give rabbits to a half-dead halfbreed and they hadn't enough nourishment for a horse-fly. He came back a few days ago much to my delight. He says he is frightened to death but he is always wanting to charge somebody somewhere.

Another officer, Crabbe, has gone "off his nut" on the way to the trenches and has been sent back to hospital. I am not feeling particularly well myself these days. I wish I could have something. I want to get to bed and just lie there and do nothing and think of nothing. I am the only officer now who has been through the whole show and I don't suppose there are more than 20 men who have been through it either. This is just pure wonderful luck so it's not boastfulness to mention it. More than anything I wish to go home and make speeches. My profession is "speeching," not fighting. I hate this murderous business. I have seen so much death, and brains and blood, and marvellous human machines suddenly smashed like Humpty-Dumpties. I have had a man in agony bite my finger when I tried to give him morphine. I have bound up a man without a face. I have tied a man's foot to his knee while he told me to save his leg and knew nothing of the few helpless shreds that remained. He afterwards died. I have stood by the body of a man bent backward over a shattered tree while the blood dripped from his gaping head. I have seen a man apparently uninjured die from shock as his elbow touched mine. These are but a few examples. Never shall I shoot duck again or draw a speckled trout to gasp in my basket. I would not wish to see the death of a spider.

I have just been summoned to see the General! I will finish later.

I have just returned after a long conversation. The matter was a very delicate one. We have unhappily an officer who has been for some time under suspicion as a possible spy. I am very loathe to form an opinion. However, the Germans are clearly in communication with someone here. Last night a

message from them was intercepted. Translated it meant "Message received."
It's a nasty business.

The table is being set for luncheon. I am famished. Our dining room is six
feet below ground, beams overhead, then galvanized iron sheets, sandbags,
bricks and earth. It would be blown to bits if a shell hit it. I am just told we
shall be relieved tomorrow night, which is pleasant, and will be inspected by
Sam Hughes on Sunday, which is not so pleasant.

The sun is shining and the dugout is becoming warm. You have probably
fallen asleep over my letter or have cried "enough!" I ask only toleration for
my letters but I should delight in replies.

Very sincerely,
Talbot Papineau

In the Trenches,
France, August 14, 1915.

My dear Miss C.

Yesterday there came your excellent letter of July 26th. The ration party
brought the mail in about nine in the evening but it was not until eleven that I
was able to lie down in my dugout and treat myself to the reading of it. My first
impulse was to be ashamed of my last letter. You will think me a faint-hearted
soldier. Yet it is monotony that was ever my greatest trouble. The tiresome
inaction of the last three months has worn out my patience. We are constantly
in face of the enemy, much occupied during the unnatural hours of the night,
and nervously affected by desultory shelling, intermittent sniping and vague
rumours of an impending catastrophic bombardment. I cannot say I am
longing for a desperate hand-to-hand encounter but I do wish we could be
forced into some mad activity and be done with it.

It is over a year now since I volunteered and since then life has seemed like a
ball in a game of roulette, trembling uncertain on the edge of either Beginning
or End. For in effect Life will be again at the Beginning if I survive. All
opinions, ambitions, decisions hang suspended awaiting the verdict of chance.
In the meantime I have moments of gaiety with companions, moments of
sadness when I think of home, moments of terrific anxiety and black, black
moments when I question myself, my courage and even the final success of our
cause. Recently I have been tired but more confident and ready to face the
issues. For a while I thought too vividly. I pictured the homecoming, the glad
celebrations which you too promise, the widened fields of action, the possible
realization of some ambition, then the wish to live became maddeningly dear.
The wider my horizon, the keener my perception of self and the possibilities of
life, the more horrible appeared death, the less I wished to put my head above
the parapet and the more acute the inner throb when a machine gun barked

and I though of the time to come when I should have to charge into that rain of bullets, and then suddenly cease to be, or slowly in pain realize the coming end of all things. It is a great mistake for a soldier to have too keen an imagination or to allow his thoughts to dwell morbidly on his dangers. I now cultivate a sort of daredevil carelessness.

I am not by nature intrepid, not even quarrelsome enough to make fighting enjoyable. On the contrary, I shrink from the naked disclosure of human passions, drunkenness, insanity, hatred, anger, they fill me with a cold horror and dread. But to see a man afraid would be the worst of all. To have to kill a man in whose eyes I saw the wild fear of death would be awful. I almost think I should stop and let the fellow kill me instead.

There should be no heroism in war. No glorification, no reward. For us it should be the simple execution of an abhorrent duty, something to be ashamed of, since by reason of our human imperfection we would rather kill and torture than accept conditions of life we have not been taught to regard as good. Had I been born under Prussian influence I should have believed their cause just and fought for it, but I have been differently trained so I fight against it.

Probably I have bored you with these half-thought impressions or else antagonized you. You may have much of the savage glee and delight in combat left, as I have too when my mood is not reflective or when I am moved by martial music or the sight of armed men or the turmoil of a victorious charge. You may think me a sorry soldier.

You have famous friends. I am inclined to wonder if I have not treated you too lightly. I have formed the opinion that you are a natural, healthy, fun-loving girl with something more than usual intelligence and yet without the oppressive seriousness of conceit. You have maintained your sense of humour and proportion.

Bobs has grown into a sturdy, attractive little fellow. Your suggestion of sending him to you isn't practicable but I like you for having made it. Somebody accidently poured boiling tea on his back so like myself he has scars. Perhaps they will wear off. I have a little snap of him and myself which I shall send you. He is only a friend and I am sorry to say not my exclusive loving companion. I have been too occupied to feed and cherish him. My servant is very fond of him and by doing all this has prevailed on his affection. He is nevertheless a comfort and I can put upon him some of the accumulation of love which finds no other outlet in this barren life.

You must send me a photograph. You say you will "if you like my future letters." I can only hope you will. I have no artifice to make them different. I only write as I am impelled and as I know so little of your likes and dislikes I can only be myself alone and trust it pleases you.

I wonder who was laughing at you for writing such a long letter. What would they say of mine? No doubt you were in the midst of gay young people full of life and laughter. You should see me in similar circumstances. I defy anyone to be gayer or more ridiculous.

I liked your description of drifting in a canoe. I am generally too energetic to drift. I have not that capacity for the silent enjoyment of beauty that most people make much of. If the beauty is of nature, sounds well into my throat formlessly, if the beauty is of the ballroom I am frightfully talkative. I lose my steps by reason of my impulsive conversation and the beauty is frightened away like Miss Muffet!

Confound it. I must stop though only half-emptied. Until next time. You must reply, mustn't you?

Yours very sincerely,
Talbot Papineau

August 23, 1915.

My dear Miss C.,

The sinking of the *Arabic* has filled me with apprehension. I noticed that she carried mails and I am disturbed to think that some at least of my recent letters to you have been destroyed. What I said may be utterly valueless for others but its worth is inestimable in our own personal progress. To verify my fears you must acknowledge individually the letters you receive if only by a picture postcard. I sent a souvenir of Ypres in a long letter. Then I sent a long letter in a souvenir of Armentieres. Before and after I wrote ordinary letters of extraordinary length. No matter how many you receive I shall always mourn the loss of some.

I have been riding this afternoon. The crops are being taken in by the women and old men and boys and the fields are magnificent for gallops. There are no wires except the field telephones. I have just bet forty francs on myself against the grey with Crabbe up. I think my lighter weight will just make the difference and my black is in better form. Charlie and Crabbe are giving me 2–1 odds. We may race tomorrow. I have to be up at 5 a.m. to take a party to the trenches which we came out of last night, but I expect to be free in the afternoon.

Bobs is in great form. He is really quite a little beauty and I shall do my best to get him home. Perhaps I should have his tail cut. What do you think? I secured a collar for him, a rather ornate thing of tan leather lined with blue flannel with scalloped edges like a petticoat and studded with little brass stars.

I am restless and uneasy today. Nothing pleases me. I hate bridge although I have just won nine francs from Charlie. We return to the trenches tonight for four days. There is no hope of hearing from you again. I shall have to write to others. This is enough for today.

Talbot Papineau

August 24, 1915.

My dear Miss C.

Just another line to let you know that I lost the race and forty francs! Everybody bet against me but I maintain that if I'd managed a better start I would have won. In any case it was very exciting. I have also been unfortunate at bridge. It will not be a lucky day for me unless I get a letter from you this evening. Going into town to get some ink and a pen.

Talbot Papineau

August 26, 1915.

My dear Miss C.,

My letters are really degenerating into a diary. I should feel they were outwearing their welcome if I did not believe you to be interested in the War. I cannot hope for more personal interest, but impersonally you may be willing to know some detail of our life at the front. It is true that I have written more to you than any other single person excepting Mother, but you have interested me unusually.

The day has been gloriously warm and flooded with sunshine. The observation balloons have hung motionless in the hazy unclouded blue. I fretted and fussed all morning. We are confined to billets to be ready in case of attacks so I cannot roam. After luncheon the restraint became unbearable. I was wild for exercise. All about us there are these marvellously cultivated fields. Some are green where potatoes have been grown, otherwise they are peroxide blondes. The grain is being cut by hand and piled in small stacks of smaller bundles. In one field I saw an old man with two enormous loads of sheaves building a wheat stack. It was irresistible. I tramped over, took off my cap and belt and coat, rolled up my sleeves and told the old chap that I would take his place. He capitulated at once. I climbed on the load and seized his longhandled pitchfork. The heads of grain were so full and ripe I hardly dared move and felt clumsy and brutal to stand upon them. My task was to spear a sheaf and toss it to a boy who stood near the top of the stack. In turn he tossed the sheaves to a couple of ancient farmers who shaped them and place them, building the stack in a solid sturdy mass that would resist storms and wind and rain and protect the grain until threshing time. I began very merrily chatting with the men. I learned how to move my feet so I should not stand on the end of the sheaf I was trying to toss. I learned to shorten or lengthen the handle to reduce the effort. I learned to give a little shove at the end of the stroke to disengage the fork, just as we used to hoist the pole at Oxford when punting.

We finished the first great load very pleasantly. The farmer's wife came out with a jug of cool beer and a china bowl. I hate beer. I've never taken more that a mouthful all my life but I felt too much a part of the picture not to join in the drinking. So we all sat wiping our brows and passing the china bowl. Then the horses drew the big clumsy lumbering wagon away. Close by another fully loaded waited its turn. Once more I climbed up and we commenced with a swing. I wondered if they would notice I was tossing more slowly. To my shame blisters came on what I thought were my calloused hands. The perspiration soaked and dripped about me and the sheaves grew heavier and heavier. But it was magnificent. It was an Adventure in Contentment. I am happier for the work and have promised to return tomorrow. Our men, heaven knows, have enough hard work to do, digging, digging, digging, carrying pit props and steel girders and sandbags and rations, but we officers have no exercise. We do without sleep to patrol the trenches and we walk and talk but otherwise we are like gang bosses. We stand about and grow soft. We are to have two solid weeks in reserve so I shall try hard to get in shape again.

We have wild rumours this morning, that we have won a decisive victory in the Dardenelles, that Bulgaria has joined us, that America has declared war, and that Russia will desert us and make a separate peace. Something has pleased the Germans. They are cheering all along the line. A wild tale comes also that over a million Japs are crossing Siberia to the assistance of the Russians, a situation full of suggestions if true. I wonder when I shall hear from you?

Talbot Papineau

September 7, 1915.

My dear Miss C.,

I am off today for London for a few days leave. At two o'clock this afternoon with a haversack containing my washing things I shall ride to the rail head at Steenward and at 3 a.m. tomorrow I should reach London. Yet I am sorry to be leaving just now. After some cold rainy days it has become serene and beautiful. There is a "gentleness of heaven" brooding today. A few lazy clouds and here and there in the clear spaces a few speckled rows where the anti-aircraft guns have vainly pursued some aeroplane with their shrapnel. This afternoon will take place our regimental sports, which I shall miss. I was to have run as leader of our company squad in the cross-country half-mile full-equipment race. I am so stiff and sore from our football game yesterday that I am hardly as sorry as I would be otherwise. We played English rugby of course and one or two of our men were new to the game. However we have splendid material. We have to a man the championship teams of Alberta and British Columbia and many of the best McGill, Toronto and Queens University players to choose from.

My letters will be not forwarded to me in London, so it will be some time before I can hear from you even if you have written. Also I wonder what you have done about the promised photograph. I have innumerable commissions for other officers, from hats to whisky, to fill and I also plan a strenuous round of baths, lunches and dancing at night clubs. I am principally looking forward to getting my soiled old uniform off and into a white collar and a pretty blue suit again!

Talbot Papineau

2

Ludlow, Colorado; September 20, 1915

Junior Rockefeller has dirt down his collar and dirt in his shoes. He has dirt on his hands and behind his ears and in his eyes and every time he smiles he gets dirt in his mouth. He kicks up dirt with every step, and the steady wind that blows across the coal fields of Colorado spins it into whirlpools around the small group of men standing beside the charred wooden cross marking the site of the Ludlow massacre. He reaches for his handkerchief to hold over his nose, stifling the smell of charred earth that comes from the shallow pit where two women and eleven children were burned to death, but Mackenzie King's hand touches his arm, and his head nods, ever so slightly, towards the silent group of miners gathered outside the remaining tents, watching, and Junior Rockefeller quickly puts the handkerchief away. He bows his head and closes his eyes. He feels another one of his headaches coming on. He prays that the day will pass quickly and that he will not be shot.

A photographer from the New York *Times* snaps a picture and the little group moves solemnly off towards the cluster of ragged people by the tents. Two years have passed since the Colorado coal miners went out on strike and fled the company camps to set up their own tent city on the open prairie. Most of the strikers have drifted away, driven out by starvation, but a few have clung stubbornly to the land, living as best they can from their little gardens, and odd jobs, and whatever the women can bring in peddling eggs and sex and moonshine to the scabs in the camps. They are blacklisted by the companies and deserted by their union, which cut out when the bullets started to fly. They are alone, too proud or helpless to run, silent now as John D. Rockefeller Jr., the richest man in the world, makes his way across the field towards them, rubbing his hands nervously against his coat.

"H-h-how do you do," says Junior, offering his tiny, pink hand to a tall, grizzled man pointed out by Mackenzie King.

"I'd like to introduce Archie Mercer, Mr. Rockefeller," says Mackenzie King, "and this is Mrs. Mercer and the Misses Mercer and young Master Mercer...."

Junior shakes hands all around, repeating the names, smiling graciously as the women giggle into their aprons and the men puff up their chests and blow through their moustaches and mumble "Pleeztameechasur," holding their hands stiff afterwards as if they'd been burned.

"...and this gentleman is known simply as Ol'Mose."

A great black paw swallows Junior's hand. It is attached to a long, black arm belonging to an enormous Negro with a shock of grey, frizzy hair, grinning yellow teeth and rolling yellow eyes.

"Ol'Mose has prepared an address of welcome, sir," says Mackenzie King.

Ol'Mose steps forward, flings his arms wide, raises his right hand high in the air and looks dramatically around at the crowd.

"Yo see dat hand, gennelmen!" he cries. "Dat hand has just shook hands with Mr. John D. Rockefeller!"

Junior winces at the laughter and applause, finding ridicule more painful to endure than obscenities or blows, but Mackenzie King is grinning too, and clapping, so he forces a smile, and wonders whether Mackenzie King is deliberately making a fool of him.

Ol'Mose waves his arms to command attention, thrusts out his chest, opens his mouth once or twice, rolls his eyes to Heaven and clutches his thatch of hair in despair at having, in all the excitement, forgotten the address of welcome Mackenzie King had so patiently coached him with.

"Mr. Rockefeller," he cries at last, "Yo is not great in stature, sir, but yo is surely great in fame!"

Junior bows in acknowledgement of the applause. He accepts a small bouquet of wild flowers from a little girl and quite impulsively bends down to kiss her grimy cheek. A photographer from the Denver *Post* snaps a picture.

"Good Lord," Junior thinks on his way back to the car, "I've never shaken hands with a nigger in my life. What would Father say!"

He looks surreptitiously down at his hand, hardly knowing what to expect, but it is as pink and perfect as before, with only a faint, white line showing where he had removed his heavy gold signet ring, on Mackenzie King's advice.

"To hell with Father," he smiles to himself as they thump over the rutted roads on the way to the head office of Colorado Fuel and Iron. "I have been to Ludlow, and I am alive!"

How he had dreaded coming! He had delayed, and made excuses, for almost a year, invented pressing business and hidden himself in his office, shuffling paper from one side of his desk to the other, until Mackenzie King had cornered him, and told him that unless he made this Christian gesture of conciliation in Colorado, unless he led the crusade to humanize industrial relations, he, Junior Rockefeller, would become the storm centre around which all the prejudice against rich and powerful corporations would be certain to gather, and he would become, whether he liked it or not, the leader of the forces opposing the great struggle of the people, a struggle leading to certain and inevitable revolution.

"Revolution!" he had written in his notebook with his silver pencil, underlining it three times.

Junior was terrified of Revolution. He had lived with this fear all his life. Revolution was a black, bearded thing lurking just outside the green hedges that surrounded the Rockefeller family estate at Tarrytown, a ravening monster ready to leap out at him from dark alleys and doorways if he varied one iota from his inflexible daily routine, an enemy more deadly, as he grew older, than his other great foe, Germs. As a child, an only son, he had never been allowed playmates for fear of Germs, nor been permitted to visit a zoo, or a theatre, or attend a birthday party, or learn to swim, or go to school, and later, as a man, he had never left his house or office without a bodyguard, or taken a taxi, or a streetcar, or entered a tavern, or taken a vacation (apart from his honeymoon), or walked into a theatre or restaurant in New York City without a glance over his shoulder and a cold lump of fear in his gut. In fact he never would have met his wife, his sole companion, had he not, at twenty, defied his mother and gone to a dance.

Junior was being perfectly truthful when he told Mackenzie King he derived no pleasure from his money. He led a life of rigidly disciplined tedium, chained like a wretched clerk to a shabby desk in an office at Standard Oil, signing letters written by people he didn't know to people he'd never met about transactions he didn't understand, justifying his existence by meticulously correcting punctuation and sending the letters back, as much as three times, for retyping, before sending them on to Father for final approval. He applied himself earnestly to his work, making something of a fetish of his meticulous routine, refining and polishing his chains until they shone like the brass plate on his office door. He believed his unhappiness to be his own fault. Junior had no head for business.

He had humiliated himself at an early age by losing $4 million in a stock market swindle and had never recovered his reputation. He was hated by the poor, but he was laughed at by the rich, and in his heart of hearts Junior found the snickers of his peers more painful to endure than the black and bearded bogeyman outside the gates. He wasn't even very good at giving money away, since no matter how many millions he donated to medical research or the

China missions, to education, to the arts or to the poor, the fund of the Rockefeller Foundation continued to swell. His father had been patient with him, rewarding him, in lieu of salary, with substantial cheques, or blocks of shares in various corporations, one of which had been Colorado Fuel and Iron, an insignificant company considered so marginal to the Rockefeller interests it would be safe enough in Junior's hands. Junior had paid no attention to it at all, dismissing the strike as another incarnation of Revolution, until, after Ludlow, he found himself portrayed as the very personification of capitalist corruption: he, Junior Rockefeller, the most incompetent capitalist of all!

"It's n-n-not fair," he told Mackenzie King.

Junior had been shocked by Mackenzie King's defence of unions until King had pointed out the difference between good unions, led by honest, hard-working, God-fearing men, and bad unions, led by Revolutionaries and troublemakers, who should all be locked up. The troublemakers were few, said Mackenzie King, the decent men were many. The logic of this argument, to mobilize the organized mass of good workers to expel their own agitators, struck Junior with the force of revelation.

"Conciliation!" he wrote in his notebook with the silver pencil and underlined it twice.

"Be yourself," Mackenzie King had said when Junior testified before the Senate committee on industrial relations. Even the most hard-bitten labour leaders were stunned by this shy, stammering, naive young man who believed in unions and loved the poor; this smiling, sweet-faced Sunday school teacher who brushed away tears when Ludlow was mentioned could not possibly be the bloody fiend who fed on the flesh of the exploited masses. Mother Jones, the infamous agitator, had come up and shaken his hand, and wished him well, and said if she'd only had the chance to meet him before she never would have said all those awful things, or wished him dead. A photographer from the Washington *Post* had snapped a picture of Junior with his arm around Mother Jones. Junior had vomited in private before every appearance, and shaken for hours afterwards, but he had triumphed. Mackenzie King had convinced him that he, Junior Rockefeller, was an honest man, a good man, a Christian, and when Junior read Mackenzie King's little book, *The Secret of Heroism*, he screwed up his courage and resolved to plunge into Colorado as Bert Harper had plunged into the icy Ottawa River.

Father told him to take a revolver and a dozen Pinkerton men. No, said Junior, he would go alone and unarmed. It was the first time he'd said no to his father, but the imperative of God's will was stronger. If the cause of capitalism required it, Junior Rockefeller was ready to be its martyr.

Mackenzie King has dirt down his collar and dirt in his shoes. He has dirt on his hands and behind his ears and in his eyes and every time he smiles he gets dirt in his mouth. Mackenzie King hates dirt. He can't help it. He has tried to overcome his revulsion. He has visited fetid sweatshops in Toronto's Ward and written about them in the newspapers, he has interviewed girls in the Eddy match factory dying from phosphorous poisoning, he has lived in a Chicago slum and spoken to countless meetings of working men, he has slept in mean bunkhouses and filthy hotels, he has accompanied prostitutes to their squalid rooms and tried to turn them to God. He has toured mining camps and London slums and country hovels in the backwoods. He has dedicated his life to the poor. And the poor are dirty.

He used to think his fastidiousness a fault, and tried wearing soiled shirts, and going a week without a bath, and became unhappy, until he perceived that cleanliness was really a form of prevention, a way of keeping himself healthy and ready for the work to which God had called him. The proof was that he, of all his family, was the only one still well and strong. If only Bella had taken proper care of herself and not worn herself out lifting heavy ledgers at the bank, if only she had told the manager she had an enlarged heart, and couldn't do heavy work, instead of concealing the truth from him for fear of losing her position, she would still be alive, and able to help Mother and poor father around the house, instead of leaving them helpless and alone. He had always considered Bella a selfish, headstrong girl, thinking, because she was a year older, she could ignore his advice, when it was clear he was right, and she was wrong, determined to make her own way in the world although it cost her her health and her prospects for marriage. He'd told Bella she would have collapsed even sooner had he not persuaded her to give up nursing and care for Mother, although for all the thanks he got you'd think he'd ruined her life. A little foresight did no harm. He made a mental note, on his way home, to stop in at Johns Hopkins for a thorough medical checkup.

As Mackenzie King guides Mr. Rockefeller from camp to camp, he takes care to stand slightly apart and to one side, so that a bullet intended for Mr. Rockefeller will not claim him by mistake. He did not, he confesses, foresee that championing Mr. Rockefeller would involve actual physical danger. It had only been by chance one day, in New York, when the chauffeur had not been waiting in the agreed-upon spot, that Mr. Rockefeller explained how he never went anywhere alone but always with a companion or two, and took a different route every morning and left at a different time, by a different exit, every evening, and met the car somewhere on the street, or walked if the streets were not too crowded, and Mackenzie King had realized, with a cold feeling around his heart, that Mr. Rockefeller's hospitality, his insistence that Mackenzie King accompany him to lunch, his delight in inviting the lonely bachelor home to dinner, was not the passionate expression of friendship that he had supposed, but that he, with his extraordinary resemblance to Mr. Rockefeller, formed a sturdy shield and a perfect decoy. Since then Mackenzie King has taken to dining alone more often, and seldom uses his office at the Rockefeller Foundation, which bears the unfortunate number 13. Mackenzie King desires immortality, but not just yet. So when he introduces Mr. Rockefeller to clusters of curious miners, he stays close to the photographer from the New York *Times*, who is really a Pinkerton man in disguise, with a bullet-proof vest and a revolver concealed in his camera, and he makes sure that Archie Mercer and other company agents are stationed in their appropriate places, and the company detectives have a sharp eye out, and that he is wearing the working-man's soft cloth cap he's adopted in Colorado, the cap that shows his support of the working class, the cap that no assassin, however crazed, could mistake for Mr. Rockefeller's elegent snap-brim fedora.

As Junior makes his way around the mining camps of Colorado Fuel and Iron, encountering nothing more troublesome that a few surly stares and the occasional stream of tobacco juice aimed at his retreating feet, he experiences an unexpected elation. Why, he has stared the black, bearded monster in the face and found a pussycat! He has sat on broken chairs in squalid shacks and shared miners' suppers of beans and potatoes, mopping up the gravy with a slice of bread, he has shared a drink from a common cup, and when he found it was whisky, swallowed it. He has dressed in miner's overalls and a miner's cap, and gone down into the mine shaft and walked for miles along the black coal face, talking to men as they worked, and changed in the common wash house, he has visited schools, and saloons, and sat on rough boards in primitive privies, and patted mangy dogs, and conversed with men who spoke no English, and on Saturday night, at the Cameron camp, he danced the polka with every miner's wife and daughter in the hall, and when the music ended he'd jumped on a chair, and promised them a bandstand and dance pavilion, at his own expense, and the story of John D. Rockefeller Jr. dancing with the poor had made the front page of nearly every newspaper in North America.

"Why, this is fun!" he'd said to Mackenzie King, who was dancing as hard as he was, his round face red as a tomato.

Junior is profoundly grateful to Mackenzie King. King's faith in him has given him courage, King's advice has, to use a western vulgarism, saved his bacon. Junior is generous in his public praise, referring to Mackenzie King as his "godfather," elevating him over the heads of the Foundation executives to the position of honour at his right hand, making no public statement or public gesture without consulting Mr. King, to the point where it is said that Junior even pees on Mackenzie King's advice. After more than a year of Mr. King's close company, Junior himself has to admit that he wishes Mackenzie King were not always *there*.

Junior is by lifelong habit a solitary man, his own best company, and he finds Mackenzie King, on long acquaintance, uncomfortably cosy. He has no taste for long, philosophical discussions about Christianity, or politics, but prefers pragmatic problems and simple Bible reading and a good night's sleep. On several occasions, as Mr. King talked on into the night, Junior has yawned, and turned out lights, and announced his intention of going to bed, and the butler has hovered at the door to see Mr. King out, but Mr. King has seemed quite oblivious to these hints until finally Junior instructed the butler to call the car, but still it was almost another hour before he was finally out the door. Junior fears he was a little indiscreet when he spoke to Mr. King about the Rockefeller "brotherhood." He had meant it in a symbolic way, a polite way of saying he expected loyalty; but it was clear that Mr. King interpreted it quite literally, and would, at the slightest sign of encouragement, move in, bag and baggage. He had an embarrassing way of talking about himself and his dreary family, and when his sister Bella had died, last April, at the same time as Junior's mother, his tearful commiserations had driven Junior nearly to distraction. Junior believed that if any Rockefeller made it to Heaven, it would be his mother. He was quite confident about her angelic status and rejoiced in it. But he found Mackenzie King's suggestion that Bella and his mother would be singing hymns together on the far side of the pearly gates more than a little presumptuous, and he'd suggested that Mr. King proceed immediately to Colorado to investigate the coal mines.

Originally he had not intended Mr. King to visit Colorado. The strike there had already been broken. He had advised him to visit Europe, but the war had made that impractical. He'd expected, actually, that Mr. King would return to Canada, to take up the political career he was so anxious about, and would pursue his research in libraries, and Junior had become a little suspicious when Mr. King appeared to have no political career at all. It had been part of his father's genius, as a businessman, to take an interest in politics, so it was said there wasn't a politician in the United States, from president to dog catcher, who wasn't in the Rockefeller pocket. His father had been pleased, in view of Mr. King's past credentials, to get him on board for $12,000 a year. But when Junior made a few inquiries through Colonel Foster, the American consul in Ottawa, he found that William Lyon Mackenzie King was considered a lightweight with little political future.

"Unless Mr. King makes a brilliant marriage," wrote Col. Foster, "which seems unlikely in view of his romantic notions about women, he does not possess the financial resources to pursue a political career with any success. He is, however, an energetic young man, and I have never met anyone more anxious to please. Mr. King takes a very broad, North American view, is truly democratic in his principles, and, in view of his family history, naturally sympathetic to the ideals of the American Revolution. He is one of our few friends on this side of the border. I have suggested to Mr. King that he take a position in business, to secure the necessary finances and influential friends, and I know that handsome offers have been made to him by the Canadian Pacific Railway, and the Canadian Manufacturers' Association, but he clings stubbornly to the 'cause' of the working man, who cannot help him in a practical way, and his radicalism makes him something of a joke in sophisticated circles, although in Ottawa, sophistication is a joke itself.

"The future of the Liberal party, however, is bright. The Conservative government is riddled with corruption over war contracts. It is common knowledge that the Canadian Ross rifle, which the Minister of Militia, Sam Hughes, insisted upon, is worse than useless. I have it from a good source that during the Second Battle of Ypres, last April, in which the Canadians distinguished themselves so bravely, the troops threw away their Ross rifles and picked up Lee Enfields from the bodies of fallen British comrades. General Hughes boasts quite openly that patronage goes only to 'friends' of the government, particularly his own, and I believe it will be only a matter of months before it is revealed that Hughes, and the rest of the Tory gang, have been lining their pockets. Certainly some vast fortunes have already been made by those fortunate enough to acquire contracts for shells and other supplies. Although the casualties have been much higher than anticipated, the war has had a remarkably stimulating effect on the Canadian economy, and with the 'right' government in office, the opportunities for development will be enormous."

Junior is prepared to overlook Mackenzie King's bad taste (why does he wear that appalling cloth cap?) and bad manners (he dropped Abby's dear friend, Miss Ruth Fitch, like a hot potato, after rushing her off her feet for a week, and pretended he didn't see her when they passed by accident on the street), but Junior is not prepared to be manipulated like a puppet on a string in front of his own employees. And he has the uneasy feeling, as his tour nears its end, that Mackenzie King has somehow taken control, and that he has come to Colorado not to get Junior Rockefeller out of a tight corner, but to build himself a political platform on Junior Rockefeller's reputation and Junior Rockefeller's money, a platform to be called the Rockefeller Plan for Industrial Representation, already drawn up and waiting for his approval, which looks to Junior, the more he studies it, like an unnecessary and dangerous sellout to Revolution.

Has he made a terrible mistake? Could William Lyon Mackenzie King possibly be a Socialist spy?

Government House
Ottawa
September 28, 1915

Mr. William Lyon Mackenzie King
c/o Colorado Fuel and Iron
Ludlow, Colorado, U.S.A.

Dear Mr. King,

Their Royal Highnesses have asked me to thank you for your kind gift of the photograph of yourself and Mr. Rockefeller Jr. taken by the mine shaft at Ludlow, Colo. It took us a moment to recognize you in your overalls and we would not have known Mr. Rockefeller Jr. in his miner's cap had you not identified him on the back. He seems, as you say, perfectly ordinary.

I have looked through all the Ottawa newspapers for a story about Mr. Rockefeller's visit to Colorado but have failed to find a word. There is little in the press here but war news. If something is mentioned I will clip it and send it to you.

His Royal Highness has asked me to express to you his opinion that the quick entry of the United States into the present war would do much to achieve industrial harmony. In his exact words: "It would knock all that bolshie nonsense on the head." Wages here are so high, especially in the shell factories, that there is some worry it might cut into recruiting.

My own feelings about the war are now much closer to your own. I hate it.

We all wish you a successful conclusion to your mission.

Yours very truly,
"C"

Pueblo, Colorado, Friday, October 1, 1915

"A union if necessary," Mackenzie King explains patiently to John D. Rockefeller Jr., "but not necessarily a union."

Mackenzie King wipes the sweat from his forehead and loosens his collar. It's nearly midnight. In less than twenty-four hours his Industrial Representation Plan, the brilliant compromise that will make him the toast of the industrialized world, is scheduled to be presented to a mass meeting of miners in the Pueblo hall by its patron and chief benefactor, John D. Rockefeller Jr. But Mr. Rockefeller Jr. has developed cold feet. He is not smiling.

"The men will be free to join a union, yes, as they are free to join the Baptist church or the Odd Fellows lodge," says Mackenzie King, "but you do not have to *recognize* the union, any more than you have to negotiate with the Odd Fellows or the local bishop. All grievances and complaints will be taken before the joint management-labour committee, to be settled there in a free and reasonable way, so the men will feel no need for a union, and a firm sense of friendship and trust will grow up between your superintendents and their employees. It is not Socialism, Mr. Rockefeller, but it's Democracy."

Junior is Republican. He is also politically astute enough to sense that Mackenzie King has missed the point, that the real socialists, the militants, the troublemakers, will not be bought off with better wages, or wash houses, or clean streets, or good schools, or garden plots, or polite foremen, they want *everything*, and the more you give them, the more they'll take, until they have everything. And once you open the door, even a crack, and they get their dirty foot in, there will be no stopping them, and the sensible thing to do is to crush them, kill them, exterminate them from the face of the earth. But it's almost impossible to do the sensible thing in a democracy, so Junior is sitting here with a headache, in a stuffy room, trying to decide between two equally unpleasant alternatives.

"I believe in l-l-liberty," Junior says. "An open shop. My men are free to f-f-form whatever associations they please, as long as they do their w-w-work and don't break the law. Now that we have taken steps to improve our organization and supervision, I see no reason why things cannot be left as they are. My visit here has done a world of good. The camps are in tiptop shape. Why do we need a p-p-plan? Everything has been f-f-fixed."

Mackenzie King stares unseeing through the grimy window of the mine manager's office, trying to control his temper. What a hateful, hideous place this is! What a fool he's been! He has sacrificed his political career, soiled his reputation, wasted his energies doing the Rockefeller dirty work in this black, Satanic hole, hoping, in the crucible of Colorado, to institute some basic principles of reform, principles that could be applied far beyond the Rockefeller empire. But instead he has been nothing but a hatchet man, an errand boy, begging, bargaining, buying, feared and mistrusted on all sides, the kind of man he most abominates, a bought man, a fixer. Of course everything's fixed! He's fixed it! Who does Mr. Rockefeller think got the shacks painted? And fences put up around the yards? Who rounded up old oil drums for garbage cans, and had the roads graded where the spring run-off had washed them out, and ordered new wells dug, for fresh water, and had wash houses constructed where there were none, and had the saloons turned into community halls, and persuaded the company stores to drop their profit from twenty per cent to ten? Who got rid of the most vicious superintendents, and persuaded the others that miners were men, not cattle, and paid Mother Jones' way from New York, and put her up at a hotel, so she could tell the men what a fine fellow Mr. Rockefeller was? Who, after six weeks of pleading and cajoling, persuaded Mr. Rockefeller to donate $100,000 in relief because the unemployed were starving, and when the district manager put them to work, building a road to his ranch, had the work transferred to the camps, where it was needed, and who soothed the ruffled feathers of the bosses, and calmed their fears, and listened endlessly to the miners' grievances, and promised them, in the name of John D. Rockefeller Jr., redress?

Did Mr. Rockefeller not realize what a hell-hole this had been when Mackenzie King had arrived, last April, a year after the Ludlow massacre? He had been nearly sick with shock. But he had convinced himself, after a few weeks, that the fault was not with Mr. Rockefeller, or the mine managers, but with the type of men the mines attracted, bohunks, Galicians, niggers, wops, rough, illiterate peasants right off the immigrant boats, men with no choice but to take the dirtiest, poorest work available, men who, unless they were organized and educated and controlled by the decent white men among them, would drag the camps down into a cesspool of vice and savagery. The poor, Mackenzie King concluded in Colorado, were not dirty because they were poor, but they were poor because they were dirty.

He had reasoned with Mr. Rockefeller explaining how higher wages and clean, democratic camps would attract a better class of man, and the scum would drift off elsewhere, and he'd thought Mr. Rockefeller had understood. But he was aware that Junior had a very brief attention span, an almost manic obsession with his own sense of injustice and, in spite of a college education, no interest at all in political, moral or philosophical questions. Mackenzie King had been saddened that their relationship had not developed the intimacy and mutual understanding he had so desired (he had asked Junior to call him Rex, but Junior had stammered so badly over it that they had reverted to the more formal Mr. King). Mr. Rockefeller's praise had been so warm, his declarations of trust and confidence so unequivocal, his personal generosity so unstinting, that Mackenzie King had never imagined for a moment that he would, at the very climax of his career, after compromising his ideals and humbling himself, be, by the man he loved like a brother, so coldly and brutally shafted.

He notices, as he fights to control his panic, a shadowy figure in a tweed coat and slouch hat standing in the pool of yellow light beneath the yard lamp, gazing up at the window. He rubs at the windowpane with the heel of his hand to get a better look. Yes.

"Mr. Eugene Williams of the Associated Press is waiting in the yard," Mackenzie King says harshly, turning on Junior. "I shall call him in this moment and announce my resignation. I have promised the men the Rockefeller Plan. If I cannot present that plan, I can no longer remain with the foundation, or continue to allow my name to be associated in any way with the Rockefeller interests."

He walks quickly across the room and opens the office door.

"S-s-s-s-s-s-stop!" cries Junior. "Not the p-p-p-p-p-p-press!"

Next to Germs and Revolution, the mean-spirited, muckraking, miserable

Press has been the scourge of Junior Rockefeller's life, and without hesitation he would prefer death by cancer, or bullet, to being once more pilloried as a coward and a cad on the front pages of the nation's newspapers. It is a martyrdom that he, with all his merciless self-denial, finds intolerable to contemplate.

Junior flips open his little notebook, as he often does, in times of crisis, with his Bible, looking for guidance, and reads:

"C-c-c-conciliation."

It is a sign. The true way, the Christian way. Charity, that's the ticket, that's his business, isn't it, charity? Perhaps the black, bearded bogeyman can be bought off after all. It's worth a try. He must consider his own future, his reputation, his sons. Now things are going so well, he can work behind the scenes, increase the surveillance, the bribes, just to make sure, perhaps the plan will make it easier, bring the agitators out into the open....

"P-p-p-please, R-R-Rex," says Junior, "Let's r-r-reconsider."

Just after midnight, on the dusty unswept floor of the mine manager's office at the headquarters of the Colorado Fuel and Iron Company in Pueblo, Colo., John D. Rockefeller Jr. and William Lyon Mackenzie King, weeping tears of relief and gratitude, kneel together and ask God's blessing on the Rockefeller Plan for Industrial Representation.

In the yard below, huddled in his old tweed coat against the night wind, Mr. Horace Jamieson of the Pinkerton Detective Agency, alias Eugene Williams of the Associated Press, wishes those two little farts would pack in it so he can go home and get some sleep.

London, October 2, 1915

My dear Miss C.,

Because I have spent one wholesome day in the country and have been with wholesome people for a few hours I have at last the courage to write you. Since my last writing your letters have come to me, several of them, and I have been almost ashamed to open them. I have been ashamed to answer them. They have meant a great deal to me. In the trenches they have helped me face danger. Here perhaps they have helped me avoid it. But I have not avoided it, not entirely. You have already provided me with inexhaustible "munitions" as you called it simply in the acknowledgement and discussion of what you have written. I have recently done much that I would not care to write you about.

How I hate London! Not so much London's fault I suppose as my own, but for me it has come to mean long walking in an alien crowd, the ceaseless flow of money, innumerable dashes in taxicabs, feverish excitements of music halls and night clubs, health-destroying restaurants and lounges, the ceaseless passing of painted faces, the hideous pageantry of commercial affection. If I have been drawn into much of this side of life I blame myself but I also blame the disturbing influences of the war, because with war I have ceased to dream of princesses and I have sought the hollow shams of easy and immediate gratification. Because life might suddenly end I have not waited for the slow and doubtful realization of dreams. I wanted affection, beauty, laughter, companionship. I wanted them immediately, and so I bought them, the cheap, ready-made articles, and so have cheapened myself until I am sick with disappointment and glad that tomorrow I go back to the front and so perhaps end it all. The offensive has begun. We may break through but the price will be a heavy one. I shall arrive just in time. It seems curious to be here tonight in such peace and security and the day after tomorrow to be again in the middle of death and destruction.

I have liked all your letters. There have been no jolts or jars. You have seemed always to say the right thing. I am deeply grateful for the good fortune which has made you a correspondent. As you say the circumstances are unique. I can write to you almost as to myself. I have all the interest of reading between your lines and trying to discover your character. I write freely without evasion to permit you an equal discovery.

Your letters came this morning like a breath of freshness and hope. I was shocked with my own shame. I can think of nothing else until I have told you so I have come to write you, but not until I had bathed in cold, clear water and shaved and brushed myself and dressed as particularly as if you were here for these things seemed necessary as a sort of ritual. My resolutions have already been taken. Please don't think I shall attribute reformation to the influence of your letters. I have always scorned such Sunday school sentiment and would place no reliance in the good resolutions of a love-sick youth. I shall be different whether you write to me or not. But at the same time you have helped me. You have cleared the clouded atmosphere that obscured my star. If now I must die I shall die as I would like to have lived.

Curiously in these last two days your personality, so far as your appearance is concerned, has almost disappeared. I was first interested in the texture of your hair, the colour of your eyes, the expression of your face, and even as to how you dressed, and now I do not care. That part of you has ceased to exist. You have become only a mind, a mind answering to mine in whose processes I am interested. I want to know what you think, not what you wear. I am indifferent to your hair. I am only interested in how you will treat certain subjects. How do you like being a mere disembodiment, a sort of ghost! I only regret that our spiritual seances are so separated by time. If I could have immediate replies to my queries how truly exciting it would be.

You appear to have had a wonderful journey. I can visualize a good part of it. Your little haphazard illustrations are like a moving picture machine. When I read your description of the woods and wild things my silly eyes grew warm and moist. I wonder if you love them as I do. Mother tells me in her last letter that 2,000 acres adjoining the maple wood at Montebello have just been sold. Some lumber people bought it, not Booth thank god, and I suppose the trees will be cut. And I had planned it as a sanctuary for trees and living things but I will get it back some day. So we are left with 800 acres. I think had I been home, we would not have sold. We would have been more land-poor than ever but happier.

Talbot Papineau

Pueblo, Colorado; Saturday, October 2, 1915

The meeting hall is jammed to the rafters, more than two hundred miners' representatives from across the state, every manager and superintendent, a crowd of curious onlookers packed into the standing room at the back, the press hovering outside the door.

Junior Rockefeller, standing behind a small table on a platform at the front of the hall, is telling the men how deeply touched he has been by their kindness and hospitality during his visit to Colorado.

"I have gone into your wash houses, and talked with the men before and after b-b-bathing," he says. "As you know, we have pretty nearly s-s-s-slept together! It has been reported that I s-s-slept in one of your nightshirts. I w-w-w-would have been proud had this report been true."

"I tink we're gettin' somewheres," calls a voice from the back of the hall.

"You think we are getting somewhere, sir," cries Junior. "You know d-d-damn well we are!"

He waits for a moment for the sky to fall, but his first swear word of a lifetime brings only grins and wild applause from the men.

Encouraged, Junior reaches into his pocket and piles a handful of coins on the table. The clinking sounds very loud in the silence.

"You all know," he goes on, "about those awful R-R-Rockefeller men in New York, the biggest scoundrels who ever lived, who have taken m-m-millions of dollars out of this company, who have oppressed you men, who have cheated you out of your w-w-wages and 'done' you every way they could, well, let's say this pile of c-c-coins represents that R-R-Rockefeller company, Colorado Fuel and Iron."

With a flick of his hand Junior sweeps half the coins to the floor. He listens as the last copper spins away across the boards and plinks against the wall. Not one man bends to pick up a cent.

"That is the share you men get," Junior says. He removes a smaller stack of coins from the pile.

"This is the s-s-s-share of the company officers." He takes away the last few coins. "And these are the directors' f-fees."

All eyes are rivetted on the empty table.

"Why, hello!" cries Junior. "There is nothing left! For never, since my f-f-father and I became interested in this company as stock holders fourteen years ago, has there been one s-s-s-single cent for the common stock! Put that in your pipes and smoke it, when you hear for the R-R-Rockefellers are oppressing you, that the common share holders have put $34 m-m-m-million d-d-dollars into Colorado Fuel and Iron without receiving one c-c-cent of d-d-dividends!" One or two of the men whisper that if Rockefeller doesn't make any money out of them, why does he own the company? But since the miners of Pueblo don't subscribe to the *Wall St. Journal*, they are unaware that Junior is telling the truth, that the Rockefeller investment is not in common stock, but in interest-bearing bonds, and their bonds, over fourteen years, have yielded a profit of $9 million from Colorado Fuel and Iron.

Junior reaches into his pocket and places another pile of coins on the table.

"There are men going around the country," he cries, "clever, charming, talkative men, who will tell you that you should demand the highest wages, and do the least amount of work. It sounds like a good deal, doesn't it? Well, let me tell you, those men are not your friends! They are your deadliest enemies!"

He slips his fingers under the edge of the table and tips it forward. The coins clatter to the floor. He waits until the last copper spins away. Not one man bends.

"That's what will happen if any of us demands more than our fair share! There will be nothing left for anyone!"

Mackenzie King leads the cheers and applause, delighted at the way Junior has delivered his speech, so simple and natural you'd swear he'd thought it up himself, off the cuff, and so passionately committed at the end that his stammer completely disappeared! The miners give Junior a standing ovation. When they leave, Mackenzie King retrieves the coins from the floor.

The Rockefeller plan is put to a vote at every Colorado Fuel and Iron Camp. Every one of the nearly five thousand miners is given two ballots, one marked "For," the other "Against." Since so many men are ignorant, the "For" ballot is printed on white paper, the "Against" ballot on red paper. Of the 2,846 ballots cast, 2,404 are white.

"I have been trying to decide what to investigate next," says Mackenzie King as he sees Junior off on the train to New York.

"N-n-next?" says Junior. "N-next?"

"I thought perhaps Pennsylvania, the steel industry, then I should touch on the railways, textiles, oil of course...."

"Oil?" says Junior. "*Standard* Oil?"

"I have something very broad in mind," says Mackenzie King, "a definitive study, possibly a book, a straightforward, honest statement of the humanitarian aspects of industrial...."

"Mr. King, your energy and enthusiasm amaze me. I cannot afford to lose you! You must take a rest! Got to California! San Francisco! There is no hurry now, is there? Why, everything's f-f-fixed now, isn't it?"

Mackenzie King slips the familiar white envelope into his breast pocket, on top of his wallet with the photograph of Mother, which he carries over his heart.

"Yes," says Mackenzie King.

3

Boulogne, Oct. 5, 1915.
11:30 p.m.

My dear Miss C.,

Here I am once again in France. My train does not leave until 1 a.m.

This morning I went off in my uniform to do some final shopping. I bought a new revolver holster and a haversack and a warm "wooley" to wear under my coat and also four bottles of whisky for Charlie! Then I went by myself to tea at the Piccadilly and gradually an unpleasant mood came upon me. I disliked everything and everybody, the contrast between the soft lights and comfort of the tea room and the trenches. I grew especially angry with the women, some very pretty ones too, who seemed so pleased and placid with themselves while I knew of the carnage at that moment going on. Women swarm everywhere, breezing about the shop windows, covering bus tops, dashing across the roads and flashing by in cars. What are their purposes? They seem ineffective and inane. And there I was to leave in a hour and not a soul to speak to! I was sorry for myself. I was better pleased to be left alone.

I arrived at the station just in time. There were crowds of soldiers returning by the same train, a larger crowd still of weeping women. I was so bitter I laughed at them all and their silly tears. What difference does it make if a few more of us are killed? It was raining. I read the evening news and ate some cold chicken on the way to Folkestone. At the boat it was still raining. I went below and lay down but could not sleep. All lights were extinguished so I lay in the black darkness and was nearly as gloomy myself. The boat was filled with drafts of eager young officers going out for the first time to their great adventure full of nervous enthusiasm. I felt like a senior among a lot of freshmen. I disembarked and came to this little hotel grandly called Le Louvre next to the Gare Centrale from which I leave. The quays are lined with thousands of Red Cross ambulances. The streets are in almost total darkness. After ten, only beer and sandwiches can be procured. My example of writing seems to have been followed by a number of boyish officers. It's hard to believe that a nation of such healthy, brave youths is being defeated. Surely we must win.

I noticed late last evening — your letter was the last thing I read after getting into bed — that you had written at the top of some of the sheets "I love you," "I love you not," "I love you a little," I am inclined to be a little sentimental tonight, because I am so tired I suppose, but I wonder if you were testing me and what the result of the test was. It would be rather comforting right now to have Fate compel you to the "I love you," but I am absurd, and you will register a dig at my sentiment later on, I feel sure. I had better stop. So goodnight. You are sleeping better this evening than I expect to.

Talbot Papineau

October 6, 1915

My dear Miss C.

Some day I shall not call you Miss C., but perhaps simply Lily, for you sign yourself so and it is ridiculous to commune as we do yet retain all the formalities.

I am not only in the trenches but I have found there your photograph and a number of letters. If only I could get my letter to you immediately. I hate to keep you waiting so long for an acknowledgement of the many nice things you have said and done. You are the best correspondent I have ever had. You are almost a dream come true!

At first when I saw the "feathers and fuss" photograph I was depressed — you were a wedding group! Fortunately I see the difference. You have a rather stern expression, but I like the firm mouth and honest, intelligent eyes. Of course you have an absurd amount of material in the dress but have quite the appearance of a Princess. Altogether it is a picture that I should like to have in an expensive frame in my room at home and if I ever love you it would be a shrine. It is all very well to say that Bobs can chew it up but I tremble to think of the danger you run. When we move I carry you in my pack. If we are shelled you will be destroyed. However let me assure you that you will have my most respectful protection and no harm will come to you while I can help. I like your fun and I like your serious criticism and I like your opinions so far as I know them. Sometimes you have misunderstood me. When I said you were "absurdly young" I meant only in comparison to my thirty-two and in relation to your mature expression and achievements. How could you take such exception to my phrase!

You did not quite understand what I meant about mother. I do not particularly wish her to see my letters now or ever. They are written to you and for you alone. I meant if I were to be suddenly killed, it might be quite possible you would have the fullest description of my "last moments," and this I know mother would give anything to have. Please do not think I don't appreciate your offer to make copies for her. I do very much, and it seems part of the sweet sympathic nature that you have. I place you under no obligations. Perhaps you will be more inclined to tear up my letters than to typewrite them, since I have said some miserable things to you, haven't I? Your letters are so loyal and good. You do not harbour all the doubts and scepticisms that assail me. You accept me in a generous and friendly spirit and I am a wretched fellow to be so unkind in return. It is because I have presumed upon this singular position of ours and felt at liberty to speak my very true thoughts whether your vanity should be wounded or not. I think we can share a great deal and make a valuable exchange of some of our deeper feelings.

I am seated at a nice, round mahogany table, before a crackling wood fire, in a spacious room! Our present line runs through the heart of a pretty little French village on the border of a canal and we simply occupy the houses. Of course there are bullet holes in the walls and some of the window panes are broken but we have chairs and candles and crockery and mirrors!

A telegram has just come in from headquarters to take every precaution this evening. Perhaps they expect retaliation for our attack last night. My revolver has been lost during my absence so I am at present armed with a big policeman's baton studded with large nails — a good weapon if I get close enough but poor in the daylight.

It is now 10:30 p.m. and no attack. Our patrols have reported the Germans to be singing and playing instruments in the trenches. Perhaps like savages they are working themselves into a fury by songs, dances and firewater!

Since you think it melodramatic of me to leave you off when an attack is expected, I shall finish tomorrow when the sun is shining again and all is serene.

Oct. 9, 1915

Broad daylight and no attack! So I am glad I did not finish my letter last evening. I have reread all your letters, at least all the recent ones. My baggage is limited to only 35 pounds so there is little room for accumulation. I am obliged to destroy letters after keep them for rereading. I try to memorize them but I am sure I must forget a lot.

I have the cutting from *Midnight* before me — "Is the fascinating Miss L.C. getting ready to leave her Court for a King?" I tell you it makes no difference, yet I am interested to know if you are engaged. Indeed I would throw up my hands in despair and cry *"Voila, une autre!"* if I heard you were and never would I write again. I have honestly no expectations, no, I will say intention, of falling in love with you, principally because I am certain you won't fall in love with me! Why is the cutting not complete? I want to know more about this "devoted admirer" camping on your trail. Is he good-looking? Is he blond or dark? Does he write letters?

I am glad that somebody thinks your heart is in the trenches. I wish I did! Would I be mentioned in *Midnight*? I notice the "L. still holds out." Bravo! Keep it up! Stand to your guns. Hold your trenches. Beat back the encamped admirer until at least we have romped together in the snow at Montebello, until we had laughed together over Leacock, 'til we have danced together at a *Bal Masque*, til we have conversed at Zoé's lunches and somebody else's breakfasts. Then you may surrender if you wish, but surely we owe it to the fate that made us correspondents that we should meet still with the possibility of possibilities.

You have sent me a pin and I return the penny. May we rarely quarrel — and always make up! I kept your tic-tac game for some time but it is lost. I enclose a fresh one. Of course you had taken the centre!

Have you thrown all this in impatience aside, I wonder? I will spare you further, for the present.

Talbot Papineau

Oct. 11, 1915

My dear Miss C.,

I want you to thrust two misconceptions out of your head, both of which, by your own admission, are preventing you from being perfectly natural with me. The first, that because I was a Rhodes scholar I am saturated with learning and uncomfortably clever, is quite wrong, I assure you. On any one subject of importance I am deplorably ignorant. In the second place, you think me so critical that you are to be stilted and unnatural. You even threaten to run away and avoid me. Surely there is no reason to worry over what I might think or say, if I do not praise you as perfect and divine. Have I not more cause to fear that you will not be satisfied with me? I have written of myself and my thoughts and my belongings with no more than a hope that thrown into the unknown, like the call of a wireless operator, they would find an instrument attuned and so gain me a perfectly adjusted reply. I am always in doubt as to when I will strike the jarring note and suddenly break the lovely, filmy web that we are spinning between us.

I am wounded. I have wounded myself. I was wearing my dagger and absent-mindedly pulling it out I jammed the point into my thumb. It will add another little scar to my collection. I have a few of which I am proud when it comes to the exchanges of scars and illness that boys delight in. When I was ten, I was one of the first cases of appendicitis. Two years previous to that I slid down an old board playing tag and drove an enormous splinter through my thigh. When I was fourteen I took a running dive into shallow water and pulled up short with my head on a rock. At school when the ground was frozen hard I fell and rolled on my thumb. I went on playing football and by the end of the game my thumb was bigger than the rest of my hand. I still have a lumpy thumb; then there are the scars of my Winchester burning and I also broke a bone in my left hand skiing.

I am writing near midnight by the light of a candle. The others are sleeping heavily. Outside it is inky black. The rats are trying. Bobs is with me again and I hope he will be a good ratter. He seems very keen but the poor little fellow has had distemper. We have no medicine so he is simply weathering his own storm. I enclose a couple of sketches I made for you today. They are the first I have attempted since the war. I thought you might be interested. I will send you some more from time to time. There is a rat persistently trying to enter my room by way of the wall near my bed head. Charlie is groaning in his sleep. Outside there is an intermittent rifle fire. In the cellar I hear a signaller trying to get some message on the phone. I must away. May this reach you safely and join with all its fellows to make a path into your affections.

Confound this war. It's horrible. I hate it. Heavens, what a peace lover I shall be afterwards!

October 14, 1915

I am sending you the leather seat of a chair from the chateau of Hooge on Bellwarde Lake near Ypres. I know every foot of ground in that unhealthy vicinity. The chateau has been reduced to a heap of stones and this chair was the only piece of furniture left. Our line was merely a narrow trench, so narrow two men could not pass. The chateau since we were there has been taken and retaken. It is on the Menin road. If you read the official reports you may be familiar with these names.

I have now set my expectations so low that nothing can disappoint or dishearten me. I am going to steadily believe that the war will be over before Christmas and when that hope proves vain I shall believe something else.

Talbot Papineau

October 19, 1915

Dear Lily,

I am glad you like the way I write. I look in fear and trembling for your next letters. What a fool I was in London and perhaps what a bigger fool to tell you that I was. The mischief is done. I hope you care sufficiently to scold me and not too much to drop me. I promise you my reformation is now complete as far as intentions go, and my intentions go pretty far. If one good can come from war to a nation, it's the purifying influence of sorrow and sacrifice. It should be the same for individuals but it isn't.

You see, I am getting old and crusty and since the war I feel a certain quarrelsomeness that befits a soldier. You have asked that your letters should be mine and mine alone and I assured you that no one has seen them and no one shall. You may take full advantage of the freedom that our peculiar circumstances permits and I shall understand. I know I shall. I know from the answering chords your letters have struck, from the echo in my mind as I have never known before, it is not love, it is understanding. I feel perfectly at liberty to fall today or tomorrow in love with someone else, with some pretty little fair-haired creature with a taste for music and smart clothes, for instance, affectionate but shallow. Similarly you this winter may write me of your engagement to a stock broker or something else, and so our correspondence can be free from sentimental misunderstandings.

I am not a little worried over your work. I am interested in it. I want to hear more about it. I want you to send me some photographs. Truly you are not going to prove a monomaniac after all. All I want you to do is retain a sense of proportion, which I know a woman is very likely to lose. My fear is perhaps unfounded but you will forgive its expression.

You prefer me clean-shaven. So do I myself. So when the war is over my upper lip shall again be disclosed. I shall give myself every advantage.

I have been offered a staff appointment with promotion. I think I will accept, since I think I can do good work in that way. Sir Max Aitken made the offer when I was in London. He said it was most depressing to belong to a decaying empire.

Talbot Papineau

Rideau Hall,
October 20, 1915

Dear Mrs. Papineau,

I am sorry that Talbot's letters have upset you. I would not have sent them had he not asked me to do so. I am sure he has not intended to hurt you, or slight you, but simply to let you know the truth. He treats me almost as a "comrade-in-arms" because of my association with the regiment and there-fore perhaps speaks more freely than he does to others. Who can he speak his heart to over there?

We are so proud of him! He has brought such honour and distinction to both himself and the P.P.C.L.I. His achievements will never be forgotten. I do not see how he could have made any choice other than the one he did. I would give anything to be in his place.

I will not send any more letters if that is what you wish.

Please do not be angry with him.

Your truly,
Lily Coolican

Oct. 22, 1915

My dear Lily,

Today I received a letter from mother. She speaks of a very nice letter from you and of the receipt of your copies which she says are very interesting. Just as I feared, she continues "I note you have written more frequently and at greater length to Miss Coolican than to me and I am furiously jealous!" Dear old mother, who has always been a sort of a deity to me, is I find a woman after all, but I love her the more for it. To me, who could never waver in my devoted love for her, it seems entirely unnecessary to mention my love and yet mother delights in its expression — just as my wife, I suppose, will some day.

Bobs disappeared last evening. I am growing worried. We may be moved at any moment and the hope of ever finding him in this poor turbulent land would be nil. I already miss him considerably. He used to cuddle up every night on my blankets. He followed me everywhere and was a real companion. I know you will feel quite as sorry as I do, perhaps more because I have seen so many friends come and got out here that one more or less does not seem to matter. It's all in the game, all a part of this horrible procession of events to which our hearts must be hardened and our minds deadened. He has in all likelihood been carried away by some of the troops that are constantly passing through this village.

The day has been perfect, the sun warm enough to rouse the sluggish flies, the trees shining in many colours 'tho less brilliantly than ours at home.

You have asked me to be "honestly candid" in picking to pieces what you "think and say." My dear Miss C., even with my limited knowledge of your sex I fully know the terrible risk of doing as you ask. I am quite willing to imagine you a pampered pet of society surrounded by social sycophants and flattered by much attention and many fulsome compliments. You are too sensible, or too intelligent, to believe even the sincerest of your admirers and you would like to hear the opinion of an entirely honest observer. But, and here I endanger myself, your object is insensibly dictated by vanity, for you would like to receive compliments whose hallmark of honesty you might trust. I doubt very much that you would like to hear any uncomplimentary truths. All I can do is to avoid paying you any unnecessary and untruthful compliments. I can have the desperate courage of the martyr who being condemned to die dares to speak his mind and needs not by pleasant phrases to propitiate the executioners.

I can understand your sense of negation but you yourself are to blame. It is the artificial limitations of society which you tire of. You are like the Persian cat impelled by half-felt instincts to get out into a broader life. But you will not be able to escape and you would be unhappy if you did. You are bound by fetters of your own forging. You may be dissatisfied with dinners and teas but you will be still more dissatisfied without them.

You will never really be natural until you are deeply in love and it is quite probable that you will be denied even that remnant of Nature's creation, for you will choose to love not by instinct but by intelligence, choosing to mate with someone who is presentable at your house parties and who can supply you with the degree of comforts you are accustomed to. Presently I hope the day will come when women will be sufficiently developed to create their own outlets and satisfy their own ambition, but as things stand today your best opportunity is to marry a successful man and through him achieve your purposes.

Have I been disagreeable enough? At least I have written enough for one letter. Besides the evening is dead.

I have been playing more bridge and again losing. It has become late and I am sleepy. I use the pen for your letters only.

Bobs is definitely lost. I can find no trace of him. Poor little chap. I can only hope he is being well looked after. He was an amiable soul and has no doubt made new friends and forgotten old.

Talbot Papineau

Hospital, Havre, Nov. 18, 1915

My dear Lily,

This will be a surprise to you. I was shipped off to hospital more than two weeks ago and have been on my back with bronchitis ever since and so thoroughly disgusted with life I couldn't think of writing anyone, not even you. I am sure you don't want to hear about such a miserable existence as this. You have been wonderfully good about writing. I am very glad to have the little picture frame and the four-leaved clovers. Both for Bobs and myself they arrived just too late. I have very much enjoyed your letters. I have an idea my last one was rather objectionable. Please forgive. It was more or less done on purpose.

I have amused myself in bed drawing silly things but just to show you I send them on. I may be another month in this wretched hole. I am writing a treatise on trench warfare and reading immeasurably, mostly rotten stuff. Please forgive my ill temper. I will feel better later on, I dare say, and will try to make up for it. In the meantime, farewell.

Talbot Papineau

Hospital, Havre, Nov. 23, 1915

My dear Lily,

I am a miserable worm! You may trample upon me and if I ever turn it will only be to squirm under your foot. I have no sooner sent my letter of yesterday when yours of Nov. 1st and 5th arrived and they left me with a wholesome sense of unworthiness. Our communications are those of the Dark Ages! What misunderstandings must have arisen between a Crusader and his fair correspondent, all due to the tardiness of the Post Office! How can I compete with Billy on the spot who can splutter explanations the very instant of his transgressing? Or what chance have I with Ted who can whisper seductive apologies during entreactes or with Edward who can roll his eyes, bare his teeth, figure skate and otherwise show his appreciation after falling from grace? Poor Talbot can only send slow-footed letters to be the belated ambassadors of his repentance.

You object to my vacillations, my withdrawals! You wish the moving finger to write and having writ to quit! What would be the consequence? You would compel me to an unnatural discretion, to a studied consistency of emotion that would make my letters impersonal chronicles of personal experiences. I might even be driven to copying-paper and duplicate files!

What has our correspondence meant to me? It has meant receiving frequent letters and so being kept cheered and interested in these trying times. It has meant the charm of possible romance. It has stimulated my imagination and has given me letters to write that, as they seemed to touch an answering chord, added fresh fuel to my enthusiasm. It has been a pleasant plaything and filled a want. Has it not been written "There are two things which a true man loves, danger and play, and he loves woman because she is the most dangerous of playthings"? I should like to write love letters, but you would not permit unless I really was in love and was prepared to be bound to the very letter of my expressions. And because I love your compassionate heart and your bounding, all-embracing energy and your hair excelling human beauty, am I to love irrevocably the remainder? I may not be Methuselah but neither am I adolescent in my experience of love, and too well do I realize that the ardent youth rushing on to Ottawa expecting to complete his heart's devastation might suddenly seek only the friendship of Lily and the love of someone else.

At the same time, and here is a very honest confession, I shall be properly enraged if before my visit I should find that Lily had succumbed to the good looks of Stanley or the love songs of David or the emergency rations of Joe or the attractiveness of Billy.

And worse still would be to have you carry into effect your threat of withdrawal. Please keep on amusing a soldier no matter what he says or does. Quite independently of your feelings for me as a man, I appeal as a military unit. But of course I am not gainsaying that I should be glad to have you develop an interest in me personally, not that I expect of you what I do not expect of myself. In the meantime it is pleasant to dally with the preliminaries of love. I know 'tis well said that "*il ne faut pas badiner avec l'amour*" but surely such a disembodied sort of *badinage* can work no harm.

Do you want to know the principal characteristic that exists in my mental picture of you? It is of tremendous, all-embracing energy. I visualize you as an object in constant motion, and like Leacock's horseman you "ride off in all directions." You make me think of a box I had as a boy with a glass cover. Inside were several little Chinese figures, and when the glass was rubbed with a glove the figures rushed about with intense activity. Somebody never stops rubbing your glass cover!

I cannot picture you in repose. I do not think of you in hammocks or on sofas or even seated. Your chairs look like spring boards to me and your sidewalk like a scenic railway. You bang a hat on, jamb four long pins into place, hurl furs all over you, then dash down a flight of stairs three at a time. You meet five friends. You say, "Oh my dear, how are you, isn't it warm, I'm in such a hurry come to luncheon Sunday isn't the war news good goodbye." You hurl through a shop. You say, "I want the whole of your stock how much allright." You fly to a platform. You deliver an oration. You leap into three or four taxis. On the way you invent a machine. You have tea. You speed to the dressmakers. You interview a row of reporters. You answer twenty-five telephone calls. You leap into a new winter suit, which you suddenly discard for a tea gown then another dress and another. You whirl into the dining room an hour late. You speed up and catch the theatre before it closes. You are seated before a typewriter. For hours you ceaselessly and rapidly pound the keys. You read half a dozen books. Finally, staggering but still energetic, you seize a pen, an enormous sheet of paper, and you begin "Dear Captain!"

Such is my visual impression. Of course I am wrong but there you are. I thought it might amuse you to know. And if you don't invent a shorthand typewriter, you will succeed with a perpetual motion machine.

I am getting very interested in my book. Will you type it for me? Mother and I have appreciated your goodness of heart in sending her the painstaking copies of my letters. You have shown an unusual sweetness of disposition.

You must not reproach yourself for sending mother the violets on my behalf. I have actually accepted mother's thanks for them, and had I only been more thoughtfully, it is exactly the thing I might have asked you to do for me. For Heaven's sake do things you are moved to do. I like a girl with native impulses stronger than social education — provided the impulses please me! I am inclined to trust your impulses. Thank you for doing it. But I am already bankrupt in your debt. What can I do in return? At least, if it were of value, I should like to give you my love.

I am feeling better today but I have been quite miserable and more hurt in mind than body.

Talbot

Christmas morning,
Havre, Dec. 225, 1915

My dear Lily,

I am convinced there must be a large number of letters and parcels for me somewhere but they are not here. Not a single letter, not a single present. Only one parcel from mother containing "undies" which are not meant for a present and which I do not want. I have in 32 years never experienced such a complete lack of attention from Santa Claus! Yesterday the orderlies hung up in the ward two pathetic red, blue and white paper chains but a pillow fight developed in the evening and they were destroyed. I have, in common with all the others, received a small box of chocolates from Cadbury's Ltd. I also received an invitation to church service, which I did not accept. I enjoy sometimes the combination of good music and architecture and a comfortable pew but the solemn recitation of ridiculous prayers in unnatural tones in a cold tent does not appeal to me. I am something worse than a pagan but I should have gone to the Cathedral if I had been in Amiens. That interior is enough religion for me.

And you are sending me something for Christmas. You even asked me to guess. I think of a photograph, perhaps a coloured one, or a marble bust of yourself, or knitted mittens, or a book shelf, or embroidered hankies, or rubber boots, or home-made candy! Anyway I am waiting impatiently. A big box arrived from you which I assumed was things for the men, so I have sent it on to the regiment and have instructed Charlie to attend to the distribution. I believe the regiment is now in the trenches so the things will be greatly appreciated.

Tonight eight of us arranged a Christmas dinner. We have purchased a turkey and a few other delicacies. I have a little headache but I must observe the Christmas ritual as best I can. I also have a little heart ache.

I have a confession to make. I have lost your pages of Walt Whitman. I blame the orderlies who moved my things from one ward to another. I am very apologetic and very sorry for your sake and mine. I wanted to know the poem better. The last verse particularly I wanted to commit to memory. It is a beautiful verse. I should be very happy if someone I loved ever sent me that verse. I must stop. May the New Year have much in common store for us both.

Talbot

4

Rideau Hall, Ottawa
Thursday, January 6, 1916

I have a gun. It's a service revolver, a Colt 45, very big and heavy but smooth, glossy, the colour of raw silver. We have all been given them, the staff, the footmen, the maids. We have not been told exactly why, whether it's to shoot Germans or to preserve our honour or to shoot ourselves.

The Duke has set up a shooting range in the tent room. It was originally built as a games room, or gymnasium, by some governor-general who had children, and now that the hideous red-and-white canvas has been taken down it's wonderfully bright and airy. We were all driven in there this afternoon, although we had to wear coats because there's no fireplace, and the Duke stood on a chair and showed us how to load and point the pistol, turning our bodies sideways and holding it out straight, at arm's length, as if we were in a duel. I guess he forgot he was on a chair because he suddenly cried "Ready!" and spread his legs to steady his aim, and fell off. His pistol went off and blew a hole in the skylight. Two of the maids were cut by falling glass. Now we have to wait until it's fixed.

I keep my pistol in my desk. I am very fond of it already. It cheers me up. Madame Pacquette, the cook, put hers in the flour bin. I said it wouldn't be much use there but she just shrugged and cried *"Foo! Foo! Maudeezanglais!"* and rattled the stove lids.

Patsy is painting something green and pink. It is not going well. She is poking at the canvas with her brush, scowling. I have drawn a picture of her in her smock for Talbot. He looks at me solemnly across my desk. His jaw is clenched and his eyes are full of pain. Where is he tonight? Somewhere in France? I pray not. Pray. Bloody God. Bloody war. How long do wars last? There was the Thirty Years War and the Hundred Years War. I should read *The Iliad.* That would last the winter. Willie is bound to have it, although I might not see him again for a long time. He says he is giving up social engagements until his book for the Rockefellers is finished. I saw him on the toboggan slide with Miss Chadwick yesterday. Duty? Am I jealous? I could strangle him sometimes, he's so annoying, but he does make things interesting in a funny way. You never know what he's going to do next.

"I think I ought to enlist," he said at the Duke's New Year's levee.

"Don't be an ass," I said and started to cry.

He was quite speechless. It's usually Willie who does the weeping.

Is he lonely too?

Snowing again.

R.H.
Friday, January 7, 1916

The snow is more than four feet deep in the park. It has drifted almost to the roof of the conservatory. We have our tea there every day, among the hyacinths and the banana trees, next to a pool of goldfish. Today it was like being in an igloo, snug and warm with a lovely soft sheen from the ice. Tomorrow Joe, the gardener, will have to shovel off the snow to let the sun in. The Duchess wants to close the conservatory, as an economy measure, but Joe says the water pipes will freeze and the glass will break, so she's taken her revenge by shutting down the long gallery at the back of the house, and by rationing the coal so I have to wear woolies and heavy socks to work in, even though I've pulled my desk as close as possible to the fireplace. She spends most of her time in bed, snug as a bug, smoking. Miss Yorke says she's dying but she looks exactly the same as she did when I first came here, and I wonder if her ailment isn't just opium.

Tomorrow we'll go skating again if Patsy can persuade the new aides-de-camp to shovel the rink. They landed in last week like a flock of jays, tall and fair. Their ruddy cheeks remind Patsy of Rupert Brooke, and they tumble around outside, throwing snowballs like a bunch of boys. They are unfit for service at the front. I expected them to be wounded, but Patsy says it's nothing more than a weak chest or fragile nerves and their rich mummies just don't want them getting killed. She is bitter about it since Alex Ramsay is still at sea, and the Duke as set against the marriage as ever, and when the naval ADC struts by she makes clucking noises behind his back and flaps her elbows.

Monsieur Nazaire, the skating instructor at the Minto Club, is coaching her on figures, but I'm afraid it's hopeless. She practices very hard, two or three hours a day, and I'm sure she thinks she looks graceful, but she is simply too tall and too awkward, and something that supposed to resemble a dying swan comes out looking like a dead duck. I have made a million excuses to avoid taking pictures but I don't see how I can hold out much longer. I'd rather go skating on the Canal, like everyone else, but she's not allowed. "If I mix with people," she says, "I shall have to accept invitations. If I accept, I shall have to return the courtesy. Where do I draw the line?" She can't even give her clothes to charity in case one of her cast-off dresses turns up on the back of a cleaning woman, or, worse, a woman of ill repute. They say the Russell Hotel is full of prostitutes, now that the House is about to open again.

The park in the snow reminds me of Montebello, and Talbot bundled up in his scarves and mitts in his little wooden sleigh. He doesn't mention snow in France. I'll take some pictures tomorrow to send. Maybe I'll send one of Patsy as a dead duck on condition he doesn't show it to anyone but Charlie.

The ADCs are outside, in the dark, making a snowman in the driveway. It's supposed to represent someone, but I can't make out what they're saying, they're laughing so hard.

R.H.
Saturday, January 8, 1916

More snow. Packed a Valentine box for Talbot, cigarettes mostly, and magazines, a flashlight, pencils, a thermos bottle, a leftover Christmas cake from Madame Pacquette (did she hide it?), a book of Rupert Brooke's poems from Patsy, a beautiful pair of fur-lined gloves from a woman in Quebec who read about his Military Cross, and an enormous heart-shaped box of candy I found yesterday at Page and Shaw's, seven pounds (!) and simply slathered with ribbons and lace. I was lucky I asked, because they weren't on display yet, but Mr. Page said there was a great demand for candy for overseas, the troops seemed to like it more than anything. I'm glad now we sent the maple sugar for Christmas, although it took us nearly six weeks to address the 38,000 boxes, one for each man overseas, individually packaged, but I never, ever want to see or smell maple sugar again. It seems so pathetically little when it's all packed together, and I'd feel more useful sending a box of shells, but everyone says "morale" is so important and a letter is as good as a rifle.

Sometimes I think Talbot is only writing me to amuse himself or pass the time, or to have some "purple prose" he can put into a book when he comes home, to make himself famous. He can be so self-centered, so cruel, although he says he's only teasing. I get angry, but I'd feel like a traitor to break it off. It would be easier if I didn't love him, if he didn't *demand* that I love him, then tell me I'm misguided, and he's going to die anyway. It's only true, I guess. It must be awful living there in the ground year after year, so if he wants to imagine he's in love with me, even if it's not true, then the least I can do is go along. It's not so big a sacrifice, is it?

Patsy gets two or three prosposals of marriage from the soldiers every month, strange, misspelled little notes printed in crude letters with indelible pencil, usually from a hospital, offering her eternal bliss and a simple life on a homestead when they come home. She always replies, except when we've seen the name in the casualty lists before the letter arrives. We read the casualty lists first now, then I file the names by regiment. I wonder why they always print the casualties in the classified ads or the sports pages? Do they think only men read them? Or do they think the dead soldiers will be happier there, between the horse races and the baseball scores? We don't reply to the dirty letters. There seem to be a lot of them, crazy scrawls telling Patsy what they are going to do to her, or she to them. I can usually tell them by the finger marks on the envelopes and throw them in the garbage. Some men have the most amazing imaginations.

There is not much to do. All the social events are cancelled. Mrs. Freiman has taken over the Red Cross. She was blackballed last year so she formed her own chapter. The Disraeli chapter raised more money in a month than all the other Ottawa chapters combined and sent five times as much stuff to England. Miss Yorke says it's because they're all rag pickers. Mrs. Freiman says it's because they are businesslike. She has installed thirty brand new Singers in her drawing room and every afternoon the women make dressing gowns, one on the sleeves, one on the collars, one on the seams, like a real garment factory. She got the standard pattern from the Duchess of Connaught hospital at Cliveden, and found the blue flannel in New York, very cheap because it was so ugly, and they can rattle up thirty dressing gowns on a good day, except for the High Holidays. "At the May Court," Mrs. Freiman whispered to me, "they are still stitching shirts by *hand*. By hand! Can you imagine! I ask you, is this a war or a wedding?"

The snowman looks like Sam Hughes. It is funny, with a big pot belly and fierce jaw and two coal eyes and a rusty old sword. Why do they hate him so?

R.H.
Wednesday, January 19, 1916

I am to go to the House of Commons tonight to "observe" the debate. It seems certain that the Liberals will try to bring down Sir Robert's government. They apparently "have the goods" on Sam Hughes, but nobody knows what the "goods" are. Ena McAdam is going to take notes because Sam's in England but I am to sit in a corner of the press (!) gallery. The car will take me to the Governor-General's office at 7 p.m. and a guard will see me up before the reporters arrive. I am to wear my old black dress and the cloth coat I came to Ottawa in, and look as inconspicuous as possible. It seems ridiculous because I've been in and out of the *Citizen* and *Journal* offices a hundred times and everyone knows who I am.

I expected everyone here to be very upset, since Sir Robert and Lady Borden are such good friends, but lunch was very jolly. We even had champagne! It was Ribbentrop's brand, I'm sure, and it gave me a pang of nostalgia. Where are you now, Joachim? Dead, I hope.

R.H.

Thursday, January 20, 1916

I had a very good seat, right at the end of the gallery, which is very small and crowded but gives a good view of the whole chamber. In fact the whole place is disappointingly small, and cramped and dirty, and there are spitoons everywhere for the Members to spit into! It was stifling hot and very crowded and almost impossible to hear because of the echo and the noise the Members make pounding their desks and screaming. I was shocked. I had no idea Parliament was anything like this! It was worse than the Renfrew Hotel on a Saturday night. Sometimes the yelling and banging went on for minutes at a time, with the Speaker yelling and banging back to make them stop, and no one paying the slightest attention.

Mr. Pugsley, of the Liberals, made a long speech accusing Sam Hughes of profiteering on shell contracts, although he didn't seem to have any proof, except that a Colonel Allison had been overheard in a New York club bragging about the profit he'd made thanks to Sam. The Liberals kept shouting "Resign! Resign!" even though Sam wasn't there, and the Tories screamed "Slander! Lies!" until they all got tired out. Ena was sitting in the Conservative gallery, right over Mr. Pugsley's head, and she stood up at one point, and I thought she was going to hurl herself down on him, but she sat down again. She says if Sam has made a single dishonest penny she'd like to know where it is, because he lives in an awful fleabag of a room, he doesn't smoke or drink, he wears the same uniform from one month's end to the next, and she sends his entire paycheque home to his wife. "Why do people think war is a holy crusade?" she asked me afterwards. "Sure, it's full of graft and bribery and favouritism, but so's everything, and if the job gets done, and we win, what's the harm? Why should we be noble and pure when it comes to killing Krauts?"

Miss E. Cora Hind of the *Free Press* was behind me in the gallery. She didn't recognize me at first.

"You look so remarkably much cleaner," she said.

"Aren't you an agricultural reporter?" I asked.

"I am," she grinned, nodding at the chamber. "Oink, oink."

She very kindly took me to the telegraph office so I could write down Mr. Pugsley's speech in longhand while she read it to the operator, and then we went up to her room for tea. It was a cold cheap room (the *Free Press* is stingy) but she had her frying pan and made us some bannock on the hot plate. She has really come for a suffrage meeting, and did the speech as a favour, because of the crisis.

"When we get a few women into that barnyard, they'll clean things up," she said. "Men are such shits."

It was a good thing I had the speech written out because the Duke was waiting up and I would have had to yell in his ear for an hour. He drives everyone crazy.

R.H.
Friday, January 21, 1916

Went with Miss Hind to the suffrage meeting. A very small group, from across the country, older women, all tremendously stout and homely except for Nellie McClung, who's stout but pretty. Mrs. McClung explained how the war has brought women out of the kitchen and the nursery into the factories and the sewing rooms and the hospitals, how we have built great enterprises like the Red Cross, and how we have already shown the men that we can organize, and raise money, and keep accounts, and make speeches, and open our own doors, and there is no reason at all why we should go back to pouring tea and baking dainties. And not only have women done all this on their own, they have given birth to those boys fighting in Flanders' fields, and nursed them, and dried their tears and blown their noses and raised them to be strong, honest men and sent them away, with breaking hearts, to die for Canada, and if, by the end of the war, the love and courage and sacrifice of Canadian women is not recognized, if we are not given the equality before the law that is our right, then we must rise and occupy the Houses of Parliament, the legislatures and the city halls and remain there until justice is achieved.

It was tremendously inspiring. Mrs. McClung is so good-humoured, so full of enthusiasm, so *confident*, she makes it all seem like fun. I came away feeling quite elated. Can it be that the war is a good thing after all?

R.H.
Saturday, January 22, 1916

Sam Hughes is returning from England this week to face a parliamentary inquiry into the shell contracts. Ena says Sam was always too busy to be bothered with office routine so he left her in charge of the patronage. "Just check the list," he said. There was a white list (Tory) and a black list (Grit). It was simple, Ena says, since most of the applications for contracts came with a note attached from Sir Robert Borden, or R.B. Bennett or another cabinet minister, and she would just make it formal, like giving the bacon contract to Canada Packers, and the longjohns to the Stanfields.

"Sam is innocent. He doesn't even *know* about most of the contracts. He was never there. We couldn't afford to wait weeks until he returned from England, or wherever he was, so I did a terrible thing, Lily. I forged his name!"

R.H.
Sunday, January 23, 1916

Went to church. Knelt at the back. Bishop Ralph prayed for peace. "It's a good thing I left the Methodists twenty years ago," he said, "or those warmongers would hound me out for sure now." His windows have been broken and the sign on the front of the church defaced with dirty words. He is the only minister of the Gospel in Ottawa to preach against the war. He looks much whiter, thinner. I can't imagine ever being afraid of him.

Church was full. Walked home. Very cold. The ADCs were trying out their new skates. I promised that Jack would teach them hockey when the Canadiens are back in town. I offered to show them myself, but they found that so frightfully amusing they all fell down and "Bunny," the naval attache, cut his leg and bled all over the ice so Joe will have to scrape it off and flood the rink again. Bunny is now on crutches, poor lamb.

R.H.
Monday, January 24, 1916

Sir Robert was here today. The Duke demanded his resignation. He refused. There is talk of bringing in some Liberals and forming a National government, on the theory, apparently, that once the Grits get their hands in the pie they'll stop making trouble. It seems to me that once you let the Grits in, you'll never get them out.

R.H.
Friday, February 4, 1916
3 a.m.

The Parliament Buildings have burned down! It was the most spectacular fire! The water froze almost as soon as it came out of the hoses and a great lacy sheet of ice formed over the outside of the building but the heat was so intense inside that the windows glowed orange like a jack o'lantern. The stone walls are still standing but the inside is completely destroyed.

I was at the Russell Theatre with Willie, watching Madame Edwina, a

dreadful Frenchwoman who sings to a cat, and the sound of the first fire
engine clanging past was a welcome diversion. Fortunately we had seats on
the aisle so we were able to slip out quietly after the third engine passed,
although the whole theatre had emptied, I am told, before 9 p.m. There
wasn't a great deal to see when we got there except clouds of thick, black
smoke. Sir Robert and several MPs were standing around outside in their
shirtsleeves. Mr. Burrell, the Minister of Agriculture, had the hair all burned
off his face and head. Some had escaped with bits of furniture and typewriters
and there was an enormous portrait of Queen Victoria propped up in the
snow. It was very dark, and trying to snow, and with the steam from the hoses
it was impossible to tell if everyone had escaped. Ena came running up saying
"There was a man in the office! There was a man in the office!" and I thought
she meant that someone was trapped, but she said no, he got away. Sam
Hughes came galloping up on a horse and pushed us all back behind the iron
railing because the glass was beginning to explode out of the windows. Ena
tried to tell Sam about the man in the office but he couldn't hear over the
noise, being up on a horse, and shouting so much himself, so Willie took us
across the street to the Rideau Club, which doesn't let ladies in normally, but
made an exception because of the emergency, and we watched from the
windows.

Everyone gathered around Ena, who had actually been *in* the building
when the fire started and had actually met a strange man sitting at Sam's desk
going through his drawers.

"I am the *only* person with a key to the inner office," she said, "and I have
the lock changed regularly, but when I let myself in, just after eight-thirty,
there he was, just as cool as you please, with the file drawers open and papers
all over the desk. 'Who are you?' I said. 'Who are *you*?' he said. Well I told him
who I was and I was going to report him to the guard that very instant, and he
said 'You better not do that if you value your life,' and then I heard shouting in
the hall, and Sir Robert came running in, crying 'Fire! Fire!' and we all ran
out, not even shutting the door, but by the time I got outside, the stranger had
disappeared."

Ena kept insisting that the stranger did not have a German accent, and that
his clothes were English in cut, a houndstooth check coat and a cap, but that
was taken as evidence that we were up against a diabolical German spy, and
several men rushed off to guard the waterworks and other public buildings
against a mass attack and we all peered anxiously in the direction of the
Chateau and the Union Station, expecting at any moment to see them go up in
sheets of flame.

Ena was on her third brandy and describing the spy to Charlie Bowman of
the *Citizen* when she suddenly pointed at a man in formal dress who'd just
come in and whispered "That's him! That's *him*!" He was a tall, lanky young

man, with thinning pale hair and a long pale face. He had a toothpick in the corner of his mouth and there was something about the way he languidly picked his teeth that seemed familiar to me.

He took the whole thing as an enormous joke.

"A houndstooth coat?" he drawled. "How perfectly grotesque. I ask you, have any of you ever seen me in a houndstooth coat and a *cap?*" There was a lot of laughter at this, and back-slapping, as if that was the craziest idea in the world, and then the man reached into his pocket and produced two ticket stubs which he held high in the air. "Why," he said, "I have just seen a delightful companion home from Madame Edwina's concert."

Ena looked very red, and crestfallen, and said the brandy was making her dizzy, and she couldn't remember *exactly*, it had been quite dark, and she was sorry if she had embarrassed anyone.

"Who *is* that?" I asked Willie.

"Oh, that's Constable Dempster, of the Dominion police," he laughed.

We watched the flames creep from the second story to the third, then up the clock tower, the clock still chiming the hours, until it caved in at last just after 12:30 a.m. The flames started to die down then, and nothing else exploded, so we took Ena home.

Ena was giddy, and we thought it was shock, or the brandy, but she grabbed my arm at the door of her rooming house. "Isn't it true that I can't be convicted of a *crime*," she whispered, "if there's no *evidence?*"

"Jesus," I said. "You didn't do it, did you?"

"No," giggled Ena. "It was an acc...acc...act of, an acc...accident!"

Willie thinks the fire was an Act of God, a sort of miniature Armageddon sent to purify the political life of the nation, to cleanse the ground for his return to politics, whenever he finishes the book he's writing about the Rockefellers.

"Sabotage?" Arthur bellowed when I shouted the news in his ear. "Damned right it's sabotage! Just what this country needs. A damned fine kick in the ass. Didn't think Sir Robert had the guts."

6 a.m.
Can't sleep. I keep thinking about Captain Dempster. What was he doing in there? What can we do?

10 p.m.
A lovely, clear, cold morning. Took the streetcar. Wellington St. was blocked off by the police so I went down Elgin and walked across Sparks to Metcalfe, hoping to get a good shot up the street. Oh, a dazzling lake of ice, a sea of light! And, perfectly framed by the wrought iron gate, the ruined building glittered

like a huge wedding cake, half-eaten, the icing all melted and runny, the
library perched at the back like a chocolate cupcake, sooty but safe. The whole
mass was still smoking, glowing orange in the rising sun, even the trees were
hung with icicles, bent low, like Willie's mother washing her hair, and small,
black policemen stood in rows, disappointed bridegrooms slapping their
chests with their arms to keep warm.

A crowd of children was gathering at the corner where the Speaker's
apartments had been, hoping no doubt to see the charred remains of Madame
Morin and Madame Bray, who had gone back for their fur coats. Sam Hughes
charged at them and chased them off. He looked cold and very tired. There
were still three men missing, he said, one of then an MP who had an office on
the third floor. It was obviously the work of the Huns, he said. I told him
about Captain Dempster but he just said, "never heard of the bugger," and
rode off.

I took dozens of pictures. The light was perfect and the icy trees formed
natural frames. I was walking around the back to get some photographs of the
library, when I ran into Willie. He was bent over, tugging at some chunks of
carved stone that looked like they had once been a window arch.

"Guard these!" he puffed when he saw me. "I'll go for the dray!"

So I stood there feeling like a fool in the middle of mountains of blackened
stone. Quite a few people were poking through the rubble, MPs mostly, from
what I could tell, although what they could expect to find I don't know. I
didn't see anybody carting off stones. A gargoyle stared up at me out of the
snow, its neck broken. It had a mischievous grin on its black, monkey face.

"That's D'Arcy McGee," Willie said when he came back with two men and
a wagon from Shenkman's Junk Yard. "All the Fathers of Confederation had
their portraits carved on the buttresses."

I certainly couldn't leave D'Arcy McGee alone in the snow, so I had the
drayman load him in too, alongside the better part of two windows and a
doorway. Willie and I got up beside the driver.

"Where are we going?"

"Kingsmere! I am planning a modest ruin there, something to give a
religious atmosphere, a small shrine for quiet meditation. Think of it, a piece
of real history on my own grounds! The stones of British parliamentary
democracy framing the unspoiled beauty of the Canadian woodland!"

"Shouldn't you pay for them?"

"Pay? But they're ruins!"

I got off.

Printed up my photos this afternoon and took them to the *Citizen*. They
bought ten at $2 apiece. Not much money, but they're the first pictures I've
sold to a newspaper.

Sir Robert has announced the fire started under some newspapers in the

Commons reading room. Someone had probably left a cigarette butt in an ashtray. The flames were out of control before the guards could reach the fire extinguishers. It sounds reasonable. Nobody believes him.

It still seems like theft to me.

R.H.
Saturday, February 5, 1916

My beautiful pictures came out dark and blurred, and the *Citizen* left my name off the bottom.

Madame Edwina and her accompanist were arrested this morning crossing the border at Niagara Falls. (He was "uncovered" hiding in her berth. O scandal!) It appears he is an Austrian travelling on a Belgian passport. The *Citizen* says it is forged. All the foreigners in Ottawa are being rounded up and the trains searched. We have received dozens of telephone calls about suspicious strangers and explosions and overheard conversations. I tell them to telephone the police, but they say the lines are busy, so I have to take the information down, and their names, and addresses. It is difficult, being polite.

The House of Commons is going to sit in the Invertebrate Fossil Room at the Victoria Museum. I laughed when Ena told me but she didn't think it very funny. Of course she and Sam Hughes have a "thing" going, Alice says. Alice had taken some letters over to Sam's office one afternoon last fall, and forgotten her coat, and when she'd gone back for it that evening, "there they were, on Sam's couch, stark staring, Sam with his boots on and his breeches down, his rump as white as his hair, going at it furiously *on top of my coat!*" She never mentioned it and neither did they.

There wasn't a word in the *Citizen* about Ena or about the man in the houndstooth coat.

R.H.
Sunday, February 6, 1916

Took some of my pictures over to Mr. Booth, thinking he'd be downhearted, he was so proud of that building. He took me on a tour on my very first day in Ottawa, board by board, every railing, every panel, every desk and chair and carving, oak in the Commons, walnut in the Senate, pine in the Library, telling me where each tree had come from, and the names of the men who had brought it down the river, all prime timber he had selected himself, matching every board for colour and grain, standing over the carpenters for eight years while they sanded and whittled and polished until the rough boards glowed as soft and smooth as satin.

"'E's out," said Old Martha at the door. "'E's measurin'."

"Measuring?"

"Up the Hill."

"Measuring a hill?"

"No, no! Measurin' the buildin'. The lattytude and the longytude. The horizontal and the perpendicular!"

"What building?"

"The *parlymint* building."

"But it's burned down!"

Old Martha rolled her eyes and flapped her apron with exasperation.

"The *new* parlymint buildin'. 'E says it's gonna be *twice* as big an' *twice* as grand!"

I brought my photographs home again.

France, Feb. 7, 1916

My dear Lily,

I am alone in a big old farm house, generations old. There are a couple of pewter plates and some large china plates with a flaming pattern of red roses that I should like to have. Otherwise the ornamentation consists of cheap religious prints and very ugly statues of the Virgin Mary. Marching we pass innumerable shrines generally with the device "*Sacre coeur de Jesus aye pitie de nous.*" The house is full of children, home ones and refugees. I have met them everywhere and everywhere they are taken in and become like members of the family.

We arrived late last evening after an exhausting march. I was utterly played out. I feared for a while I was going to have a breakdown. I could eat nothing. I couldn't move and the tears were trickling helplessly down my checks. Then I was too tired to sleep. I am so depressed about myself. I have always prided myself on my endurance. I liked marching for the sense of power it gave me. I now can only manage it after painful persistence. However, my strength will soon return. I stayed in my sleeping bag until after eleven this morning and I shall get back in early after dinner.

Your letter of December 29 came the day before yesterday. It started off so nicely but ended rather alarmingly. I wonder what letter you received in the meantime to cause the change. I am an idiot. I am really not worth knowing, Lily, I promise you. However, it is so pleasant hearing from you that I shall continue to write. It appeals to my sense of romance. Really I have progressed so far that I like the things you have given me not so much for themselves, as because you have sent them. This little pen I truly cherish. I am actually wearing the leather jacket, for there is no heat in the room, and in my pocket is the little silver shoe for luck. At my elbow I have your Christmas card with the picture of Bobs. It was a kindly thought and I am more touched by it than any other thing. The gloves are perfect beauties but too fine for the trenches, so I will keep them in my valise until my staff appointment. Whether I shall get it or not is still a question. I don't want it any longer. Part of my changed character is that I care not at all whether I survive this winter or even the coming tour of the trenches. I am too tired to care. I don't tell anyone this but yourself, because by the time this reaches you I shall be quite strong again and I should not wish people here to think I wasn't.

I am sending you a couple of handkerchiefs. I bought them in a house at Neuve Eglise, a house that boasted the only unbroken pane of glass. You can find Neuve Eglise on the map. There is nothing "neuve" about it. Only a few houses remain and they are battered and torn. The battle line is only a short distance away yet these lace makers are there still making the lace. The handkerchiefs were made on the spot. The old woman takes refuge in the cellar when the shells come over and isn't a bit frightened.

I am not in very good shape but can carry on. Perhaps I shall hear from you soon. I hope so.

Talbot

Trenches, Feb. 19, 1916

My dear Lily,

I am feeling awfully depressed at this moment so I thought I should write you a letter. You are a very sympathetic person, though I daresay your sweet sympathy will arrive too late. Last night young Parlett was killed. He was one of the patrol that I had personally taken out and placed a couple of nights before and he was shot through the head just above the right eye while patrolling in the place I had selected. I have a sense of responsibility for his death. Then little Cpl. Millen, a fine young boy, has just been killed, shot through the head. I enclose a little sketch of trees I made this morning just before he was killed behind the tree in the left top corner of the page. I cannot grow accustomed to these losses. It is horrible, this killing in cold calculated blood, this deliberate lying in wait, as though we were hunting animals, which itself is bad enough, Heaven knows.

I finally found the courage to tell Charlie I was leaving for the staff. He was decent about it but I think feels it very much, and makes me feel badly. Several of the men have spoken to me about it. They all say I should go but they will miss me. I hate like poison to leave them and live in comfort and safety while they go on here without me. Of course there may be a hitch in the appointment. I have just received such a pathetic letter from mother. She is almost overcome with happiness and pride and said her fingers were shaking so with joy she dropped her pen several times while writing. She has an enormously exaggerated idea about me, I'm afraid.

We shall be relieved in a couple of hours. I should hate to be hit now. I wonder what you would think if you could look in here at this moment. I am pretty muddy but I have shaved! I am planning my beautiful new uniforms when I am summoned to the General. Good night, my dear Lily.

Talbot.

P.S. Your letters are not censored and no one sees them at all. I am obliged to destroy them after reading.

France, Feb. 24, 1916

My dear Lily,

Here I am an A.D.C. to General Alderson and, as far as I can make out, a combination between a fashion plate and an orderly! I was summoned yesterday and since then you can imagine me dining with nothing less than Generals! We are in an enormous house and the translation between the two conditions is positively stunning. We have napkins at all meals and I am so unaccustomed that mine slips continually to the floor. Also I shall have my own horses and cars at my disposal. Tomorrow a car comes for me and I drive to Boulogne, catch a special boat and then to London for ten days. And yet I am not happy. Yesterday I cried like a baby when it came time to say goodbye. All the N.C.O.s in my company paraded to say goodbye and I couldn't say a word. I felt like the devil! Now I would return if I could, but I cannot give this position up until I have made good at it. Then back I shall go to the good old crowd with a light heart. But my heart will be broken if any are lost in the meantime. I had no idea I was so bound by ties of affection to the Regiment until it came time to leave. Poor old wicked Charlie. I miss him dreadfully.

I want to let you know my new address:

General Headquarters Staff

Canadian Corps, C.E.F.

I hope you will have received the lace handkerchiefs from Neuve Eglise. I do hope you have written to me recently.

Talbot

General Headquarters Staff
Canadian Army Corps
March 7, 1916

My dear Lily,

May I call you darling? Surely, if I am your Valentine, I may be permitted at least once this very natural outburst, for this morning I received your beautiful box of cigarettes so beautifully wrapped and so extensive as to ensure me "smokes" for a long time to come. Together with the heart-shaped box of candy they ornament a large chest in the corner of my "sitter." How can I sufficiently thank you and how can I ever hope to be a deserving Valentine? You do love to do things on a regal scale, don't you? I have already read three of the magazines and they are now in our stately mess room for general consumption by generals.

My new clothes are quite a success. They ought to be, as I went to the tailor for the Guards and the King. I have not dared to ask for my bill. So far a lazy, idle life. I simply eat and talk a very little in awed whispers and walk in stately fashion. No more weary marches and glorious rests, no more exciting escapes. I wonder how long I can stand it. I am not built for this sort of thing.

I am very glad you said in your last letter that our correspondence was now on a different footing and no longer merely for the entertainment of a "lonely soldier." I am glad you agree we are to become interested in each other as definite personalities. I am proud of your work and your success and I want to remain connected no matter what may change in my own life, place or *affaires de coeur* or anything.

Tonight as I walk through the black streets I carry your electric lantern and wherever I turn I have evidence of your too generous friendship. You will have become a habit. I shall not be able to think in any other terms than you presently. I am thankful for the kind fate which made us known. Whatever the ultimate end, the in-between time has been most pleasant and helpful. I love the little touches of feeling you sometimes manifest. Truly they go straight to my heart and then it is that I wish to call you a darling or some other term of endearment. Remember I am soon to send you another photo of myself and shall wish an exchange. I must go now to my dinner, so farewell, my dear Lily.

Yours devotedly, Talbot.

R.H.
Thursday, March 9, 1916

Jack came this afternoon to give his hockey lesson. He was a big hit. The ADCs were taken with his gold teeth. None of them had met a real prospector before. They kept calling him a "sourdough." They seem to think Kirkland Lake is in the Klondike. Jack strung them the most awful yarns, how he and Harry ate off solid silver plates they found lying among the rocks, and how they'd been in the very saloon when Dangerous Dan McGrew was shot and had put the body outside to freeze, and it had frozen so hard they could break the arms and legs off just like twigs, and make a neat parcel out of him, so he could be shipped out south in a suitcase because there was no wood in the north to make a coffin, and how they'd gone fishing one day, and been blown out to sea, and drifted for three days and nights before reaching shore and only realized when they saw little yellow men in fur hats running along the beach that they were in Siberia.

He sold them a lot of shares in his mine for $1 each, even though he'll give them to anyone else for 25 cents. He also took nearly $500 off them at poker. Bunny says Jack is the first "authentic" Canadian he's met. He asked me if Jack were a "Red Indian." I said I didn't think so. He seemed very disappointed.

Constable Dempster and two friends made up the rest of the team. I watched from the window.

Got two bullseyes on the target range today, shooting from the hip, cowboy-style. It's enormous fun.

R.H.
Friday, March 10, 1916

Patsy is painting my portrait for the next Red Cross bazaar, although nobody will recognize me with an eye in my forehead and my nose in my ear. I asked her what happened to Pre-Raphaelite and the bullrushes, which I sort of liked, but she says that's passé now, and cubism is the thing. It is to be called "Young Widow." I wear my old black dress and the hankies from Neuve Eglise at my throat and pull a long face. I hate black. It's all the fashion now, although there's black and black, the rusty black worn by the poor women who come to the back door looking for work and Patsy's black velvet with the Russian sable trim around the cuffs and skirt. You can't tell the real widows any more except that nobody talks to them. You'd think they were witches or lepers. Bad luck. You don't notice at first. They simply disappear. Then somebody says, "where's Mrs. So and So?" and somebody else whispers, "lost her husband," as if it were a terrible scandal, and nobody asks after her again until six or eight weeks later she reappears, the same as if she'd had a baby, only sallow and silent, all in black, like a puff of smoke. I wonder if the other women wear black out of sympathy or jealousy.

R.H.
Sunday, March 12, 1916

The first trainload of wounded came in this morning. We met them at Union Station, along with the May Court and the Red Cross, a great crush of women in new spring hats and galoshes. The wounded looked thin and lost, but they seemed cheerful and smiled all the time, like broken dolls. Patsy gave out daffodils and cigarettes. Several Pats were there. One of them was George Bennett, Dickie's younger brother. I hardly knew him, he looked so old and dirty. He seemed quite drunk although it was only ten o'clock. He lurched up to me as we were leaving, the pockets of his shabby greatcoat clanking suspiciously. He'd expected Dick at the station, he belched. Needed a few dollars to tide him over. He held out his hand. The index finger was missing. He noticed me hesitate.

"Don' worry," he said, reaching into a pocket. "Got it right here."

He pulled out a glass jar. One pickled finger.

"Picked it off the window ledge, when they blew up H.Q.," he said proudly. "My counting finger."

I gave him a five-dollar bill and tried to point him towards the rotunda where the men were lining up to parade through the square. I could hear the pipers tuning up inside. The platform was almost deserted. As I turned to go, a line of ambulances drew up at the far end of the platform and the steps of the last coaches were lowered. I noticed that the blinds were drawn. I had assumed they were empty.

"Jesus," I said. "We've missed some!"

"You don' wanna see them," said George, pulling my arm. "An' they don' wan' ya to."

Several large wicker baskets were carried gingerly down the steps. Each basket contained a large, squarish, khaki object. I would have taken it for a pack sack or dunnage bag except each bag had a human head, with a cap on it, and a human face, with eyes that moved and a lighted cigarette in its mouth.

"The basket cases ain't as scary as the nut cases," George said with a hard, dry laugh.

I turned away quickly.

"It would be a kindness to shoot them," George said.

I ran all the way through the station and got to the reviewing stand just as the parade started. It was cold and slushy underfoot and I worried that the men on crutches would have trouble, but the pipers took it slow and the men swung along with amazing skill, an army of grasshoppers. People cheered and clapped but some were silent, and I noticed that a lot looked down, or turned away, ashamed, as I had done. I was watching a grizzled old kiltie, straight as a rod, head up, eyes front, swinging up the street on a leg and a crutch, a grin on his face and his chest bright with ribbons, when there was a flashing arc through the air and the clink of a silver coin at his feet, and a shout "jolly good show! God bless you!" from the sidewalk, a tall, ruddy man in a black overcoat, smiling, arm raised in salute. The kiltie stood there, stock still, while the parade went past him, tears streaming down his face, then he raised his crutch and threw it towards the man and fell, and lay there, screaming curses, until two soldiers rushed back and led him away, still crying and cursing. I put my camera away and came home.

R.H.

Monday, March 13, 1916

Alice and I put George Bennett on the train for Calgary today, but not before he'd shown his finger to Sir Robert and Sir Wilfrid and every living soul in Ottawa. Dick refuses to speak to him. He'd told everyone that George was suffering from trench foot. Alice says that trench foot is just a face-saving word for cowardice or drunkenness or stupidity and that George actually cut his finger off himself to get out of the army. Dick is paying him $50 a month to stay away from Ottawa.

Major Hamilton Gault has sued Marguerite for divorce. The case goes to the Senate tomorrow. Alice says that Gault has accused her of "openly fornicating" with wounded men in the same military hospital where he was recuperating from an amputated leg.

"You mean he had to watch?"

"Worse," Alice whispered. "It wasn't *real* sex."

"Real sex?"

"She used her *mouth*."

Alice blushed beet red. I had a vivid mental picture of a long, dark hospital ward with rows and rows of narrow white beds and a small, solitary figure in a white cap making her way from bed to bed, carrying a lamp. Could *that* have been the secret of the Nightingale legend?

"It's not *funny*," said Alice. "It's the Red Cross!"

"The Red Cross sucks! The Red Cross sucks cock!"

"I don't believe it," Patsy said when I broke the news leaving out the details.

"Perhaps she was simply trying to bring succor to the suff...."

"It's not *funny*," Patsy said severely. "Think of the regiment!"

"I am!"

Part III

WILLIE

1

Easter, 1916

"W.L. McK.K. loves C.C."
  "Rex loves Cookie."
  "W.L.McK. King and his wife, Lily."
  "Mr. and Mrs. W.L. McK. King."
  "William Lyon Mackenzie King and Mrs. King."
  "Prime Minister W.L. Mackenzie King, K.C.M.G. and his charming wife."
  "Sir William L.McK. King and Lady King."
  "~~Lord and Lady Kingsmere~~" (No! Never!)
  "The Kings."
  "The King."
  "God Save ~~the~~ King."
Willie King puts down his pencil, rests his aching head on the desk and cries.

He is on a station platform. He is carrying a large, heavy hamper of food. Cookie is there. He can't see her. The train is full of soldiers. He and Mother are going to Kingsmere for a picnic. Mother is leaning from one of the windows, waving. He begins to run as the train starts to move but the hamper is too heavy. He cries out as he runs but no one hears. The train goes faster and faster. The soldiers all laugh and point. He looks down and realizes he is wearing only his undershorts. Now the train is just a small speck in the distance. The platform is dark and deserted. He is alone.

He wakes up in a cold sweat. He has this dream quite often. It fills him with utter mortification and despair, a feeling of desolating loss that leaves him frightened for days afterwards. Why, nobody could be more meticulous about his personal modesty! Even in the warmest weather, he never goes for a walk without a collar and tie and proper jacket, and while he doesn't spend a great deal on clothes, he takes great pains to wear the appropriate thing for the occasion. It is true that his suits have become very tight, like the skin on a sausage, and last week a button popped off his vest into his soup at the Rideau Club, and he made a little note to give up hot chocolate and sweets and to take more exercise. Dempster has recommended horseback riding. Willie dislikes horses, but Jimmy Dempster has assured him he has an ideal build for an equestrian, and talks of putting together a polo team in the summer, and has offered to give him some tips, to get him started.

Willie has become quite fond of Jimmy. He was surprised at first that the man was friendly. So many of his old friends, the jingos particularly, snub him now, because of the Rockefeller work, even though they all have safe jobs in Ottawa, that he has become accustomed to avoiding the "brass hat" crowd at the Rideau Club, and would have given up going altogether except for loneliness and the need to remind Sir Wilfrid constantly of his continued existence. Of course Jimmy was only a policeman, but he moved in those fast, hard-drinking circles that made Willie so uncomfortable. Oh, Willie had been something of a rake at college, leading the Hallowe'en pranks, but he'd never had a head for liquor, or a talent for games, and once he'd begun doing well at scholastic work, he'd been shunned as a swat. Even his nickname, Rex, had been bestowed by the *Varsity* newspaper as a jibe at a pompous speech he'd made, but he'd taken it in good form. At least everyone knew who he was, and it sounded a good deal more masculine than Willie.

Willie knew he was thought a prig because he didn't smoke or drink or swear or gamble or tell dirty stories. He found the company of most men boring, so, rather than seem a snob, he avoided them. He preferred the company of women, not only because they were attractive and amusing, but because women read books and talked about Philosophy and listened. Men never listened. He had been startled then, and grateful, when Dempster had shown a genuine interest in his book, which he had tentatively entitled *Industry and Humanity*, and had shown moreover a true appreciation of the philosophical aspects of industrial relations. Why, Willie hadn't had such a sympathetic and understanding companion since poor old Bert had died. He found it a great joy, in the course of their walks along the Rideau Canal, to confide in Jimmy Dempster his hopes for the future and his worries about the present.

"How does one get married?" he blurted one warm March evening when the melting snow was running in the gutters.

"How?" said Dempster. "Well, you just do it!"

"What if it's a mistake?"

"Hell, they're *all* mistakes!"

That wasn't much help. Willie asked Junior Rockefeller how he'd nabbed Abby.

"Oh, m-m-mother did it!" said Junior. "I couldn't make up my mind, and things were dragging on, so m-m-mother arranged it. I didn't have to s-s-say anything at all!"

"Mother, I have met a young lady here, you'll remember, Kingsmere, the summer before...yes, she is much younger...I have become very attached to...No, no! I haven't proposed, I haven't proposed yet, that's why I'm telephoning, to ask...she is *not* a stenographer, more of a compan — no, she is not German, I know how you feel about the...I am not rushing into it, Mother, we have known each other for.... Mother, I am not ungrateful! I know my first responsibility is to you and Father, but a wife would *help*...Yes, I know it's a difficult time but I simply can't...well, I need someone to take care of the social end of things, the letters.... Yes, I know you'd do a splendid job but your strength...Mother, you are the dearest, sweetest, most beautiful of women, no one can even hold a...I couldn't possibly love anyone more than you....Please don't...I'm sorry...please don't cry...no, no, I won't...I love you, dear, I love you."

He had been thoughtless and cruel to upset Mother. It was not a time to be thinking of his own happiness. Mother had been perfectly right. Why that very night, March 17, Princess Patricia's birthday, the night he had planned to propose, Lily had been wearing a green dress that clung in a most suggestive way and rippled when she danced, and a saying of Mother's had suddenly popped into his mind, "A snake lurks in the grass," and he'd excused himself early, pleading a cold, and come home without saying anything. It had been a narrow escape.

He did have a cold. He'd had it all winter, and terrible headaches. Sometimes he couldn't focus his eyes properly and would have to put his book down, and a panic would seize him that he was going blind, like his father. He found it almost impossible to concentrate on his work. He would waste hours staring out the window, or lying in bed, day-dreaming, indulging in the most shameful and obscene fantasies, or weeping, for no particular reason, for hours on end.

He had the "Mackenzie sensitivity," Mother always said, and she'd told him how Grandfather used to stay awake for four days and nights, feverishly writing, pouring pitchers of cold water over his head to soothe his brain, and how he put glass insulators on the four posters of his bed to help store his nervous energy, and always slept in a cold room, with the windows open. When Grandfather was still quite young, his hair had fallen out after a "brain storm" and never grown back, so he wore a red wig. Willie wondered if Grandfather too had had nightmares, hallucinations almost, that haunted his waking hours, "visions" so real he thought at times they had actually happened, and whether the Rebellion itself wasn't just a dream put into action.

Willie dreams of rape. The "visions" are always the same, although the identity of the girl changes, strangers always, girls he has passed on the street, young, virgin, schoolgirls preferably, with black stockings and bows in their hair. The rapes are leisurely, inventive and bloody. Sometimes he strangles them. Sometimes he uses a knife. When the vision ends he cries with shame and fear.

He haunts the mirror, looking for the fangs, the hairy hands that signify Mr. Hyde, but a round, bland Jekyll face peers back at him. He is losing his hair. His gums bleed and his teeth ache. His skin is sallow. He is going blind. He is going mad.

He knows exactly what's wrong with him, but the knowledge only adds to his inexpressible agony.

"Oh, Mother, it's either marriage or masturbation!"

Cultivating the confidence of William Lyon Mackenzie King is the second most distasteful of James Dempster's assignments. Courting Miss Dorothy Yorke is the worst. At least he doesn't have to kiss Mr. King, yet, and he is resolved to quit before it comes to that. He has *some* standards. Duplicity comes naturally to James Dempster, in fact he quite relishes the tissue of deceit he is able to weave around himself (he had all Ottawa searching for a mysterious foreigner in a check coat), but when he'd accepted a position in the Intelligence department of the Dominion police, he had not counted on being bored to death.

His official duty is to hunt for Huns. His friendship with Mr. King is an unofficial duty. King had come under suspicion after the shell scandal leaked in New York: King made frequent visits to New York, he had been born in Berlin, Ontario, had many German friends, had lived for a year in Germany, had been engaged at one time to a German girl in Chicago and, while he was active in the Patriotic Fund, refused to enlist or to speak at recruiting meetings. Sir Robert Borden hoped, originally, to expose him as a German sympathizer, even a subversive (he had been witnessed hanging around the Parliament buildings the morning after the fire), but Jimmy had been unable to pin him down on the leak, and had failed to extract anything but the most violent dislike of Kaiserism.

His evenings of exquisite tedium (God, if only he could drink!) had not, however, been unproductive. Mr. King had revealed himself to be a Socialist (he'd called Rosa Luxembourg a saint!), a dangerous radical dedicated to the overthrow of the British Empire. (The war, he said, was "clearing the ground" for a popular revolution, which he would lead!) He was writing, he said, a book which would be even more influential than Marx's *Capital*. Jimmy Dempster had nearly passed out. He'd always thought Socialists were Jews, dirty immigrants who worked in filthy sweatshops and smelled of garlic and didn't speak English.

His chief, Sir Percy Sherwood (knighted after the fire), had been delighted with his reports, although Miss Yorke had turned out to be a more immediately useful assignment. During one of his hockey games on the Rideau Hall rink, Jimmy Dempster had noticed smoke coming from a chimney in a wing of the building which had supposedly been closed off. He looked closely at the windows. The curtains were open but he could see no signs of life. On his next vitis, the curtains on the main floor were closed. He returned that night. The curtains were still drawn but a narrow shaft of light showed at one window.

He discovered, after picking the lock on the inside door, a secret telegraph room with two keys, filing cabinets and tables covered with messages. The cables were in code, but the ADCs had been kind enough to leave several translated transcripts around, neatly pinned to the originals. The cable traffic was with London, the War Office and the King, and from what he could tell with the aid of his flashlight, it contained detailed information about the Allied spring campaign in France. There was also a message from the Duke of Connaught to Lord Kitchener stating that Sam Hughes should be court-martialled and shot. The message was dated March 1, 1916. Ten days old. It must have been sent. He slipped it into his pocket along with a transcribed coded message, dated February 10, 1916, from the War Office. Jimmy Dempster had found an unexpected ally in his determination to destroy Sam Hughes.

Sam (Sir Sam now, after the fire) took a lot of killing. He had more enemies than the Kaiser and more lives than a cat. He had emerged from the shell scandal, in his own words, "pure as the driven snow," without taint or blemish, although Col. Allison had been found guilty of a $100,000 bribe. The fire in the Parliament buildings had unexpectedly unleashed a great torrent of patriotism. Recruiting offices were full, Sam was promising twenty-one divisions, Max Aitken's press propaganda turned defeat into victory, cowardice into courage, censorship surpressed scandal, criticism was treason. Sir Sam (ye gods, it would be Lord Valcartier next) was riding the war, and the war showed no signs of ending.

Sam went through the roof when Sir Robert showed him the Duke's secret message. In fact, Ena had to lock the office door from the outside to keep him from tearing off to challenge the Duke to a duel. As it was, he banged so hard on the Museum wall, wept and cursed so loudly, that the whole building became alarmed and within an hour the news was all over Ottawa that a murder plot against Sir Sam Hughes had been uncovered, "in the highest places," by Sam himself.

At the next meeting of the military council, Sir Robert asked the Duke if he had received any information from the War Office about Canadian participation in the spring offensive. "We have received no word ourselves," rumbled Sir Robert, "we know only what we read in the newspapers."

"Righto!" said the Duke. "No news is good news, so they say."

"You're a liar, sir!" bellowed Sir Sam, "A liar and a traitor!"

"Eh?" said the Duke, holding his hand to his ear.

The Duke demanded an apology. Sam refused. The Duke demanded Sam's resignation. Sam refused.

By April 18, 1916, Jimmy Dempster's courtship of Miss Dorothy Yorke has become so intense ("If only he weren't a *colonial*," she complained to the Duchess), his presence at Rideau Hall so familiar, that it seemed quite logical, after tea, that Jimmy should be asked to deliver a Top Secret letter from the Duke to Sir Robert, by hand.

"Righto!" he said. "Straightaway!"

He took the liberty, on his way to the Museum, of steaming open the envelope.

Private and Confidential

Government House
Ottawa

Dear Sir Robert

With reference to your interview with me yesterday, I should like to make it perfectly plain that I cannot accept Sir Sam Hughes' denial of the facts as a settlement of the outstanding question between him and myself. I must have a written apology from Sir Sam Hughes, or otherwise I shall be compelled to place my resignation in the hands of the King with a full statement of my reasons for doing so.

Believe me
Yours very sincerely,
Arthur.

Sir Robert is alone at his desk, slumped in his chair, his head in his hands.

"Excuse me," Jimmy says, offering the envelope. "Urgent, sir."

Sir Robert hardly glances at it. He rubs his face as if it were numb. His eyes are red, cavernous.

"Do you know," he says, looking into space, "that we lost six thousand men the day before yesterday, in a mud crater at St. Eloi, and six thousand men last month, and six thousand men the month before that, at St. Julien, and do you know how much ground we've gained?"

"No, sir."

"None."

The casualty lists take up almost the whole front page of the evening *Citizen*. Jimmy notices Mr. King's name on the social page. A dinner party. Mrs.

Harriss'. Of course, the *Citizen* is a Liberal paper, King's in thick with that Socialist reporter, Charlie Bowman....

Jimmy takes a file from his desk. It is marked "Rifle: Ross." His nocturnal visit to Sam Hughes' office, so rudely interrupted, had not been in vain. The file contains a report, marked *Top Secret*, dated November, 1915, from the commanding officer of the Canadian Corps, General Alderson, demanding that the Ross rifle be discarded as worthless. Yet today, April 18, 1916, the Canadian Corps is equipped with the Ross rifle, to a man.

Dear Mr. Bowman,

As you will see from the nature of this report, it is advisable that the source remain anonymous. I can assure you it is genuine.

We cannot remain silent when the lives of Canadian soldiers are at stake.

A Patriot.

He clips the letter to the report and slips it into a plain, brown envelope. He writes "Charles Bowman, Esq." on the front in what he hopes looks like a feminine script.

"Would you mind passing this along to Bowman, at the *Citizen*, next time you run into him?" he says to William Lyon Mackenzie King as they stroll along the banks of the Rideau Canal. "It's an article he loaned to Dorothy, Christian Science, I believe. Pretty goofy stuff, if you ask me."

"Yes," says William Lyon Mackenzie King.

G.H.Q.
April 28, 1916

My dear L.

Here we have a few days of glorious weather. The leaves and flowers are showing and the countryside is beautiful, at least until we reach the belt of utter desolation around Ypres. Even there I find an occasional touch of beauty. Yesterday by the ruins of a farmhouse behind the firing line I saw a fruit tree whose black branches were covered with white blossoms as thick as clinging snow.

The night before the Germans exploded a mine, bombarded and attacked. The line was held and I went over to report. An unpleasant spectacle — many unburied bodies — one officer with his head off. In front of me a man was hit and his arm shattered. Blood everywhere. Many places I had to crawl flat on my face and I was muddy and wet and sandy by turns. I went into the crater. Not a sign of all the men who had been in that line before. They simply disappeared. I wonder if they felt anything. What were their last thoughts?

Are they as conscious beings anywhere now or are they gone, knowing nothing?

The sun was broiling.

I am darkly burned but in excellent health. Tonight or tomorrow night I am going over the St. Eloi positions. I wonder how they will seem to me now, after the year since I was last there. Last year about this time I had a swim in the Ypres moat during the bombardment, but it has dried up now. I wonder who ate the swans?

I hope my photos have reached you safely. When am I to have another of yours? I await your next with pleasurable anticipation.

Talbot

Ottawa *Citizen*, May 4, 1916.

The Governor-General, H.R.H. the Duke of Connaught, has submitted his resignation to the King and will return shortly to England. His successor has not yet been announced....

Ottawa *Citizen*, May 16, 1916.
GENERAL SLAMS ROSS RIFLE

In a confidential report to the Minister of the Militia, General Sir Sam Hughes, the Commander of the Canadian Corps, General H.T. Alderson, has criticized the performance of the Canadian Ross rifle and recommended its immediate replacement by the British Lee Enfield....

Ottawa *Citizen*, June 1, 1916.

The Minister of Militia, General Sir Sam Hughes, today announced the replacement of General H.T. Alderson as Commanding Officer of the Canadian Corps. General Alderson's successor has not yet been chosen....

G.H.Q.
May 8, 1916

My dearest L.

What an impulsive darling you are! And with the kindest heart I have ever met. Moved to compassion by my loveless state, you put yourself upon the sacrificial altar and write me your charming letter of the 19th and send me gifts emblematic of your impulse. I was quite thrilled by your unusual warmth of expression. You are positively human! There can be nothing binding by the nature of things, but the contemplation of a possibility of mutual affection is a most pleasant pastime and surely we can permit ourselves the indulgence. So why not thrill me with "My own Captain" and "fiancé" and "Devotedly yours." This gives spice to my life and adds spice to your letters.

So consequently, my dear L., we are engaged. We are lovers, though I should judge very timid ones. You do indeed, in the courage of your first impulse, promise me "real love letters," but I mark the gradual oozing of your resolution. I am very happy at any rate about the progress in Romance that we have made. How much in the past two years you have cheered and comforted me and given me an interest which I should otherwise have lacked. All others I knew I did not love and would not. You were the unknown quantity, the romantic possibility, and everything I heard or saw or gathered from your letters confirmed me in that pleasing hope. That you should entertain a similar idea was not improbable. I am quite honest when I say that I should be more astonished than gratified to find that some woman was in love with me. I would be incredulous. Moreover, if you love me, I know the circumstances have much to do with it. Every woman has an instinct of affection for a soldier just as a soldier wishes to have the love of a woman. Women at home exaggerate the courage and qualities of a man who is fighting and will create Galahads from ordinary clay.

All this to show I am under no misconceptions that should cause you any maidenly confusion. You may love me and you may do so without fear or anxiety. I shall not be puffed into foolish pride. I shall not say "Poor girl, she loves me!" I shall not call you false when you tell me you have changed your mind. This is what I say, "She is a sweet, affectionate girl, clever, amusing, kind, impulsive. She is compassionate and exalted and romantic. She is a natural, healthy woman." I say, "I want to be loved" and she replies, "I will love you." Could anything be more clear or more satisfactory? So I hasten to accept the new situation. I have everything to gain and nothing to lose. We will build our charming castle, we will inhabit it for the duration, which reminds me of one of Bairnsfather's most successful cartoons. One character says to the other "How many years have you enlisted for?" "Seven years!" "Lucky, I'm duration!"

So please do love me. Love me dearly. I like it. I like it over-much. I shall like your love letters. And though you say you place no obligations on me, I shall be faithful to you as long as I can. Shall you not expect something in return really? Shall it be only play after all and shall the serious game be with someone else? We can not possibly tell, not until after the war. In the meantime it is safer to play. I am a dangerous one to be serious with. There is no reason why this evening or tomorrow I shouldn't get in the way of a shell and so cause unnecessary regrets. I want you to love me and write me love letters for they will charm and amuse me, but I don't want you to really care. I want in return to amuse and interest you. I don't want to cause you any anxiety or sorrow. It really would be better for me to say "Don't have anything more to do with me, if you are going to be serious about it." I should be beastly selfish otherwise.

I wish you would send me another photo. I have sent you five besides snapshots. I have things to do so must stop, though I feel I should go on. There is so much that should be said.

You are a darling and I am very fond of you.

Affectionately,
Talbot.

P.S. Horrors! I nearly forgot to tell you how much I am going to prize the little silver heart box and the ring and the elephant and the silver heart. They are beautiful things and I know they represent beautiful thoughts and feelings. I shall treasure them and I shall be ever grateful and better for the associations.

Your,
Talbot.

R.H.
Friday, June 2, 1916

Very warm. Everything so soft and green and smells good. Packed all day. It is still not decided if I will go to England. I would be almost afraid to see Talbot again. I'm afraid our castles in the air would crumble into dust. He would probably find me plain, unsophisticated, dull. I might find him rude, selfish. I don't think I could bear to have all my illusions destroyed.

Alice says I should drop him, he is playing with me, like a cat with a mouse, and after the war he'll laugh at me, and I'll be sunk. I suspect she's right, Alice is always right, but I just *can't*. Damn damn damn damn damn damn damn damn, damn!

Hammy Gault made a speech at a recruiting meeting in the Dominion Theatre tonight. "We are going to fight for the purest womanhood under the canopy of Heaven," he said, "We are going to fight for *our* womenfolk! Go fight for yours!" The whole audience nearly died laughing. (The divorce has been disallowed, so they're stuck with each other.)

I guess I'm stuck too. Sunk.

R.H.
Saturday, June 3, 1916

Cards with Zoé. Won a pair of earrings, lost a pair of kid gloves and the earrings. Zoé was disgusted with me. She plays remarkably well for a woman who's supposed to be blind. We have to call out the cards as we play them, but I suspect her real secret is Miss Coutu, who has an interesting way of drifting around the table, tidying, emptying ashtrays, bringing tea, not *looking*, of course, then standing behind Zoé, her hands on her shoulders, while Zoé plays. I'll bet they have a code worked out, one squeeze for an ace, two for a king, some set of signals that tells her who's got what. Nobody's going to accuse poor old Lady Laurier of cheating, not me anyway. I don't mind. She needs the money, and it isn't much.

Talbot's mother came for tea. I was shocked, she looked so much older, so strained. She asked me to walk with her back to the Chateau.

"I appreciate your kindness in sending copies of Talbot's letters to me," she said. "I admit I was somewhat jealous to begin with, that he would write so much more frankly to you, however I understand now that it is easier for him to write to someone who isn't quite so *close* to him. I want you to know that I took the liberty, when I was in England last December, of showing a number of the letters to Sir Max Aitken. He was very much impressed and suggested immediately that Talbot's talents would be put to better use as a writer and historian, possibly a successor to himself as Canadian 'Eye-Witness' at the front, and as a result Sir Max arranged to have Talbot transferred to the headquarters staff of General Alderson, to acquaint himself with the overall picture of the war before taking up his new duties...."

My letters! Sir Max! Jesus, next thing they'll be in the *Daily Express*!

"I don't think Talbot intended...."

"Talbot doesn't know. His pride would be hurt. I trust you will not betray my confidence. I have only one goal in life, Miss Coolican, and that is to see Talbot safely home again. I will do anything, *anything* to keep him alive."

"Yes."

"Will you help me?"

"If I can."

"As you know, General Alderson has been dismissed in disgrace. There is talk of a court martial, although I think it is just Sam Hughes' bluster. However, Talbot will almost certainly be returned to the trenches as soon as General Alderson is replaced. Sir Max is willing to take Talbot on the staff of the War Records Office but he can do nothing without Sam Hughes' permission. Sam Hughes goes quite berserk when anyone connected with Alderson is mentioned. He thinks the report was some sort of Prussian plot masterminded by the King. He is quite mad, of course, and his views about Liberals, and 'frogs' are well known...."

"I can ask, if you like. I'm not sure...."

"Please."

R.H.
Monday, June 5, 1916

Ena said she'd get me in at noon, just before she closed for lunch. There was a funny noise echoing through the building when I arrived, a sort of *thumpa-clack, thumpa-clack, thumpa-clack*.

"Sam's skipping," Ena said. "It calms the nerves."

He was in his undershirt. *Thumpa-clack, thumpa-clack, thumpa-clack*. I sat for quite a while, watching the map on the wall, red pins for the British, blue for the French, black for the German. They hadn't moved in a year.

"How's your papa, girl?" he puffed.

"He's dead, sir."

"Sorry to hear that, girl. Loved him like a brother, I did."

He wiped his face but I couldn't tell if it was tears or sweat.

"Papineau!" he scowled, black as thunder. "Papineau! He's a rebel, ain't he? A Grit!"

"He's a Rhodes scholar...."

"He's a Frenchie, ain't he?"

"He speaks wonderfully, and writes, in both Eng...."

Sam's black eyes burned through me like two hot coals. I thought he might hit me.

"You sweet on the bugger, is that it girl?"

"Yes. Sir."

"Ena!"

Ena sent the telegram tonight.

FRENCHMAN OK STOP PLAN TO FOLLOW

"What plan?"

"God knows," sighed Ena. "Sam will have forgotten by tomorrow."

I should be happy.

I feel terrible.

100 Cooper St., Ottawa
Tuesday, June 6, 1916

I have been dismissed.

This morning I was summoned by the Duchess. She was lying in bed in much the same position as the day I first met her, almost two years ago, only a little yellower, lines like a spider's web over her face, the first roses of the summer in a vase by her pillow.

"You were seen yesterday afternoon entering and leaving the office of the Minister of Militia, Sir Sam Hughes."

"Yes, ma'am."

"May I ask what you were doing there?"

"It was personal business, ma'am."

"You know that Sam Hughes has destroyed Arthur's career and smeared his reputation?"

"I'm sorry...."

"You know that someone in this household passed confidential information along to Sir Sam Hughes, information which was used to discredit the Royal family and damage the Empire?"

"I didn't...."

"You ought to be more careful with your possessions." She reached under the comforter and held up a red morocco notebook with "Diary, 1915" across the cover in gold lettering. "Miss Yorke found this lying on the bench in the rose garden. I believe it is yours. It says 'To Cookie, Christmas, 1914, Sincere good wishes, W.L.McK. King.'"

"It wasn't in the rose garden. It was in my trunk."

"You are a very observant...."

"It's private."

"And an opinionated young woman. It is unfortunate. I had grown rather attached to your raw, uncouth charm."

"I have *not*...."

"You have three hours to pack your things and leave. I'm sure Miss McAdam will take you in, although poor Sam might have to make some other arrangement, for a night or two. I will say, to those who are interested, that you are looking for 'a new field of service.' You may say whatever you like, since no doubt the greatest damage has already been done."

"May I have my diary, please?"

She fingered it with a tiny yellow claw, like a monkey's paw, covered with rings.

"Why don't we compromise?" she said. She put the diary on her breakfast tray, opened it, and lit it with her cigarette. It made quite a blaze.

It didn't take me long to pack. It struck me, when I looked in the closet, that I had hardly a stitch that wasn't a cast-off. I wasn't going to be accused of theft, so I left them there. I took my pistol. I'll miss the Nisam's pearls. Tough.

I went to Patsy's studio to say goodbye. She was out golfing.

While I was waiting for the taxi I scratched "Prussian bitch" on the front door with my nailfile. I was still very angry when I got to Alice's, and ranted and raved a lot, but now I feel quite giddy. I am free! Free! Free!

June 19, 1916.

Dearest L.

So sorry I cannot write, but I am working night and day and I really am almost sick with fatigue. Today my mind seems to have stopped working. When did I last write you? Do you know that I am now a Staff Officer, the official "Eye Witness," and that I have to write all official communications and descriptions, that I compile all historical records, that I am to write and edit the next books on the war? You may conceive my labour, especially at this time when so much is occurring, when so many thousands are killed and wounded. The poor old P.P.'s have less than 200 left. Buller, DeBay and Fife killed, also many friends gone from other battalions. Our men did wonderfully. I am proud of them. Charlie was away fortunately but he will be sorry to have missed it.

I visit the front line much as usual. I visit all the generals and the colonels and I have to gather all the maps and documents etc. I have a Daimler limousine and chauffeur of my own, also I am to have a secretary but he has not arrived yet. There is also an official photographer whom I am supposed to run. I write the weekly reports from the Corps to the Army and keep the diary. I have worked steadily an average of over fourteen hours a day. Not complaining. I like it. But I can't do other things I like to do. No riding, no bridge, no reading, no letters, no sleep.

Are you sorry for me? The pressure I think will lessen later. It is a special position made especially for me, or vice versa, and I am trying to make good.

In the meantime please write and forgive me if I cannot send much in reply. Such cold, rainy weather, miserable, but we are cheered by the Russian success and have high hopes for the summer.

It is most agreeable to be loved and it warms me when you sign yourself as I have no hesitation in doing,

Yours affectionately,
Talbot.

100 Cooper St., Ottawa
Friday, June 30, 1916

I asked Sam Hughes today if he would send me to the front as a war photographer.

"Do you think I'm running a fucking brothel?" he bellowed.

Tomorrow I go out to Kingsmere to type Willie's book. He's promised me $25 a week. I am to stay at the Booth's cottage across the lake. Ugh.

Kingsmere,
Saturday, July 1, 1916

Came out this morning on the train with two trunks, three suitcases, twelve big boxes, a porch swing, four folding lawn chairs, a typewriter and a bird bath. It took Billy Dunn five trips with the buggy between Chelsea and the cottage. He and Willie had a big row over the fee. "The shanty Irish'll steal you blind," Willie said. "Worse than the Jews."

I swept out the "study," which is really the only room in the cottage apart from the two bedrooms and the kitchen. Willie has a big table under the window with a nice view of the lake. I have a desk against the back wall, by the kitchen. I suggested I could perhaps use the spare bedroom but he got quite upset. It's "Mother's" room and everything has to remain exactly as it is. I found a nest of mice in Mother's mattress, funny, naked little pink things. Willie was too squeamish to throw them out so I had to do it. Tomorrow I'll get a cat from the Laroques, who live in the farm house up the hill. Julie Laroque is supposed to cook and keep house for Willie but there was no sign of her. Holiday, I guess. Willie went for water and fire wood and I made us some bacon and eggs. Once I cleaned out the soot the stove worked quite well, although I think there's a dead bird or something in the chimney. The smell of the pine trees and woodsmoke and frying bacon made me homesick.

Set up the lawn chairs on the porch, although the mosquitoes are very bad. Set off some fireworks after dark. They looked lovely arching over the water in the twilight, pink sparks against a turquoise sky, poof, *whoosh*, poof, poof, *whoosh*! Canada is forty-nine, only seven years older than Willie.

Bicycled over to Booth's to spend the night. It's only twenty minutes around the eastern end of the lake, but it makes me nervous a little at night. I could row across in five minutes but Willie doesn't have a boat. He says he might get one next year, after he builds a boathouse and a dock. He seems to have a very ass-backwards way of going about things.

I can see a light in Willie's cottage from my window. It is midnight but still quite bright, luminous, like the inside of an opal.

Kingsmere
Sunday, July 2, 1916

Unpacked the typewriter. An awful old thing. Ribbon worn out. The "t" sticks. It belonged to Bert. Got some oil from Laroque's, also Bonbon, the tabby cat. She has already delivered three dead mice and four birds to my feet. I threw the birds in the privy before Willie could see.

Spent most of the day finding a place for the bird bath. It doesn't look right sitting there in the underbrush like a mushroom.

Found D'Arcy McGee's stone head in the brush behind the woodpile, along with the other ruins from the Parliament buildings. He looked sad, so I rolled him down the hill to the lake and propped him up among the reeds at the water's edge, looking towards the cottage, like someone just coming out from swimming. Willie got quite a scare. He said it was a desecration. I said it was Pan.

Went swimming. The water is high and cold. Lovely. No leeches. Willie threw a lot of rocks out of the beach. He says he's going to make a rock garden in front of the cottage, for the bird bath, with irises and primroses and lillies-of-the-valley arranged in the shape of a clock to signify Eternity.

He has nice legs.

Kingsmere
Monday, July 3, 1916

Went up to the Herridges' cottage to pick raspberries. Got a huge bowl full, enough for a pie if I knew how to make pastry. They're better plain anyway, with fresh cream, and Laroques have an ice-cream churn. The cottage was deserted. Everything over-grown with weeds. Bill Herridge is in hospital in England with a bullet wound. He told the medical officer of the Foot Guards that his stiff back was from an old football injury so they let him in. Mrs. Herridge has had a nervous breakdown.

"Poor Marjorie was always very emotional," Willie said. "She fancied she was in love with me once. I had no idea of course. I took it as the friendship of an older married woman for a young bachelor, alone in Ottawa, suffering the loss of his closest friend. I thought nothing of it when she asked me up to the manse for dinner, or sought to comfort me in my grief with caresses. Dr. Herridge was usually there, and the children, and we sang hymns, or read aloud, in the homeliest way. It was indiscreet of me to go there so often, I can see that now, but my own innocence of purpose blinded me to her ulterior motives, or delusions, which were of a frankly sensual nature. She confessed all to me here at Kingsmere, mistaking my gratitude for reciprocal passion, and before I was able to extricate myself from this awkward situation, she'd told Dr. Herridge that she and I were going to run off together. It was only with the greatest difficulty that I convinced Dr. Herridge that poor Marjorie was unwell, and that my attentions were of the most honorable and platonic kind, the affection of a devoted son for a woman who has been a second mother to him, and that I would do my best to help the poor child see the truth and dedicate herself once more to her sacred duties as a wife and mother. Unfortunately the incident caused a breech which has never healed. Marjorie continues in the mistaken belief that I am somehow responsible for her unhappy marriage, although it was clearly her own selfishness that brought us all to the brink of ruin."

Why does Willie always talk as if he's making a speech?

Willie has a key to Herridges' and he brought down an armload of books. I am to improve my education, he says, every afternoon between four and six, starting with *Culture and Anarchy*, followed by *The Idylls of the King*.

Do I get paid for this?

Kingsmere
Tuesday, July 4, 1916

Went into town for carbon paper, ribbons. Found two letters from Talbot. One enclosed a piece of ribbon from his Military Cross. He says I can wear it attached to my P.P.C.L.I. enamelled brooch. He has told Laurier to force an election. "The army should run politics," he says. "I'm in favour of some Cromwellian stunt which will make the army all powerful — we will be when we get home." It doesn't sound like him. It sounds more like some crazy idea of Max Aitken. I can't imagine the whole country being run singlehanded by Sam Hughes, although it would be exciting.

The big push has started on the Somme. Alice says we are in reserve. Thank God.

Willie read the Gettysburg Address after lunch and showed me a plaster cast of Lincoln's hand which Mr. Rockefeller had given him. He has a photo of Mr. Rockefeller on his work table. Have you ever seen a kinder, sweeter face? he asked me. I think Mr. Rockefeller looks like a muskellunge but I didn't say so.

All Willie's notes and papers are still in boxes in the sitting room. He circles around them from time to time like a dog sniffing a lamp post. Then he finds something else to do. I finally opened one and started lifting papers on to the table. He got very upset and accused me of "messing things up," so I went for a swim and he said I was "slacking."

"Well then, let's get to work."

"It's the Fourth of July."

"So?"

"It's a holiday."

"But we've already celebrated ours...."

"You are very provincial...."

"You are very disloyal!"

He went off and sat in the privy for the longest time.

"I'm sorry. The strain...."

"I'm sorry."

We start on the book tomorrow.

Kingsmere
Wednesday, July 5, 1916

This morning we walked up the hill back of the pasture looking for the right spot to put the "ruins." Willie says it has to be a clearing, with a view, facing west to catch the setting sun through the arches. (Willie isn't up early enough to catch the rising sun.) It will be a sort of Canadian Acropolis, he says. He has two windows and a door from the Parliament buildings and a bay window from an old house they tore down last year. We didn't find the right place. It was very hot and the bugs were bad.

Started *Culture and Anarchy*. There is an inscription on the fly-leaf: "To my Sweet Child, Christmas, 1903, Your Devoted Rex." Willie said the book was a gift to Mrs. Herridge's daughter, Gwennie. Gwennie would have been six in 1903.

Raspberry icecream for supper. We have a white tablecloth now, and brass candlesticks from Willie's apartment, and the "Death of Iphigenia" etching he is so fond of — I hate it — and a big vase of lilies-of-the-valley from Herridges' garden. I feel guilty taking things when there's no one home, but Willie acts as if he owns the place.

Book tomorrow.

Kingsmere
Thursday, July 6, 1916

Went swimming. Read more Arnold. Slow going. Willie spent most of the day in the privy. He complains of headaches, indigestion. He seems feverish. Grippe, I guess.

There is nothing actually written yet. The boxes are full of notes. He showed me some diagrams he'd made, illustrating the relationship between industry and labour, circles within circles, cut into pies, scribbled over with mystical symbols like gypsies' horoscopes, with wavy lines and arrows going off in all directions.

"I am writing about Good and Evil," he said. "Life and Death, War and Peace. It's hard to know where to begin."

He has ordered a flagpole to go beside the bird bath in the rock garden.

Kingsmere
Friday, July 7, 1916

Willie has decided to clear up his correspondence before starting on the book. Some of the letters go back to April. A lot of them are from people in North York, asking if he's going to stand for the nomination again. Things would go faster if he dictated the replies directly to me at the typewriter, but he says his brain can't work that way, he has to write it out himself first, then I type it up. His handwriting looks like a mosquito got into the ink. After I type it he corrects it. Usually he changes things, or adds things, then I do it all over again. He won't let me erase if I make a mistake. The *whole thing* has to be redone. Today I typed one letter *five* times. I wouldn't make mistakes if he didn't watch me all the time.

Started *Idylls*. Rain.

Kingsmere
Saturday, July 8, 1916

Big row. Willie corrected "referendum" back to "referrendum." I had to go to Herridges' for a dictionary. Then he crossed out two lines so I'd have to type it over anyway.

Am I being paid for this?

Stopped smoking. Again.

Kingsmere
Saturday, July 15, 1916

Willie asked me what I dreamed about. I can never remember. I dream about Mum quite a bit. We're always on a ship out in the ocean, and it's dark and stormy, and there's a whale, like the one that swallowed Jonah, but I wake up before it gets me. I told him about Mum having a breakdown, like Mrs. Herridge, although it was more religion than sex. (Could it have been sex? I hadn't thought of that.) Willie dreams about trains. Oh, that's Death, I said, without thinking, although I don't know why, and I felt badly afterward.

My new silk panties disappeared this afternoon while I was swimming. Bonbon must have taken them for her kittens. I asked her but she just smirked. I felt indecent walking around without them all afternoon, not that you could see anything.

No more mice. Casualties high among the sparrows.

Kingsmere
Sunday, July 16, 1916

Walked into Chelsea for yesterday's mail and papers.

"Captain Papineau has a letter in the *Citizen*," Willie said.

Jesus, Max Aitken's done it, but it turned out to be an open letter from Talbot to his cousin, Henri Bourassa, the Quebec Nationalist who's so against the war. It was very long and high-flown, and I had a hard time following it except that Talbot seemed to think the war would be a good thing for Canada, in the long run.

"It looks as though Papineau's been taken in by the jingo crowd," Willie said. "Of course, he always did run with the moneyed interests, the Oxford imperialists, the Round Table bunch. Too bad. It's the end of him, I'm afraid."

"The *what*?"

"Politically. Militarism goes down well in some areas of Ontario, but his name would tell against him here in a campaign, while in Quebec, where his name is honoured, anything smacking of jingoism is totally disastrous. He is too close to the war. People here don't see the bravery and heroism of the fighting men. They see the ugly things, vice and graft and greed and pain. Everyone is sick of the war."

I felt sick. We walked for a long time in silence. Willie was whistling "Tipperary."

"It's too bad," he said finally. "The war could have been prevented."

"How?"

"By men of character sitting down together in an atmosphere of good will and reaching some sort of compromise...."

"What if they wouldn't?"

"Wouldn't?"

"What if one of them refused?"

"Why, then you make him!"

"How?"

"You force him."

Willie says the role of women is not to understand, but to have faith in the men who do.

Is he right? Is the war all for nothing?

Kingsmere
Monday, July 17, 1916

Finished *Idylls* this morning. I asked Willie for two weeks' wages.

"We haven't begun yet!" he said.

"We've done all the letters."

"Yes, but they're not...."

"I've worked...."

"It's been something of a vacation...."

"A *what*?"

"You hardly need the money...."

"I'm broke."

"You're an heiress."

"I'm a ward."

"Nevertheless, Mr. Booth...."

"Mr. Booth isn't dead yet."

"I thought, since we were friends...."

"It's only $50."

"I can hardly afford to waste...."

"Waste!"

"...money on your extravagances."

I very calmly went into the sitting room and started dumping out his cardboard boxes. Papers spilled out in white torrents, a waterfall of words foamed around Willie's ankles as he waded towards me, slipping on the smooth white shoals, flailing his arms to stop the waves of charts and bibliographies, index cards and file folders and notepads that slid towards him across the floor. I dumped a box of books on his feet and stormed out.

Oh Talbot, please come home.

Kingsmere
Tuesday, July 18, 1916

Arrived this morning with my suitcase and my little speech of resignation. Willie was bent over his table writing furiously. The papers were stacked in neat piles around the room. There was a sign saying "Good" tacked on the wall over one set of papers, and a sign saying "Evil" tacked on the opposite wall, over a larger stack of papers.

"It's coming!" Willie cried.

He gave me a bouquet of sweet peas and four ten dollar bills.

"I deducted $5 each, for the two holidays," he said.

He is having a telephone installed to eliminate some of the correspondence.

Kingsmere
Wednesday, July 19, 1916

Made seven jars of raspberry jam. I was going to send them to Talbot but it seems silly, they're so comfortable at headquarters, you get the feeling they live on champagne and caviar, so maybe I'll only send him one, and the rest to Charlie Stewart and the regiment. He's the only one left now, of the originals. I miss packing up the big boxes of things, and the little thank-you notes that would come back, so cheerful and optimistic. The *Citizen* says Miss Yorke is leaving for England to join the Red Cross. "Such a noble, selfless gesture," Willie said.

"She's a slut."

He always blushes furiously when I use "rude" words, but I say they're in

Shakespeare and that shuts him up. I think he quite likes it. I shouldn't tease
him. He's *such* a prude.

Started *Frankenstein* today. Not as good as the movie.

Willie spent the day on the telephone, giving out the number, although it's a
party line with six other people, so the chances of anyone getting through are
pretty slim.

Kingsmere
Thursday, July 20, 1916

Washed my hair in the lake and let it dry in the sun. Willie says I should wear it
down, with a ribbon, like Mother.

"It's too hot."

"It's pretty."

"It gets in the way."

"You look like a little girl."

Made curtains for Mother's room, white with violets. She was going to
come last weekend but Willie's father isn't well. Mrs. Laroque has given us a
lovely rag rug so we're quite homey now. I do most of the cooking. Julie
Laroque is only fifteen and has two babies to mind. She brings water from the
well every morning, and fresh milk and bread and butter, and sometimes a
pickerel or a chicken or some fresh brown eggs. I offered her $2 this morning
for a large trout. She just shook her head and smiled.

"But it's not free."

"Oui. Oui."

"Everything?"

"Oui."

Willie is paying her $15 for the whole summer! Including food!

"It's a farm," he said, "It doesn't cost them anything."

He got a cheque today from Miss Markham, in England, for $1,000, and
another from Mr. Larkin, who owns Salada Tea, for $5,000, but he says
they're for his election campaign in North York and can't be used for
"personal" reasons.

Terrific thunderstorm tonight. Read *Frankenstein* aloud. Scary.

Kingsmere
Saturday, July 22, 1916

Put up flagpole. Willie ran up the most enormous Union Jack. I think it's silly,
but he's pleased. He divided his notes into smaller piles today. The "Good"
side is now separated into "peace," "work" and "health," and the "Evil" side
is divided into "war," "strikes" and "death." The war, he says, is like
Frankenstein's monster.

He has dedicated his life to peace. I wish he'd get more work done. Only two pages today. He follows me around, kitchen to pantry to woodshed to kitchen to porch to typewriter like a big tom cat, watching me and smiling with the gap between his teeth. I always seem to be bumping into him. It gets on my nerves. "Little mother," he calls me, as a joke, but I wouldn't have to spend so much time in the kitchen if he didn't eat so much. A whole loaf of bread today. His pants are so tight his fly gapes open, and his cock jumps around as if it had a life of its own. It was a mistake to come here. I'll have to leave or marry him.

WILLIAM LYON MACKENZIE KING

Credit	Debit
Intelligent	Old (Middle-aged)
Rich (fairly)	Fat
Ambitious	Homely
Kind	Stingy (greedy)
Likes food, music, dancing	Religious
He loves me (?)	Self-centred
	Talks too much
	Doesn't drink
	Doesn't smoke
	Doesn't play cards
	Fussy
	Bossy
	Grit
	Yankee-lover
	Coward (?)
	Mother
	Strange
	I don't love him

Kingsmere
Sunday, July 23, 1916

Found the perfect spot for the ruins, a rock ledge behind Herridges'. Willie is writing to Dr. Herridge, offering to buy the property, cottage and all. He wants to buy out the Laroques too, some day, and turn their barn into a stable. The Rockefellers have a stable on their estate in New York (and a lake, and a flagpole and a bird bath and ruins).

We cranked up the Herridges' player piano, old rolls, mostly from the Nineties, but very gay. Willie found a battered straw boater and I put my hair up in a Gibson knot and we danced a soft shoe. *Skinamarink-a-dink-a-dink, skinamarink-a-doo, I love yooooooo.* It was fun. Willie can't carry a tune but he's a good dancer.

Tonight he read aloud from his diary. It was about a rich widow Sir Wilfrid had tried to set him up with years and years ago. "I must marry for love or not at all," he read. "Yet I must find a wife soon. A man in public life must have the support of a happy home." He looked at me intently when he finished.

"Why don't you read from yours?"

"My diary? Don't be silly."

"Why not?"

"Because it's personal stuff. Stupid things. I'm not important."

"Is it about me?"

"I'll never tell."

"Do you like me?"

"Yes, of course. You're very nice."

Kingsmere
Monday, July 24, 1916

Willie: "Who cooked this roast?"

Me: "I did."

Willie: "It's not done."

Me: "Yes it is."

Willie: "It's raw inside."

Me: "It's rare."

Willie: "It's all bloody."

Me: "It's delicious."

Willie: "Mother would never...."

Me: "Screw your mother!"

I thought he was going to hit me, and raised my arm, but he twisted it behind my back. Before I knew it I was lying on the rag rug and he was on top of me, so heavy I could hardly breathe, his knee between my legs, his mouth sucking hard on mine, pumping, pumping, up and down, up and down, pulling my skirt up with his free hand. The harder I fought the harder he pushed against me, his knee digging into my thigh, his hand tugging furiously at my skirt, his cock stiff and hard against my stomach, up and down, up and down, bang, bang, puffing and grunting until suddenly he groaned and a gush of hot liquid squirted through my dress and ran down my leg. He collapsed like a pricked balloon. He never even got his pants down.

He lay there moaning, his face as drained as his cock, until I finally got my knee up and pushed him off. I was gasping too hard to be frightened, or mad, so we lay there, side by side, for a long time.

Willie: "I'm a monster."

Me: "It was my fault."
Willie: "I can't *control....*"
Me: "You should get married."
Willie: "Oh, I could never inflict my...."
Me: "Isn't that what it's for...."
Willie: "I'm...not...."
Me: "Not what?"
Willie: "I'm afraid I'm losing my...m-m-my...eyesight."
Me: "Maybe you need glasses."
Willie: "Do you think so? I hadn't thought...."
He cheered up right away and went for a swim.

Kingsmere
Tuesday, July 25, 1916

I have promised to stay until Sunday, when Mr. and Mrs. King come. It's another $50 and I dread going back to Booth's mill. I work at Herridges'. We talk on the telephone. It's very hot. I'd like to work in my petticoat. I don't dare. I'd like to go for a swim. I don't dare. Besides, I'm black and blue and look like hell.

Willie has a rash. It's mostly on his legs and arms. Looks like poison ivy. I looked it up in Herridges' *Cartwright's Guide to Common Complaints and Home Remedies.* Mum taught us our ABC's from Cartwright's. A is for abscess, B is for bile, C is for cancer.... No wonder everyone said we were bloody-minded little kids. Willie is slathered in baking soda like a big vanilla ice-cream cone. Bad temper.

Kingsmere
Wednesday, July 26, 1916

Rash is worse. It's spread to his chest. (Did he roll in it?) He wears long-sleeved shirts with the cuffs buttoned up, and a stiff collar *and* a jacket. Says he can't sleep, although he was snoring away on the porch swing when I went down at noon. Spends a lot of time looking in the mirror, feeling his nose, peering into his mouth. He thinks his teeth are falling out.

Walked into Chelsea for more baking soda. Willie told me to get some rat poison.

"We don't have rats."
"Mice, then."
"We don't have mice."
"Skunks."
"We don't have skunks."

Found *Cartwright's* in Willie's privy.

Only four more days. I wish I hadn't read *Frankenstein*.

Kingsmere

Friday, July 28, 1916

Tried to telephone Willie today. Billy Dunn at the Chelsea exchange said the line was dead.

"I cut it," Willie said.

"Why?"

"There are vibrations, unseen forces at work, forces that wish to destroy me, forces that will stop at nothing to suppress my work."

He seems very frightened. He won't look at me. His hands shake. His eyes are red and puffy, as if he's been crying. He says his stomach hurts. He won't see a doctor. He stays awake all night, writing. "I must finish before it's too late," he says. "My book alone can atone for the humiliating disgrace my agonizing death will bring on the innocent heads of the two dearest, sweetest parents...."

Agonizing death? From poison ivy?

Kingsmere

Saturday, July 29, 1916

"Industry and Humanity

Chapter Nine: Principles Underlying Health

Phosphorous necrosis has been known in the match industry for over three quarters of a century. It is caused by the absorption of phosphorus through the teeth or gums. Minute particles of the poison enter, usually through the cavities of decayed teeth, setting up inflammation, which, if not quickly arrested, extends along the jaws, causing the teeth to loosen and drop out. The jawbones slowly decompose and pass away in the form of nauseating pus, which sometimes breaks through the neck in the form of an abscess. Where swallowed, as is inevitable...."

Willie: "It's A-B-C-E-S-S! A-B-C-E-S-S!"

Me: "It is not!"

Willie: "It is so!"

Me: "Not! You left...."

Willie: "Shut up! You stupid...."

He is purple with rash and rage. He crumples the page into a ball and throws it at my feet.

"You have *deliberately* tried to ruin my manuscript!"

"Ruin...!"

"You have been sent here by the Rockefeller interests to see that my work was never finished!"

"Work...!"

You have deliberately *flaunted* yourself in front of me...."

"Flaunted!"

"...like the Whore of Babylon, to distract me from my purpose in life. You have thrown yourself at me, and attempted to seduce me...."

"Seduce *you*!"

"...and drag me down into a slough of vile concupiscence...."

"Like Marjorie?"

"Marjorie!"

"The 'Dear Child.' 'From your loving Rex.'"

"It was perfectly innoc...."

"Where did you do it? On the floor? In the raspberry patch?"

"You are a vile...."

"You're a liar!"

252 Metcalfe St., Ottawa
Monday, July 31, 1916

Packed my suitcase this morning and bicycled over to the cottage, hoping to catch a ride to Chelsea with Billy Dunn after he'd delivered Mr. and Mrs. King. Willie had already left for Ottawa to meet the train. The cottage looked sad, papers everywhere, the kitchen full of dirty dishes, as if I'd never been there.

There was an envelope addressed to me on the table.

My dear Miss Coolican,

I regret that I spoke in haste and anger yesterday. I have not been myself lately. I am anxious that we do not part in an atmosphere of ill-will and misunderstanding, and I sincerely hope that we may resume our acquaintance at some later time in a spirit of amicability.

I am sincerely touched and flattered by your deep affection for me and only wish that I might return it in a way that would lead to our mutual martial (sic) bliss. It is not uncommon for romantic young girls like yourself to conceive an exaggerated passion for an older man, and to invest in him all kinds of admirable qualities, and emotions, which he does not, in fact, possess. I am not in any way questioning the sincerity of your love for me, nor do I wish to hurt your feelings, or embarrass you, or diminish the affectionate regard I have for you, but I feel compelled to say at this time that I find myself unable to recipricate (sic) your tender feelings or to place our relationship upon a more intimate footing. I feel towards you as a father towards a daughter or an uncle towards a favorite neice (sic). It is love, yes, but of a pure, platonic nature, unsullied by physical desire. I can only pray that you will not allow your own selfish feelings to interfere with the continuance of a pure and beautiful friendship. I am asking God to guide you in the ways of self-sacrifice.

Yours very sincerely,
W.L.McK. King.

I shook the envelope. Not a penny.

His own room was neat and clean, a narrow iron bed, a night table, chamber pot, the "Death of Iphegenia." The table was covered with medicine bottles. The box of rat poison was sitting next to a glass of water.

The drawer opened easily. The Bible on top, then the Diary, and *Cartwright's* underneath. The Bible fell open as I lifted it out. My pink silk panties fluttered to the floor. They had been filed at Revelation 16-18. The word "fornication" was underlined every time, in red ink.

A carbon copy of Willie's letter to me was interleaved in the Diary under July 31, 1916: "I regret that I spoke in haste and anger yesterday. I have not been myself...." I removed it and cut out all of July with a razor blade. I threw the papers down the hole in the privy.

A piece of Willie's blue notepaper was sticking out of *Cartwright's*. It marked S for Syphilis. Syphilis was underlined just like "fornication" in Revelation. The symptoms had been copied out on the piece of blue notepaper and annotated with asterisks and question marks:

Secondary symptoms:
* Fever, usually slight, malaise
** A transitory roseolar rash, chiefly on the abdomen
* Sore throat
* Cutaneous erruption. Has been mistaken for small-pox or psoriasis
* Ulceration of the skin
* Mucous patches in the mouth
(?) Soft, flat, warty growths with a greyish secretion around the anus, on the scrotum or in the groin
Ulceration of the throat
(?) Syphilitic iritis
(?) Syphilitic periostitis
* Anaemia
****** Loss of hair
*** Nocturnal headache and bone pains.

Tertiary Symptoms:
(no) Malnutrition
Cerebral thrombosis

    Jacksonian epilepsy
    Syphilitic cirrhosis
    Infantilism.
Treatment:
    Mercury
    Salvarsan
    Arsenic.

"My Dear Mr. King,
I am sorry you are not feeling well.

I notice that the rat poison has disappeared from the kitchen shelf. Please see that it is not left in the way of children or pets. It contains strychnine. An unpleasant death. (See *Madame Bovary).*

Get well soon.

Love and kisses,
C."

Imagine, four weeks on the same toilet seat!
The *bastard!*

2

G.H.Q.
France, August 26, 1916.

My dear L.

I was delighted to receive your letter of July 21st this evening. Where and when did I last write? So much has happened I am lost.

I have been to Paris! I went with Sir Sam Hughes to work with Sir Max Aitken on his next book, *Canada in Flanders*. Worked twelve hours a day and broke my heart. It's rotten. I have rewritten all I can but it is painful. Such times as I have had. Don't blame me for the book when it comes out, please. I was also taken to Paris to be shown the High Places. I may be placed there permanently as Canadian representative to the French. I shall call myself Canadian Ambassador! Now will you marry me! However it may come to nothing or I may be sent to Canada. Being greedy I tried for both, perhaps I won't get either. In the meantime I cannot tell even you of what we do. My heart is heavy for its lonesomeness and to imagine the companionship you could offer is a pleasant thing.

I love your photos and the life you tell of and indeed they do remind me of home — the pine woods might be at Montebello! I have put your little photo in my wristwatch. It gives me the greatest pleasure to look at it. I am quite in love with it.

I will know shortly whether it is Paris or Canada or more war for me. I'll write you at once. I hate to leave you my dear Lily but I must.

Very affectionately always,
Talbot

Sept. 30, 1916.

My dear L.

My letters to you these days are such horribly unartistic affairs. You won't like them any better than I do. I must have long sheets and idle hours.

I have another dog. The Twenty-Second Bn. captured him in Courcelette and presented him to me. He belonged to a German officer who was killed but he remained faithfully by the body and almost wept when he was taken away. I have treated him very kindly and he is reconciled and understands English. He plays happily with my "pot-bellied pup," Cecilia. When I take him motoring he looks eagerly about as though trying to locate himself.

Went to Amiens this afternoon for a bath. A glorious ride across the fields, partridges whirring suddenly from under foot, haystacks, woods with rabbits and turning leaves, an occasional jump, a wide, wide world.

I go into Courcelette tomorrow and beyond. The dead lie thick and unburied. A dreary battlefield. Our advance is slow, methodical, irresistible. We pound, pound, pound, blasting our way, land, houses, men, beasts destroyed. There never was a plague like it. Overhead a sky like home.

Perhaps I am going home. I have been asked to speak all over Canada in every town and village. My Corps Commander will not let me go until our share of the offensive is over. We shall meet before Christmas perhaps.

More friends have gone. By what strange law am I still here? What right have I to selfish pleasure any longer? Should my living life not be consecrated just as their dead lives have been?

Affectionately,
Talbot.

October 1, 1916

My dear L.

Three charming letters from you, all of which have given me a little heartache. I have felt a little lonesome and sentimental and want to go back and perhaps love you and perhaps be loved and so live happily for a few months at least. Yet I know it all to be hopelessly impossible.

I am rapidly getting sleepy. I was walking several hours this morning over the battlefield and was constantly shelled and badly frightened. Such gruesome sights. So many unburied in crumpled heaps, some mere chunks of flesh, black faces, flies, green, claw-like hands, and over this desolate dreary waste of shell-torn country a reek of rot and pestilence and smoke and gas. I came back with a headache from the constant crash of shells and thunder of our own guns. Had my photo taken by the moving-picture man (what, again!). I shall be qualified for the business after the war! I refrain from getting into most of them but I have been in a few, so if ever they are on exhibition you must be sure to go and see me!

If there was no question of my going to Canada, I should be greatly excited over the prospect of your coming to Paris and London. You simply must come if I don't come to Canada. I'll send you "orders," I hope, in a few days.

Heavy fighting going on. I am sitting up to get results.

Want more letters.

Shall I ever be lovingly?
Affectionately,
Talbot.

October 9, 1916

My dear L.

I am sorry you insist on our marriage being preceded by love letters because I have so little time now for such preliminaries. I am so much more sincere on paper than in conversation. I am sure if I were talking to you now I would be much more, what shall I say, emotional.

I have written an account of our big battle the day before yesterday. These accounts are published now in all the English papers as well as the Canadian and I believe the American also. I have perhaps the widest audience I shall ever have in my life! I am not a mere newspaper correspondent. Nothing makes me angrier. I write official staff documents as well. Yesterday I made a complete tour of the whole battlefront, interviewed the battalion commanders and wrote a long report which the General favourably commented on. You may think this horrible boastfulness. I don't like the sound of it myself, but I do so hate to feel that these poor devils are fighting and suffering here and myself in comfort and safety that I don't want you to think so either.

Today the regiment passed by behind the old pipers playing the old tune "The Bonnie Bonnets o'Dundee." Do you blame me for tears in my beautiful eyes and a heart of lead? Do you think I should go back to the regiment? I should really be happier there I think, but it is such a temptation to remain here and feel important. I am interested in seeing this side of the war. There will be lots of time. Sometimes it seems impossible that the war should ever end. It would be inconceivably wonderful. Such happiness would be too great to expect. Perhaps I should concentrate on this life and give up ideas of home and happiness and thoughts of pleasant vacations and trips to Ottawa.

I brought back yesterday some potatoes from a field north of Courcelette across which our attack had passed. I had intended sending them to you for your garden but a colonel walked off with them. I will get you some more.

Yours affectionately,
Talbot.

October 26, 1916

My dear L.

So much I have felt the need of you lately, yet I have been unable to write. My heart is very full and I have innumerable things to say but not the time. A line of yours and a box of candy I acknowledge with fervour.

I do not expect to come to Canada after all. Sir Max Aitken is a power in the land. He has immense influence in both Canadian and English governments and consequently the greatest influence upon the Army. This is wholly pernicious. I am deeply opposed to political influences (especially Tory!). The Canadian government deserves defeat and disgrace. They have played politics with the lives of men. It has been damnable and I shall support any movement to destroy them. Consequently I must be free from any connection with those influences. My name was becoming associated with Sir Max. I determined to break away. I was offered a promotion on the Corps staff. I accepted. Sir Max was informed. Very angry. He wrote that I must not be allowed to go. He offered the trip to Canada as a bribe. Naturally I refused it. There may be more trouble. It may precipitate an open quarrel. The Tory machine is a powerful organization to combat. I may be crushed in the effort. I also have great hopes of our own victory.

So I give up Canada and historical writing and stick to the purely military. My successor is already appointed, Charles Roberts, the animal writer and well-known novelist. I am happier.

Paris business all off also. Pity, but unavoidable. Had lunch in Amiens at Cafe Godbout. Most delicious cooking. We must go there on our honeymoon! Come over and I will meet you in Paris.

You put DSO after my name on the envelope. Not yet! Cecilia is going strong, Fritz happy. I would send him to you for safe-keeping if there is a way. When can I expect you? Shall I publish the bans? You're a dear and a comfort!

Lovingly in haste,
Talbot.

November 2, 1916

My dear L.

Little Cecilia has just been killed, run over by two wheels of a motor car while walking with me. Poor dear little thing. Everybody was fond of her. I am lonely in my office and my room. What shall I do? What will happen to Fritz? I must get him away to you as soon as I can. He is timid, seems to expect a blow, yet most affectionate and full of life.

I feel awfully depressed, as if I brought misfortune and death to those about me. It is a wretched feeling. I have arranged to buy my horses and bring them back with me after the war but I am sure something will happen to them. I hate to think about the poor pup. Couldn't even comfort the little thing. Had to tell you about it right away. It's the devil.

I may come to Canada soon after all. My law partner wrote yesterday to say Laurier had suggested to him I run as a candidate in the next election. A constituency was suggested. I have not made up my mind yet what to reply.

Five boxes of cigarettes from you. Many thanks.

Affc. Talbot

JOHNS HOPKINS HOSPITAL
BALTIMORE, MARYLAND   11/11/16

Patient:
    Mr. W.L. MacKenzie King
    Age: 41 years. Single. Occupation: Politician and public worker.

Diagnosis:
    Psychoneurosis
    Psychasthenia
    Pyorrhoea alveolaris
    Chronic sinusitis
    Pityriasis rosea

Adm. October 30, 1916. Discharged: Nov. 11, 1916.

Dr. Barker:
Patient is a member of a distinguished Canadian family. He is in good physical condition but has peculiar ideas in regard to his own person and other people. He has the idea that other people are influencing him by electrical currents. He is of a very sensitive nature, deeply religious and leads a strenuous political life. At present he is writing a book. He has fear that his present work may militate against political success in Canada. Has always been emotional and troubled by insomnia. Does not feel sick. Well oriented as to time and place. Is only disturbed by worry and feels if freed of this, he would have the power of a giant, and could undertake anything. Inclined to feel a little depressed over this. Death of his father and the illness of a brother have increased this feeling. Has no fear.
Urine: Negative.
Prostate: Normal. Small cyst in left testis. Swelling of the verumontanum and distension of the vesicles — a condition frequently found in continent males. No treatment advised.
Blood: Normal.
Blood Wasserman: Negative.

Skin: Erruption due to pityriasis rosea, which is due to gastro-intestinal
disturbance. Common lotion prescribed.

Teeth: Outspoken pyorrhoea requiring treatment. Root of the left super. first
bicuspid appears to project into sinus. Should be extracted.

Stomach and Intestines: Normal.

Nose and Throat: Chronically infected tonsils. Large adenoids. Evidence of
infection on left side.

Report of Dr. Adolph Meyer, psychiatrist:

Problem of patient due to an obvious elimination of natural sex life; the
intensely religious and spiritualized trend of affection; the strain from illness
and death in the family; an intense feeling of responsibility and of jeopardizing
his position politically; an utterly unhygenic arrangement of life, partly due to
his pathological feelings, and partly due to his excessive feeling of obligation
and the suspicion that he has been asked to make a report to test his
faithfulness to the work. Patient needs to be within the reach of a helpful
arbiter before whom he can put his impressions and reactions. He needs a
broader philosophy and an appreciation of what enters into his life and a more
placid acceptance of himself, especially the parts he has been trying to
eliminate.

Weight: 182½ lbs. Height: 5 ft. 8½ in. Ideal wt. 157 lbs.

11/6/16: Extraction of tooth.

11/7/16: Adenoids removed. Left antrum drained.

11/8/16: Patient getting along well. Feels greatly pleased over the result.
Feels the definite source of infection has been removed and this will
react favourably on his nervous condition.

11/10/16: Patient feels greatly encouraged. Feels he can go back to his political work, that he has a grip upon himself. Says he will now get rid of
his nervous troubles.

11/11/16: Patient discharged.

3

The men's lavatory of the Russell Hotel is a recognized social centre in Ottawa, so Jack's not too surprised to see that the man taking a leak in the next urinal is the Hon. R.B. Bennett, Q.C., MP for Calgary West and chairman of the National Service recruiting campaign. Jack's attention had been attracted at first by the diamond ring on the pinkie finger of the hand holding the cock, a cock as long and pink and languid as the man it belonged to, a man who, with his large, round, bald head and sloping, fleshy body looks, the more Jack thought about it, exactly like what he is, a large, erect dick.

His drinking buddy, George Bennett, had pointed out his famous brother a few times through the window of the saloon. "He's rich as fuckin' Croesus," George would say, "but tighter than a virgin's twat." Diamond Dick Bennett was pretty hard to miss. Not only did he wear a diamond ring, and a diamond stick-pin, and diamond cufflinks, but he was the only man in Ottawa who wore striped trousers, and a cutaway coat, and a silk hat, and spats, and a monocle, in public, on the street, in broad daylight, every day of the year. People called him "Mr. Peanut."

"War wound?" says Diamond Dick, nodding at Jack's claw.

"Yeah."

Jack had gotten pretty tired of explaining to strangers how he'd really blown himself up, years ago, before the goddamned war even started, and people looked at him funny, like he was lying, so he'd decided that if they wanted to think he was some bloody tinpot hero, then that was their problem. He sort of made the stories up as he went along, a shell at Ypres, a German bullet at St. Eloi, a flashing sabre during a cavalry charge at Sanctuary Wood. Christ, the newspapers described the battles in such gruesome detail it was almost like he'd been there himself, and the soldiers' lingo was pretty easy to pick up.

"Been back long?"

"Yeah. A while."

"What's your outfit?"

"Royal Flying Corps."

"The *Flying Corps*."

"Uh, yeah."

Diamond Dick's face suddenly beams on him like the rising sun.

"Boy, you have saved my day!"

"Yeah?"

"Where's your uniform?"

"I, uh, gave it to my mother, in, uh, Vancouver."

"No matter. I have one. It will do. Look, uh...."

"John."

"Look, Johnny, do you know who I am?"

"Yeah. Sir."

"I need you, Johnny. Your country needs you. What I am asking you to do is very simple. This afternoon there is a recruiting parade. A *major* event. Unfortunately our representative of the Royal Flying Corps is, uh, unable to be with us...."

"What's wrong with him?"

"He's, uh, passed away, gone west, napoo. He shot himself."

"Yeah?"

"Johnny, I am asking you to ride in a car for two hours. That's all. You don't have to say anything. Just smile and wave. Look brave."

"Umm...."

"There's $100 in it for you."

"Doncha think that maybe seein' a guy crippled might kind of *discourage*...."

"No, no! It's not the men we're after today, Johnny. It's the women. Women adore suffering."

Jack finds himself swept out of the lavatory, Diamond Dick's long, flabby arm around his shoulders, and propelled across the square to Dick's suite of rooms at the Chateau. There's a bunch of military types there and a few cripples. The uniform which once belonged to the late F/O Hubert Peacock is brought from the funeral home. (Christ are they gonna bury the bugger naked?) It's a handsome rig, nice boots and a flashy leather helmet with goggles, but even with the helmet on, and the silk scarf wound around his neck, there's not much doubt that F/O John Cuchulain looks a hell of a lot more like Silver Coolican, the star winger for the Montreal Canadiens whose picture has appeared frequently enough on the sports pages of the Ottawa newspapers to convince him he's certain to be recognized. (He'd complained to the editor about appearing next to some asshole who'd just had his block blown off. "It's a curse," he'd said, and the editor said he'd try to transfer the casualties to the foreign news.)

"Maybe I should have some bandages or somethin'?" Jack says.

"Righto!" cries Dick. "Peacock was blind wasn't he?"

"Hey, I dunno. . . ."

They compromise on one eye, and once Jack's patch is arranged, and his arm placed in a sling, he figures not even Lily would know her own brother.

Just before the noon whistle they troop downstairs and climb into Freiman's enormous black touring car. There's a banner across the hood saying "We Want You Now!" and another along the side "When in Doubt, Join the 207th!" Jack sits up on the trunk next to Major Gault. The rest of the car is full of fat guys in civvies. Politicians, he figures, but he's grateful when one of them passes up a mickey. It keeps off the chill.

They pull out towards the Byward market, a procession of six touring cars draped in flags and bunting, the band of the 207th in the lead, the three hundred poor shivering suckers who'd been dumb enough to join up straggling along in the rear. They gather a crowd along Rideau and Sussex, people pouring out of the shops and tenements as they turn into the market square, nosing their way, horns blaring, past the farm wagons and knots of shoppers. The first three cars block the north exit, the others block the south exit, the soldiers, with fixed bayonets, filling the spaces. Jack is in the last car, next to the O'Reilly Billiard Parlour. He feels thirsty. It's trying to snow.

"Ladies!" bellows Diamond Dick Bennett. "Mothers! Sisters! Daughters! Wives! Sweethearts! I haven't come to sign you up. . . ."

He laughs. The ladies don't.

"I've come to enlist your tender hearts and your generous souls. Your hearts are the most powerful weapons in our arsenal!

"Ladies, I have been to the front. I have seen our boys fight. Their courage is wonderful. Their spirit is invincible. And I have talked to our boys, in the trenches, knee-deep in mud, in the dressing stations, after a victory, smiling bravely as they wait for their wounds to be dressed. And do you know, ladies, what they say to me? Do you know the first thing they ask? 'How are things at home?' And their fingers will fumble at their jacket pocket and they'll bring out a little snapshot, all crumpled and stained with sweat, still warm from their heart's beat, and they'll hand it to me tenderly and they'll say 'That's my wife, Mr. Bennett. Pretty ain't she?' And I see a woman's face there, smiling, and children too sometimes, or maybe just a girl, no older than some of you here, who's waiting for him to come home. I'll bet a lot of your faces are in those men's pockets, eh? How many of you have boys overseas? Husbands? Sweethearts? Brothers? Come on now, hold up your hands. Don't be shy. Be proud! Because do you know why your boys are over there? Not because they hate the Huns, although God knows there's enough to hate, but men don't fight from hate. They fight because they love you! They love their wives and children, the mothers who bore them and raised them, the sisters who shared their games, the girls they're going to marry when they get home. They fight because they know what's happened to the women of France and Belgium, the women of Serbia and Russia, when the filthy Hun has overrun their villages, defiling innocent girls, raping and plundering. . . ."

"Bullshit!"

The cry comes from a tall girl in a dark coat standing on one of the farm wagons. Jack notices that she is young, with white skin and masses of curly red-gold hair.

". . .spreading filth and corruption to the wells of pure home life. . . ."

"You're a liar!"

The crowd is stirring now, murmuring, people turning to stare at the girl. The square has filled up, people shoulder to shoulder, a lot more men, it seems to Jack, than there had been, working men in cloth caps, with ruddy faces and stony stares.

". . .unless we conquer this Prussian pestilence. . . ."

"Butcher! Murderer!"

The girl suddenly disappears. Diamond Dick is sweating, mopping his face with a balled-up handkerchief. Jack notices that the door to O'Reilly's is open, and men are crowded there, watching, and faces are peering out the windows.

". . . .so how do you think those boys feel when they hear their sister's engaged to some bohunk who says he's got a weak heart, but he's not too weak to dig ditches, or his best girl's stepping out with Jimmy Brown, the biggest kid on the street, who's got himself a soft job pushing paper while he makes up his mind about going overseas? Well, let me tell you how they feel. They feel ashamed! Ashamed that any Canadian girl would be seen in public with a man not in uniform, a man like you, sir, and you, and you, and you! What's your excuse? A man who's not part of the war effort is against it! He is a coward! He is worse than a coward. He is a traitor!"

A low mooing sound passes through the knots of men. A potato sails through the air and bounces off the hood of the car. The soldiers of the 207th look at each other and shift from foot to foot.

"The real enemy in our midst isn't the German spy. It isn't the foreigner with the funny accent. It's the man right next to you who's not in uniform! Because every able-bodied Canadian man who's not in uniform is a gun in a

German hand! Any man who won't step forward and volunteer, right now, is worse than a German. He's a rebel! He's worse than an Irishman!"

"Sure, if it's a fight yer wantin', we kin 'ave one right here!"

The shout comes from O'Reilly's. The Irishmen are swarming out now, the French too, from the other side of the square, picking up sticks, staves, cobblestones. The hail of potatoes is coming thick now, eggs too, Jack takes two on the shoulder, turnips, horse buns, still warm and smoking. The women are screaming, scurrying for cover, the men pressing close around the cars, spitting, shouting curses, rocking the cars. Jack fights the urge to rip off his bandage. Christ, impersonating an officer. He'd be shot for sure. He undoes the cover on his holster. With a little luck, F/O Hubert Peacock left five shots.

Major Gault stands up on the trunk, leaning on his crutch.

"I'm Major Gault of the Princ...."

"How's the missus?"

"Fucked the whole regiment she did!"

"I have been to the front, and I am going back...."

"Atta boy, Hammy! Keep an eye on 'er!" Screw 'er with yer wooden leg there, Hammy boy!"

Jack jumps up on the seat, his arm high in the air, waving the revolver.

"Charge!" He fires two shots into the air.

The soldiers of the 207th Battalion, most of whom have never fired a rifle before, interpret this as an order and begin firing wildly in all directions. The Irishmen mill about, uncertain, confused, space opens up where men have dropped to the ground or run away.

"Let's get the hell *out* of here!" Jack yells at Archie Freiman. Archie leans on the horn, floors it, and the big Buick peels off down George St.

Jack hops out at the next corner, right behind Freiman's Department Store. He has his helmet and eyepatch off before he's pushed his way through the Saturday crowds to the front door, then the sling, and scarf, as he crosses Rideau Street dodging traffic. He tears off the jacket in the quiet of a cubicle in the Union Station men's room.

Shit. What does he do now? His clothes are across the street in Bennett's suite in the Chateau. Hell, every bloody Irishman in Ottawa will be out there now. He'll never hold his head up again if they ever find out.

He pulls off the boots and jodhpurs, which are itching like hell anyway, he never did believe in underwear, and unbuttons his shirt. He folds it neatly with the tie and scarf inside the jacket, the helmet and jodhpurs on top. F/O Hubert Peacock will have to be buried without his boots, but Jack will try to see to it that he's not buried naked. He props the boots up in the cubicle, tucks the clothes under his arm, takes a deep breath and opens the lavatory door.

Saturday, November 18, 1916; 12:15 p.m.

William Lyon Mackenzie King places his new pince-nez gingerly on his nose and peers out the train window. Carleton Place. Less than an hour to Ottawa. He'll be glad to be back in his snug rooms, among his familiar things, altogether comfortable and restored to health, ready to take a prominent place in public affairs. Monday is Sir Wilfrid's seventy-fifth birthday, a splendid occasion to renew old friendships, establish the links to the party he has allowed to slip so badly this year. It was a mistake to keep so much to himself. He had been too sensitive about the Rockefeller connection, too easily bruised by criticism. He must proceed "like a sun on its course," as Dr. Meyer had said, keeping true to his own ideals, beholden to no man. What a splendid talk they'd had together! How wrong he'd been to mistake the normal urges of a healthy man for diseased passion, how foolish to allow a little difference of opinion with Mr. Rockefeller to run away with his imagination. Why, as soon as Dr. Meyer explained that men of genius frequently suffered from "brainstorms" and emotional breakdowns, it was like a great weight had been lifted off his shoulders. Of course, that was it! He had the gift to see things that others missed, to understand more clearly, to feel more deeply. He has always felt out-of-step. Now he can see that it's his destiny to stand a little apart from the crowd, to point the way. The life of a great man is always lonely. He must accept that, remain calm, reasonable, carrying the mantle of responsibility with courage and self-denial. If he has Faith, God will guide his steps. Why even yesterday, in Toronto, a friend had whispered that Sir Wilfrid had mentioned him as a possible successor! Not that Laurier was about to step down, not immediately at any rate, the party wouldn't hear of it, but at that age you never knew, a fall, a stroke — his own father had died suddenly, in bed, without a sound, a merciful end, really, although a great shock to poor Mother.

He glances down at the little book Dr. Barker had given him, *Eat and Grow Thin*. Well, he is trying. He has given up oysters and caviar (who would have believed they were fattening?) and cocoa and sweets. It doesn't do to look fat, in wartime, especially since he is not in uniform. Of course, now with Mother dependent....

It will be a great comfort having her living with him, although he will have to clear out the study for her, and work in the sitting room, but the inconvenience will be worth the joy of having Mother there, just as they were when he was a boy in Berlin, a true, honest conscience to keep his feet on the right path. He'll get to work right away rearranging the furniture, he'll buy a proper hospital bed, with a matching table and commode, and have everything ready so Mother can be with him by Christmas. He'd quite broken down when he'd left her this morning in Toronto, her thin, frail arms clinging to his neck. "I want to die where you are, Billy," she'd whispered. How lucky he was to have such love! How could he ever be worthy of it?

He removes his pince-nez and rubs his eyes. His head is throbbing again, the left side, where Father's blindness — no, no, it's just the smoke, the noise. The train is full of soldiers, a whole battalion from Winnipeg or some such godforsaken place, and a bunch of them have camped out in the first-class coach, drinking and bellowing some filthy song about a mademoiselle over and over again. He has spoken sternly to the conductor, but the conductor just shrugged and said the men had no seats elsewhere and it was a long way to Halifax. He'd decided to skip breakfast rather than brave the rowdies but he'd gotten so hungry finally that he'd made his way to the dining car leaning heavily on his cane, affecting a limp in his left leg, with no worse consequences that a few shouts of "Hi, Dad," or "Who's the old duck?" The war was such an *inconvenience*.

He had very nearly enlisted, in August, when he'd been feeling so ill and morbid. At Kingsmere he'd had a particularly vivid dream about poor Bert, so clear it seemed that Bert was in the very room with him. He was smiling and saying "Come, Willie. Come! Come!" He'd felt such elation, such happiness, that he'd seen it as a sign, a call to sacrifice his own life, as Bert had given his, by throwing himself into the fray. He'd even taken the train to Ottawa, with the intention of signing up with the 207th Battalion right away, but when he stood for a time in front of the Sir Galahad monument it struck him that his action might be misunderstood, as his loyalty to the Rockefellers had been, not as a gesture of supreme self-sacrifice, but as support for everything wicked, hateful and corrupt about a war he despised, a sure and certain route to Hell. Who, after *his* death, would build a monument to *his* memory? He'd walked the streets aimlessly all day and taken the evening train back to Kingsmere.

Even Junior Rockefeller had misunderstood when he'd explained how necessary peace was to prosperity.

"N-n-not at all!" Junior said. "Quite the contrary! War creates demand! Ships! Shells! Guns! Food! Fuel! The greater the destruction, the greater the demand! War creates jobs, raises wages, gets things h-h-humming. Why, the war is the best thing that ever happened to Canada! We're going to have to jump in or go b-b-broke."

Junior Rockefeller had made it clear, ever so tactfully, that while the Rockefeller Foundation would pay for publication of *Industry and Humanity* it would not authorize the book, or underwrite sales, or be publicly associated with it in any way.

It had been a cruel blow. William Lyon Mackenzie King had quite broken down. The harder he tried to work, the less he was able to write; and the less he was able to write, the deeper he sank into a pit of anxiety and paranoia. In

October, when he was supposed to submit the first draft of the manuscript to Mr. Rockefeller, he had only thirty-odd pages and some typed-up notes.

"Perhaps you need another vacation?" Junior said.

He had arranged for William Lyon Mackenzie King to enter Johns Hopkins Hospital for a complete examination, free of charge, and had directed that the bills for his twelve-day stay be sent to the Rockefeller Foundation. He had invited Mr. King to convalesce in his own home for a week, and on his departure for Canada had presented him with two books he himself found very helpful, *Power Through Repose*, by Annie Payson Call, and *Why Worry?*

"Thank you," said William Lyon Mackenzie King, tucking the familiar white envelope into his breast pocket, next to his wallet and the photograph of Mother.

He fingers the envelope nervously as the train chugs slowly along the Rideau Canal towards Union Station. Expenses will be high with Mother, an election coming.... He had been quite astonished to find on his last visit to the bank that he had more than $80,000 in assets, yet he still has no job, no seat in Parliament.... It's just as well. The war seems to taint everyone who touches it. No matter how pure their motives, how noble their intentions, they emerge somehow besmirched, muddy, guilty. It will be only a matter of time before the Conservative government falls from the weight of its own corruption. Why, only last week Sir Sam Hughes was pushed out! What a crash! Who would have expected it? It was said the King demanded it, that Hughes was a madman and a menace to the war effort, and he was lucky not to be court martialled and shot. Well, no wonder, with his Prussian swagger and vile profanities and crazy ideas, like tearing up the Grand Trunk railway and transporting it to France so the war can be fought by train! And his insane insistence on Canadian armies and Canadian officers and Canadian hospitals, why it was just sucking Canada deeper and deeper into an Imperial maelstrom she was better off out of altogether.

Young Papineau is obviously a tool of the Hughes-Aitken crowd. There is no place in the Liberal Party for a man of his militarist views. What he calls nationalism is nothing but jingoism in sheep's clothing. Papineau will cause trouble, split the party, introduce Tory propaganda, conscription, alienate the French, the working class, the little people. It's a loss, yet.... Tomorrow he will warn Laurier of the dangers in offering Major Papineau a seat in the House of Commons.

Ottawa; 1:05 p.m.

Lillian Freiman is hurrying across the rotunda of Union Station. She's late. First there was Archie stumbling into the store, his beautiful beaver coat all covered with frozen egg, then such a commotion on Rideau Street! People running every which way. She mustn't miss the train. Some soldiers will be disappointed. They'll need their little comforts to get them to Halifax. God knows what sort of reception they'll get in Montreal!

As well as her heavy tray laden with apples and cigarettes and candy and magazines and soda pop, Lillian Freiman is carrying a bag of feathers. It had not been her idea to pin white feathers on men who wouldn't enlist, in fact she'd opposed the idea when it had been raised at the Red Cross.

"How do you tell if a man is a coward?" she had asked. "Maybe he has six toes, like Mr. Bennett, or a bad heart, like my Archie?"

It had caused considerable discussion, since the husbands of most of the women present were suffering from some invisible, but incapacitating, disability.

"We'll give them a 'reject' badge," said Lady Borden. "In the meantime it does no harm to err on the side of good. We must do *something!*"

The next problem had been to find the feathers. The ladies of the Red Cross purchased their chickens plucked. A survey of the Byward Market revealed that most of the live hens for sale there were brown. The few that were white were dirty. Who would pluck the chickens? Who would wash the feathers?

"My cook would quit!" cried Lady Borden.

Fortunately, a member of Mrs. Freiman's Disraeli chapter was Esther Cohen, whose uncle Sam Rabinovitch owned the Sleep-Tite Bedding Co. Sam Rabinovitch made pillows. Even better, he bought his feathers from the kosher butcher, Rabbi Rosenberg, and Rabbi Rosenberg preferred leghorns, so it is a bag of pure, white, kosher feathers that Lillian Freiman is carrying to distribute to the ladies of the Red Cross, who will pin them into the button-holes of whatever slackers, cowards and other ne'er-do-wells they encounter in the public places of Ottawa.

Speaking of slackers, isn't that Mr. King? Why, he's no doubt straight off the train from New York! Imagine, having the nerve to show his face back in Canada! Some people have no shame. And look at that coat, good thick cashmere, $7.50 a yard at least, maybe $6 in New York, and the suit, well, she could tell an expensive hand-tailored suit a mile off....

"Good day, Mrs. Freiman," smiles William Lyon Mackenzie King, reaching for his wallet. "Are you raising money for another of your charitable causes?"

"Not exactly, Mr. King," she smiles, tucking a feather swiftly into his lapel.

"What is this for?"

"It's a feather."

"Yes, but what does it mean?"

Mrs. Freiman isn't looking at him anymore, but past him, over his shoulder. Her face is pale, her mouth is open, as if to speak, and her eyes are very wide.

"Eeeeeiiii!" cries Mrs. Freiman, throwing up her hands.

A naked man is running straight towards them across the rotunda, dodging like a jackrabbit through the crowd, a policeman shouting in pursuit.

"My goodness!" says William Lyon Mackenzie King.

"Here!" says Jack, thrusting a bundle into his arms. "Keep it."

William Lyon Mackenzie King stands stock still, watching the naked man sprint out the door, holding the uniform of the late F/O Hubert Peacock, feathers settling like snowflakes on his shoulders.

"You could call it macaroni," says Mrs. Freiman.

"Macaroni?" says William Lyon Mackenzie King.

4

252 Metcalfe St., Ottawa
Monday, November 20, 1916

Sir Wilfrid's seventy-fifth birthday today. Such a ham he is, Laurier with his powder and pompadour and his funny old clothes standing so straight and proud, like a peacock. You could almost see him fanning his tail. A huge crowd. I helped with the coats and the "medicine." Prohibition is such a nuisance! We had tea and coffee and fruit juices downstairs in the dining room, but Zoé had two immense teapots full of wine in her sitting room and we had to run back and forth to her bedroom filling them from the bottles. The whisky was in Laurier's study, I think, because the men who went in there came out looking very red and jolly. It's so silly because drinking is perfectly legal in Quebec just across the river. The war is grim enough without temperance.

Willie was one of the first to arrive. He looked amazingly well. He said his "trouble" was only infected tonsils! He was very friendly and complimented me on my dress. He said I must come and visit Mother after she arrives. He seemed very happy and cheerful. I wonder sometimes if I didn't dream what happened last summer. Maybe it *was* my fault.

"The only time Mr. King speaks to me is when he's after somet'ing," Zoé said sourly. "*C'est un assassin.*"

"Assassin?"

"You will see. Look how all those near him grow sick and die, his sister, his father, his brother with the *consumption*, yet he is fat! He will kill his own mama to get ahead. He will kill Laurier. He has no feeling. You will see."

Zoé said Laurier will ask Talbot to run in Brome, in the Eastern Townships. It's a safe seat, a large English population. An election is expected in the spring.

"If the war is over, Laurier will win," she said. "If it is not, it is better that we lose."

Ottawa
Tuesday, November 21, 1916

Rowley Booth got stepped on by a horse this morning. It wasn't bad, the horse was more surprised than he was, but he was covered with manure and I had to sit for more than an hour with the stinking little brat on my knee until he stopped hollering. He's not a bad little kid, but he's only two, and full of beans, and we're all terrified he's going to fall under a wagon or walk into a saw or fall down a chute into the rapids. Nobody has the courage to tell Mr. Booth a sawmill is no place for his grandson. "Start 'em young!" he says, and that's that. He goes nowhere without Rowley. They eat their meals together, in the kitchen, cooing and giggling at each other, and before they go off to bed the old man chases him around the house on his hands and knees roaring like a bear while Rowley shrieks with delight. They'll play together for hours, but the trouble is every so often Mr. Booth wanders off somewhere and forgets completely about him. He even went home one day without him, and had to send the driver back with the buggy. Last week Rowley got into Mr. Gardiner, the manager's office and dumped his inkwell all over his desk and made nice blue handprints on the papers. "This place is a goddamned nursery!" screamed Mr. Gardiner. "Next thing we'll hire bloody women!" Mr. Booth seemed very contrite and sat and played blocks with Rowley for the rest of the afternoon, singing nursery rhymes and mumbling to himself.

It wouldn't be so bad except we're so busy. Everything's going full blast. Mr. Booth is keeping the full crew on all winter, top wages, and he's sending six gangs into the bush to cut spruce for railway ties. It's all very hush-hush but apparently the army is building narrow-gauge railways in France, behind the lines, like the Germans do.

I stink of horseshit and pee.

Ottawa,
Wednesday, November 22, 1916

This morning Mr. Booth shoved a pair of overalls at me and an ugly mob cap of Old Martha's. I put a shantyman's smock over the whole thing and shuffled after him into the mill. We stopped in the "junk" room where they cut the low-grade lumber into lathes and box boards. The saws here are small but

swift, with a horrible high-pitched whine. The old man picked up a board and
zip zip zip, cut it into perfect two-foot lengths.

"Here."

"Me?"

I slid the board gingerly towards the saw. *Whing*! It was done. *Whing*!
Again. *Whing*!

"Good, good," he nodded. "Keep at 'er. Set yer pace. Sure an' steady."

I kept at it half an hour. When the noon whistle went my back was breaking
and my head was ringing. I was soaked with sweat.

"Try 'er a week. See how she goes."

A *week*!

Ottawa
Thursday, November 23, 1916

I think I am going to die. Cut boards today from 7 a.m. until 6 p.m. with one
hour for lunch. My ears hurt. My eyes hurt. My back hurts. My whole body
aches. My hands are raw, even with gloves. The men kept looking at me,
expecting me to quit, and I got so tired I would gladly have put my neck under
the saw, but I stuck it out, although I don't remember much of the last two
hours. The men are very kind.

They think I must have done something terrible to be punished this way!

Ottawa
Friday, November 24, 1916

Washed my hair. Full of sawdust. Also my nose, throat, ears and eyes. We
come home at night all brown, like gingerbread men. Some of the men just get
browner and browner.

Ottawa
Saturday, November 25, 1916

My little pile of boards is getting bigger! I am getting the hang of it. The pain
was mostly fear.

"Ye gotta take 'er easy Missy," Joe Reilly said over his onion at lunch. "She
ain't gonna bite ya. Ya gotta kinda cosy up to 'er, listen to 'er, talk to 'er, jist
like a woman!" They all had a big laugh over that. Their saws all have names
— Millie and Rose and Jasmine and Kate — and sure enough when I look I
can see their mouths going, talking away, like they were chewing tobacco,
although I can't hear what they're saying for the noise. It's true, each saw has a
"voice" when you hear them separately. But usually the men saw together, in

rhythm, like boatmen pulling on a rope. They say it's easier that way, nobody goes too fast, and they get a split second of silence between cuts.

I call my saw Sam, in honour of Sir Sam Hughes, just a ghost now, Ena says, since his fall from power. "He wouldn't have minded being shot by the Kaiser," Ena says. "It's being stabbed by his own side that hurts so bad." I talk to him too, urging him along, it helps to take the mind off the monotony. The men tease me about Sam. "'E jiss need a little strokin' dere," says Onzième Parent. "Some guys, dey take a while t'git warmed up, but den watch out, Kaboom!"

Ottawa
Sunday November 26, 1916

Sleep all day. Stiff.

Ottawa
Monday, November 27, 1916

I am fifty boards a day behind the slowest man. He's been there two years. Mr. Booth says I'll catch up in another week or two. He whistled and rubbed his hands all the way home.

Ottawa
Wednesday, November 29, 1916

Only thirty boards behind. I am staying on. I prefer Sam to Rowley. Tomorrow I progress to lathes.

Ottawa
Sunday, December 3, 1916

Went with Willie after church to put flowers on Sir Galahad. One dozen white roses. They were turning brown from the frost even before we got there. Seems an awful waste. Nellie McClung says that chivalry is a pile of crap. It's out of fashion now anyway. You can't sit around pretending to be weak and helpless and stupid when there's a war on. Besides, it's boring.

I still dream, though, of being married, at Montebello, and lying in bed until noon, with servants, and tons of beautiful, trailing gowns, and wonderful things to eat, and nothing, nothing, nothing at all to do!

Spent two hours at the Friendless Women. The place is packed, girls and babies sleeping on cots in the halls. No one knows what to do with them. A lot of them have V.D. It's the soldiers. Piccadilly. There are brothels eveywhere behind the lines. Half the army is infected. Mrs. Fleck said how can you feel patriotic when your husband comes home with the clap? I guess that will put an end to all the talk about the war making the world "pure."

Ottawa
Wednesday, December 13, 1916

I did it! Twelve boards less than Joe Reilly, two boards more than the slowest man. They all clapped and cheered, most of them anyway. Some of them don't like me. They stay apart when we eat our lunch. Joe says they're bolsheviks. They keep to themselves. He says Mr. Booth would dismiss them except they're good hands and he needs all the men he can find. The rest are friendly. Some of them worked in the bush with Papa, years ago, and they all follow the hockey. I got five free tickets to Jack's last game and they drew straws for them. You'd think they were choosing the Pope. They are like big boys, although some of them must be close to sixty, and I feel like an only sister with thirty brothers. Sometimes they bring me little treats from home, butter tarts and cookies, to fatten me up, so I can catch a "'osbond."

"She look pretty good dress' like a man, eh?" Onzième says every day. "T'ink 'ow good she look like a woman!" They laugh harder every time. It is fun, and not at all dirty, in fact they always call me "Missy" and treat me with the utmost politeness. I have grown very fond of them, like a family, and I feel almost that I know their wives and children even though I've never met them. We don't have much time to talk. It is solitary work, each of us alone in a cocoon of noise, thinking our own thoughts, shapes in a fog of dust. I realized today that I've hardly seen the sun for a month. It is pitch dark when we come to work, and pitch dark when we come out, only the lanterns bobbing like fireflies as the men make their way through the streets of wood, their laughter slowly fading in the clear, sharp air, the crunch of a thousand boots on the snow. Only the stars are real, and the snow, and the mill.

Ottawa
Saturday, December 16, 1916

A great crowd of women was waiting at the gate this morning. I thought at first there'd been an accident, but everything looked the same, and they stood quietly, stamping their feet, and parted silently to let us through.

"We'll take on twenty for a start," said Mr. Booth, taking off his coat. "Widows first. Fifteen to forty. Start 'em slow 'til they git the feel 'o the place. Best ones move up. Rest move out. You keep yer eye on 'em."

I hired twenty women before noon. There must have been more than a hundred still waiting in the yard. A few stood there all day.

"Watch the weight," said Mr. Booth. "Don't want no brood sows. Gotta be strong, but quick. Watch the hands. No lily whites. No fists fulla spuds neither. Does she talk with 'er hands? Take 'er. She wearin' neat, home-made clothes? Take 'er. No aliens. No boozers. No blubberers. No shakers. Two-fifty a day and all the tea they kin drink."

"But the men make $3.75 and tea."

"That's right."

"But where are we going to put them?"

"Ye'll see."

At six o'clock Mr. Booth laid off twenty single men. "I won't turn ye over t' the military," he said, "but I ain't gonna let ye hide in here neither. There's a job in a shanty if ye want it, a dollar a day, or ye kin take the King's dollar overseas. That's the bargain."

Twenty men from the lathe room will move into their places on Monday. The women start on the lathes. I am foreman. Forelady? Boss.

I have printed Nellie's slogan on my looking-glass:

"Never retreat.

Never explain.

Never apologize.

Get the thing done,

And let them howl!"

I am going to need it.

Willie's birthday tomorrow. He has invited me to a little party, for Mother, on New Year's Eve. I don't really want to go, but Alice has gone home to Banff for the holidays, and Jack is God knows where, and I don't want to be alone, at Booth's. Willie is very curious about what I'm doing at the mill but I told him it was war work and very "hush-hush." Of course that just eggs him on. He's like a dog with a bone. Zoé says that when she's with Mr. King, she feels as though she's being licked.

Ottawa

Monday, December 18, 1916

We all got through the day in one piece. Nobody walked into a saw. One woman fainted, two were late and two quit so I hired five more. There were still fifty waiting in the yard. I felt sorry for those I had to turn away. Some had such flimsy coats, and sweaters that were nothing but darns on darns, and it wasn't their fault they were too old, or needed glasses. I gave them all tea at noon. They seemed so grateful. Some of them seem quite desperate. A day's wages at the mill is more than they earn in a week cleaning houses or doing laundry.

Most of them did quite well. They are very serious, very eager to learn, frightened of the saw and the noise. I tried to show them, one by one, how to get into the swing of it. One big Swedish girl picked it up right away, *whing, whing, whing*, and worked right to the six o'clock whistle without even stopping for breath, then stacked all her boards neatly in a pile!

At lunch the men sat separately, by the far wall. Everyone was very quiet. The women didn't talk to each other. They just ate and drank their tea. A couple didn't seem to have any lunch at all but they just smiled and shook their heads when I asked.

Ottawa
Saturday, December 23, 1916

Let three go. Too slow. The Swedish girl, Ebba, is nearly as fast as the men. She is just twenty, with two children. Her husband was killed last year. Mr. Booth gave all the "lasses" a bag of candy. The men got turkeys.

I have saved nearly $500. I'll have enough to get to Paris by Easter, London at least, counting clothes and hotels and meals. I suppose I shouldn't go alone but I don't give a damn. If it doesn't work out I can always come home. Maybe I could get on as an ambulance driver. Or Sir Max might find something for me. Alice says he brought down the British government and will be a great power behind the throne in the new administration. I am sorry Talbot got tangled up in that intrigue. I shouldn't have meddled. But if I hadn't.... If only there's an election soon. Zoé teases me that I'll be a prime minister's wife some day. "It is not impossible," she says. "I was just poor Zoé Lafontaine when I met Laurier, *une pauvre* like you, and now, *voilà*, I am Lady Laurier, yet I am still poor!" She is teaching me French.

A card from Willie, "Yours devotedly," (???!!) and a little book, *Power Through Repose*, by Annie Payson Call. I haven't sent him anything. He is in Toronto, with Mother, for Christmas, and will bring her back with him. Can she type?

5

Prime Ministers' Papers: Public Archives of Canada

King; William Lyon Mackenzie (1874-1950), prime minister of Canada, 1921-1930, 1935-1948. Private Diary (handwritten) 1916. p.362.

Wednesday, December 27, 1916

Mother and I arrived safely at the Union Station about 8:30 this morning having had a remarkably good night on the train. The porter brought Mother an orange at 6 and she was up and dressed when the train reached the station. Not a sign of illness, or even train sickness the whole way.

We drove to the Roxborough in a covered sleigh, and had breakfast in my rooms, before the flowers, with the bright window opening out before.

McGregor had some carnations on the table to greet Mother and myself, red and white and prettily arranged. Col. Foster sent a lovely cyclamen, to me, a box of sweetmeats to mother. The servants were all pleasant in expressing their thanks for 'Xmas gifts.

I went through a pile of letters and cards awaiting our arrival — such a lot of beautiful cards from friends in the United States and Canada and England. Among the letters were three from Mr. Rockefeller, one acknowledging my letter proposing two months salary off, which he said must be placed before the Committee, one enclosing his cheque for $365.00 in payment for the expenses of my illness, & one informing me tentatively of renewal of my engagement with the Foundation for another year. All were beautifully expressed, & in most considerate and kindly terms. The last rests my mind for the coming year. It gives me that time to complete the work in hand for the Foundation & lets the year's events intervene, with a chance to be governed by them as to what may be best at the close. Truly I have reason for profound gratitude at this great good fortune, and at possessing so loyal and true a friend. How grateful I am that everything has worked out. Instead of being poor and stranded as we once feared & might have been but for the care and foresight of recent years under the Providence of God, the independence I had hoped for as a basis of public life is gradually being accumulated. I am trying to put my affairs on a solid basis, providing for Mother and myself in the event of politics and marriage come what may.

I wrote thanking Mr. R. and answered other letters.

This morning and afternoon I got busy with McGregor and two servants, and pulled my office out of the room in which I have had it & which I changed into a room for Mother & converted my bedroom into an office & bedroom combined. It was a heavy and dirty job but we made splendid progress and by evening I was able to show Mother into the little room I have tastefully arranged for her, and to give her a welcome to it, which as I expected, would be appreciated so feelingly that words could not be expressed. She has been wonderful all day, went downstairs to both lunch and dinner.

After dinner, when I spoke of going out for a little walk, she asked if she could come along. A perfectly wonderful spirit. If the body were only strong, it could achieve anything. It gives me a great deal of happiness to have her near me, and now I shall provide for her happiness always. God grant she may be long spared. God has answered my prayers in letting me see father's affairs well straightened out, during his lifetime, and provision made for his age, free of debt and obligation of any kind, and He has answered it, in preserving Mother for me, and restoring my nature to its noblest self, where I find the highest joy in unselfish service for her. For all this my heart is filled with a gratitude beyond words.

To bed at 11.

Thursday, December 28, 1916

The maid in the rooms has a cough and I gather has tuberculosis. She said "Wherever you go you have to work." What a lot the poor have! I feel I should like to give my life in service to help improve theirs, that is my real ambition. I wish I had the right person with whom to share it.

Most of today as been spent continuing yesterday's arranging of furniture and belongings. Also some little time spent shopping. Bought a brass bed (single size) mattress and springs for Mother's room for $35.00. Then I attended a meeting of the Patriotic Fund. Met the new Governor-General, the

Duke of Devonshire. I thought he was a man of force of character and ability, essentially practical and with a good business head. He spoke very well. One million Frenchmen have been killed in the war so far! What a sacrifice! How can men love war, how can nations tolerate it!

At the Rideau Club I had lunch with Mr. Fraser and Sir Henry Egan, two of Ottawa's millionaire lumbermen. Both very modest and agreeable men. After lunch I wrote letters of condolence to Frank Oliver, Col. J.W. Woods and J. Turiff, MP, on the loss of their sons in the war.

Took Mother with me for a little walk between 4 and 5. It was not too cold and she enjoyed the air, but she is very frail. She came down to dinner but did not each much. Tonight she went early to bed after we finished reading the balance of *A Sunny Subaltern*, a splendidly written series of letters & wonderfully descriptive of the boy's experiences in all phases of war.

The Tory papers are beginning mean attacks on me because of the Rockefeller association. Trying to raise enmity with Labour because of this association. How sinister and cruel the world is to those who would befriend it!

Friday, December 29, 1916

Today has been spent putting things away. McGregor and I have worked like Trojans cleaning cupboards and drawers from the bottom up and putting in the storeroom below everything we can manage to get along without. We have had shelves put in below and are removing all our transfer cases there, the entire correspondence of past years is now in the basement. Also we packed away many of the pictures which I have had since coming to Ottawa. I am trying to 'put behind those things that are behind' that I may the better 'press on to the mark of the calling in Christ.' Mother has developed a heavy cold which threatens bronchitis. Mother took both meals in bed and ate very little at either of them. I have sought to get her the things required, fruit, medicines, etc. but I find it difficult to remember, and with the cramped quarters doubly hard. I try not to be impatient, but somehow illness in others is very hard for me to bear. Still, I shall seek to be brave in this, and overcome myself, realizing how great is the privilege. No joy can equal making her remaining time peaceful and happy. I fear greatly at times that it may not be long, yet if I do keep her bright and of good cheer it may be for years. God help me to do this with all the love of which my nature is capable, love worthy of her dear life and love. Mother will I think throw this cold off soon.

Hon. Mr. Casgrain, Postmaster General, died today from pneumonia. I liked him & he was one of the best of the present government.

Very cold tonight — to bed 11:45.

Saturday, December 30, 1916

Today McGregor and I continued our task of cleaning up. We spent part of the morning completing the correspondence and this afternoon we worked in the storeroom downstairs, hauling boxes, sorting papers etc. By 8 o'clock we had every cupboard & drawer in the place cleaned out, its contents duly sorted and packed, and the rooms transformed in appearance. I purchased a few articles for Mother's room, a little wagonette to cook on & serve meals on, an umberella (sic) stand for the Hall, and gave McGregor a small gift in recognition of his faithful services through the year. Mother is better but still has a heavy cold. I veritably believe she could not have lived long and might not have been alive now had she remained where she was. I got in a few groceries.

It was about 1 a.m. when I got to bed this morning having cont'd to work getting off cards and letters and straightening out things. It is a duty job well out of the way. So far as I know not a single business matter is outstanding or a single business communication unanswered or a single account unpaid (the club and Roxborough excepted). We end the year with a perfectly clean slate.

Sunday, December 31, 1916

All day I have worked very hard to clean the slate of all obligations. I *owe* no man or woman living a letter or a cent, nor even an acknowledgment of a kindness done or a courtesy shown. *Everything* has been acknowledged though it has taken a herculean effort and has prevented me enjoying Mother's society through the day.

Have had breakfast & tea in my rooms & greatly enjoyed sharing them with Mother and having them cooked on our little electric heater. C. came for tea. She brought Mother a perfectly lovely violet in a pot, a mass of blooms & just right for the sunny window. She is a sweet, modest girl, quite transformed now she is out of the 'royal' set. I can't help but feel she may be the one to share my life's work. I have in the past perhaps been a little too critical and missed opportunities that way.

Tonight I found a five cent piece in the snow in the middle of Sparks St. Picked it up, was surprised to see the King's head. If it be an omen it may mean a King's commission with sufficient to carry it out in the New Year.

My last thought in the year was of dear old father and little Bell, and the loved ones still on earth. We are all one family although two have gone before. I thank God for sparing me Mother, and for restoring me to a nobler manhood than any I have hitherto known. Withal God has been kind and good. I see life more clearly. My faith is stronger, my life purer, my character nobler than a year ago. Passing through the furnace of physical and mental suffering has taken some of the dross away. I look out on life with a wider vision and spiritual insight and have greater self-control & a greater faith in God. Good-bye old year, and God forgive all that has been amiss in it and bless the good that He has sent. All we owe to Him.

252 Metcalfe St., Ottawa
New Year's Eve, 1916

The party turned out to be just Willie and Mother and me. A quiet tea, cosy fire. The place has been cleaned up wonderfully, quite bright, masses of flowers. The "Death of Iphigenia" has been replaced by a "Crown of Thorns," which is even more awful. The room smelled of antiseptic, medicine and furniture polish, like a funeral parlor. Willie read some Burns. I sang "Annie Laurie." Mother had a good cry. "This is my last Hogmannay," she kept saying. "I won't live to see another." She refused to be cheered up. Poor Willie.

On the way home he found a five-cent piece in the snow. He thought it was a message from the King. "Maybe he wants you to enlist," I said. He put it in his pocket.

Last night Mr. Booth cut all the men's wages to $3 a day. There was a lot of grumbling and more than five hundred men gathered in the yard at quitting time. We were scared of a riot. "They'll want t'git home 'n drink," said Mr. Booth. "They'll be no trouble." A group of them came into the office to plead with him. "Ye'll take it," he bellowed, "or I'll close the mill!" There was a lot of shouting and cursing. "Git out, then, if ye don't like it!" he yelled at them. "An' don't come back!" On Tuesday we'll take on twenty more women for the lathe shop.

Whisky and haggis for dinner. Drank a *lot*. Feel terrible. Wrote Talbot. He has his DSO now and a six-week course at staff college. The Pats have asked him to return to the regiment. He will go if they make him second-in-command. The regiment is his home now.

G.H.Q.
January 1, 1917.

Lily dear, my first letter this year shall be to you, and it is very little I can do to thank you for the thousand kind thoughts and deeds which have given me so much pleasure and have marked for me friendship, perhaps the most precious I have ever had. Yesterday I received your last letter and it was the kindest and loveliest you have ever written to me. I had not heard from you in ever so long, but in the meantime your beautiful clock had come. It will be wonderfully useful, so handy, and I only have to wind it once a week. I rise and descend by its time, I dine, I wash, I go to lectures, by its command. You have ordained my life. With every tick I must think of you! Really, Lily, I feel most unworthy of such goodness. You have all the attributes of a fairy godmother and I love you as I would a fairy — except when I peep into my watch and see your sweet, grave face and honest eyes — then I love you — as a photograph.

You certainly have been frank about marriage, haven't you. You say I am not "serious" and "don't know you" even though I feel I've known you all my life. I am not blaming you a bit. Marriage is such a terrible finality. I am however, mortally jealous of Sam and Joe and Charlie and Onzième (imagine numbering your children!) and all your thousand and one stalwart beaux. I can imagine how devastating you are in your mob cap and coveralls, but I can't imagine you throwing great boards about and churning up masses of sawdust. How strange things will seem when I get home, all the dainty girls I knew great beefy slabs of sinew and muscle!

Shall I make you jealous of my whirl in London? Luncheon, tea, dinner, theatre, supper, dance every single day, always with different people. Ran into Doris from Winnipeg and I'm not quite sure I am not engaged to her. I was engaged to Martha for a few days. May still be, not sure. Martha was quite the best dressed girl in London and drives her own little car, a Fiat, and a beauty. Dorothy was sick in bed but I went and had tea one time. Prettiest thing you ever saw, all pink and white and blue and golden pigtails with pink bows on and white fluffy fur and a bad cough — put Mimi right out of business. However she would not consent to an engagement at present. Doris is the best dancer in Canada and quite an amateur actress. A little politician and very fascinating — a narrow escape. What the dickins was all the talk about the "girl in Montreal"? There is no such girl. I write to no one regularly except you, and if only you knew, my dear Lily, how gladly I would give myself to you entirely, for I am a sad, silly gadabout and allow too many of your attractive persuasion to divide my affections. In consequence I despair of myself. Shall I make resolutions for the New Year?

Thus has my New Year's Day gone by. At nine this morning we all left in an old London motor bus to "A" where we saw a pack train unload into wagons boxes of rations and hay and oats and straw and cheese from Montreal. We munched sandwiches on the way home and at three had lectures with a break for tea until 6:45. Then dinner in the mess until nine. Then here in my room. What have you done? Shall I hear? Last evening three of us dined with Col. Sims — an excellent big dinner — and afterwards played billiards upon an indifferent table. Now I must lay me down to sleep, being tired and the morrow will be long.

You are a darling my dear Lily and in my inner heart I love you.

Talbot.

6

Dominion Police Force
File #3782

BULLER, Annie S.
Sex: F. Height: 5′8½″ Weight: 140 lbs. Eyes: Blue. Hair: Red/gold
Date of birth: Dec. 9, 1896.
Place of Birth: Montreal, Canada.
Residence: Suite 3, 104 George St., Ottawa.
Occupation: Salesgirl, china dept., Ogilvy's Dept. Store.
Race: Hebrew.
Religion: None.

Charges: Seditious utterances, inciting to riot, public mischief.

At approximately 12:55 p.m. on Saturday, November 18, 1916, I observed a young woman shouting from the back of a wagon during a National Service recruiting rally in the Byward Market. Observing her remarks to be of a seditious and inflammatory nature detrimental to the purpose of this public meeting, I apprehended the young woman with the aid of Constables Perry, MacIntosh and Spence of the Ottawa City Police. On her person were found several leaflets advocating resistance to National Registration, a number of publications in a foreign language and a copy of *The Red Flag*, a well-known Bolshevik newspaper, all of which are banned under the terms of the War Measures Act.

Under examination the young woman freely confessed to being a Socialist and opposed to the War Effort, which she described as "a war against the working class." She also admitted that her actions were intended to "stir things up" and she seemed pleased when informed that a riot had, in fact, ensued.

In view of the provocative nature of her conduct and the undesirability of her political opinions, I recommend immediate deportation.

> Respectfully submitted,
> W. James Dempster.

Annie: "You can't deport me."
  Jimmy: "Why not?"
  Annie: "I'm a Canadian."
  Jimmy: "You're a Jew."
  Annie: "I'm a Canadian Jew."
  Jimmy: "We can intern you."
  Annie: "No you can't."
  Jimmy: "Why not?"
  Annie: "I'm not an enemy alien. I was born here. I'm a domestic enemy."
  Jimmy: "Well, we can lock you up then."
  Annie: "For what? Speaking my mind? I thought this was a free country. Isn't that what the war's all about? Freedom?"
  Jimmy: "You were carrying a German publication...."
  Annie: "Yiddish."
  Jimmy: "...and a Russian-inspired newspaper...."
  Annie: "They're our allies, aren't they?"
  Jimmy: "Shut up!"
Trial: Ottawa City Police Court, November 26, 1916.
Sentence: Reprimand; One month probation.

Ottawa; Saturday, January 13, 1917

Annie Buller wasn't a Kraut, that's for sure. Damn, he could've sworn when he saw her, big, buxom, blond, white skin, who ever heard of a Jew with blue eyes, and tough as hell, Christ she'd given him a good whack on the shins and a black eye before he'd got her off that damn wagon, and the language! Jimmy Dempster had never arrested a woman before who didn't burst into tears, or wheedle, or try a bribe, money or sex, but there wasn't much chance he'd get into that broad's pants, or out again in one piece if he ever did. But like Sir Percy said, if she was a spy, she wouldn't go around advertising it, would she, and the tough news was there just wasn't much interest in Bolsheviks these days. With the Socialists in Germany doing their damnedest to bring the Kaiser down, nobody wanted to lean on them. He'd expected a promotion after bringing in the goods on Mackenzie King, but Sir Robert Borden had just sighed in his rumbly way and said that branding Mr. King a socialist would only do him good with the working men, and push the trade unionists into the Liberal camp, and that wouldn't do the government much good, would it? Weren't they having enough trouble already with these bloody women all going Liberal because of Mrs. McClung? If Sir Robert knew of Jimmy's role in exposing the secret Rideau Hall telegraph room, he had chosen to forget, and he spoke of the Duke, now that he'd gone, only in terms of the highest regard, and described Sir Sam Hughes, who'd driven him nearly mad with his careless flamboyance as "my beloved friend."

So on Saturday, January 13, 1917, Constable Dempster is still Constable Dempster, assigned to the unpleasant task of rounding up deserters, quelling riots, dragooning reluctant volunteers out of church services and keeping an eye on Annie Buller. She hadn't been up to much. A lecture by Red Emma Goldman on birth control. Half the Red Cross had been there too, so there wasn't much he could make of that, they were all sex-crazed, being around naked men so much. Annie had smoked a cigar at a tea dance in the Russell House, blowing perfect smoke rings at the orchestra, and raised a ruckus when she got thrown out, demanding to know the difference between a cigar and a cigarette, but he'd kept her name out of the papers, saying she wasn't a suffragette but a nut case, a friend of the family, so embarrassing.

He sure hadn't expected her to turn up at a hockey game, but there she'd been, right ahead of him in line for tickets at the Auditorium, so he'd followed her in, suspecting a dodge, and taken a seat three rows behind and a little to the right, realizing when it was too late to flee that he was on the Montreal Canadiens side of the arena surrounded by a howling mob of crazed peasoupers. Well, a job was a job, so he'd turned up his coat collar and pulled down his tocque and hollered along with the rest of them, feeling like an asshole since his original purpose in coming had been to watch the team of the 207th Battalion, who occupied the opposite side, beat the living piss out of the Frenchies.

"Come on, Hymie!" yells Annie. "Come on, Hymie! Kill the bastards!"

Jack hears her from his spot on the Canadiens bench and recognizes her right away, even though his right eye is almost swollen shut from a stick he'd taken across the face in the first period. He's never heard anybody cheer for them in English before. He and Hymie are the only two *anglais* on the team, except for George Kennedy, the owner. Kennedy figured if he had a couple of English on the team they wouldn't get beat up so bad, by other *anglais*, maybe score a little better, but it didn't work out that way. If anything they got beat up worse. It's shitty hockey anyway, so much tripping and slashing they can't mount a rush, crap raining down on the ice, pennies, overshoes, fish. In Ottawa a fresh carp on the blue line is a big joke.

"Hey, Hymie! Who's the blond dolly?"

"You mean Annie?" Hymie shouts over the screech of the 207th Battalion's brass band. "Shit, she's my *sister*!"

With less than a minute remaining in the game Jack takes a hard rebound off the boards beside the 207th net, draws the goalie and neatly tucks the puck in the corner of the net. Canadiens-12; 207th-4.

Jack loses sight of Annie in the deluge of bottles and popcorn, fish and flags and furious fans that pours on to the ice after the referee calls the game. By the time Jack fights his way to the dressing room he's covered with spit. Silently the Canadiens put on their boots, slip their overcoats over their jerseys, form a solid phalanx, sticks high, skate blades out, and charge for the exit.

Annie is waiting across the street in a taxi when he and Hymie stumble out in a hail of broken glass. They dive for the back seat.

"You guys shouldn't put up with this!"

"So, it's a living."

"You're being exploited."

"Aw, c'mon, we cleaned those guys!"

"That's not what I meant. You're being treated like bums. Thugs."

"Money's okay."

"You're bought and sold. Cattle."

"Yeah. So what do we do about it?"

"Strike!"

"Yeah? High-sticking? Clipping? We're pretty good at that...."

"Hymie, be *serious*."

"We're not a union for Chrissakes! We're...We're...We're stars!"

"You're assholes. Here you are getting your heads beat in for a measly, what, $1,200 a year? And how much is Mr. Kennedy taking home? Twenty thousand? And does Mr. Kennedy get his head beat in? No. But Mr. Kennedy likes a fight because fights bring the crowds and the crowds pay the gate."

"He'll blacklist us."

"He can't blacklist *all* of you."

"For Chrissakes Annie, you'd organize the birds in the trees."

"The birds are organized. *You* are the problem."

"You can organize me if you like."

She gives Jack a long, hard stare, her face passing from black to white, black to white as the taxi passes under the street lights. She is not pretty, but she has the high, Slav cheekbones and wide mouth he liked so much in the Polack girls back home, and wow, that hair! He reaches out and brushes a loose curl from her cheek. She shrugs.

"Sure."

"My place or yours?"

Face down on the ice, his cheek resting in a puddle of blood from a gash across the back of his head, rests the unconcious but still breathing form of Constable W. James Dempster, one of the thirty-six casualties, twenty French, sixteen English, of the most memorable battle ever fought by the 207th Battalion, which will, upon its arrival in England a month later, be dispersed among other regiments as reinforcements, remaining only a lingering memory to the twelve men, of the original 305 recruits, who come home.

Ottawa
Sunday, January 14, 1917

Found Jack in bed at noon with *another* blond.
"Annie's a Socialist."
"That's not what I call it."
"I am *not* a tart!"
"She's just sociable."
"Virginity is a bourgeois myth to keep women enslaved. Free love is a necessary step towards sexual equality."
"Up the revolution!"
"Women must liberate themselves from sexual taboos."
"Besides, it's fun."
"Cheap at the price."
"You have a very reactionary attitude."
"Lily's just jealous."
"I am not!"
"My sister likes *old* men. Can't get it up...."
"Oh, bugger off. You've liberated half the girls in the Ottawa Valley. I don't see any revolution. All they get are broken hearts and babies."
Annie groped under the covers and held up a concave, pink circle, all dripping and slimy.
"Rubber. It's called a cervical cap. Ninety-nine per cent foolproof. Want one?"
"Well...not right now."
She lay back against the pillow, stark naked, calm as you please, and lit up the most enormous Havana cigar.
"I rolled these damn things at Macdonald Tobacco, in Montreal, when I was a kid, twelve hours a day, two hundred of us at long trestle tables in a dark warehouse. They liked little girls because our fingers were small and quick. I was an 'apprentice' for almost five years at half wages until I turned seventeen. Then they fired me. That's why I smoke these things. That's why I'm a Socialist."
"Do you know Mr. King? He's a Social...."

"Like hell."

"Pardon?"

"He's a Rockefeller socialist. Socialism for the rich."

"Well, he's written about sweat shops and phosphorus necrosis and better working conditions and preventing strikes...."

"Liberal reform strengthens capitalism. It deludes the workers with trivial gifts, while keeping power and profit in the hands of the bourgeois exploiters. Bread and circuses. Have you read Marx?"

"What's that?"

"*Karl* Marx. *The Communist Manifesto.* I'll lend it to you. You will see things differently when you've read it."

"It's kind of like the Bible," Jack says, "except instead of angels and devils, there's workers and bosses, right? And they fight each other until the Revolution comes, which is sort of like Armageddon, and the workers win, and there's Heaven on earth."

"You sound like Bishop Ralph."

"Well, sort of, except...except...we don't have to die!"

"Jack is a worker," says Annie, blowing a smoke ring. "What are you?"

"Me? Well, I guess...I work...but I'm sort of a boss, too...I've never thought much about...."

Annie listened very carefully as I talked about the mill, glad of a chance to tell *somebody*, bragging a little about how we can cut more lathes in a day than the men ever did, taking only thirty minutes for lunch instead of an hour, no point wasting time gossiping, everything neatly stacked and swept at the end of the day, Mr. Booth so pleased he gives us extra bread and jam for lunch, because some of the women have so little, only a cold potato, or an onion....

"Does he pay you more?"

"More?"

"More than the men. For doing more."

"Well, no."

"Less?"

"Yes."

"Why do you work so damn hard then?"

"I...it's...pride. We want to show...."

"Or else you'll get fired?"

"They *need* those jobs. It's a lot of money for those women."

"They're scared?"

I thought of those fifty tired, dirty faces leaning against the wall at lunch, eyes closed gulping their war bread and scalding tea, how silent they were compared to the men, hardly looking at each other, or at me.

"I hadn't thought about...."

"What do the men think?"

"They don't like us."

"Should they?"

"No."

"What do they call you?"

"Dirty names."

"Finks? Scabs?"

"Cunts. Bitches. Whores."

"Are you?"

"No! We work hard...."

"For less."

"Well, we don't fucking *give* it away, like you! Aren't you scabbing on the whores?"

Such an infuriating girl! Where does Jack find them? This one's the strangest yet, worse than the Spanish Inquisition, plain as a board fence except for her hair. Well, I *am* jealous of girls with blond, curly hair, so there.

Ottawa

Monday, January 15, 1917

Went tobogganing with Alice at Rideau Hall. Sore bum. Met Jack Munro on Elgin St. coming home. He was wearing his Pats' greatcoat, the empty right sleeve pinned up on the shoulder. It gave my heart a bit of a tug. He still had his big yellow dog, Bob.

"I'm on my way to Kirkland Lake," he grinned.

"But you can't...."

"Oh, it's not to dig! Your brother has another wee operation up there that requires a man of my long experience and specialized...taste."

He winked and smacked his lips.

Me: "Jesus, Jack, are you bootlegging?"

Jack: "Well...uh...."

Me: "But you own a gold mine!"

Jack: "Yeah, but we can't get the damn stuff out. Nobody but Harry Oakes believes its there. You know what they call it? The 'Hoax Mine.' Funny eh? I want to sell out but Harry won't. Who'd buy the damn thing? Rockefeller?"

Ottawa

Tuesday, January 16, 1917

Annie: "I wish to apologize."

Me: "Apologize?"

Annie: "You are right."

Me: "About what?"

Annie: "Only yesterday I came across a letter from Comrade Lenin to Comrade Inessa Armand, our great leader in the free love struggle. Comrade Lenin states that free love is an expression of philistine individualism leading inevitably to moral degeneracy. What matters in affairs of love is the objective logic of class relations. Free love is a bourgeois, not a proletarian demand."

Me: "Jack will be disappointed."

Annie: "Nothing is lost if we are able to learn from it and correct our errors."

Me: "Maybe Lenin is wrong."

Annie: "Lenin! Never!"

Me: "Actually, the idea was beginning to appeal to me."

Ottawa
Friday, January 19, 1917

Went with Alice to the Dominion theatre to see Talbot's movie, *The Canadian Army in Action,* although his name wasn't on it anywhere, only Max Aitken's, Lord Beaverbrook now, but it was about Courcelette, and the French Canadian regiment, *les Vingt-Deux,* although the battle scenes were staged. Everything was staged, Talbot said, but it looked pretty realistic and awful.

"That's him, Alice! I'm sure that's him!"

"Where?"

"There! The major, see with the armband, and the tin hat."

"How can you tell?"

"I'm *sure.*"

"You can't see his face for the hat."

"Look, he has a moustache...."

"They all have moustaches."

"It just looks like him."

"They all look alike to me."

Alice doesn't think I should go to London.

"You shouldn't go chasing after a man."

"I am not chasing. He invited...."

"It's not etiquette."

"Etiquette! Alice, it's *war.* There may be no *time* left! Why should I sit here and wait, and wait and wait? I want to grab my chance now, before it's too late."

"It may be too late already."

"What do you mean?"

"The U-boats are sinking everything in sight. It's not safe."

"I'll take my chances."

Ottawa
Monday, January 22, 1917

I have cut off my hair. I did it this morning at the mill, on the spur of the moment. We all did. It was a crazy irresistible impulse, like a fever, that spread from one to the other. Ebba's long, blond plait fell down and she accidentally cut off the end in the saw. She started to laugh and before I knew it she'd turned around and flicked the whole thing off under the saw, zip, laughing and whooping around waving her braid like an Indian waving a scalp. Everybody looked up and started to laugh and dance around, *woo-woo-woo-woo*, and in a flash caps came off and the braids came off, *zing, zing*, hair flying through the air everywhere, everyone giggling and galloping around waving their switches, tearing the caps off the girls who held back. They grabbed me last, and I thought for a moment they might take my head off, but it was fun, and over in a second, and I felt ten pounds lighter but half-naked. And I laughed so hard I had to sit down in a pile of sawdust to catch my breath. I was afraid Mr. Booth would be furious but he was quite pleased. Keeps the hairpins from dulling the saws, he said.

Alice has snipped at me with the scissors to trim things up. She says I look like Theda Bara in *The Eternal Sappho*. I think I look ghastly. I sail for London March 26. Will it grow in time?

Ottawa
Friday, January 26, 1917

Annie: "What the hell happened to you?"
  Me: "I cut my hair."
  Annie: "I don't mean your hair. I mean your eye."
  Me: "I got hit. By a piece of wood."
  Annie: "Who slugged you?"
  Me: "Nobody *slugged* me. It was thrown. Some of the men were waiting for us when we came off work. I'm okay."
  It wasn't some of the men, it was a great mob of men waiting in the yard when the six o'clock whistle blew, chanting and cursing and shouting. Mr. Booth had to call the police to make a path for us to get through. It was Onzième Parent who threw the block of wood. I saw it coming and stood there, frozen.
  Annie: "Why do you fight each other? Why don't you fight Booth?"
  Me: "How?"
  Annie: "Demand equal pay."
  Me: "We'd be dismissed."
  Annie: "Shut the place down."

Me: 'We'd *all* be dismissed."

Annie: "Crap. He can't afford it. He's building the Parliament buildings. He needs you. And there aren't enough able-bodied men left in Ontario to take your places."

Me: "Well, I can't strike."

Annie: "Why not?"

Me: "Because I'm...I'm...the boss."

Annie: "So quit."

Me: "I can't quit."

Annie: "Why not?"

Me: "I need the money."

London will take every cent I have even if I stay with Caroline Papineau in the Dorchester. Am I a fool? What if he thinks I'm ugly and stupid? What if he's stuck-up?

And yet what is there to lose? Love? Letters? Lies? I can't go on spinning dreams. It's too hard, when such frightening things are happening, and I feel like a liar concealing the truth. Dreams don't seem to be enough any more. I can feel him drifting away, out of touch, into a world where I can't go, the lifeline between us growing thin as a spider's thread. When I saw the moving picture it seemed that those flickering patterns of light representing men were more real than the men themselves, or that they weren't men at all, but shapes of men, imaginary men, black-and-white men in a black-and-white universe, gnomes in funny hats jumping out of the ground and jumping back in again, running and shooting and doing things that people in the real world wouldn't think of doing, ghosts playing fairy games in a wild wood. And it seemed as if I had seen Talbot's spirit, and he was already dead — no, not dead, but that his spirit had left his body and was living in a different place, far away, and would never come home.

I have to know.

Ottawa
Saturday, January 27, 1917

Annie: "You shouldn't let them beat you up."

Me: "It's not my fault."

Annie: "What's old Booth ever done for you?"

Me: "It's not him. It's my girls."

Annie: "*You're* girls?"

Me: "Well, I like them."

Annie: "How many did you let go this week?"

Me: "Three. Six quit."

Annie: "I bet your heart bled."

Me: "I felt badly, but...."

Annie: "I bet your major whatshisname feels bad too when he's butchered a dozen kids in a good day's work."

Me: "Talbot is not a butcher!"

Annie: "How many men has he killed? Fifty? A hundred? He must be good at it, he's damn near a colonel."

Me: "Shut up, Annie. *Shut up!*"

Suite 3, 104 George St., Ottawa
Sunday, January 28, 1917

I quit last night.

"I suppose yer gittin' married," Mr. Booth said when I told him.

"No."

"Well, you oughta be! Yer damn near an old maid."

"You're an old fart," I said but he didn't hear.

"Bye, bye," said Rowley.

And that was that. I am staying with Annie. Tomorrow we're going to look for jobs in a munitions plant out past the Experimental Farm. There's a waiting list, but Ena McAdam awarded the contract last year and she'll give me a letter to the manager.

Me: "I thought you were against the war."

Annie: "I am."

Me: "Then why are you making shells?"

Annie: "Comrade Lenin tells us to go where the workers are. They are making shells. A woman who makes shells is a strong woman, a militant woman, it's simply a question of directing her fighting spirit into the correct channels, so she finds her place as part of the mass proletarian revolution, and identifies with her fellow workers in the struggle against capitalist exploitation."

Me: "Like me?"

Annie: "Like you, comrade."

7

Billy: "Mother, dearest, perhaps at last I have found the girl to share my life...."

Mother: "Oh, Billy! How you flatter an old lady like me!"

Billy: "But...but...but you *are* a girl in spirit, Mother! And in appearance too, by far the loveliest young girl in Ottawa!"

Mother: "Well, once I'm better, and able to dress up a little...."

Billy: "I'll take you waltzing at the Country Club!"

Mother: "Oh my!"

Billy: "Perhaps, Mother, you will waltz at my wedding!"

Mother: "Wedding?"

Billy: "I have quite made up my mind, Mother. I am determined to marry. It is a necessary step."

Mother: "You're not going to marry that Irish girl are you?"

Billy: "Well, I...she...she loves me, I think...."

Mother: "But *I* love you! I've always loved you best, Billy!"

Billy: "And I love *you*, Mother! I am only thinking of you."

Mother: "I'll just be in the way, a nuisance."

Billy: "Not at all! I couldn't live without...."

Mother: "I'll go to the hospital. I don't want to be a trouble, Billy. You have your own life to live. I'm just a burden. I only want what's best for you."

Billy: "Mother, you are *not*...."

Mother: "My days are about over."

Billy: "Mother, please...."

Mother: "I want to die. I don't want to be a burden to anyone."

Billy: "You're not going to die, you're getting well...."

Mother: "Only for you, Billy, dear. I live only for you."

Billy: "And I for you, Mother."

Mother: "We were happy here, together, just the two of us."

Billy: "We *are* happy."

Mother: "I've only wanted what's best for you, Billy. But I'll be dead soon. Then you can have your fun."

The Roxborough; Monday, January 29, 1917

Mr. King: "I thought Mother looked remarkably well this morning, Doctor."

Dr. Gibson: "Yes. She seems quite bright."

Mr. King: "How long, then, do you think, before she is up and about again?"

Dr. Gibson: "Up? Well, possibly a wheelchair...."

Mr. King: "I meant the use of her legs. A good brisk walk would do a world of...."

Dr. Gibson: "Mr. King, I am afraid you are being overly optimistic."

Mr. King: "She *is* getting better, isn't she?"

Dr. Gibson: "Mr. King, your mother will be seventy-four years old next week. In addition to the usual frailties of old age, she suffers from hardening of the arteries, which causes the occasional lapses in memory, headaches...."

Mr. King: "That's just nerves. Mother's very sensitive. She's always had headaches. She simply needs rest, peace and ..."

Dr. Gibson: "As well, you will recall, we located a number of growths in her abdomen, one of which appears to impinge on the spine. This mass is interfering with her powers of locomotion and is no doubt responsible for the pain she experiences in her stomach and legs."

Mr. King: "Oh, her legs are much improved! She was able to move them a little this morning. With exercise, and proper nutrition, the muscles will gain strength...."

Dr. Gibson: "Your mother is too weak to survive an operation."

Mr. King: "Yes, I wanted to mention that. Perhaps we might start her again on solid foods, she is particularly fond of sweetbreads...."

Dr. Gibson: "Yes, if she wants."

Mr. King: "Good! With the proper diet, exercise, plenty of rest, she'll be up and about in no time!"

The Roxborough; Thursday, February 1, 1917

Mother: "Do you like me, Billy?"

Billy: "I love you."

Mother: "I always loved you best, Billy. You are so good. I had a good mother. I have a good son."

Billy: "You are the best of all, Mother. You are perfect."

Mother: "I've tried to be good. God knows, it's been a struggle. People haven't understood me."

Billy: "They didn't understand Christ, Mother. He suffered too."

Mother: "I am not very brave. I am trying so hard to get well, Billy, yet it seems to be one thing after another...."

Billy: "You need rest."

Mother: "I am so tired. So tired."

Billy: "You must try to sleep."

Mother: "Kiss me good night, Billy my boy."

Billy: "I feel like a boy again, with my head on your lap."

Mother: "Imagine, last week I thought I was dying, and here I am, holding the hand of the future prime minister of Canada!"

Billy: "Oh, Mother, now...."

Mother: "You want me to live until you're prime minister, don't you? Well, I will, I will live, Billy. I'll do it for you."

Billy: "And I will live for you, Mother. I consecrate my life to you, and God's holy service. May I be pure in thought and deed, worthy of your love and God's blessing."

Mother: "How I love you, Billy dear! Kiss me good night."

Billy: "Don't cry, Mother. There's nothing to be sad about."

The Roxborough; Tuesday, February 6, 1917

William Lyon Mackenzie King kisses his mother gently on the lips and lies down on the bed beside her, scarcely able to breathe for fear of waking her, his body tense, rigid, listening to the steady, shallow rasp of her breath in the darkness and all the intimate sounds so familiar to him now after so many sleepless nights, the quiet ticking of the little clock on his desk in the other room, *work Willie, work Willie,* the hot water chuckling in the radiators, the frost crackling in the wall next to his ear. He pulls the quilt up against the chill and closes his eyes, tired, so tired, yet afraid to sleep, afraid that with the slightest lapse of wakefulness, the slightest relaxation of will, she will slip away on him. He has kept her alive this long, hasn't he, through sheer force of will, and prayer, prayer certainly, long hours on his knees at her bedside, imploring God please, please let Mother live, let her live at least until today, her birthday, and God has answered his prayer, just as He had years and years ago when Billy had prayed to God to save his kite, when he'd let the string go, and the string had tangled in the grass, and when he'd prayed to God to find his dog, Gyp, and the dog had turned up the next day in Waterloo, and when he'd prayed to God to make Max well, and Max got better, and now, surely now too Mother would get well again, if he can only find the strength to keep praying.

"Billy?"

"Yes, Mother."

"Are you awake?"

"Yes, Mother."

"I'd like a little milk, and one of those pills Dr. Gibson left...."

"I've thrown them away, Mother."

"Away?"

"They weren't helping you. They put you into a coma."

"I don't remember."

"You must remain strong and alert, Mother, if you're going to fight this illness off."

"I'm so tired. Tired. I'm not sure I can find the strength. The pain...."

"God is strong, Mother. God will make you better."

"God. Dear God."

"Would you like me to sing to you, Mother?"

"That would be nice. I'm just a big baby, aren't I, Billy? I even wet the bed again."

"Shhh. The new doctor I've found will have you up in no time."

"I would like to be a bird, Billy, and fly away."

He sings softly for almost an hour, going through all the hymns and lullabies he can remember, his hand holding his mother's thin, bony claw. She seems to be asleep but every time he gently pulls his hand away her fingers tighten around it. He thanks God for the will to live for them both, and the wisdom to have exposed old Dr. Gibson for the charlatan he was, a complete fakir with all his gloomy talk of Mother's "hopeless" condition, one dreadful symptom after another, washing his hands of a cure, prescribing nothing but morphine tablets and bromides when it was plain they nearly killed her, in fact he wouldn't be surprised if the morphine hadn't caused the trouble in the first place, worsened the chill she'd taken being too close to the window, the pains in her legs and head nothing more serious than rheumatism, a touch of neuralgia, bound to clear up with the spring. Her bowel obstruction is a kind of nervous colitis, the new doctor, McCarthy has said, an altogether different man, cheerful and helpful, just the sort of doctor to brighten Mother's spirits and take her mind off her legs, not dour like Gibson, and rude. Imagine telling him, William Lyon Mackenzie King, that he was "irrational!" He had spoken out sharply to Gibson that he was a Harvard man, and something of an expert on economic questions, a scholar good enough to be employed by the Rockefeller Foundation on an independent inquiry, and certainly rational enough to know the value of fresh air, and wholesome diet and good, earnest prayer, and Gibson would see his Mother safe and well at Kingsmere this summer, no thanks to his care, but thanks to the divine power of love and faith and prayer. "Well, King, your mother has to die some day," was all the boor had managed to reply.

When the nurse comes at seven o'clock he goes out for a walk, hoping the
cold wind will clear his head, a fugitive from his mother's suffering, yet
hearing still her cries of pain as the nurse administers the enema. His is hungry,
dizzy, an unshaven scarecrow in clothes that hang too loose now, too
depressed to eat, to work, not a single page written in six weeks, praying for
the strength to endure, to triumph, not break down again, gulping deep
breaths of air to help him steady his nerves, get a grip on himself. He walks
fast, head down, in the first faint light of dawn, afraid that someone will
recognize him, and speak to him, cause him to burst into tears.

At breakfast he gives Mother the brooch he'd hidden under her pillow at
midnight, a black onyx, for father and little Bell, who've gone before, surrounded by a gold band, for the glory in which they dwell. He lifts her into a
rocking chair he's had set with a silver plate:

> "To Mother
> On her 74th birthday
> With Willy's love
> Ottawa, February 6, 1917."

He carries her, chair and all, before the fire, in the faint light from the window,
where she looks sadly into his Brownie as he takes her picture. He shows her,
one by one, the bouquets that have come in, seventy-four red roses from Mr.
Rockefeller, a mauve cyclamen from McGregor, sweet peas from Max,
daffodils and iris and hyacinths and harebells and violets and spring daisies
and the loveliest white gardenia from Lily. Mother plucks the largest bloom
and tucks it in her hair over her ear. Then he brings in the birthday cake, six
lighted candles, one for each member of the family, and "74" in pink icing on
the top, and steadies it in her lap while she blows out the candles, and cuts it,
placing the pieces in tiny boxes to be sent to the others, and takes a few bites,
and then he kisses her once, twice, seventy-four times, one kiss for every year,
and a few more for the years yet to come, and kneels at her side and thanks
God for the suffering He has sent to purify his nature, and asks God to spare
his mother long enough to see her beloved first-born son, William Lyon
Mackenzie King, prime minister of Canada, amen.

It is nearly midnight when he slips out for his evening stroll. He walks north
on Elgin, and stands for a long time in front of a house on George St. looking
up at the darkened windows, wondering if Christ in the Garden of Gesthse-
mane was ever this cold. An hour later, in a shabby room on the third floor of
a Patrick St. brothel, a nameless, naked woman kneels at his feet, takes his
cold cock into her mouth like a sacrament, and swallows it. It's over quickly
and he hurries home to record the transaction, directly beneath "Birks,
brooch — $50.95", in the little ledger Junior Rockefeller had given him for
Christmas:

"$2.00 — Wasted."

Ottawa
Tuesday, March 13, 1917

Annie: "The Revolution has come!"
  Jack: "Hey, we won the Stanley Cup!"
  Me: "I threaded a hundred shells today."
  Talbot: "My mind is all fallow. It's maddening to be getting middle-aged and nothing accomplished. I have been of utterly no value in the world. Created nothing. I have drawn pictures in the water with a stick."
  Willie: "Have spent today changing the rooms about so that I can give Mother the bedroom I now occupy, and have the front room to work in in the mornings and at night. I think she will be as well with this change, and the large bedroom will be comfortable for her, did I not think so I would not make the change, but I long for the sunshine to work in, and less confusion than at present exists. The bedroom looks very pretty and cheerful. If I didn't think so I would not let her remain there, but I really think it is going to be most satisfactory, and there will be a better chance of getting on with work in a quiet and orderly way. I bought curtains for this room, and after dinner continued the hanging of little pictures, taking out the home photographs that I had put away when Mother was so ill, and the little ornaments which were without charm at the time. How different the world looks when overcast with despair from what it is when brightened by hope!"
  Annie: "The Czar has abdicated! All power to the Soviets!"
  Me: "The Duchess of Connaught has died."
  Jack: "The score was 7-6. I scored the winning goal."
  Talbot: "I am feeling so full of life today that I want to go back to the regiment. Mother says it will kill her if I am killed and I believe her. I cannot get her to accept the situation with any philosophy. It is only thirty or forty years sooner and what is that."
  Willie: "In my own heart I have felt strange sensations today. When the beds were out of the study and Mother in the other room I felt almost as if I would break down. Part of this feeling is due, I think, to a sense of joy, that it is possible to make the change without danger of setback, part to the coming back to my own true self which the room as a study always brings to me. I am at rest in mind and heart here as I cannot be when surrounded by disorder. Mostly however the feeling is due to the strange atmosphere of the room after the sickness there has been, and the miracle that has been worked in it. I cannot but know that dear Mother's life has been saved here by the grace of God. The picture of "The Crown of Thorns" over her bed was very real to me through that terrible crisis. As I look at it now I think the vows made then, and since broken, and it is the grip at heart of these broken vows that more than all else makes me sad. I have slipped away when I should have held to the life of Christ more strongly than ever, a life more consecrated than ever before. May

God forgive me and help me to rise again. Dear little mother is so gentle, so tender, so wonderfully patient. I almost break down when I see her doing all this thro' her love for me. I feel I am not enough with her, while she is still with me. I shall begin anew. God grant that I may do His will better than ever before. First & foremost I must again become calm and peaceful at heart, earnest in thought, vigilant in act and reverent in all things."

Jack: "Hey, your boyfriend, whatshisname, the fat one, he knows Rockefeller doesn't he?"

Annie: "If you fools got organized you could own the National Hockey League."

Me: "Two more weeks and I will be in London!"

Talbot: "I have become very sleepy so I shall turn in. My bed looks very cold. Lovingly."

Willie: "Spent $2.00. Worse than wasted."

8

Plymouth, England; Saturday, March 31, 1917

She is wearing a dress the colour of spring leaves, a matching hat with a feather tilted over one eye and cream kidskin gloves that are warm and soft in his hands. She seems taller, straight, self-possessed, her face no longer the round face of a girl but all angles and planes, flesh on bone, definite, defined, the face of a woman whose secrets he will never share no matter how hard he tries, and he cannot help but try.

"You've cut your hair."

He is standing towards the back of the pier, near the door to the baggage shed, alone, looking very stiff. I see the red band on his cap first, then the gold braid gleaming against the black wall. He looks very thin and taut, tired. His face is drawn and lined, splashed white where the burns have scarred him. His eyes are black, secretive, only the crinkles at the corners are the same when he smiles.

"You've grown a moustache."

Dorchester Hotel, London
March 31, 1917

Caroline: "We'll ring for the maid to press your evening gowns."
 Me: "I don't have any."
 Caroline: "Pardon?"

Me: "I don't go to parties. At home."
Caroline: "We dress for dinner here."
Me: "I'm sure any nice dress will do."
Caroline: "I think not."

Talbot goes to these hateful dinners in uniform, straight from Corps head-quarters, and leaves as soon as possible, pleading work. He wouldn't go at all except his mother, during her winter in London, has acquired an insatiable appetite for army intrigue. The invading force of sisters, cousins and aunts far outnumbers the Canadian Corps in England. In formidable phalanxes the women troop from shop to tea to drawing room, making a fearsome racket with their tongues and leaving a debris of ruined reputations and crippled careers. Men are no match. His own Corps Commander, Sir Julian Byng, suffers silently the siege of the worst bedroom general in the entire army, his own wife Evelyn, the dreaded Memsahib.

Talbot's mother is triumphant. Talbot is safe. He is on Staff.

But he cannot play the game. Poor Colonel Farquhar, long since blown up by his own stupidity, had been right after all. Talbot had thought for a long time that once he knew the rules, he could play and win. His association with Max Aitken, Lord Beaverbrook (did his mother arrange that too?), appalling as it was, has given him a reputation as a brilliant strategist. Yet his taste for the game has disappeared.

The game is not war. He had misunderstood. The British Army does not exist to win wars, wars exist for the British Army. Casualties create fortuitious vacancies, vacancies create enviable promotions; the greater the casualties, the more promotions. A long, unsuccessful war is therefore preferable to a quick victory, and to achieve this end ineptitude and inefficiency are entrenched as the very bedrock of the British Army. One only has to look at the new Commander-in-Chief, Sir Douglas Haig, butcher of the Somme, a pig-headed incompetent who remains convinced that a single cavalry charge, with sabres, will win the war.

Look at him, Major Spitandpolish Papineau, master of the military memo-randum, commander of a corps of typewriters, officer in charge of carrier pigeons and telephone cable for the Vimy assault, safe and snug drawing lines on a piece of paper, red and black and blue, lines that mean a ridge captured, an objective taken, a promotion. Brigadier Papineau, Lieutenant-Colonel Papineau, oh how they must hate him, his old comrades, whose lives to him now are only numbers on a page, in triplicate.

And how *he* hates the redcoats! The realization has welled up slowly from his heart, feared and familiar, his father's dark shadow on the snow. He is a *Patriote* after all, rebel to the core, a Papineau fighting the same old battle, captive in the enemy camp paying with his own life the debt *Le grand Seigneur* had evaded, happy only in the fields of France among the ruined farmyards of his adopted home, happy in a dirty ditch with primitive men, *les habitants*, who fight because they have no choice, to stay alive.

His heart today is with the army in the chalk catacombs in front of Vimy Ridge, the great, pale caves lit by flickering fires, the air thick with smoke and the smell of fear: men milling, murmuring, mole-like, shadows against the walls, creatures of the underworld, troglodytes. For six months Talbot has been planning the assault on Vimy Ridge. He knows this labyrinth better than he knows the streets of Montreal. He has mapped it, measured it, excavated and explored; he has read the history of the war on its walls, the names of men lond dead, their regiments, battalion crests, poems and popular songs, instructions, messages, jokes, the initials of unknown girls pierced with arrows, a Bayeux tapestry of obscenities.

The assault is a diversion to pin the Germans to the ridge and distract their attention from the British and French advance to the south. It is not expected to succeed. It has become therefore something of an experiment, an artillery battle, guns timed with mathematical precision to the split second, every step of the assault rehearsed so every man knows exactly how many steps it is to the top of the ridge and how many minutes he has to get there. Talbot has studied aerial photographs until he knows every rock and bush. He has invented signals for the aircraft. He has visited Marconi at Poole and acquired a wireless, a bloody great cumbersome thing but, if it works, a wonder. He has drawn up plans and revised them and discarded them and started again. And again. And again. For the past week he has lived at Corps H.Q. catching odd hours of sleep on a camp cot, lights never out, telephone never ceasing, starting awake thinking the battle has been fought, remembering an oversight, panicky. He is no longer needed at the front. Everything is in place. He is long past the battle. He is planning the retreat.

She has come too late. There is no time for courtship. He has been irresponsible, self-indulgent, babbling on about love. There is no time for love. Did he propose marriage? There is no time for marriage. No time for life. Too late.

Talbot says he has no time to show me the sights. I don't want to see the sights. London looks exactly like it's supposed to.

I have come at the wrong time.

She smiles at him from a long way away. He sees her as if through the wrong end of a telescope, too far away for him to speak or hear or touch, or feel anything beyond helplessness, a vague regret that he seems to have lost something that doesn't matter any more.

We walk, in the odd hours he can get away, bobbing along in a sea of humanity, shouting at each other over the rumble of trucks and the blare of horns. London is in flood. Even the parks are full, every bench taken, the bushes spoken for, the maze at Kew too crowded for kissing, the grass too wet, perambulators on the paths, not a seat or a room or a corner that isn't occupied. If only we could be alone.

Even the poor whores in Piccadilly have to turn their tricks standing up, in doorways, in daylight. He hopes she didn't notice.

Imagine doing it right out in public like that with thousands of people walking by and gawking!

She stirs the ashes in his soul, probes among the dead roots, searching for tender shoots.

The French will mutiny without a victory, he says, and the Russians will make peace. The real winners will be the Americans, the Reds.
   "They'll fight."
   "Americans, yes...."
   "The Russians."
   "How do you know?"
   "Annie says...."
   "Have you turned Red, then?"
   "Oh no. They won't have me, I have too many sins...weaknesses...bourgeois attitudes. It's very hard to be a Bolshevik, you know. They don't take just anybody."
   "It sounds like McGill."

I made him laugh, at least.

Today she wears a dress the colour of wild violets. He buys a bunch from a girl in Trafalgar Square and puts them in a jar on his desk.
   "Pretty, sir."
   "I didn't know you cared for flowers, Blatchford."
   "I mean the girl, sir."
   "Does it show?"
   "Yes, sir."
   "I thought war would be the hard bargain, Blatchford."

"Not at all, sir."

Caroline: "Have you set the date?"
Talbot: "Monday. The barrage will open up at exactly zero five hours and...."
Caroline: "Your wedding."
Talbot: "I have nothing to offer a wife."
Caroline: "Why did you bring her here, then?"
Talbot: "I didn't bring her."
Caroline: "Why did she come?"

Why did I come? It has been a mistake.

She passes him a plate of cakes. He takes the lemon tart on the left, near her thumb. The thumbnail is broken, blackened at the edges. She pulls the plate away and puts it down. He grabs her wrist, turns her hand over and pries the fingers open. The ridges of her fingers are blackened, rough, swollen, the nails worn to the quick.
"Grease," she says, looking away, "soaks through the gloves."

He gives me a strange look and kisses my hand.
"I am an idiot," he says. "I'm sorry."

Sunday, April 8, 1917 midnight

There is nothing more to be done. The orders are going out. Men are standing up, shuffling into line, creeping out of caves, crawling along tunnels, rising up from ditches and dugouts, slipping out of woods: silent, stealthy, rifles swaddled, boots muffled with mud, sworn not to speak or smoke or swear, thousands of men filing steadily along the saps leading to the jump-off points facing Vimy Ridge, four divisions, the entire Canadian corps, full strength, forty thousand men on a four-mile front, the First Division to the south, towards Arras, then the Second, the Third and the Fourth on the north, near Givenchy, where the hill is steepest. They will not have far to go, only one thousand yards, all uphill, under fire. For all the preparations it will come down to the same thing, the bayonet in the belly, guts.
Talbot turns out the light and closes the window against the north wind. Cold. The moon is out. Bad luck. There is nothing more to be done but bring Lily home from the High Commissioner's reception and say goodbye. He leaves for the front tomorrow night; she sails the next morning.

The windows of the great house are blacked out. But inside, the chandeliers are blazing and a band is playing in a distant room. If they play "Tipperary," Talbot says to the footman, "I'll kill them." The footman nods and bows. Chatter, champagne. The usual English delight in a show, *une divertissement sanguine*, jolly good.

Where is she?

The Prince of Wales is in the drawing room, near the brandy, holding a cigarette gingerly between thumb and forefinger. The tiny white hand trembles and the prince sways on his feet. Poor kid, so desperate to be *Coeur de Lion*, such a small, sad little lamb. A king for our times. Talbot sees a livid face in a mirror, his own, beside it a walrus in a field marshal's uniform.

"Brandy?" says the Duke of Connaught.

Talbot drinks it at one gulp.

"Another?"

They stand together in a corner, Talbot clutching his glass, hefting it, testing the weight, one good grenade in the middle of the crowd, right there between the King and Lloyd George, he could blow the bloody Empire to bits.

"Victory," says the Duke, raising his glass.

"*Maudizanglais*," says Talbot.

"Eh?" says the Duke.

She is in the library, on a sofa, next to Memsahib, her head bent in an attitude of silent resignation. Her bare back makes him think that Mary of Scotland must have bowed her head this way beneath the blade.

He has such a look of fury that I jump up and follow him without a word. His office is very small and plain. It smells of wax and Exports (my cigarettes!) and violets. He rummages out coats and socks and rubber boots and takes a set of keys from the pocket of a soldier who's sleeping on a cot in the corner.

The car is big and very fast. We rocket out of the city into the night, tunnelling past hedges, swooping around corners, an endless void opening in front of our lights. I have no idea where we are until we come to Canterbury.

"Will someone write about us some day, do you think?"

"We write to each other."

"A Soldier's Tale. What shall we make it? Heroic? Absurd?"

"It depends how it ends."

"Do you like happy endings? Sad?"

"Serials. They never end."

The sky is greying when they reach Dover. He pulls her up innumerable stone staircases until they come out on the battlements of the castle high over the

Channel. Clouds are scudding across the moon. The wind is freezing. He points towards France.

I'm freezing. I can't see a thing. Why has he brought me here?

Five twenty-eight. Five twenty-nine. Five thirty. Now!

A pale glow lights up the sky directly to the east. It flares, dims, flickers, flares again. Sheet lightning. A faint boom. Thunder. Storm. Fire. Firestorm. Guns!

A curtain of fire sweeps towards Vimy Ridge like a summer shower across a lake. Talbot times the advance on his watch.

He looks at his watch. At the sky. His face is rapt. He is smiling.
    "You like it, don't you."
    "It has a certain simplicity. I'm good at it. It's my life. I enjoy it, yes. Does that shock you?"
    She stares at the sky, watching.
    "I am old, crippled, monstrous. You waste your time on me. Find yourself someone worthy of you. A young man."
    "There aren't any."
    "I know. I have killed them all."

She turns away and walks along the battlements still looking towards France, as she had at Montebello, so long ago, so far away. It strikes him that perhaps her journey here has been as long and hard as his own, requiring equal strength and courage and made at even greater cost. He waits for her to raise her arms to the wind, but she remains hunched in his greatcoat, huddled like a sparrow against the grey stones.
    "I love you," he shouts, flinging the words like pebbles towards the sea.

Pte. P.V. Blatchford, P.P.C.L.I.; Monday, April 9, 1917:
    "Well, I tracks the son-of-a-bitch down at long last after combing half the bleeding countryside. It's coming up to fourteen hundred hours and it's the fifth bloody pub I've tried since I hit Dover. 'The Pigs' Knuckles' it was, something like that. Don't matter. 'Why yes,' the landlady says, bless her, 'staff officer, red patch on his sleeve, come in early, well before seven, wanting a room, at that hour, mind, had a lady with him wearing an evening gown all wet up to the knees, run off together if you ask me, not my business, first flight up, second on the left.'
    I'd soon as died as knock on that door, but damned if I didn't have to near kick it down before I gets a sign of life.

'Time to go, sir.'

'Bugger off, Blatchford.'

'Orders, sir. Sorry.'

'Bugger the orders. Go away.'

'We've taken Vimy Ridge sir.'

'You're lying, Blatchford. It's a trick.'

'Not at all sir. We're over, sir.'

Well I could tell from the quiet that I'd got him. Sure enough.

'Five minutes, Blatchford.'

'Very good, sir.'

She wasn't at all like I'd thought, didn't look more than a kid. I never did see nothing like what went on in the back seat of that car — I mean, I seen it all right, but not in a car, if you know what I mean, with a third party present. Not that I was watching, mind, me with my eyes on the road and my foot on the floor and my fist on the horn, even the coppers pulling over most respectful, like I was carrying the King.

Vimy Ridge! Nobody thought they'd do it, poor bloody Canadians. But it's a great day for England, I'll drink to that."

Dorchester Hotel, London
April 9, 1917

Lord Beaverbrook and the High Commissioner were in the hotel room when I got back. A policeman from Scotland Yard was sitting on the sofa taking notes.

"We have been to Dover to see the war," I said. "It's wonderful!"

I have shut myself in my room. Not another word will they get from me.

9

26 Besserer St., Ottawa
Saturday, April 21, 1917

"Penises."

"Eh?"

"Shells," said Flora. "That's what they are. Rows and rows of penises."

"I hadn't thought of it that way."

"A lot of boys peeing at each other. That's war. If women ran things, we'd have peace."

"Why don't we, then?"

"We're slaves. What is marriage but imprisonment? A life sentence. What rights does a housewife have that a slave doesn't? None."

"What about love?"

"Love is crap. Worse than religion."

"You're very cynical."

"Realistic."

"What can we do about it?"

"Fight! Rebel! The vote's a start. We'll win too."

"But that's sort of war, isn't it?"

"Bloody right. Cut their balls off."

Flora Denison is very peculiar, that's for sure. In the evening, when the shop's closed, she wears her hair down, past her waist, and a long, loose, blood-red dress, and a necklace of bear's claws, and bare feet. Sometimes she goes around stark naked, like lumpy porridge with legs. She says she's a shaman, an Indian priestess, even though she's Scotch, and she learned the

secrets of the spirits from an Indian called Sunset who still visits her even
though he's dead. She says she can talk with the dead, and foretell the future,
and travel around the universe in her imagination, when she's asleep. She
burns tobacco in the cook stove as an offering to the Great Manitou, and
thinks Christianity is the greatest plague ever visited on earth because it
deprives women of our rightful place, except among the Iroquois, where
children are born into their mother's clan, and where women choose the chief,
and throw him out, and generally tell everyone what to do. Flora's clan is the
Turtle, the Great Mother of the earth, and strangely enough with her small
eyes and beak nose and snapped-shut mouth she *looks* like a turtle. Her Indian
name is Wazahoniung, which means "Little Flower." It makes me laugh
because she's at least 200 pounds, but she takes it very seriously.

She calls me Anungpikobeesae, "Star Who Fell into the Water," after a
beautiful Ojibway maiden pursued by two suitors, Winter and Summer, who
fought over her so long and bitterly that she grew old and sad, and to end the
fight her parents took her away to a remote bay, and built her a house on the
water where she lived, alone and unfulfilled, until she died. Then she was
transformed into a water lily, endlessly drifting to and fro, a symbol of the
futility of seeking love from war. Not too cheerful.

I have lived here since I got back from England. Flora's son Merrill, who's
my age, is in the ambulance corps, so I have his room. It's on the third floor,
next to the attic. Flora lives on the second floor, and the dress shop, "Denison,
Couture," is on the main floor, the reception room at the front, with its stacks
of *Vogue* and display cases of stockings, the fitting rooms behind and the
workroom in the back with bolts and bolts of the most wonderful silks and
muslins stacked around the Singer, although Flora says business is bad this
year, with the war, and not being able to go to Paris. And the Yanks are
coming in now, which will mean the end of Seventh Avenue, and everybody is
pinching pennies and not wanting to put on a show. The new styles with the
short skirts scare the old ladies, who have no ankles, while the young girls with
the good legs prefer to buy ready-to-wear flapper styles at Freiman's. So if it
wasn't for the mourning, she'd be broke for sure, although working with black
every day is going to ruin her eyes if the war doesn't end by summer.

"I'm banking on your tits," she says.

It feels strange walking around half naked, being stared at and pulled and
poked and twanged, but the brassieres seem to be catching on. We sold a
dozen this week, mostly to ladies with no tits at all. Flora showed them how to
fill the cups with handkerchiefs.

I help in the shop from 11 a.m. to 3 p.m., taking coats mostly, serving tea,
creating the right sort of servile mysteriousness that Flora thinks is seductive.
"Stroke 'em," she says. "If they feel sexy in the dress, they'll like it. It's not the
'mode' I'm selling, it's the mood." She really does stroke her customers,

patting their hands, tidying their hair, fussing with necklines, pinning sleeves, her tiny hands flitting here and there, all the time making sympathetic cooing noises in her throat. Women without any clothes on are certainly ugly, all flab and rolls and wrinkles and moles and folds of flesh as thick as cold grease. What do men see in us?

My shift at the plant is four o'clock to midnight, although it's almost an extra hour each way by the time I've taken the streetcar and changed into my overalls and boots and walked through the maze of machines. We're packed in so tight we have to line up in order of our position on the assembly line and walk in single file. Once we're in place we don't leave all night, except for one ten-minute break at 7 p.m. and another at 10 p.m. We even eat at our seats. It's worse than the mill but it's $25 a week, and I have the rest of the day free. I don't get as tired now as I used to. The work's not hard, the machine does it all, it's all those shell cases coming at you, and the strain of having to fit each one into place without missing a beat, and the awful grinding sound the blade makes as it cuts the steel, not that you can hear it for the racket but you can feel it in your hands, and you can't make a mistake or the whole line has to stop and everybody glares at you. If we're not up to quota on the line we'll all get the sack, even though it's often the machine's fault, and a bad shell will kill more of our own soldiers than Germans. When the machines heat up, there's a little tap we can turn to spray them with some sort of liquid chemical that smells awful and eats through our overalls and trickles down, so by the end of the shift we're standing in puddles of water and out boots are soaked and our feet are cold, even though we're sweating from the heat of the blast furnace in the next room. It's going to be hell in the summer.

Annie is busy agitating for a canteen where we can get hot drinks and soup and sit down for a while and talk a little, but it's hard to get people interested when the only time you can see them is on the streetcar coming home and by then everybody's half asleep. But she has a committee organized on the day shift, and nobody seems to be against it, and they're going to approach the Women's Canadian Club to run it, which seems like a good idea because they're spending all their time arguing about whether to sing "O Canada" or "God Save the King" at their meetings and the whole city is disgusted with them. I said I didn't think a canteen was very revolutionary, but Annie just gave me one of her withering looks.

26 Besserer St., Ottawa
Sunday, April 22, 1917

A beautiful day, warm wind from the west, sun, smell of fresh earth. How dirty the city is after the snow has gone, dust and cinders and manure and old papers blowing every which way. Walked along the Canal past the Rowing

Club all the way to Lansdowne Park and back. The ice is still in the Canal. It looks strange, all white against the dry brown grass, like Willie's mother's hair blowing out behind her from the open carriage that passed me on the Driveway, Willie sitting opposite, stiff and attentive like a suitor. They didn't see me, or pretended not to. I've obviously been "dropped." Zoé says Willie is hot after Miss Carnegie, in New York, and Lady Maud Cavendish, the Duke of Devonshire's eldest daughter. Come into the garden, Maud.

I wonder if the sun is shining in Paris, or London, or wherever Talbot is, and I am not.

26 Besserer St., Ottawa
Tuesday, April 24, 1917

All the lights were on when I came in at one o'clock this morning. There were a dozen people in Flora's sitting room sitting in the dark, with candles, and Flora was got up in beaded buckskin with her bear's teeth and her hair in braids, so I thought it might be a seance, but it was just a meeting of the Whitman Club and they were working their way through *Leaves of Grass*. I wasn't going to go in but Flora insisted. There was wine, from Hull, and lovely little cakes full of unpatriotic sugar, so I sat in a corner awhile and listened. It wasn't at all dirty, but very high falutin', a rhythmical chant, like parts of the Bible, a sort of moving picture show, from God's point of view. I thought that pretty presumptuous, but Whitman was a Yank, after all, so what can you expect? I still like the one about the lilacs best.

Coming home, I saw Willie again, from the streetcar. I'm sure it was him, standing on Rideau Street talking to a girl in a long fur-trimmed coat. He turned away as we rattled past but I caught the flash of his cane in the light from the street lamp. It reminded me of the night we met, almost three years ago, on the bridge, and how frightened I was, and how pleased with my position in life. And here I am, in a factory after all!

Jack left for Kirkland Lake this afternoon. I gave him Rockefeller's address in New York. He says Harry's going to write, being a Yank and a college man too, and offer Rockefeller 49 per cent of the mines for $1,000,000. Fat chance.

Ottawa
Saturday, April 28, 1917

Rain. Went to the Byward Market looking for hyacinths for Flora, but they were all sold out. I like it there when it's wet. Eveything looks shiny and smells good. Earth. Fish. Smoke from the little charcoal stoves under the wagons. The farmers look like monsters huddled under their slickers, hands thrust out offering potatoes, grasping money. Chickens sad and silent in their cages. A big woman in a babushka standing by a wagon holding a cabbage in each hand, round as her head, big as her tits, thrusting them out as if she were going to juggle them, head, tits, cabbages and all, and toss them, one after the other, into the sea of umbrellas. I would have liked to take her picture but it's almost impossible here. As soon as they see a camera they go all stiff and shy. I'd rather get them haggling and cursing with their mouths open and their arms waving. Every wagon has its place, English to the west, French on the east, Irish to the south and the foreigners on the north, with the Chinamen and Jews in the little shops all around the sides. Mum used to say that the Chinese laundries were the gateways to Hell because of all the steam coming out, and the Chinamen were devils being punished for their sins. She was just jealous, I think, because their wash was always so much whiter than ours, and she could never figure out how they did it. Every Chinaman in Renfrew was called Scotty McLeod because he was black and yellow, like the tartan.

The Jews are black and white, like photographs, black hats, white faces, white hands stitching black cloth, sitting crosslegged on long trestle tables, fingers flying. They always look dressed up, with their hats on, as if they're just about to leave for a party. I always look in the windows of the junk shops. Who can make money selling stuff nobody wants? Old eyeglasses. Soiled dancing slippers. Fur pieces with the eyes missing. Tarnished jewellery. Violins with missing strings. Bilsky Jewellers had a big gold watch in the window just like Papa's. I stood there for a long time looking at it, knowing it couldn't be, but wanting to see. So I went in. A little bell tinkles. No one is there. The shop smells of old leather and glue and tobacco and dust and the most wonderful fresh, hot cinnamon rolls. I peer through the glass counter at a row of daguerreotypes in velvet cases, shimmering silver faces, unsmiling, unknown, plain, proud people, dead now, or very old. Who would sell their own kin? Who would buy them?

"Most people buy them for the cases. They throw the pictures out."

A tiny, fat white palm cradles a heavy silver case, monogrammed, with blue velvet lining. The palm flips over and the daguerreotype clinks on to the counter.

"For this we are asking $20, but . . ."

"Mrs. Freiman!"

She closes the silver case and rubs her thumb over the monogram.

"My father does not work Saturdays. I mind the shop."

We go behind a curtain into a small back room filled with broken-down armchairs and ticking clocks. There's a kettle singing on a hotplate and a table covered with a red rug and, in the middle of the table, a plate of cinnamon buns.

"We will have tea. You are my first caller. My other friends, they come here to market, yes, but they pretend not to see me. I am just Lillian Bilsky, the pedlar's daughter from Mattawa. They go by the window, whoosh, with their hats over their eyes."

She hunches over, her head tucked between her shoulders, fiddling with an imaginary pair of gloves and winks at me out of the corner of her eye.

"Maybe they are ashamed I should see them, the great ladies. They come here in their dirtiest clothes, holes in the elbows, pretending to be poor, thinking they can fool the farmers, as if even a simpleton doesn't know silk when she sees it, even when it has a hole in it, haggling over ten cents, while all the time the chauffeur is waiting around the corner in the car. And then, when they are all loaded up with chickens and fish they have stolen from the poor farmers, they go to the drygoods store for a spool of thread and ask to have the whole kaboodle sent to the house, for free! And the fools do it!"

She throws her hands up, as if she were tossing rice in the air, and looks at me with her soft brown eyes.

"Not all of them do this, of course. Some send the cook."

The tea is hot and strong. We cut it with cream. I have two cups and three buns slathered with butter. Mrs. Freiman's voice patters on like the rain on the roof, calm, melodious, full of sad laughter.

"I have something you will like," she says, going to a cupboard. Watches. Rings. A tray full of gold teeth. She brings out a small package wrapped in heavy brown paper and tied with twine. She puts it on the table and I wait for her to unwrap it. Instead she tucks it under her arm and points it at me. A flap opens in the front. A lens opens and shuts. Click. The flap closes. Thunk. A camera!

"It's supposed to look like a parcel of books," she shrugs. "But nobody in Ottawa carries books."

It carries six small glass plates that slip into place automatically. The shutter is released by a small string at the bottom. The only thing that gives it away is the loud thunk when the fresh plate drops into place.

"It's lovely. How much?"

"It's yours. I will have it cleaned up."

"Oh, no...."

"You must come and photograph my baby. What do you charge?"

"I...I don't...eight dollars?"

"Tomorrow? I would like something nice. Every photographer in Ottawa I have tried...."

She throws her hands up again, scattering seeds to the wind.

Ottawa
Sunday, April 29, 1917

Baby turned out to be a fat, five-year-old boy with ringlets and a brown velvet
suit. Baby was to be photographed at the grand piano, seated on a big cushion
on the stool, his little hands resting on the keyboard.

"Like Paderewski," Mrs. Freiman beamed.

We pushed the piano over to the window to catch the light. The maids took
down the dark velvet curtains. The soft reflection from the polished mahogany set off Baby's brown velvet beautifully, but nothing I could do, no riddle,
rhyme or joke, could crack the stubborn rage on his blank white face.

"Play, Babykins!" cajoled Mrs. Freiman. "'Mary had a little....'"

Chocolates disappeared behind the clenched rosebud lips. To no avail. The
eyes filled. The chin began to tremble. Paderewski was about to have a fit.

"You see?" cried Mrs. Freiman. "Nothing works."

We tried the nursery. A wonderland of toys, lifesize stuffed dogs, rabbits,
ducks, an electric train with a whole village and mountains, a playhouse,
shelves full of blocks and puppets and trucks, shiny miniature automobiles,
the latest models, toy soldiers, everything brand new and neatly put away, and
in the middle room, Max, a rocking horse made of real leather, with a real
horsehair tail and a real bridle made of red leather with stirrups and brass
fittings and red lockers. Baby is changed into a tweed jacket and jodhpurs
and a starched collar and a tiny peaked cap, and set upon the horse. Rock
rock. Rock rock rock rock. Bounce bounce bounce. He grins from ear to ear,
banging the sides of the horse with his little heels and slapping its rump.

"It won't work, I'm afraid...."

"Stay still, babykins, please. Gentle as a lamb now...."

Washed in the blood of....

"Jesus."

"Pardon?"

"Your son, with his curls, reminds me of baby Jesus. Perhaps a simple pose,
in shepherd's dress, with a lamb...."

Baby Jesus stops rocking.

Sweeney, the Freiman's chauffeur, is despatched to a farm for a lamb, nice
and white, not too big, and some shavings, and the cook comes up with a clean
flour sack, and within an hour Baby is seated on the conservatory floor under
a palm tree, among the shavings, wearing his ragged shepherd's smock,
hugging the sweetest little lamb you every saw and smiling like a cherub.

"Perhaps a Moses now, in the bullrushes," cries Mrs. Freiman, clapping her
hands, "or a David. I wonder who has a harp...."

I do Moses tomorrow. Flora is lending an Indian reed basket and the
bullrushes. I can use the laundry room as a darkroom without much trouble.
She says I am launched on a brilliant career.

Ottawa
Monday, April 30, 1917

Saw Ruth Fleck on Sparks Street today. I expected she'd go by with her nose in the air like the other May Court girls, but she deliberately stopped me, and complimented me on my hair, and asked where I'd had it done.

"I hear you are working at Daddy's shell factory," she said.

"Ummmumph."

"I think that's so exciting! So avant-garde! You must be thrilled."

"Umumph...well...."

"It's like those Russian women who go into battle, what are they called, the Legion...the Legion of Death isn't it, isn't that simply heroic? Do you wear those swishy overalls, with the bib? Aren't they simply swagger!"

"It's just to protect...."

"I'd simply love to have a pair! Imagine wearing pants!"

"They're very heavy, and coarse."

"Oh, I'd have mine made up in something sweet, gingham would be nice, don't you think? A little blue check with white piping, and lovely big pockets, and a sweet white blouse, a Huckleberry Finn look. Just perfect wth bobbed hair, don't you think?"

Me: "Do you think overalls are chic?"

Flora: "*Your* overalls?"

Me: "Something custom-made, a little blue gingham perhaps, with white piping, a lace blouse, a matching bow for the hair...."

Flora: "Bernhardt did well in pants."

Me: "The military look is very 'in' this year...."

Flora: "And that other French woman with the man's name...."

Me: "Maybe a nautical touch, cotton duck, with brass buttons...."

Flora: "Bernhardt's were satin, *so*...."

Me: "They *are* comfortable."

Flora: "They're not indecent."

Me: "Practical."

Flora: "Sensual."

Me: "Huckleberry Finn."

Flora: "Where are my scissors?"

Ottawa
Tuesday, May 1, 1917

The German workers will rise today and overthrow the Kaiser, Annie says. That would be nice. For a country that's supposed to be beaten they're fighting very well. Every day our casualty lists get longer and longer and longer, twelve thousand since Vimy Ridge. I feel as if I've been there and know them, every one. Flora is up to her knees in black crêpe, and gingham overalls. They're a big success. She's sold at least two dozen, including a peach satin pair to Mrs. Harriss, who's almost sixty and stout. Flora calls them "Walt Whitman's" and tucks a few stanzas of "Song of Myself" into the pocket of every pair. I love her.

We had our own little May Day dance at the plant. We have a canteen now, just a big covered wagon with primus stoves in the back that parks in the yard out front, but we get a half-hour dinner break at 7:30 p.m. and we can have tea and lie down on the grass and look at the sky. The robins were whooping it up tonight and one of the girls just started to sing, something silly, I've forgotten what it was, and in a minute we were all whirling around the wagon so hard we fell down, and lay there, our arms out, like angels in the snow, giggling. The foreman checked the wagon for liquor but all he found was tea and Campbell's tomato soup.

Ottawa
Friday, May 4, 1917

Annie is organizing a baseball league for the Queen's Birthday holiday. We're supposed to play some girls who make uniforms in Hull, and a bunch from a boot factory in Prescott. Our team is called the Ottawa Whiz-Bangs. Our cheer goes likes this:

> "One, two, three, four,
> Who are we for?
> Whiz-Bangs! Whiz-Bangs!
> Kill! Kill! Kill!"

Ottawa
Saturday, May 5, 1917

Mrs. Freiman has ordered ten Baby Jesus, six Moses and even two Paderewskis, which turned out better than I'd expected. I have appointments now with Shenkmans, Rosenbergs, Waismans and Davidofs.

Ottawa
Sunday, May 6, 1917

Sweeney arrived this morning with a $100 cheque, a matzoh and a box wrapped in red-and-white candystripe paper with "Freimans — For Smart Shoppers" printed along the side and all tied up with red ribbon.

Ciick. Thunk. Who will ever guess!

Went to Holiness church. I felt I owed it to Jesus. I still have a lot of trouble with God. Bishop Ralph said Mum was doing good work among the returned soldiers in the asylum. I should visit her, he said. I said I couldn't afford it, then realized that I could, in fact, so I said I'd try.

No letter this week.

Ottawa
Thursday, May 17, 1917

We've got the vote! You expect the sky to fall, bells to ring, yet everything goes on as before, except Flora, who's whirling around like a dervish. It makes you think. I guess I'll vote Liberal. Such wickedness! Annie isn't going to vote at all.

Ottawa
Sunday, May 20, 1917

Loaned Annie *Leaves of Grass*.

Ottawa
Saturday, May 26, 1917

Riots in Montreal over conscription.
   "It's throwing good bodies after bad."
   "But we need the men, Flora...."
   "What for?"
   "We're *losing*."
   "Quit then."
   "We can't."
   "Why not?"
   "Do you want to be a German?"
   "Do you want to die?"

Ottawa
Sunday, May 27, 1917

Annie returned *Leave of Grass*. She says its "imperialist rubbish."

G.H.Q.
May 27, 1917.

My very dear Lily,
   I have not received any letters from you lately but then everything seems to be going wrong with me. A sort of judgment come upon me! Last week I

supplied a whole series of orders, schemes and accounts of operations for the Americans at the request of our Canadian representative, and afterwards General Byng asked upon what authorization I had done so and there was an unpleasantness. Then he said he could not recommend me at present for Brigade Major, so I am making arrangements to go back to the regiment. I shall be in charge of a company and probably second-in-command since I am senior to Charlie.

I have been offered my old job back at War Records but I am reluctant to get involved with the Aitken-Hughes crowd again and there seems more future reward in going on active duty. I shrink from the fresh discomforts and fatigue and the narrowness of the existence, yet I cannot be truly happy with security and comfort. I must choose the hardest alternative, perhaps the one I dislike the most. It is better to share in the making of history than in the writing of it.

Brave words, aren't they? Not false, I hope. Our brief time together has helped me to see that I can be of most use with the men in the field. It is they who will win this war. They must be encouraged. Their dangers and hardships must be shared and lightened. I can no longer bear the pettiness and hollow vanity of London. My place is with the Regiment. I could only entertain any other alternative if I should receive definite orders, such as a call from the government, that I could do nothing other than obey. There's not much chance of that, is there, under the present regime? And I am not going to turn myself into a drummer to keep the Conservative crooks in office. I know my principal reason for wishing to return to Canada was war weariness and homesickness. That has passed now. You are always with me, no matter how far away.

Tomorrow I go to the Corps school to brush up my drill for a week or two, then I will assume my job in the Regiment. This is, I think, better than any job in Canada, military or diplomatic, and in the long run I think I shall be happier and more content.

I made three bets today, each for five pounds.

1. Lille taken by August 1, 1917.
2. English on German soil by September 1, 1917.
3. Fighting over by February 1, 1918.

So good night, my dear Lily. May all be well with us in these stirring times.

Your
Talbot

Ottawa
Saturday, June 16, 1917

Flora: "you're unhappy."
Me: "How do you know?"

Flora: "Your aura has turned blue."

Me: "Cerulean?"

Flora: "Indigo."

Me: "I've tried everything, Flora. Nothing works. He seems determined to die."

Flora: "Tobacco? That's important."

Me: "Tons of cigarettes."

Flora: "Food? The spirits like to eat."

Me: "Chocolates. Maple sugar. Cakes. Raspberry jam...."

Flora: "Prayers? Incantations? Spells?"

Me: "Shells."

Flora: "Shell. Excellent. The Indians normally use a sea shell, however I don't see why.... Charms?"

Me: "Snapshots. Letters. My gold turtle...."

Flora: "Turtle! Splendid! What's your totem?"

Me: "My what?"

Flora: "Has an animal ever spoken to you? That's your guardian spirit."

Me: "Oh, come on Flora...."

Flora: "Do you feel any particular kinship with any animal?"

Me: "I don't...I...well, I've always been rather fond of frogs."

Flora: "Good! Good! Strong medicine, frogs. Amphibious. Earth. Air. Water. Fertility. You must make a sacrifice."

Me: "But we've already given up sugar, and white bread, and meat twice a week, and...."

Flora: "No, no. I mean a *sacrifice*. An offering. You see, if someone is killed *in his place*, he will live. It must be someone close, a shadow...."

Me: "But I can't *kill* somebody, Flora! I'll be hanged!"

Flora: "You don't have to actually *do* it. It can be symbolic, like celebrating mass. Nothing more than cannibalism, Christianity."

Me: "I'm not going to eat somebody, Flora...."

Flora: "First you have to be initiated. We could use some mistletoe...."

Me: "Jesus, Flora...."

Flora: "Pine boughs will do. Can you bring me a shell? That's the key."

Me: "But...."

Flora: "You'll have to fast seven days. Too bad you're a virgin. However...."

Me: "I'm not...."

Flora: "Really? What a stroke of luck!"

Me: "Look, Flora, I don't...."

Flora: "Are you scared?"

Me: "I'll starve."

Flora: "Have I starved?"

Me: "No...."
Flora: "Come on, then, we'll shake the earth!"

Ottawa
Friday, June 22, 1917

Starving. Soup for seven days. Giddy. Ate one hundred morning glory seeds
an hour ago. Supposed to bring on "visions." Feel sick.

Rain. Flora's step on the stairs.

Yikes!

A hideous monster in the doorway holding a candle, a mountain of flesh
painted green with black stripes, and circles everywhere like the rings on a
snake, black hair flying, its face painted half-red, half-green, naked except for
the paint.

"Flora?"

"I am Makinauk, your guide," it says with Flora's voice. "Come, we will
enter the womb."

She opens the attic door. Smell of lilacs. She goes ahead, holding the candle.
We're in a narrow passageway, hung with red flannel. The passage twists and
turns. I lose all sense of where I am. Mirrors are hung here and there and we
catch sudden glimpses of ourselves, me in my black cotton shift, representing
the dead self I am to leave behind, Flora in her paint, which ripples and folds
into curious patterns as she walks. She walks slowly, chanting, a weird
keening noise in the back of her throat, keeping time by shaking an enormous
tortoise-shell rattle in her right hand. We walk for a minute, an hour, a year.
The smell of lilacs gets stronger. We come to a bend in the passage.

Yikes!

Bears. Giant brown bears on their hind legs block our way. Paws. Claws.
Maws.

Flora cries out and strikes at the first bear with her rattle. It topples over
with a terrific crash. All the other bears topple at the same time. Mirrors.
We're in a tiny room lined with mirrors. There is only one bear and it lies
across the entrance, paws still raised. One eye is missing and it has a big "A"
shaved on its chest.

"Hey, this is Geordie, the Rideau Hall bear!"

"Shhhh."

"The Duchess donated him to the Red Cross rummage...."

"Where else would I find a bear?"

There is a post hung with pine boughs in the middle of the little room, with a
primus stove at its base. The floor is covered with fresh-cut grass and lilacs are
banked around the sides, masses and masses of huge purple blooms. The smell
is suffocating.

I am tied to the post, my hands behind my back, in front of the little stove. I say my lines:

"I come to die.

I come for life."

Flora the frog leaps around me, shaking her rattle, her wild black hair flying in all directions, chanting:

"It's easy to die.

It's hard to live."

She lights the stove with her candle and sprinkles leaves on it from a skin pouch. The smoke curls slowly up, sweeter than tobacco, fresher, greener, more like tea, or incense.

"Is it opium?"

"Grass."

"Ordinary grass?"

"Sacred grass."

She stuffs some in a clay pipe trimmed with feathers, holds it up towards the ceiling, then to the floor, then to the four corners of the compass, intoning a prayer, then takes a deep pull. She holds the smoke in a long time, releasing it slowly through her nostrils, eyes closed, then puts the pipe in my mouth. The smoke is dry, sharp. I hold it it, feeling light, like a balloon, and dizzy as I let it out.

The frog pops a strawberry in my mouth. The fruit of wisdom, she says. It is wonderfully tart and wet after the fire. We smoke the whole pipe this way, slowly, turn-about, pipe, berry, pipe, berry. I close my eyes. I feel very light, as if I'm floating, light as a leaf on a wave, drifting, easy, carefree, rocked on the bosom of the sea. The air is thick with smoke but I seem to see everything very clearly, the bright red of the strawberry, and the little bumps on its skin, the tiny, curled petals of the lilac, violet in the centre fading to pale mauve at the edges, the bright, glass brown eye of Geordie the bear, the little rivulets of sweat on the frog's belly, everything swollen, pregnant, bursting with happiness. I want to talk, tell the frog how lovely her shade of green is, but my tongue is thick, and words too much of an effort, and my thoughts seem to travel without words, on tendrils of smoke.

She slips off my black shift. The air feels cool on my skin. She empties the pipe into her palm and rubs the ashes on me, still hot, then crushes the last of the strawberries and smears the juice on my face, and between my legs, her fingers light and slippery, so I hardly feel her tongue at first, licking, a little fish. I should be frightened, or angry, but I'm too lazy, it's not important. I am floating somewhere outside my body, watching, feeling, my body heavy, stiff, unable to move, left behind, mine and not mine, her tongue like little waves lapping the shore, water meeting rock, meeting earth, eternal. . . .

Something cold. Hard. The shell.

Yikes!

"Stop it."

"It won't hurt."

"You'll blow us up."

"Eh?"

"It may be live."

"How can you tell?"

"I can't. I just stole it from a pile."

"Well, we'll never know what hit us."

I see us all blown sky high, me and the Frog and the bear, rocketing out over the city like a shower of sparks from a roman candle, up, up, up until we're only specks of light, tiny stars winking in the clear night sky. I ride the shell through the galaxies, hot now, and sharp, so I cry out, down, down, riding a silver ship in a blood-black sea, down, down, sucked, swallowed, submerged in the blood, the blood of the Whale, drowning, dying. . . .

I feel the pole shake. The floor beneath my feet trembles and heaves. The mirrors tilt, all at once, and then come crashing down. The whole house sighs, and heaves, and shivers.

"Hail Mary!" says the frog and crosses itself.

We huddle on the floor amid the broken glass and fallen flannel walls of the womb. Suddenly everything is still.

The frog stares at me, its eyes round with wonder.

"It did move!"

"It's the morning glory seeds. I think I'm going to throw. . . ."

Ottawa
Saturday, June 23, 1917

It *was* an earthquake.

The whole city felt it. Not much damage was done, a few chimneys came down, knick-knacks fell off.

Flora brought me breakfast in bed. She says I have great powers.

Me: "Is that all it is then, sex?"

Flora: "What more do you want?"

Ottawa
Wednesday, July 18, 1917

We are not getting the vote after all, at least I'm not! Only the wives and mothers and daughters of soldiers are getting it, so they'll push through conscription, Alice says, although all the girls at the shell factory are for conscription anyway, except me and Annie. It's infuriating! Imagine treating us just like all the hunkies and foreigners who aren't allowed to vote because they're traitors!

"So what did I tell you?" Annie said.

"If the Russians would fight we wouldn't need conscription."

"The Russians are smart."

"They say you're friend Lenin is a German spy."

"They say that about your boyfriend, the Rockefeller patsy."

"He is *not* my boyfriend!"

Flora is leaving for New York to work on the suffrage campaign there. If she stays here, she says, she'll kill somebody. We've tried everything else, except blowing up the Parliament Buildings, but that's been done, hasn't it, and it's only half-built now, and Mr. Booth would only build it up again and make more money, and we'd all be in jail.

Flora is closing down the business. Things are slow anyway. Everybody's at the cottage. All I have to do is clean the house and tend the Victory garden. She showed me the sweet grass plants, planted in between the rows of corn so they wouldn't stand out, although nobody's likely to notice anyway, and I could always say we were going to make rope.

Dreamt about Kingsmere last night. It was pitch dark and I was swimming in the lake. There was a dark shape beside me on the water, a canoe, or a boat, but I couldn't see who was in it, and no matter how long I swam I never got close enough to touch it. The water was warm and I swam effortlessly, never tiring, never getting any closer to the shore, but not caring, perfectly happy and content, quite cross when I woke up and it was broad daylight, and hot.

I wonder how Willie's book is doing. Zoé says he's been snubbed by Lady Maud and Miss Carnegie so he's courting the three Lynch girls, simultaneously. The youngest is only sixteen.

Ottawa
Saturday, August 25, 1917

Annie is organizing a study group among the Jewish and Russian girls at the plant. They meet every Sunday night. It's called a "language class." They read Marx in German, Lenin in Russian, and Annie lectures in English.

Ottawa
Sunday, August 26, 1917

Three years ago tomorrow I met Talbot.

Walked with Alice out to Lansdowne Park and back along the Canal. Same hot sun, damp heat, same grass, same white figures playing tennis at the

Rowing Club, same gumdrop boats on the water, same women shading their eyes with their big straw hats, same men in shirtsleeves rowing, *scree-thunk, scree-thunk*, same children laughing under the trees, same soldiers snoozing, same me.

"Men are strange, aren't they Alice?"

"Perverse."

"Romantic."

"Irrational."

"Solitary."

"Selfish."

"Careless."

"I warned you."

I got out my map of Belgium with the red pins and the black pins and Alice helped me line them up, the red pins curving to the west and south of Ypres, the black pins to the north and east, exactly where I put them three years ago.

Cut the grass.

10

William Lyon Mackenzie King is at Buckingham Palace, in a large anteroom, a ballroom, with red walls and gilt mirrors. There is a great crowd of people in formal dress, all of whom have come to see him receive a decoration from the King, yet none of them pays the slightest attention to him. He calls out "Hey, it's me! I'm here!" but no one hears. He has put on his Windsor uniform with its high, stiff collar and gold braid and white satin stockings and patent dancing shoes with brass buckles, but when he looks down, to make sure everything is in place, he realizes he has forgotten his breeches. If only there is time to return to the hotel! He tries to push his way through the crowd, but everyone is surging towards a great golden door crying, "The King! The King!" and the sound of the King's approaching footsteps can be heard on the other side, louder and louder....

Bang. Bang. Bang bang bang. Bang bang.

He opens his eyes. A shaft of sunlight falls across his bed. The sheet is in a knot around his neck. He lies quietly, waiting for his heart to stop pounding. *Bang bang. Bang bang bang.* A hammer. Of course! It's Johnny Dunn, finishing the dock! Today's the day, the christening, the start of a whole new life, a clean slate, a chance to rededicate himself to God's great purpose in life!

He pulls on his bathing suit and tiptoes into the sitting room. The nurse, Miss Purdy, is snoring gently on the cot. He peers into Mother's room. Her eyes are closed, her ravaged face sallow against the crisp white pillow, her breathing slow, harsh, the deadly sleep of belladonna. He had stood out stoutly against morphine all spring, but then the hemorrhages had started and

Mother bleated so with the pain, like a little lamb, that he had quite broken down, although he hates the way drugs make Mother drowsy and stupid when she should be so bright and gay, and he's frightened by the way she seems to be drifting away from him, farther and farther, into a vague, private world of memories and regrets, so sometimes he shouts at her, and is cruel to her, to call her back. But she'll only smile at him, and call him "Dear Billy," and talk of unhappy things that happened long ago, before he was born, as if he weren't in the room at all. If only she weren't so obsessed with her illness, so morbid, she'd soon be able to shake off this mucous condition and be her old self again.

A robin is splashing in the birdbath. He walks softly across the grass towards it but it hops on the edge and flies off, singing. A divine omen! What could be a more perfect expression of God's grace than this innocent songbird enjoying the little gift from Mr. Rockefeller he had set up with his own hands a year ago?

His heart is full of joy as he watches Johnny Dunn nail the last of the floorboards onto the dock. How fitting an end to the summer, this little addition to his property! It had seemed at first such an extravagance, $400 for a boathouse and dock and a set of wooden steps leading up to the cottage, but he'd put the steps off for another year, and got the rest for $360.68, including the two gallons of Canary Yellow he'd had McGregor bring out from Ottawa because the first coat had a greenish tinge that didn't go well with the pale green roof, and now his boathouse shines in its fresh paint like a beacon of hope in the dark, a symbol of Mother's own bright and beautiful personality, the trim as white and sparkling as the lace around her throat, the new little flagpole at the end of the dock a testament to her unflagging spirit.

He places his towel and soap on McGee's head and wades into the water, submerging, then floating on his back spouting like a whale. The water is colder than it was last week. The sky is pale blue, the tops of the birches turning yellow. A year today since father died. Another summer gone. He will stay until the end of September, if the nights aren't too cold, and Mother is strong enough. He dreads returning to the rooms at the Roxborough, the stifling heat, the nurse underfoot, the smell of medicine, Mother's whining, no, no, that's not true, she is very brave, it's his own fault that illness in others get on his nerves so, he must strive to be patient, not lose his temper. If only he had some privacy, so he was not driven out into the street. He must think about getting larger rooms, perhaps a servant, it will be an expense, but all to the good if it keeps him in his proper place, by Mother's side. He will reject all invitations of a social nature until she is well enough to accompany him. This will keep his evenings free and his head clear for work the next morning. It was a mistake, spending so much time at the Country Club, although he'd considered it a kindness, a duty almost, there were so many grass widows in the city, who otherwise would have had to sit alone at home. He hadn't the heart to deny them a little pleasure, their hearts were so heavy, with their husbands at the front, and there was no danger, of course, of an "involvement," but he'd fallen into the habit of drinking too much, another mistake, and spending his days in a haze of exhaustion, and when he got himself into this restless condition he lost control of his passions and selfishly indulged himself, while Mother lay alone and suffering. He'd tried placing lengths of string in front of the door, after dinner, to keep himself from going out, and would have had the telephone disconnected except for the need to call the doctor in an emergency, and Mother had complained when he replaced the electric hot plate with a kerosene stove. So he'd had to give in, and content himself with putting glass insulators on the four posts of his brass bed, but even Grandfather's spirit seemed powerless to prevent him sliding down the slippery road to Hell.

He had almost welcomed conscription. Discipline. Routine. Exercise. Drill. Cold showers. Exactly what he needed. He would welcome death, especially a heroic one, and he was quite cast down in May to find that he was only Class Nine, way down the list, and almost certain never to be called. He had kept the flying officer's uniform that had been thrust on him so strangely in the middle of Union Station, certainly a message from God, and got into the habit of putting it on, under his overcoat, when he went for a stroll, finding that the subterfuge aroused an almost delirious excitement, a sensual passion so intense that simply by opening his overcoat in the dark, when no one was watching, was enough to make him explode in flames. He amazed himself with the risks he took, venturing out even in daylight, the silk scarf high around his neck, his legs strangely stick-like in their walking boots and heavy socks under his coat, daring anyone to question what he was wearing. But although he passed many people he knew, and some looked at him oddly, no one said a word, and he would return, weak and trembling but triumphant, with a sense of indescribable relief.

To William Lyon Mackenzie King conscription had seemed so sensible, so logical in view of the appalling casualties, that he had been flabbergasted when, having expressed this view to Sir Wilfrid, the old man had turned on him a baleful eye and said that conscription was totally repugnant to him. It was unacceptable in Quebec, and he, as a French-Canadian, would never betray his people, and if the Liberal Party wanted conscription it would have to find a new leader. He had waited, breathlessly, for Laurier to place his hand on his shoulder and say that he, William Lyon Mackenzie King, grandson of the great rebel, must assume the mantle of leadership, but the old man had just sighed, and rubbed his eyes with his long, graceful fingers, and William Lyon Mackenzie King, realizing he'd made a blunder, had taken pains to explain his views more clearly. He had said that of course conscription was a desperate measure, a form of coercion, a typical example of dictatorial Tory practices, and the government was clearly in the wrong to impose it without an election, or at least a referendum, and any measure that weakened national unity in this time of crisis would only damage the country and harm the war effort. Sir Wilfrid was perfectly right to oppose the manner in which it had been brought in, and he, William Lyon Mackenzie King, would nail his colours to the mast, and stand fearlessly by his leader, a true and noble friend who had been like a father to him, a guide and an inspiration. He, for one, would fight the good fight, win or lose, a Laurier Liberal to the end.

Laurier had thanked him, and walked with him to the door, stooped, shuffling, complaining of the pain where his teeth had been extracted, his handsome, arrogant mouth shrivelled, shrunken, old, powerless, sunk in despair, his long, slim hand cold and dry to the touch. As he took it, and expressed his loyalty, William Lyon Mackenzie King said to himself "Laurier is dead" and he saw, in the grey fog of his frustrated ambition, a tiny pinprick of light. It was a bright beacon of opportunity that, in the long, quiet weeks at Kingsmere, had grown, through no effort on his part, miraculously brighter.

All his rivals for Laurier's mantle, the strong men of the Liberal Party, Guthrie, Graham, Fielding, the members of the inner circle, Laurier's most trusted lieutenants, deserted the old man for the conscription cause, compelled by their own convictions or greed or opportunism, or by the promise of a plum post in Borden's new Win-the-War Union government. Laurier is betrayed, bitter, alone. No, not alone, not quite, for one man, one loyal colleague stands fast by his side, Sir Galahad by the aged Arthur, fighting the good fight against the forces of reaction, true to the death, and it will be death, defeat, disaster for the party, Laurier, himself. He has been shaken, frightened by the strength of the conscription hysteria, but he has heard too the voices raised against, it, the voices of working men, and farmers, the voices of the poor and disenfranchised.

The war will be won. What then? What sort of man will the people be looking for? Why, a man of peace, a man of the people, a young, progressive man, untainted by corruption, uncompromised, a man who knows how to solve the problems of reconstruction, a man with a vision, an English Protestant, Laurier had said, acceptable in Ontario, sympathetic to Quebec. A man therefore bearing a great liberal name, true to great Liberal principles, author of the world-famous *Industry and Humanity*, the Member of Parliament for North York, the Hon. William Lyon Mackenzie King, Prime Minister of Canada.

He wades ashore, the pebbles hard and slippery under his toes, dries himself and inspects the dock to make sure Johnny Dunn is using the two-inch nails, not the expensive three-inch ones he'd started with. The boat house had been a bit of a worry, first the plans, then the constant supervision, running back and forth to make sure the walls were straight, and the siding not warped, and he had accomplished little on his book, not having anyone to type. He had rearranged the furniture in the cottage, and considered taking down the white curtains, with violets, in Mother's room, and removing the other traces of Lily's presence, but he hardly knew where to begin, and worried that it might cause questions. He had even decided not to burn her silk panties in the kitchen stove as he had intended, in case Miss Purdy, or someone else, found the charred remains, so he'd left them where they were, in Revelation, something of a solace at night, when her image floating before his mind's eye drove him almost wild with longing.

He had caught a glimpse of her in April walking alone by the Canal, her dark hair tousled by the wind, and it had struck him with some surprise that she might be as lonely as he was. He'd felt such a pang of regret he could hardly keep the tears back, and he'd mentioned her to Mother at dinner, feeling the need to share his unhappiness, but Mother had only stared out the window, saying she'd caught a cold on the drive and he should have hired a closed carriage. He'd gone out and walked along the Canal where he'd seen her and sat on a park bench until it was dark, but she hadn't returned, and he'd ended up, against his will, at Patrick Street, where he'd stayed too long, rushing home just after midnight to find the doctor on the telephone. Dr. McCarthy had been trying to locate him at the Rideau Club. Poor Mother was gasping for breath, having suffered an attack, and nearly died, at the very moment he'd been selfishly indulging in shameful pleasures. He'd taken her in his arms, and kissed her, and wept. But to his dismay, in the days that followed, the awful fear that he'd be away immersed in sin when Mother died only added a keener, more compulsive edge to his nocturnal wanderings, even at Kingsmere where, lacking more serious temptations, he'd taken to courting the Lynch girls across the lake, sitting up in the moonlight until all hours, reading the *Idylls*, then dashing home cold with sweat, his heart in his mouth, expecting to find Miss Purdy on the veranda, calling, and Mother gone.

He dips a pail of water from the lake and fills the birdbath, bending over, as he does every morning, until his round face, wrinkled with ripples, smiles up at him from a halo of golden leaves. He waits until the water is calm, a round brown mirror, a heavenly eye, and repeats like a benediction the little verse Mother taught him as a boy:

> Only as the heart is pure
> Shall large visions still be mine
> For mirror'd in its depths are seen
> The things Divine.

"Billy!"

He waves to Mother sitting on the veranda in her wheelchair, a pale shadow in the shade, and carries the pail around to the kitchen door. He's changing into his Brooks Brothers blue suit, an exorbitant price, but a good investment if saved for special occasions, when Johnny Dunn comes to the back door. Johnny wants his pay, grumbling that he lost money on the job, if he counted labour, with the price of lumber being so high, but when William Lyon Mackenzie King recalls the keg of nails Johnny accidently dropped in the lake, and the money he'd wasted buying cream paint when the instructions had clearly implied yellow, Johnny falls silent and pockets his $360.68 without another word.

He had planned to carry Mother down to the dock for the little ceremony, but finds her so heavy, with the swelling, that he has Miss Purdy help him with the stretcher. They make her comfortable on the little bench Johnny has built at the end of the dock, beside the boathouse, but she seems so tired, so far away, so indifferent to the beauty of his creation, the little "spiritual child" of their summer together, he is tempted to put it off to another day. But to lose the association with father, the anniversary of his death, would ruin half its meaning, so he puts his arm around her and calls to her.

"Mother, dearest, what shall we sing?"

She looks past him, out across the lake, where a sailboat is scudding along before the breeze, and begins, quite suddenly, in a high, childish soprano,

> Jesus loves me,
> This I know,
> For the Bible,
> Tells me so.

He joins in the chorus, his tenor bray making up in volume what it lacks in tune, his heart bursting with joy, his face radiant in the glow from the boathouse, turned in gratitude towards the Almighty God who in His mercy has swept his enemies from his path and made his way clear, so that after lingering in the wilderness for forty days and forty nights, he may emerge, like Christ, triumphant.

> Yeeesss Jeesus loves me!
> Yeeesss Jeesus loves me!
> Yesssss Jeeeesus loves me!
> The Bible tells me so.

He helps Mother dip her hand in the water, prompting her as she waves her fingers over the dock:

"I christen thee...John...King."

Mother gives a strange little cry, half-laugh, half-sob.

"This must be Bella," she says, sprinkling the little bench, "and the boathouse, is that really me, Billy."

" 'The Isabel Grace Mackenzie,' dearest."

"But you, Billy, where are you?" she says, touching the yellow boards with her wet fingers, as if they were hot.

"I am right here, Mother, beside you."

"No, I meant. . . ."

She gazes out across the lake again. Her eyes fill with tears.

"I'm dying, Billy, aren't I?"

"No, Mother, you promised."

"Promised?"

He leans close, her arms around his neck, his lips close to her ear, sound-lessly forming the words.

"To see me prime minister."

"Yes, but that's so. . . ."

"Hold on, Dearest, it won't be long."

P.P.C.L.I.
Belgium, Aug. 26, 1917

My really dear L.,

There came several nice letters from you this week and a huge box like a Christmas stocking. I had a wonderful time hauling the different things out. All of them will be most useful. I still have quite a piece of the original bath soap — you remember the big cake — as my baths at present are few and far between and bath soap has a long life. The little kettle will be useful. Certainly if I find no need for it myself some of my men in the trenches will be very glad to have it. These are new trenches so they have no modern conveniences!

I cannot thank you enough for your thoughtfulness. Your letters are the only ones I receive with any frequency or regularity. It is now three years since I left Canada and friends have changed and married and died and I have had no chance to make new ones. The old ones are still good ones, I am sure, but they have other and more commanding interests. I am resigned, however. It is a minor affliction.

Aug. 27: Last evening came your letter about returning to the Corps staff. You and Zoé are wonderful and full of energy and ingeniousness on my behalf! I met our new commander, General Currie, several times in Van-couver, before the war, and I realize he is a staunch Liberal, and a friend, and I know he wanted me to stay on last spring, but honestly, Lily, I cannot undertake to leave the Battalion again before I am at least wounded. Here I am busy building up a company esprit de corps and a loyalty to each other and all that sort of thing. I become very fond of my men and I cannot endure to allow them to go into the trenches without me. It was hard enough last time when I was not a company commander and when most of my men were strangers, but now that we are strong friends and allies we have got to fight together. This is probably foolish and senseless of me. Mother is constantly begging me to return to the staff. Why should I? Except for her I don't mind a bit being killed. I should positively like to be wounded, provided I wasn't maimed in some horrible way, and I certainly am going over the top next time we go in. Nonetheless I deeply and sincerely appreciate your thought of me. I do love you as much as I possibly can anyone.

By the way, I am not going to be a major after all. The regulations have been changed and no new majors are to be made. Consequently I must wait my turn, but since promotion must mean the elimination of those above me, you understand that I am content.

I was desperately tired this morning and stayed in bed until 1 p.m. We have had a succession of late dinners and concerts and very full days and I am worn out. I have had to make several speeches. If you want to send me a Christmas present I would appreciate a pair of running boots, not shoes, size 7. I have tried everywhere in London and cannot find them. I want them for races, football, etc.

The situation in Canada is grave, is it not? If only I could be wounded out I would go to take part in the show.

> With my best love,
> Affectionately,
> Talbot.

P.P.C.L.I.
Belgium, Sept. 8, 1917.

My dear Lily,

I am almost a broken-hearted man today and I want the consolation of telling you about it. This morning Charlie Stewart was taken away in an ambulance, I fear never to return. He is found with Bright's Disease. Only his extraordinary powers of endurance and his remarkable will and his copious consumption of whisky have kept him going. Now when he is *most* needed, when the command of the Bn. appeared within his reach, he has suddenly to give it all up and go away to die a slow lingering death deprived of all the good cheer and company which has meant so much to him. I was devoted to him and I think he was to me. I depended enormously on him. To my mind this poor life so wrecked is the greatest tragedy of the war. Hamilton Gault has come to stay with us for a few days but I need more than that to cheer me up.

When did I last write? I have bought a new dog, a little black and white terrier called Tony. I suppose something will happen to him despite all the care I take. We are out of the line temporarily but we had a fairly hard time of it. Did I tell you? My company suffered a number of casualties. It is so discouraging to build up an esprit de corps and get to know all my men and then have them dwindle away. However, men may come and men may go but the company goes on forever.

Did I acknowledge the new pine pillows? They are beauties. So fragrant. I sleep on them tonight and every night I can. You really are a darling and extraordinarily good to me. I wish I had the heart to reply more appropriately but I simply cannot. Charlie and I went for a motor ride the other day and had a game of golf. He beat me. We were very happy. I have made a number of sketches which I will send you some day.

I am going to bed now. Sorry to write such a perfectly rotten letter but this is a blue moment and I am simply unloading on you.

Affectionately,
Talbot.

I have some souvenirs I am sending you soon.

11

26 Besserer St., Ottawa
Sunday, September 9, 1917

I took Flora's sign down from the front window today and put up my own
card:

PHOTOGRAPHS BY LILY
CHILDREN A SPECIALTY
REASONABLE RATES.

I wanted to paint an orange lily on it but Zoé said it would scare the
Catholics away. I've mounted six of my best in the window. The smaller
"carte" size I've put in the display cases where Flora used to keep her
stockings and brassieres. I've put Jack on the wall, in his Canadiens uniform,
and Willie's mother, by the sun dial at Kingsmere. I have some good "detective" snaps too, but I don't want to give myself away, and the girls at the
factory will kill me if I show them all smeared with grease and dripping with
sweat. I should really give up my job there, I'm so busy, but I'd miss the
company. It's like a family, although we know very little about each other,
and never see each other outside. May be that's why it's easier to talk. We get
$30 a week now, and I've made nearly $1,200 from my photographs since
spring. I'm getting to be a wealthy woman! Things will probably slacken off
now. I can't pose the children outside, without any clothes on, when it's
freezing, although Christmas is coming, and bathtubs are still popular. It's
cost me a fortune in rubber ducks but the results are glorious!

Marguerite Gault has been granted a divorce and $1,400 a month alimony.
Everyone is astonished. It appears that Hammy Gault was the adulterer,
wooden leg and all. Well, you never know.

26 Besserer St., Ottawa
Monday, September 10, 1917

Was in the bathtub just after one o'clock this morning, dead tired, when the
doorbell rang. I was going to ignore it. Then I thought, "Talbot has been
wounded," so I threw on my housecoat and went tearing down. It was Willie!

"I was out for a stroll," he said, "and I thought I'd...."

He just stood there, looking distraught, not saying anything. I thought
maybe something terrible had happened so I asked him in. He wouldn't let me
take his coat.

He sat in the sitting room. I made some tea and laced it with a good jolt of
Jack's whisky. He drank it down at one gulp! So I poured some more, and a
good shot for me too. His hand was shaking so hard the cup rattled against the
saucer.

"Are you okay, Willie?" I said.

He nodded and burst into tears.

Jesus! What was I to do? So I just sat there like a dummy, in bare feet, with
my hair all damp, and waited for him to stop.

"I don't know what to do," he said at last. "I want...Mother wants...Mother
wants me to help her...."

"Help her?"

"Help her...die. 'I want to die, Billy,' she keeps saying. 'Please help me.' She
is suffering...so...I cannot bear...I have tried...but the harder I...."

He closed his eyes and leaned back against the sofa. I noticed how much
thinner his hair was, and paler, not blond or grey, no-colour. I poured us each
another whisky. He gulped it down. I sat by the fire in Flora's Morris chair
and closed my eyes, not knowing what to say, wishing I could go to sleep and
never wake up. When I opened them he had unbuttoned his overcoat and was
wiping his eyes with a long, white scarf.

"Willie, have you been conscripted?"

"No...I...."

"Are you Home Guard then?"

"No...."

"But what *is* that?"

"It was given to me...."

"Given?"

"Sort of...a gift...from God."

"God?"

"It was quite miraculous...in Union Station...I noticed that the hands of the
clock were quite together...."

"But you have no *right*...."

I stood up, seized by a wild fury, and grabbed at the khaki jacket, trying to
tear it off his back. I could hear my voice, very loud, but a long way away:

"Coward!"

He grabbed my wrist and twisted my arm away.

"Hoor!"

I pulled free and flung open my housecoat.

"Is this what you came for then, soldier?"

He fainted.

I left him there and came up to bed. He's still there as far as I know. That should be the end of Mr. W.L.McK. King.

Ottawa

Tuesday, September 11, 1917

Willie was back tonight.

"Look, Willie...."

"Please...."

"What do you *want?*"

"Help...."

I was feeling perfectly murderous, after the way he had treated me. Imagine the nerve, standing there on my porch, in the middle of the night, everyone will think it's a cat house.

"Go away."

"I need...."

"Look, are you completely out of your mind?"

"Yes...I...I'm afraid...."

The cringing look on his face only made me more furious. I figured I'd give him a real scare.

"You have to take off your coat."

He hesitated, then took it off.

"And your socks and boots."

He took them off.

"Thank you," he said.

The womb was warm and stuffy, full of summer heat. Flora had hung up the red flannel again, and the bits of shattered mirror, which made it even spookier. Willie was breathing so hard behind me I thought he might have a heart attack. Then I'd be in trouble!

"AAAAHHHH!"

The bloody bear. I'd forgotten all about it.

"Push it away," I said.

"No no no no no no no no no...."

Willie's eyes were round as saucers.

"Push it."

"It will kill me!"

"Push it."

"I can't!"

"Are you scared?"

"I...I...."

He swallowed hard and gingerly stretched his hand out towards Geordie's shaven chest. Drew back. Stretched. Touched. Drew back. Touched again. A gentle push. Geordie didn't move. Harder now.

"*Push* it!"

Geordie thumped over backwards.

I lit the stove, sprinkled it generously with sweet grass and left him by the post, with a single candle, staring at his reflection in the broken mirrors.

"Breathe deeply. You'll have a vision."

"I feel...dizzy."

I ran down to Flora's room and put on the scariest of her false-face masks, the leering one with the glittery copper eyes and the scraggly white hair. With a bed sheet and the turtle rattle the effect was pretty stunning. I crept back up the stairs quietly, trying not to giggle, and leaped out at Willie from behind the post.

"Mother!"

Jesus, I hadn't expected that.

"Billy? Billy King?"

"Yes, Mother?"

He hung his head and shuffled his bare feet, one on top of the other.

"You've been bad again, Billy."

"Yes, Mother."

"What do you say?"

"I'm sorry, Dearest, I...."

"You know what I have to do."

"Yes, Mother."

His eyes were full of tears. I undid his belt buckle and pulled the belt off. He fainted.

Me: "Did she whip you often?"

Willie: "Yes."

Me: "With the buckle?"

Willie: "Yes."

26 Besserer St.

Friday, September 14, 1917

Got the jacket off. He talked a lot about things he'd done as a boy, stealing apples, fighting, failing at school, telling fibs, things all kids do, stupid things, yet he *wept* as though they were enormous sins. Such a memory for vice!

Bishop Ralph would like that. Why, Willie would *live* at the penitents' bench!
"I love you, Mother," he keeps saying. "I love you." But she is implacable.
"You don't love me, Billy," she says. "If you loved me you'd be good." He
seems to really *believe* I am his mother. So do I. It's like a Pearl White serial. I
can hardly wait to see what happens tomorrow.

26 Besserer St.
Wednesday, September 26, 1917

Snipped his suspenders with Flora's sewing scissors. He fainted. His cock was
so hard his breeches just hung there, like moss from a branch, then gradually
slid to the floor.
    Me: "Did the sky fall?"
    Willie: "No...."
    Me: "Are you still alive?"
    Willie: "Yes...I guess...."
    Me: "Is it still there?"
    Willie: "Yes...."
    Me: "Did it hurt?"
    Willie: "No...not this time."
    Me: "When?"
    Willie: "She caught me. My...my buttons were undone. My...it was...stick-
ing out."
    Me: "All by itself?"
    Willie: "No...I was hold...she said I was dirty. She smeared my face and
hands with...p...p...p...from the chamber pot...."
    Me: "'Poop?'"
    Willie: "Yes. Then she marched me downtown, down the main street of
Berlin, to show everyone what a d-d-dirty boy she had."
    Me: "With your buttons undone?"
    Willie: "Yes."
    Me: "And it sticking out?"
    Willie: "Yes."
    Me: ""How old were you?"
    Willie: "Eight. She said that if she ever caught me again she'd cut it off."

26 Besserer St.
Thursday, October 18, 1917

"Please don't touch me, Mother."
    "Why not Billy? You're my own wee boy."
    "I've grown up now Mother...."

"Give me a kiss, Billy."

"I...I can't...."

"No kiss for little Mother?"

"I...."

"Don't you love me any more, Billy?"

"Yes...of course, I...."

Sweat stings his eyes. His throat is dry. Mother's hands are soft, slippery against his skin, stroking, slithering, her hideous leering face pressed close to his. He strains against the post, shaking, suffocating, sucking for life....

"No!"

The forbidden word comes out round and flat as a stone from a cold, deep well.

"No. No, I don't love you."

"Do you hate me then, Billy?"

"Yes."

"You want me to die."

"Yes."

"You would like to kill me."

"Yes."

When he opens his eyes his mother is standing across the room, a white shape in the smoke, quite small, still. She is holding a revolver. She raises it, aims it at his heart and fires.

26 Besserer St.

Friday, October 19, 1917

He fainted. Good thing too, because I'd forgotten the pistol was loaded, and the bullet creased the post right beside his neck.

What have I done?

How do I get out of this?

12

Trenches
October 19, 1917

My dear L.

Ages since you wrote. Many moons since I did myself. Why? What new trouble has come upon us? For myself I have lost the capacity. Often I have been seated to write to you and I cannot. I live in a world so apart. Why write to people on the moon? I have done long days in the trenches. I have missed no day since the middle of May. I am here now, happy in the middle of a small dugout where I sleep excellently on hard boards. The nights are cool, but as we never take clothes or even boots off, I am warm enough. We sing, sleep, eat, recite poetry and generally pass the prison life away quite pleasantly. This is like living in a mine gallery exactly. I really don't expect peace. This life simply has become the normal existence. I live only for the great defeat, the pursuit, the utter humiliation of the Germans. I want to see them slaughtered and surrendering in the tens of thousands. I want to see them running scared to death. I would not miss participation for all the love and money in the world.

I am hoping for leave towards the beginning of next month.

I have a number of sketches that I hope to show you some day.

What are you doing?

I owe letters to all my relatives. I receive none except from mother.

Do hope I will hear from you again soon.

Forgive my brevity. I think at greater length.

Always devotedly,
Talbot.

26 Besserer St.
Wednesday, October 31, 1917

I had the most astonishing experience yesterday. It was just after midnight and
I was coming off shift, trudging along as usual with the girls on my line, too
tired to talk very much. We'd just come out the door, hunched against the
wind, when I felt someone standing by my left shoulder and a voice said,
"Hello, Lily." It was Talbot! *His* voice, clear as a bell. He was *there*, just
behind me, in his uniform, and I could smell the khaki and leather and his
Export cigarettes. I stood absolutely stock still, afraid to break the spell. His
presence seemed to surround me, warm and tender and happy, as if we were
back at Montebello, among the birches, and the sun was shining through the
golden trees. "Remember," he said, "I love you." I could see his face for a
moment, scarred, drawn, but smiling at me in his mischievous way. I stood
there, very still, for a long time, so excited that I missed the streetcar and had
to walk all the way home, but I was so thrilled, so wonderfully happy, I felt I
was flying through the air. He's coming home! I'm sure of it. His letter came
today, mentioning leave, he's probably on his way already, in London, at sea.
Oh, I've been so afraid that we would be strangers, or hate each other, but now
I'm sure that's not true. Nothing's changed! Nothing! Oh, I can hardly....
There's the telephone. Damn. Oh Talbot, I love you!

The Roxborough, Wednesday, October 31, 1917

William Lyon Mackenzie King grins at himself in the bathroom mirror. The
wig had been a masterstroke. He looks like a child again in the torrent of
golden curls, the gilded laurel wreath riding on top like a halo on a cherub.
Actually it wasn't laurel, the florist had said, but some sort of dried weed, but
it serves the purpose and creates the right impression, and it's only a Hallowe'en party after all, for the Patriotic Fund, and one is expected to look a little
foolish. The wings have given him more trouble. He had purchased actual
chicken wings from the market, with real feathers, but they were too big, and
he found no way to attach them securely to his heels, so Mother had cut him
out a pair from cardboard, and covered them with silver foil, and stapled them
to the thongs he is wearing Greek-style on his legs. He feels a little nervous,
appearing in public with bare legs, but it is no worse than a bathing suit, and
they *are* his best feature, next to his long, thin, Christ-like feet, and it will be
hot in the ball room at the Chateau. And who will recognize him as Apollo?

He adjusts his mask, straightens the scarlet tunic Miss Purdy kindly cut out
from an old bedspread, tucks his ukulele under his arm and flies down the hall
to say goodbye to Mother.

"You are my golden boy!" she cries, clapping her hands.

He kisses her lightly on the cheek, being carefully not to smear greasepaint on her reading glasses.

"I'll try not to be late."

"Never mind. I'm going to finish Miss Chadwick's column and go to bed."

Miss Purdy helps him into his coat. His feet are going to be cold. He'd thought about wearing socks underneath his sandals but they spoiled the effect. Well, it's not far to the Chateau, and he'll take a taxi, stopping first at Besserer St. It will be an expense if they have to wait, but it can't be helped, and it is a good cause. He waves to Mother.

"Sleep tight, Dearest."

"Oh, isn't that too bad," she says, glancing up from the newspaper. "The Papineau boy has been killed at Passchendaele."

William Lyon Mackenzie King feels faint. He closes his eyes. The blood pounds in his ears. Oh dear Lord. Oh merciful Lord. His last obstacle. His last rival. Oh blessed Lord!

"What a tragic loss," he says, kissing Mother once more.

Oh Hallelujah! Another lucky stroke! Oh the hand of God doth move in wondrous ways! He flies down the stairs aflame with excitement. He must win! He must! With the election called for his birthday, a splendid omen, just King and Laurier alone, against the Forces of Evil, they'll sweep the country, already the crowds are flocking to see Laurier, Laurier and King, the old man and the young heir, triumphant together under the banner of Liberalism. He will give a great victory speech, a program for a new era, a new leader, a man reborn, a young prime minister with his young bride by his side, Laurier's disciple wedded to Lady Laurier's protégé, the old hag will have to come round, she'll have no choice. He'll pop the question tonight! This very night! The shroud of nervous anxiety that has made his life such a hell has evaporated like mist on a sunny morning. He is bursting with confidence, bursting with optimism, bursting with joy!

"I'm in love!" cries William Lyon Mackenzie King.

He's startled to find the house dark when he drives up. He's left his watch at home, having no pocket, but the taxi driver assures him it's half-past eight. Right on time.

He rings. Again. Again. He can hear the bell echo in the hall. Knocks. No light, no life.

"Maybe she's gone on ahead," says the driver.

They dash over to the Chateau and he bounds up the steps, realizing only when he sees the great milling crowd of Snow Whites and Louis XIVs that Lily hadn't told him what her costume would be. It was to be a surprise. So was his.

He shoves through the throng, puzzled, panicky, frightened by the leering, laughing gargoyle faces. Where is she? Why has she done this? People stop him, admiring his costume, but he pushes them rudely aside, peering over their shoulders, searching. Where is she, where is she, what's wrong, what's wrong? He stands alone in the corner of the ballroom watching the swirling faces, deafened by the noise, sickened by the laughter, angry, ashamed of his nakedness.

Had he made a mistake? Was it the wrong house? Perhaps she was late...the time was wrong...a prank.... He dashes back down the steps, and runs all the way over to Besserer Street, rehearsing his apologies, certain to find her furious, his heart pounding with expectation, tonight, later tonight, if things go well, tonight they might, he might, together it might, he might *do* it!

But the house is still dark and there is no answer.

William Lyon Mackenzie King stands on the porch until his feet are so cold he can no longer feel them. He walks back to the Chateau, intending to go in, but he stops at the bottom of the steps, outside the circle of light, hesitates, and turns away.

26 Besserer St.
Wednesday, November 7, 1917

Still raining.
    Passchendaele taken.

26 Besserer St.
Thursday, November 8, 1917

Sleet.
    Flora telephoned. Suffrage won.
    Flora: "You sound peculiar."
    Me: "It didn't work."
    Flora: "What?"
    Me: "The sacrifice."
    Flora: "I'm coming home."
    Me: "It's too late."

26 Besserer St.
Friday, November 9, 1917

Bolsheviks have seized power in Russia.
    Annie delirious.
    "Our workers will rise!"
    "They're not starving."
    "Not for long."

"They're scared."

"It will come."

"This isn't Russia."

"It's the same."

Lost my job. Absent without permission. Don't care.

26 Besserer St.

Thursday, November 15, 1917

Letter today. Forgot about the mail.

Trenches
October 21, 1917

My very dear Lily,

Two nice letters from you at last and also the boots. They are the most wonderful things I have ever seen! But my dear Lily how could you think I would deliberately ask for anything so expensive? I only meant a pair of canvas running boots with the rubber sole. I am positively ashamed that you should have sent such an elaborate gift. Your "Quest of the Boots" was so diverting that it seemed a real shame all the fun should be for my personal enjoyment only. How do you think of so many amusing things? If all else failed, you could still be sumptuous as a writer!

I am on the eve of great events and I have only a short minute in which to write but I wanted to make sure you heard from me. Please dear L., don't think you mean any the less to me but I have rather felt the strain recently and somehow I have lost interest in everything except my work. Please don't desert me 'tho I should not blame you. But you are really all I have left on that side of the water.

A couple of days ago I sent mother a P.P.C.L.I. sofa cushion that I had made out here to be sent to you. I hope you will receive it in due course. Whatever happens you must realize that I have thought of you and been happy and grateful for you now and to the end.

We are to be inspected by the Duke of Connaught tomorrow.

I am sorry this has to be such a short letter and I have to be so reticent. Better wait for my next letters before replying. I am in excellent health and spirits. There is a rumour that we first arrivals are to be sent back to Canada for three months at Christmas. If so I shall see you then. Wouldn't that be great!

Believe me, always affectionately and gratefully,

Your
Talbot.

No more letters.
No more.
Never.
No words.
No kisses.
No life.
No love.
No hope.
Nothing.

13

Ottawa
Tuesday, November 20, 1917

Laurier's birthday. Sam Hughes there. Sam looked very old. Thin. He said that if Sir Robert hadn't kicked him out of the cabinet, he would have made Talbot Canadian representative in Paris. He said that Byng and the British deliberately "cleaned out" all the Canadians. It's probably just Sam's bluster. Didn't make me feel better. He put his arms around me and wept. I nearly broke down too.

Sat with Zoé most of the evening telling her who was there, how they looked. She is quite blind now, but her ears are sharp, and her tongue. Everyone admires the way she's come out against the Liberal traitors, an old lioness protecting her cub, wild with rage and merciless. Fleas, she calls them with a curl of her lip, *les puces*, who rode Laurier's back to power and have jumped to another dog. "Who is this Mr. Fielding," she says, "who dares to demand Laurier's resignation because Laurier is too old, then calls him a coward, a Kraut, because he is Québécois? Before Laurier found him, before Laurier raised him to the cabinet, before Laurier made him Finance Minister, Mr. Fielding was a journalist. *Rien!* Phht! And how young is Mr. Fielding? Seventy-two!"

"I have lived too long." Sir Wilfrid said, smiling, when I wished him happy birthday. "I would rather be dead."

So would I.

Ottawa
Monday, November 26, 1917

Cushion cover came today.

Montebello,
Nov. 22, 1917.

Dear Miss Coolican,

Talbot's personal effects have been returned to me, among them this small gold chain, which he wore always on the strap of his wristwatch. He said you had given it to him and I thought you might like to have it back. The turtle has lost its emerald eyes, I am afraid, but I am sure they can be replaced.

Talbot was killed at dawn on October 30 leading the attack on Passchendaele ridge. He was hit directly by a shell. The chain was all that was found. He will have a grave in the military cemetery there. I will send you the location later in case you might wish to visit it on a future trip to France.

Talbot always spoke of you with the highest regard. Your generosity and kindness on his behalf were very greatly appreciated, especially in view of your association with the formation of the Regiment to which he became so deeply attached. I hope you have taken his letters in the flirtatious spirit in which they were intended. Talbot was always something of a "ladies' man." He could have made any number of brilliant marriages but he enjoyed the game of courtship too much to give it up. He told me shortly before he was killed that he regretted not having married, but that he had never been in love and was too much of a romantic to marry without it. You need therefore feel no regret or remorse at "what might have been," although I am sure you share the grief of all those who knew Talbot at the loss of a brave and brilliant man. I, for one, shall never been reconciled to his death. Nothing can make me believe it was worthwhile.

Yours sincerely,
Caroline Papineau

Zoé: "I don't think she meant to be cruel."
Me: "What did she mean then?"

26 Besserer St.
Wednesday, November 28, 1917

"I'm sorry, Willie, I didn't mean...."
  "You've been away?"
  "Yes."
  "Mother is dying."
  "Yes."

"I feel so...alone."

"Yes."

"Except for our...."

"Yes?"

"I have been think...wonder...it seemed if we...I...were joined...our resources...in holy...divine...together...."

"Are you proposing?"

"Yes, I guess...I...we know each...I've missed...need to share...help...I'm...I love...."

"Don't look so miserable then."

"You...will?"

"Yes, of course. Why not?"

26 Besserer St.
Thursday, November 29, 1917

Annie: "Don't be an asshole."
  Me: "He loves me."
  Annie: "Balls."
  Me: "He understands me."
  Annie: "Yeah."
  Me: "We understand each other."
  Annie: "So?"
  Me: "What's so awful about it?"
  Annie: "You're selling out. Bargain basement."
  Me: "It's my life."
  Annie: "You shouldn't marry for grief."
  Me: "I do love him, in a way."

26 Besserer St.
Sunday, December 2, 1917

We were married this afternoon by Bishop Ralph at the Holiness church. It was an impulsive thing. Everything's a secret. Willie wants to make the announcement on his birthday, at his victory rally. He left tonight for North York. He seems very happy.

So here I am.

The Roxborough,
Thursday, December 6, 1917

Put a dozen roses on Poor Bert. He looked cold, standing there in the snow.

I am sitting up with Willie's mother so Miss Purdy can have the evening off.

It's her first time off since August. "Mr. King is such a busy man," she said, "away so often, and he so dreads his mother being left alone. He has quite a morbid fear that she will die when he's not at her side, but she insisted, absolutely insisted, he go off to campaign. 'I will live to see you win,' she said. Isn't that wonderful?"

She is asleep, a skull and crossbones, propped on pillows, breathing noisily, her body beneath the blanket bloated, rotting, a living corpse. The stink is almost unbearable. She woke up about an hour ago. She didn't recognize me.

"My name is Bird," she said matter-of-factly.

"King," I said. "Isabel King."

"It used to be Bird," she said firmly, looking at me with her round, hawk's eyes, her little nose even sharper now. "I used to be a bird." She closed her eyes and lay back, struggling, pressing her skinny arms convulsively against her sides.

"Are you all right?"

"My wings are very strong. I am trying to hold them down. It's not time to go yet."

I gave her a glass of champagne. She went back to sleep. Finished the bottle. Wish Willie was here.

Ottawa
Saturday, December 8, 1917

Alice Millar left for Calgary today. Arbee has given up politics. He was dropped from the Union cabinet in favour of a Liberal. Alice says he was so enraged she thought he would have a stroke. She's just as glad to be out of it.

"Conscription is fine in principle," she said, "but think of the paperwork!"

She wants me to come to Banff in the summer.

"Do you remember how the sun shines in Alberta?" she said. "The sun never shines in Ottawa."

I will miss her.

Ottawa
Sunday, December 9, 1917

Willie telephoned from Newmarket. Things are going badly. The Toronto *Star*, his loyal friend, has come out against him. Everyone is afraid to speak out against conscription for fear of being put in jail. Squads of returned soldiers go around from meeting to meeting in uniform, shouting him down.

"It's working in my favour," he said. "People will see that Union government means thuggery while Liberalism stands for peace and democracy. It's a question of Fear versus Faith."

He sounded quite cheerful and confident but Laurier says defeat is almost certain, it's only a matter of the size of the deluge. Ontario hates the French. The foreigners in the west, all Liberals, have been disenfranchised. The women are solidly for conscription. Only Quebec will be true.

"So Mr. King has not abandoned ship?" Sir Wilfrid said this afternoon.

"He says he's trying to steer a middle course."

"*For* conscription *and* against it?"

"For the principle, I think he said, but against the method of implementation. He has a phrase to describe it...."

"Conscription if necessary...."

"...but not necessarily conscription. That's it."

"Mr. King doth bestride the world like a Colossus," said Sir Wilfrid, waving his arm, "always a foot in each camp."

I don't think that was fair. Willie didn't have to run. He could have gone to work for Standard Oil, he told me, but stuck it out from loyalty. He *is* standing up for the French and for peace, and the only other man I know brave enough to do that is Isaac Pedlow, who's running as a Liberal in Renfrew and there are a lot more French Canadians in the Valley than there are in North York, that's for sure.

Went over to the Roxborough to sing hymns with Miss Purdy and Willie's mother. She was sitting up and seemed stronger. "Here is the angel of death," she said when I came in, "the angel of mercy." I was going to leave, not wanting to upset her, but she held my arm. "I am glad to see you," she said, "stay." We sang "Jesus Loves Me," over and over again, and I played Chopin on the Victrola until she fell asleep.

"She will go soon," said Miss Purdy. "I'm afraid, in a week, I don't know."

The Roxborough
Saturday, December 15, 1917

Mother unconscious. Willie speaking at Newmarket tonight.

The Roxborough
Sunday, December 16, 1917

Expected Willie home today. We are *frantic*.

The Roxborough
Monday, December 17, 1917
2 a.m.

"Willie, where *are* you?"

"...is Mother?"

"I can hardly hear you! Where are...."

"...she awake?"

"No, she's. . . ."

"...good...rest is good...do good. If only she. . . ."

"When are you coming home?"

"...tomorrow...the campaign...need one more day...win. . . ."

"Willie, I think you should. . . ."

"...can't leave now...run...must win...grandfather...give my love...birthday ...did she... love...?"

"Willie, the doctor says. . . ."

"...did she send love...what did she...?"

"Yes, she sends her love."

"...win...happy birthday. . . ."

"Yes, I am sure it will be."

Miss Purdy is praying. "It's worked before," she said. "Mr. King has brought her right back from the grave."

I am drinking champagne. Can't let it go flat.

10 p.m.: Willie has been beaten. Only 500 votes. Less than many others. Union government has swept all but ten seats in Ontario. Isaac Pedlow has won Renfrew. Renfrew Grit! Papa will be spinning in his grave.

Streets are full of drunks singing "Rule Britannia." Zoé says the Win-the-War committees bought up all the bootleg whisky in Ontario. Jack will be happy. And drunk.

Miss Purdy is opening the last of the champagne.

The Roxborough
Monday, December 18, 1917

No Willie. Met the morning train from Toronto and the late train. Where can he be? Doctor is here. Mother very low. I've telephoned everywhere, Newmarket, Barrie, the Liberal Club in Toronto, even the Toronto *Star* and the CPR, thinking there might have been an accident. He has simply vanished. Can he have slept in?

The Roxborough
Tuesday, December 19, 1917

1 a.m. Mrs. King died just before midnight. No Willie.

2 p.m. No Willie.

The undertaker came to remove the corpse. The doctor said it was too decomposed to be allowed to remain.

We have burned the bedding and disinfected the room. I opened the window for a few minutes. Very cold. Could Willie be frozen in a snowdrift somewhere? Murdered? Suicide? Miss Purdy says I should call in Willie's friend, Constable Dempster of the Dominion police. Like hell. "We don't want a scandal," I said.

4 p.m. Sent Miss Purdy home. Her fussing and chatter were getting on my nerves until I realized what she wanted. She hasn't been paid since Thanksgiving!

"Mr. King is such a busy man," she said, "I thought at Christmas...."

I gave her $22, all I had in may handbag and an I.O.U.:

"Two months plus one week...."

"That's $78, less the $22...."

"Per month?"

"Oh, no! Altogether. If you think it's too...."

"It's starvation."

"Oh no! I took several of my meals here. I'd cook up little omelettes on the hot plate, such a handy thing, with toast, Mr. King did so enjoy the homey little...."

"You cooked for Mr. King?"

"And Mrs. King, malted milks, and eggnogs, she was fond of sweetbreads, in a cream sauce...."

"Miss Purdy...."

"You see, it was actually quite an economy, staying here, and a privilege, being near two such lovely people, such a devoted son, and so famous! Did you know that Mr. King is going to be prime minister soon? Mrs. King told me. She was so proud! It's only a matter of time, she said, after Laurier...."

"After Laurier...."

"After Laurier resigns! He's finished now, isn't he...?"

The apartment is very quiet. The radiators gurgle. I'll have to get that fixed, clean up the bric-a-brac, get rid of the hideous fumed oak. The wing chairs can be recovered, velvet, a cinnamon shade would be nice with the walnut, a Chinese silk on the sofa, yellow, very light and delicate. I wonder if we can get a bigger suite of rooms. I'd love a house with a lawn, and French windows....

"Hello, Mother! I'm home!"

"Willie, where on earth...."

"Mother, dearest...."

"Willie, please sit...."

"I thought she'd be sitting...."

"Where have you *been*?"

"Mother? Hello, hello...."

"She's gone, Willie."

"She's gone out? In this weather...?"

"She died, Willie, last night, very peace...."

"Mother?"

"Yes."

"But I wasn't here!"

"No."

"But she can't. She promised...."

"I tried all day to reach you. I tried *everywhere*. We thought you had been kill – ...."

"But she's not *here*."

"She's dead...."

"But *where is she*!"

"The undertaker."

"No! No!"

"The doctor insisted, Willie...."

"I must find her!"

"Willie, please sit...."

"Mother! *Mother*! MOTHER!"

6:30 p.m. He's still not come back. I might as well go home. He must have taken his defeat very hard. Stank like a brewery. Poor Willie.

Ottawa

Thursday, December 20, 1917

"Willie, your mother's wedding ring is gone."

"Yes."

"Shouldn't we report it stolen?"

"She gave it to me."

"But she was wearing it when...."

"She promised it to me."

"You took it?"

"It's mine."

We spent the morning arranging all the photos of Mother around the room, the big Forster oil over the fireplace, the bronze and marble busts on the mantlepiece with the portrait photographs in between, except the one in evening dress, which Willie dislikes, the snapshots and albums on little tables: Mother with Willie as a baby, Mother with Willie in the garden, Mother with Willie at Kingsmere. It gives you the creeps, all those bright, beady eyes staring out from the corners. We just get them all arranged when Willie jumps up and changes them all around again.

"Everything will have to be...postponed."

"But we *are* married."

"...it would appear as though we were dancing on dear Mother's grave...."

"But we were married *before*...."

"...worse, indulging ourselves in sin...selfish pleasures while poor Mother was on her deathbed...."

"What pleasure?"

26 Besserer St.
Christmas Day, 1917

Telephoned Willie first thing this morning. Miss Purdy answered.

"Mr. King's in bed," she whispered, "terrible pain, the doctor thought appendicitis at first but it's the left side, the same as where Mrs. King's trouble began, and he has the same stopped-up feeling, enemas don't help, and the doctor can't find anything. He's quite delirious at times, I'd put it down to grief, people behave in strange ways at times, except for the rash on his chest...."

Willie was huddled under a blue eiderdown like a sparrow with a broken wing. When he saw me he just turned his face to the wall and cried.

"I wonder if a male nurse wouldn't be more, more appropriate," Miss Purdy whispered in the hall.

"He has great confidence in you, Miss Purdy."

"It's just that when, when I administer the enema, he becomes quite, how shall I say, *stimulated*, and, I'm afraid, refers to matters of a physical nature which are rather *indelicate*, me being a single woman, and him a bachelor, and he uses language that, well, I'm surprised that such a decent man like Mr. King would even know such words, of course I am perfectly able to defend myself...."

"Does he swear at you?"

"Oh no, I wouldn't call it swearing, he's not angry, oh no, quite the reverse, very humble, remorseful about his wicked deeds, it's just that he says the same words over and over, dirty words, they all mean the same thing...."

"Don't worry, Miss Purdy. It's in the Bible."

"Bible? Sex in the Bible?"

"Revelation. Look it up."

"Well, I shall. Thank you. That's a comfort. I've never been as religious as I might be."

14

Ottawa
New Year's Day, 1918

Midnight mass with Zoé. I thought she'd be tired afterwards, but she invited me upstairs and we sat in the dark, by the fire, drinking sherry.

"This is my birthday," she said.

"I didn't know...."

"I keep it quiet. I was an old maid, over thirty, when I married Laurier. Today I am eighty-five."

"But it was a love match!"

"Ah yes, everyone says so, eh? How the handsome young lawyer from Arthabaska eloped with little Zoé Lafontaine, the piano teacher. *Quelle romance! Quelle amour!*"

"But you were in love, you still are...."

"Ah, yes, I was, I am. I have been in love with Laurier since I first saw him. *Un coup de foudre.* Bam! They say it can't happen, eh? Pfft. He was a student at McGill, brilliant, so tall, so proud in his old homespun clothes, so beautiful, pale, consumptive everyone said, would not live long, so thin and delicate. I lived only for him. He came to the house often, not to see me but to talk with Dr. Gauthier, and to eat, he was always hungry, and I played for them while they talked, and hung on the sound of his voice, low, like a cello, and brought his coat for him when he left, and prayed for a smile, and blushed when he told me how beautifully I played, and if he kissed my hand I didn't wash for a week. And I dreamed, and I prayed to the Blessed Virgin that Laurier would live, and love me as I loved him.

"But he went away to Arthabaska, to set up his practice, and I saw him only once, twice a year. I wrote. He replied. The letters became fewer. Shorter. I became engaged to another man. *Un cochon.* An oaf. It was an arranged marriage. I had no dowry; he did not mind. He would 'take me off Dr. Gauthier's hands.' I tried to be brave. I tried to do my duty. But a week before the marriage I broke down. I wept. I raved. I confessed all to Madame Gauthier. The days went by. I did not eat. I threatened suicide. Then, the day before my marriage, *miracle!* Laurier was there, in the sitting room, and Dr. Gauthier said he'd come to marry me! I was delirious! I threw myself on him. I told him how much I loved him, how happy I was that he loved me, oh *quelle brouhaha!* I hardly stopped for breath. The Blessed Virgin had answered my prayers! I was so happy, so naïve, I paid no attention to Laurier's grave white face, thinking it only shyness, and I did not think he might have been summoned there by something other than my desire.

"We were married that afternoon. He left by train after dinner, having to appear in court the next morning. I arrived in Arthabaska three days later. Oh, the whole village was there to see the handsome lawyer's new bride! He met me with a buggy, and drove me to the new house he'd rented, a little cottage, with a garden. I was like a fairy tale! He showed me all the tiny rooms, then his study, full of books, and our bedroom. 'This is your room,' he said. 'I shall sleep in the study. We shall live together *comme frère et soeur.*'

"I thought it was his health, that he would change his mind when he got better, that it was for my sake, to protect me. I nursed him. I babied him. I knit scarves. I mended socks. I made soup. I prayed. Still he got sick. In the winter I would give him the bed. He would lie there for weeks, coughing, so at last I wired Dr. Gauthier to come, Laurier was dying. Dr. Gauthier came. 'He is not dying,' he said. 'It is not consumption. I told him that when I examined him on your wedding day. I told him what he needed was a good wife, that Zoé Lafontaine was crying her heart out for him, and if he had any brains he'd make a match of it. He said he'd discuss it with you, but when we saw the two of you together, anyone could see there was no need for discussion."

"You mean he didn't. . . ."

"He didn't love me, no. He was trapped."

"But why did he go through. . . ."

"Would he break my heart? Laurier? Never! *C'est l'honneur!*"

"Did he love someone. . . ."

"Someone else? Who knows? He has never spoken of it. There have been 'friends.' There are children in the village, grown men now, people say they have 'Laurier's curls', or 'Laurier's lips' or 'Laurier's voice.' I do not see it myself. Because he is famous, people want to identify. I do not think he is a ladies' man. He prefers the company of men. That's what makes him a great leader."

"And you, you've lived all these years. . . ."

"*Toute vierge.*"

"But you could have got an annulment."

"What for? I loved him!"

I laughed. Zoé cried. I told her everything.

She shrugged. "You could 'blow the whistle,' as they say. Tell Lady Borden. The world will know within an hour. Force his hand."

"I've thought of that."

"You want out?"

"Yes."

Ottawa

Sunday, January 13, 1918

"What are we going to do?"

"As soon as my health is restored, and *Industry and Humanity* has been published, and I have found something in the way of work, and cleared off the debts, we should be able to clear the slate, make a fresh. . . ."

"We could get an annulment."

"Don't be a fool."

"Why not?"

"Everyone would know."

"So?"

"We'd both be ruined."

"We'd be free."

"It would destroy my political career."

"You don't have a political career, at the moment."

"Are you prepared then to drag your name through the mud, to make yourself the subject of filthy jokes and scurrilous gossip, the laughing-stock of Ottawa, like the Gaults?"

"No."

Ottawa

Wednesday, February 6, 1918

Willie's mother's birthday. Her rocking chair is by the fire, with her shawl and lace collar on it, the sitting room is full of flowers. Willie got upset that some people didn't send flowers this year, as they had last, and I said maybe they were saving them for Mother's Day, and he seemed content. A little sparrow came and huddled on the window ledge for a while and Willie wondered if that might be Mother's spirit, but I said I thought she would be a more brilliant bird, a canary, perhaps, but he preferred a robin. We talked about birds for a long time and played Parsifal on the Victrola. He pesters me mercilessly for details of her last moments, what she said, how she looked, and won't accept the fact that she died in her sleep. So I have invented a whole death-bed scene, with dialogue, worthy of Little Nell, and it seems to comfort him. He doesn't notice that I forget some details from telling to telling, or add others, or else he doesn't care.

I think he is quite mad. He conceals it in public, dresses in an ordinary suit, does all the proper things, talks quite reasonably about commonplaces, lunches at the Rideau Club, argues about politics, goes through all the boring rituals of polite society so perfectly that polite society considers him boring. Perhaps we are all mad.

Tonight we are to attend a seance. It's at the Chateau, a Mr. Benjamin from Toronto. He's been here a week and caused a sensation by raising the spirits of soldiers killed in the war. Of course everyone is reading *Raymond*, Conan Doyle's book about his son, and it is hard to believe that the creator of Sherlock Holmes would be duped. Flora speaks very highly of him, and she knows almost all the mediums in Canada. He has promised to "materialize" Willie's mother. Apparently this is very difficult, and he's charging $200. Mrs. Benjamin came this afternoon to collect the money. She likes to meet the sitters in advance, she said, so she can pass their "psychic vibrations" on to Mr. Benjamin. She was a shabby little woman in a purple coat and a peculiar hat, with feathers sticking up all over, and an old wolfskin around her neck with the tail hanging down and a matching muff with the wolf's head still attached, eyes and all, and jaws that opened and shut with a crunching sound.

"Don't tell anyone, dear," she said, "but it's German. One never need be afraid alone on the streets with a muff like this."

She took a great interest in all the pictures, picking each one up and holding it between her palms, eyes closed, head back, to get the "vibrations," then replacing it on the table, exclaiming "Beautiful! Beautiful! Such a beautiful soul! Oh I am sure we shall have great success, Mr. King! Great success!" until Willie was simply hopping with delight. He showed her all his mother's things, her clothes, still in the closet, her reading glasses on the night-table, her wedding ring and the lock of her hair. He even allowed her to sit in Mother's rocking chair. She sat down gingerly and closed her eyes rocking slowly at first, then faster and faster.

"Your mother is near, Mr. King. Very near. She is in this room. I feel her spirit close to us. I see a light, a beautiful, radiant light. She wants to speak to you. She will come tonight. She will come."

Willie knelt and Mrs. Benjamin placed her hands on his head.

"Your mother had a favorite hymn, that she sang with you, before she died. . . ."

"*Jesus Loves Me.*"

"Yes. *Jesus Loves Me*. Let's sing it together."
"Jeeesuuus loves me,
This I know,
For the Bible tells me so...."
I checked carefully after she left to see if anything had been taken, but everything was exactly in its place.
I'd rather not go.

Ottawa
Thursday, February 7, 1917

There were three other people there, an older couple, Mr. and Mrs. Patteson, who lost their little girl, Rose, years and years ago, and a Mrs. Ross, a pretty woman, heavily made-up, whose husband was killed in the war. She asked me if I had lost someone and what regiment he was with, but Willie came up so I let it drop. She suggested we have tea and a chat later but it's the last thing in the world I want to do.

Mr. Benjamin was much younger than I'd expected, dark, sallow, with penetrating brown eyes and very dirty fingernails. He spoke very softly, so you could hardly catch what he said, and moved as if he were in a trance. The room was dark, just a small oil lamp in the middle of a round table, and we all sat around, our hands overlapping on the tabletop, Mrs. Ross and I on either side of Mr. Benjamin, then Mrs. Benjamin next to Mrs. Ross, then Mr. Patteson, Willie and Mrs. Patteson. We sat in silence for a long time, Mr. Benjamin with his head bowed on the table, then he blew out the lamp and began shouting an invocation to the spirits. It was absolutely pitch dark. Nothing happened at first. I don't know if it was a minute or ten minutes, then the room seemed to be filled with a strange vibration, a crackling in the air, so that my hair stood up at the roots and my whole body tingled, as if an electric current was rippling down my spine, and then I felt a rush of wind, a strong gust, and Mr. Benjamin's chanting got much louder, and then something wispy passed across my face so I almost screamed, and Mr. Benjamin cried out: "The spirits are here! Welcome! Welcome!" and Mrs. Patteson cried out "Rose? Are you here, Rose?" and then Mr. Benjamin cried "Let us sing!" and we all started in on "What a friend we have in Jesus" at the tops of our lungs. Mr. Benjamin and Mrs. Patteson were rocking and moaning on either side of me. We were just underway when there was a strong smell of smoke, gunpowder, and Mrs. Ross cried out "Peter? Is that you?" and a strange voice answered "Aye."

"Are you happy, dear?" she said.

"I am happy," the voice said. "We are all happy here. Tell the others."

The voice didn't sound at all like Mr. Benjamin, much deeper, with a burr, and I was quite sure there was someone else in the room, an invisible presence. Mrs. Ross talked about friends who'd died, asking how they were, and each time Peter Ross said: "She is well. She sends her love." He spoke in a very formal, stilted way, not like real people, and kept saying "I am happy. Tell the others. There are many here with messages." He seemed so perfectly *real* that I felt I could reach out and touch him.

Rose came next, a woman's voice, not a child's, saying: "I am here, Mummy. I am always near." Rose seemed quite far away, behind Mr. Benjamin, and I was straining my eyes over his shoulder when Yikes! a translucent white face appeared floating in the darkness, a young woman's face, pretty, wrapped in a white shawl. The face seemed to fade in and out, brighter and dimmer, always fuzzy, and while Rose spoke, the lips never moved. I got impatient with Mrs. Patteson who chattered on and on about trivial family things while I was desperate to know more about Heaven, and were the streets really paved with gold, and what did you have to do to get there, and was there a Hell too, but it didn't seem polite to horn in.

Mr. Benjamin suddenly cried out: "Isabverl is here! Isabel wishes to speak!"

"Mother!" Willie cried.

"She needs help," said Mr. Benjamin. "She is asking us to give her strength. She has a hymn she wishes us to sing together, I can't quite make it out, she is getting weaker...."

"'Jesus Loves Me!'" Willie cried.

"Yes! She is nodding her head. She is coming back."

We all sang "Jesus Loves Me" at the tops of our lungs. During the third chorus there was a strong smell of gardenias and Mother's face appeared behind Mr. Benjamin's shoulder. She was in profile, facing left, the nose was unmistakable. Her head was wrapped up in something thick, white, like cotton batting, not transparent but bathed in a halo of light.

"I love you, Billy," she said. "God is love."

The voice was not hers, but an old woman's all the same, and the illusion was overwhelming.

"Are you happy, Mother?" Willie said.

"Yes. I am happy. We are all happy here. Father sends his love."

"And Little Belle?"

"Little Belle sends her love. Grandfather is here too. He says you fought the good fight in North York."

"Oh Mother, I'm so glad! Do you forgive me?"

"Yes, Billy. I am always with you."

Willie burst into tears, laughing and crying at the same time. Mother faded and Mrs. Benjamin turned on the lamp. Mr. Benjamin was slumped over the table. Mrs. Benjamin put her fingers to her lips and motioned us to leave quietly. "He lies like this for hours," she said. "He is quite exhausted."

The seance had lasted only thirty minutes.

Me: "Your mother's face looked like the Forster portrait."

Willie: "It was facing the other way."

Me: "Reversed."

Willie: "The portrait is hanging over the fireplace. Mother was *there*. I spoke to her."

Me: "Why would she materialize like a painting?"

Willie: "Mrs. Patteson explained it perfectly sensibly. Spirits do not materialize as themselves, only as representations, symbols, so to speak, so they can be easily identified. Her own daughter, for instance, appears not as a child, but as a young woman, the age she would be had she lived."

It's all very mysterious, especially my own message. I hadn't expected anything, since Mrs. Benjamin had paid no attention to my vibrations, but right after Rose disappeared Mr. Benjamin suddenly started groaning and writhing and all of a sudden the table lifted right up! Whoosh!

"There is a strong spirit here," he said, "an angry spirit, a spirit that knows no rest. There has been trouble, yes, violence. This man has been murdered!"

The table started rocking violently from side to side.

"Push!" cried Mr. Benjamin. "Hold the spirit down!"

We all pushed and the table slowly came back to the floor.

Mr. Benjamin grasped my hand like a vise.

"The spirit has a message, a life-and-death message, for someone in this room. He is smiling. He is saying 'I'm glad you have come, Cookee.'"

I nearly fell out of my chair.

"That's you!" Willie cried.

"Who is it?" I said, shaking like a leaf.

There was a long silence, with the tingling vibrations, and a strong smell of kerosene as if the lamp had been tipped over.

"Was it Mum, Papa?" I found myself saying.

"No."

"Who?"

Silence.

That was all. It doesn't make sense. But if it's a fraud, how did he know my name?

The Roxborough
Sunday, March 3, 1918

Had the Benjamins for tea. They are leaving for Montreal "to carry the happy news of eternal life." Willie has been to five seances. Mother has materialized four times, each time in a different pose. They have had long talks. He says he has asked intimate questions about Kingsmere, the family, that no stranger could possibly guess, and she's been right every time. I've never seen him so happy. He is actually finishing his book! Mother's "spirit" is urging him on. McGregor is typing it up, poor fellow. I am checking for errors. I find it difficult to follow. It reads more like one of Dr. Herridge's sermons than a book about industrial war. I don't see how Faith is going to raise wages. Am I a Bolshevik after all?

Ottawa
Saturday, March 23, 1918

Talbot's birthday. Received a photograph of the cemetery from his mother, a forest of crosses, white, like the birch wood at Montebello.

26 Besserer St.
Victoria Day, 1918

Bought Flora's house for $2,000, an investment, as Willie would say. Even the oysters he eats by the dozen are an "investment in health." Flora has bought an old tourist lodge in the middle of nowhere. She expects to make enough from summer guests to live there year round. She tried to persuade me to come but I'm not going to be anybody's cook and bottlewasher, especially not the Whitman Club's! I've had it with hocus-pocus. Willie's mother is more of a nuisance dead than alive. He and I are considered engaged, although there's no talk of a wedding, thank God.

26 Besserer St.
Saturday, May 25, 1918

Cleaned out the womb today. Burned all the red flannel. The attic will make a wonderful studio once I have a skylight put in. I'll make my bedroom into a darkroom and move down to the second floor. In the autumn I'll hire an assistant to do the framing, make prints, all the joe jobs that take so much time, and with people coming here it will save all the lugging of stuff around. I'll leave the attic perfectly empty, just a big, bare room with a single chair, and the camera, and sheets hanging like washing to reflect the light, and maybe Geordie in the corner to make people laugh so they're not all hysterical as if they're at the dentist. Everyone wants a "classic" portrait now, a close-up, in profile, against a plain white background, very austere, stunning if the girl looks like Princess Patricia but otherwise an agony of lighting and wounded vanity. Ottawa girls should only be photographed out of focus. Now there's an idea...!

Ottawa
Monday, May 27, 1918

I am to be a war photographer after all. I have been commissioned to photograph the plastic surgery cases at Mrs. Fleck's convalescent hospital. Most of them have been burned in aeroplane crashes and hideously disfig- ured. "It takes time to build a new face," said the doctor. "There is no reason why these men can't be discharged during treatment but they refuse to leave, or go out only with their heads swathed in bandages. No one comes to visit them. I thought that by having their portraits taken they might become accustomed to being *looked* at, which will inevitably happen, even after we've done our best for them. They can't hide in there forever. We need the beds."

We went over this afternoon. The patients were all out on the lawn, each one in pyjamas and an electric-blue Freiman's dressing gown, sitting in a semi-circle staring idly out over the Canal. They covered their heads with shawls or put their hands in front of their faces when they saw me, peeking out between their fingers like a row of oysters, all except one, a squat, square man who stared at me defiantly. He had no left ear and only half a head covered by a steel plate that glittered in the sun. His name is Skull. "If you've come here lookin' for a husband you must be pretty hard up!" he called out. The oysters shook with laughter. The doctor explained that I would take their pictures for the medical records, before discharge, so the progress of their treatment could be documented. There was dead silence. Then Skull turned on his heel and stalked back to the house and all the oysters rose as one and followed, two by two, in perfect step.

"I have never in all my life encountered such a rude, ungrateful group of men," declared Mrs. Fleck. "We have done everything for them, *everything*. The May Court spent hours this winter, *hours* teaching them to weave baskets, and decorate biscuit tins, and they made the prettiest little lampshades out of chintz, and they could have brought in quite a bit of money at the Red Cross bazaar but the night before do you know what they did, do you *know*, they put everything in a pile on the lawn and burned it! *Burned* it! Well the poor girls were simply heart-broken, so insulted! They simply *wept* with rage. And do you know what those soldiers did? They laughed! Well, those girls have not been back since, nor any others I can assure you. The language in this house is not fit for female ears, I warn you. I have informed the medical staff I want those men out of here, *out*, by the end of June, when we leave for Murray Bay, and as far as I am concerned they can be dumped on the street. Malingerers that's all they are, cowards, freeloaders, and I'll tell you quite bluntly that they ought to be shot."

"The wounded are no longer fashionable," the doctor said later, "especially the unpleasant ones. The novelty appears to have worn off. Perhaps people are worn out. They used to be in great demand at recruiting meetings, you know, and we'd get them up there on the stage, and sometimes they'd make a little speech, and everyone would sing and cheer them on, and they'd come back just on top of the world, but now, with conscription. . . ."

I set my camera up in the sunroom, on a tripod. I waited an hour but nobody volunteered. I left the camera where it was. It's a brand new folding Kodak portrait camera but it's worth the risk. Who can resist it?

Ottawa
Friday, June 14, 1918

Not much progress. They grin and leer at me now but it's hard to know if they're making faces or being friendly. They're certainly trying to get rid of me. They sing all the marching songs with dirty words. It's an improvement. I always hated "Tipperary" and Skull's version of "Abide With Me" is very funny. He told me to bugger off today and swore a blue streak but I waited until he'd run out, then gave him a stream of my best, English and French, Protestant and Papist, Irish, Scotch and Ottawa Valley, plus a few I learned from the Duke of Connaught. Two of the men applauded. That's something. Skull's the boss, the commanding officer, although he's only a Sergeant, Sgt. Mahoney. They're organized into a kind of platoon, with ranks and duties and nicknames, "Red Baron" for Tim, whose face is red and crinkled like a lobster, and "Cy" for Hal, a blond boy from Napanee who has only one eye and not much face. They do everything together, although they don't do much except eat and gamble and tell stories. They never talk about fighting, only about silly things, goofs that officers made, or girls they met in Piccadilly, or flea races on hot tin plates, and they laugh every time, even though they must have heard the story a hundred times before.

Me: "They won't even talk to me."
Annie: "Of course not. They're on strike."
Me: "But they're just sitting there."
Annie: "It's a sit-down strike. Peaceful occupation. Very effective."
I have to admit it is a nice place to live.

Ottawa
Sunday, June 16, 1918

Willie came with me today. I tried to persuade him not to, afraid there'd be a scene, but he insisted, and everything turned out wonderfully. He shook hands all around, very easy and relaxed, and then sat right down beside Skull and asked about his mother! You should have seen the bugger's face! Well, before long Skull was rummaging in his pocket for a letter from home, and telling all about his brothers on the farm, and his married sister in Pembroke, and then the others started chiming in about their families and pulling out letters and snapshots and passing them around. We had tea, and chocolates that Willie had brought, and he sat very attentively and listened to their grievances, and promised he'd speak to Sir Wilfrid about compensation, and finding work, and perhaps Laurier might drop by himself. Well, that created a stir! Skull told the doctor that Willie was the first politician to visit them.

I have never seen Willie in his "politician's suit" before, so calm, so gracious, so sensitive, a different man. I could hardly believe it. He was excited afterwards. "The plight of the returned man, *that* will be the great issue after the war!" he cried. "Reconstruction! Rehabilitation! A splendid opportunity! A noble platform!"

Ottawa
Wednesday, June 19, 1918

Sir Wilfrid and Lady Laurier visited today, Laurier in silk hat and tails, Zoé all in grey, streaming scarves like a moulting pigeon, the men at attention, faces uncovered. Skull explained the routine of the establishment in the most officious detail, Mrs. Fleck looked like Medea at the thought of a Grit under her roof. Laurier said little, but listened carefully, his head cocked to his good ear, and made a little speech promising to raise the matter of disabled pensions at the next session of Parliament.

"If any of you is discharged without work, or without a decent pension," he said, "I will make myself personally responsible for your welfare."

He was cheered to the rafters.

Cy touched my arm as we were leaving. "She's blind, isn't she?" he said.

Ottawa
Thursday, June 20, 1918

Cy showed me a photograph of himself taken three years ago, before he joined up, a fair, smiling boy in a hockey jersey, holding a stick. "I was just a kid then," he said. "I'm nearly twenty now."

When the others marched out to sit in the sun he stayed behind, pretending to be asleep, then came over and looked at the camera. I showed him how it worked and let him look through the viewfinder.

"It has only one eye, doesn't it?"

"That's why photographs look different from the way we see."

"Except me."

"Yes."

Ottawa
Friday, June 21, 1918

When I arrived this afternoon Cy was dressed in his kilt and bonnet and waiting on the chair in the sunroom.

"I want to go home," he said.

He shook, and kept closing his eye, but finally Skull yelled "Cheese!" and I got it.

Ottawa
Monday, June 24, 1918

A line-up today, all in uniform. Big crowd of spectators. Whistling, catcalls, insults. We are having "a freak show" on Sunday, very exclusive, very private. Cy is helping me print. A.Y. Jackson, the war artist, will be the judge and the prize is a copy of *The Secret of Heroism*. Sir Wilfrid and Lady Laurier will be the guests of honour.

"But I can't see a damn t'ing!" Zoé said.

"That's okay."

15

King Edward Hotel, Toronto
Sunday, August 25, 1918

Went to see Mum. I couldn't believe it when the streetcar conductor pointed
to this enormous building with a dome. Imagine a looney bin looking like St.
Paul's! The rotunda seemed as big as Union Station and the gibberings of the
patients shuffling around echoed off the walls in the spookiest way. The
patients were all dressed alike in shapeless grey sacks. The women's hair had
been cut short, the men's heads shaved. The matron said Mum was outside
with her Bible class.

She was sitting under a tree with a group of patients gathered about her on
the lawn, silent and still as monks, their bodies contorted into peculiar
positions. Mum was in white, a nurse's uniform, with a little white cap with a
red cross on it, and her Bible was open in her lap. She closed it as I came across
the grass, threw her arms wide, and the familiar lilt of "Amazing Grace"
drifted towards me, Mum's strong contralto booming high over the others.
Suddenly one of the monks leaped up, threw up his arms and pitched
backwards on to the grass, back arched, stiff, shrieking, thrashing like a fish,
beating the ground with his arms and crying out in a voice shrill with fear.
Some of the others glanced at him and groaned but did not change position
and continued to sing as if nothing at all were happening.

"...'tis grace hath brought me safe thus far,
And grace will leeead me hoooommmme."

Two orderlies bundled the man into a straightjacket and carried him away
into the cathedral.

"Hello, Mum."

"I've been expecting you. Your father said you were coming."

"Papa?"

"He comes quite often. And General Gordon too, of course. Such an interesting man. Then Miss Nightingale is with me at night. I couldn't manage without her. Who is the young man with you?"

I looked around.

"I don't see anyone, Mum."

"Oh, too bad. He's quite clear. He's wearing a striped jersey. He says he's lost his glasses."

"Jesus."

"Oh, our Lord would never wear a jersey!"

She seemed very small. Her hair had turned quite white and her face was white too, translucent, illuminated by the sunlight on her white dress.

"Are you happy here, Mum?"

"Oh yes! Mind you it's very hard work. Not a moment's rest. But it's my duty to stay. They'd quite go to pieces without me."

A young man came hesitantly towards us leaning on a cane, his right leg stiff and his body wrenched painfully to one side.

"Here's Freddy!" Mum said. "I must go. I have a most important message from his father."

"Your mother has become more or less a member of the staff," said Dr. Livingstone, the psychiatrist. "She has been night supervisor on the shell-shock ward for two years. Few trained nurses can last that long. She has an unusual rapport with the other patients. Of course she attributes it to the Lord Jesus but my assessment is that she has natural talent as a medium."

"Mum?"

"She believes that she died and went to Heaven and has been sent back to earth with 'messages' from various 'spirits' with whom she is in continual contact. It is a pentecostal version of the Benjamin technique, although her success has been greater...."

"You mean they've been *here*? The Benjamins?"

"Oh yes, we use mediums fairly often, although I'd appreciate it if you didn't mention it. Do you know them?"

"Oh yes, Mrs. Benjamin is a strange old duck...."

"Old? I shouldn't think so. I found her most attractive, rather theatrical perhaps, but then she trained as an actress in Great Britain. They're all show people of course...."

"*Actors*?"

"Illusionists, magicians if you like. Spiritualism is simply an illusion. I'm not sure how they do it, one of those tricks of the trade they're secretive about. But if you observe closely you'll see that the 'spirit' does very little speaking and the 'sitter' a great deal. It's a form of psychological projection. The sitter, or patient, thinks he is conversing with someone outside himself, but he is really talking to his own psyche, trying to argue out some inner anxiety. It's very useful in our line of medicine since 'shell shock' patients are nothing more than extreme hysterics, taking refuge, very logically I may say, in paralysis or deafness or fits, from which it becomes difficult to dislodge them after the immediate danger has past. Freudian psychoanalysis is the accepted method, but psychiatrists are scarce and the treatment very time-consuming. Spiritualism is cheap and effective, at least as a start. Your mother has had astonishing success with several cases I would have believed hopeless had I not see the cure occur. If she were a Roman Catholic, I would say she was a saint."

"Who is curing her?"

"She may cure herself, that's really all that happens in the long run with anyone. I'd be disappointed, of course. We'd really find it hard to replace her."

An old woman was sitting very quietly by the door as I came out. She leaped up and stood in front of me, her face eager.

"Is Rex here? Has he come?"

"No...I'm sorry. . . ."

"He'll be here soon then. We're going to run away together, you know, to New York, start a fresh life. . . ."

"A clean slate?"

"Why yes! Those were his exact words! Dear Rex! He said the summertime, when the doctor had gone. I'm all packed. . . ."

"I'll tell him. He's very busy."

"Yes, such a brilliant man! Thank you! He'll come soon. He loves me, you know. He told me so."

Ottawa
Sunday, August 26, 1918

Me: "You should visit Mrs. Herridge."
Willie: "Marjorie is...deranged."
Me: "Maybe that's why you should visit her."
Willie: "How was your mother?"
Me: "Wonderful. The Benjamins have helped her."
Willie: "The *Benjamins*?"
Me: "Yes. The woman we know as Mrs. Ross is really Mrs. Benjamin. I figured it out on the train. The old woman is probably his mother. They sit together around the table so one of them is free to get up in the dark and work the projector."

Willie: "Have you lost your wits?"

Me: "Mr. Benjamin has dirty fingernails...."

Willie: "So do you, when you're working...."

Me: "...and one of the smells, besides the gun smoke and gardenias, was developer fluid...."

Willie: "...but *how*?"

Me: "The muff! Gnash, gnash, click, click. I must tell Mrs. Freiman."

Willie: "You are perverse. I don't believe a word of it!"

Me: "That's okay. Mum's psychiatrist says it's very therapeutic. Faith vs. Fear. You'll be fine. Have you ever heard of someone called Freud?"

16

John D. Rockefeller Jr.'s ears are cold. His fingers are cold. His toes are cold. His balls, if he dares to think about them, are cold. He hunches against the piercing wind and stamps his feet impatiently in the snow. Behind him his chief mining engineer, his assistant mining engineer, his accountant, his assistant accountant, his secretary, his personal physician and his Pinkerton bodyguard all stamp their feet impatiently in the snow.

"Cold, eh?" says Jack Coolican.

Junior gives him a wintery smile.

"It'll be warmer down the hole. Just wait, Mr. Rockerfeller, it'll knock your eye out."

Junior shows his teeth again. Don't Canucks know anything? Peasants. Savages. The whole Lakeshore Mine is nothing more than a little hole in the ground, less than five hundred feet deep, and they dug the whole thing by hand! He should have known better, traipsing up here in the dead of winter, it's just a swindle, like those stocks he got stung on years ago, everyone knows gold mines are disastrous investments, only one in a million pays off, he'll fire his engineer tonight. It was *his* fault, going overboard on those ore samples Oakes sent down, fool's gold, he should never have come himself, wouldn't have except his physician said the cold would kill the influenza germs and it would be safer than New York. But when they stopped in North Bay, in the middle of absolutely nowhere, he'd seen a whole pile of coffins on the station platform. Junior would have turned around right then except it would have meant having his private car uncoupled, and he would have been stuck there among the coffins until the next train came, so he'd pressed on, but there were coffins at Swastika too, and half the miners at Lakeshore were quarantined in the bunkhouse.

Junior had decided to visit Canada incognito, to avoid curiosity on Wall Street, and had run up an enormous bill outfitting the Standard Oil advisors as a party of American moose hunters from Harry Oakes' home town, figuring that makinaws and leather boots would also blend in ideally with the local population of Kirkland Lake and avoid the attention he so much dreaded. But Junior had not figured on the impact his stainless steel railway coach would make on the natives of Swastika (pop. 306), and had failed to realize that his crisp plaid shirt from Abercrombie and Fitch would stand out in the wilderness like a tulip in a cabbage patch, summoning the residents of Kirkland Lake (pop. 76) to follow the richest man in the world wherever he went.

There wasn't far to go in Kirkland Lake. A few log huts, some tarpaper shacks, the filthiest Chinese restaurant he'd ever been in (germs *everywhere*), packs of dogs snapping at his heels, mountains of tin cans, outhouses (Junior had, for the first time since Ludlow, used an outhouse, germs and all, because the only alternative was to poop in public), Red Indians with no feathers and not a single Mounted Policeman to be seen — only Chinks and bohunks, foreigners of all kinds, worse than Colorado, and freaks, cripples who work at the Rainbow Mine under a foreman with a steel head they call Skull, more sullen than Roza, the crazed cook, wrapped in a Union Jack and shrieking "Yankee Go Home!" Dear God, Junior had thought, I'd love to.

"Here she comes!" cries Jack, blowing his nose into his fingers and flinging the snot to the ground before grabbing the hoist as it rattles to the surface of the mine shaft. Harry Oakes and Rockefeller's chief geologist get off.

"I think you should go down, sir," says the geologist.

Junior does not like holes. He licks his lips and steps reluctantly into the cage with Oakes. When he opens his eyes at the bottom he is dazzled by the light from their lanterns reflected off the shards of quartz. Why, it's not like a coal mine at all! It's light, clean, the stone pale pink and hard, glittering in places like diamonds. At the end of a long walk down a narrow tunnel, Oakes suddenly stops and stands aside, holding his lantern high.

"Ooooooh," says Junior. "G-g-goodness!"

The gold vein runs from floor to ceiling, a foot wide at the centre, gleaming like the stairway to Heaven. Harry scrapes a leaf off with his penknife.

"Souvenir," says Harry, holding it out.

Junior takes it gingerly, rubs it, smooth, soft, like Abby's, Abby's skin.

"I've never actually seen g-g-gold before, you know," he says, "not pure g-g-g-gold."

"It gits t'ya," says Harry.

Junior continues to rub the flake of gold long after the train pulls out for Toronto. He can buy 49 per cent of both mines for a little over $100,000, not much more than he's invested in Mr. King over the years, including expenses, and that was money badly spent, wasn't it, that frightful book, nothing but a Bolshevik tract! He'd considered having the whole print run bought up and burned, but his press agent, Mr. Lee, had warned that might create a bad image if it got out. So he'd contented himself with putting the word about in the right circles, Harvard, the Foundation, the New York *Times*, to make sure the book wasn't talked up in any way, pointing out that while he had the utmost respect for Mr. King's intelligence, he was a rather woolly-headed intellectual and a foreigner besides, quite out-of-touch with American ways, with a somewhat unstable political background, an idealist, unable even to hold his seat in the Canadian government. Fortunately the approaching armistice in Europe has distracted attention from industrial problems, and even Junior's most virulent enemies among the press have failed to pay much attention to *Industry and Humanity*, or to the windfall profits accumulated by Standard Oil during the eighteen months America has been at war. What better place to bury some of those profits than in a hole in Canada? And what better bet, when the war debts are called, than gold?

Junior is annoyed when Jack bursts into his private car at North Bay and plunks himself down in the next armchair.

"Have we got a deal, Mr. Rockerfeller?"

"You will be a m-m-millionaire," says Junior, showing his teeth.

"Yeah? I could use some cold cash."

Junior hands him a $100 bill.

"It's a deal, Mr. Coolican."

Junior had hoped Jack would go away, but he sits back and takes out a cigar, spitting the end into a corner of the car. Junior ponders with distaste the mystery of a Divine Providence that permits a crude, illiterate, backwoods Canuck to rub shoulders with John D. Rockefeller Jr. simply by picking up a handful of moss. Can they all be so rude, so simple, so lacking in a sense of place? Oakes at least is a Yankee like himself, an educated man, fine family, somewhat rough in manner from years in the wilderness, but nevertheless sound, mature, not soft on labour.

"Do you by any chance know Mr. Mackenzie K-K-King?" asks John D. Rockefeller Jr.

"Yeah," Jack winks, lighting his cigar with the $100 bill, "met him once or twice. Not my type."

"Do you agree with Mr. King's political views?" Junior coughs.

"Never knew he had no views, none that I can figure anyways. Least he ain't featherin' his nest at the country's expense like the rest of them buggers."

Only at mine, Junior says to himself bitterly.

"And what do you think of his political prospects?"

"Oh, he'll be prime minister soon. Everybody says so."

Junior sits up straight.

"W-w-why?"

"Who else is there?"

John D. Rockefeller Jr. pours two shots of his very best old brandy. He gets his secretary out of bed and tells him to inform the conductor they will not be crossing via Niagara, as planned, but at Ogdensburg, with a stop at Ottawa. He has been hasty. Canucks are a peculiar people, foreigners, not like Americans at all, so who better to advise him on labour problems at Kirkland Lake than his peculiar foreign friend, William Lyon Mackenzie King?

Junior opens his little notebook.

"Prevention," he writes with his silver pencil and underlines it twice.

Chateau Laurier, Ottawa; Saturday, November 9, 1918

"You got one of those royal rooms?"

"Pardon?"

"You know, the place where the King stays if he comes here, the nobs."

"We have a Vice-Regal suite, if that's what you have in mind."

"Yeah, I'll take it."

"I'm sorry, sir, it's locked...."

"Somebody stayin' there?"

"No...."

"I'll take it then, couple nights."

"It's thirty dollars a night, sir."

"Okay."

"In advance."

"Mr. John D. Rockerfeller Jr. does not pay in advance."

"Mr. Rockefeller?"

"Is here, in Ottawa, just arrived at the station. Check it out if you like. I'm a business associate of Mr. Rockerfeller's. Here's his card."

"Yes, sir! Right this way, sir!"

Jack is dismayed to find that the Vice-Regal suite of the Chateau Laurier is furnished exactly like a classy but not too clean Montreal brothel. Homey enough, but lonely without the girls. He telephones Lily at the studio. No answer. Shit. He's got to tell *somebody* the good news. He runs a scalding bath and soaks for half an hour. He hasn't had a bath since when, freeze-up, six weeks? You could grow potatoes in the ring around the tub. The bellhop brings up flowers and a mountain of fresh fruit.

"Is Mr. Rockefeller expected soon?" he asks.

"Yeah. But no fuss, understand. He's travellin' in disguise."

Jack has a haircut and shave in the Chateau barbershop. He's the only customer. The place is spooky. Even the Grill is closed.

He stops by the studio on his way to Ogilvy's department store but it's shut up tight. Funny, Cy's always there, especially on Saturdays, but then a lot of shops are closed, not many people around. He buys two suits at Ogilvy's, one slate grey, with a matching fedora, the other navy with a matching stetson, a dozen hand-stitched shirts, two pairs of shoes, ties, socks, vests and an overcoat. The bills comes to just under $500. He wears the slate grey. The clerk wraps up the rest.

"Send it over to the Shadow," Jack says, "care of Mr. Rockerfeller, Vice-Regal Suite."

"Yes, sir!"

He telephones the Minister of Railways to get an appointment about the spur line into Kirkland Lake. "I'm sorry," the secretary says, "the minister is not receiving. It's the influenza."

"Fuck the influenza!" says Jack. "I need a railway!"

"Click," says the telephone.

Goddamn country, some asshole throws up and it comes to a stop. Not that it goes much as the best of times.

Jack wanders down Elgin to Sparks Street. Theatres closed. Restaurants closed. Goddamn bars still closed. What the hell are healthy people supposed to do? Christ, he's a millionaire and he's got nowhere to spend it!

He finds a poker game in the back room at the Russell but his mind's not on it and he loses his stake on the third hand. Fuck it. He goes back out, spoiling for a fight, but there isn't even anyone to fight. You could shoot a cannon down Sparks Street and not hit a soul. Saturday night in the big city. Even the dance halls are closed. Shit. The tolling of the church bells is getting on his nerves.

He goes back to Besserer and bangs on Lily's door. Nothing. He rattles the knob. Hey, it's open. Half way up the stairs he hears voices. Christ, what the hell is she up to? He stands on the landing, listening. Women's voices. Angry. Crying. Some sort of argument? Christ, the house is cold. He tiptoes up.

Lily is huddled under a blanket on the bed, alone. The room reeks of puke. Piss. Oh, Christ. She stares at him, blind, babbling, her head and arms jerking compulsively as he drags her out of the stinking sheets and wraps her in her sealskin coat. Christ, she's hot as a live coal. He carries her to the sofa and drags it in front of the fireplace. Thank God there's wood. He lights the fire, stokes the furnace, boils the kettle and pours half a cup of hot whisky down her throat. She stops shaking.

"Room service?"

"Yes, sir."

"What's the soup?"

"Beef broth, sir."

"Okay, I want a big pot of it, hot, and the best meal you've got, okay, roast beef with the works, apple pie, two Havanas."

"Your room, sir?"

"26 Besserer St. It's just around the corner. There's $10 in it for you. Charge the food to Mr. Rockerfeller's room."

"Yes, sir!"

The bellhop arrives in twenty minutes with a silver tureen of soup on a silver tray and enough roast beef to feed the Canadian Corps. Jack tips him with $10 from Lily's cash drawer. She'll never notice.

By midnight the room is hot as the pit of Hell. "I feel like a fucking Finn," Jack mutters but Lily is too absorbed in her private argument with death to even know he's there. He plays the gramophone, smokes, wipes her face, feeds her soup and whisky, stokes the fire, replaces the covers she tosses off, dozes, watches, waits and curses.

"Fucking flu, goddamn fucking flu, god fuck the goddamn flu."

7 a.m. The bellhop is back with breakfast. Lily is quieter but breathing hard, gasping, rasping, coughing, he can hear her all over the house as he paces, prowls, breathing in unison with her, tense for her sudden silence.

6 p.m. The bellhop is back with roast chicken and four Havanas.

"Are you all right, sir?"

"Yeah."

"The armistice is expected sir, tonight. If you keep a lamp on, it will blink. That's the signal."

"Yeah? Thanks."

Her head feels a little cooler. Maybe he's just imagining it. She takes almost a cup of soup.

He dozes off in the armchair, half-asleep, still listening. He wakes up with a start to the sound of the telephone. The lamp is flickering.

"The war is over!" says the operator. "God save the King!"

"Fuck the King," says Jack. It's a quarter to four and he can hear the automobile horns outside, and the muffled sound of people yelling, running, church bells clanging.

Lily is watching him, her sunken eyes clear and sharp.

"The bells have changed."

"The war's over."

"Did we win?"

"Yeah, I guess so."

"You look different, Jack. Are you dead?"

"Hell no! I'm rich!"

26 Besserer St.
Tuesday, November 12, 1918

"You killed Papa, didn't you?"
　"Who told you?"
　"Mum."
　"It was an accident."
　"A fight?"
　"Yeah."
　"Money?"
　"Yeah. What the hell's the use of hidin' it in the ground?"
　"You took it?"
　"Yeah. You know what I got? $150 in bills, $300 in tokens on the Booth
stores, and $1,000 in I.O.U.s."
　"Papa wasn't much of a businessman."
　"You gonna turn me in?"
　"No."
　"I didn't mean to. I got kind of souped up on Polack rotgut. What can I do?
Hang myself?"
　"God will forgive you, if she exists."
　"Fuck God."

The Roxborough,
November 13, 1918.

My Dear C.
It came as a great shock this morning to learn that you have been unwell,
but I am very much relieved to hear that you are over the worst. This dreadful
disease has taken a terrible toll. I have taken the precaution of confining
myself to my rooms as much as possible to avoid the spread of contagion. Had
others followed this course earlier, I believe the plague would have been
arrested before it had brought suffering to so many homes. McGregor is able
to go to the bank, the post office, etc. etc. so I have been able to make
substantial progress in mailing out *Industry and Humanity* to the Members of
the House of Commons and the Senate and to the senior members of the Civil
Service, as well as to influential members of the press and the academic
community. It has been a difficult chore, and an expense, amounting to over
500 copies in all, but I believe it will be a good investment in the long run to get
this book into the hands of people in a position to put its principles into action.
　I have also been taken up with an unexpected visit from a Most Influential
Friend who has come to Canada on a matter of the greatest significance to our

industrial development, a project which could mean *unparalleled opportunities* now that the war in Europe has ended. The nature of our discussions must remain secret but I am pleased to say that I have been able to put my old friend Constable Dempster into an interesting line of work with respect to the prevention of labour strife in some of the more remote parts of the Dominion.

I have asked Miss Purdy to stop by and offer whatever assistance she can. I am confident God will hear my prayers for your complete recovery.

Yours,

W.

26 Besserer St.

Nov. 14, 1918.

Dear Willie,

It was thoughtful of you to send Miss Purdy but I am quite strong now and she is needed more elsewhere.

Thank you for the champagne. It reminds me of the early days of the war.

Jack and I are leaving soon for Kirkland Lake. The fresh air will do me good. I long for the peace of the pine woods. There are only six women in the whole place, I understand, so I'm sure I can make myself useful. Lady Borden has promised me the post office.

I don't know when I'll be back.

Goodbye,

C.

26 Besserer St.
Monday, December 2, 1918

Our anniversary. Dinner with Willie. Oysters, poached salmon, chocolate mousse. I am still hungry! He talked about moving to New York in January, once the book is mailed, and the Christmas cards acknowledged, and the New Year's telegrams out of the way, and the Governor-General's levee is over. Mr. Rockefeller will take him on at Standard Oil, we'll make a fresh start, turn over a new leaf, a new year, a new life.

"A clean slate, Willie?"

"Yes, that's it, that's exactly it!"

He said he was pleased to see me laughing and bright again.

Willie is like a burr. The harder I try to shake him off, the tighter he clings. He wears me out.

I think he is glad to see me go.

26 Besserer St.
Friday, December 6, 1918

Jack came home tonight with a big bouquet of white roses all brown around the edges.

"Some asshole left them in the snow next to that cocksucker with a cape on Wellington Street. What a dumb thing to do."

"That's Bert."

"Who's Bert?"

"A sort of a dog."

"Yeah? You kiddin'? Pretty weird."

"I love you."

26 Besserer St.
Saturday, December 7, 1918

Paid Jack's bill at the Chateau. Jesus. Why do millionaires never have any *money*?

Club car, Timiskaming and Northern Ontario Railway,
     near North Bay, Ont.
Monday, December 16, 1918

Left Ottawa this morning.

Mrs. Freiman: "When you're making chicken soup, don't forget to put in the feet...."

Annie: "I've told the Wobblies to send a man up, he'll be there before spring...."

Willie: "...so upsetting, birthday tomorrow...poor Mother...all alone...Gethsemane...."

Laurier: "King is licking his lips, but I'm not dead yet...."

Zoé: "*Plus ça change, plus c'est la même chose.*"

E. Cora Hind: "I have asked Eaton's to send you a stout, cast-iron frying pan...."

Cy: "Please call me Hal."

Jack: "Listen, next year I'll *buy* the Canadiens."

Tired. Can't sleep. Wheels are going *clickety-scree, clickety-scree*, frost, very cold. I'm glad of my fur coat. It's an extravagance, but Mrs. Freiman got it for me at half-price, a New York import, the only chinchilla coat in Ottawa. "If you are rich," she said, "why dress poor?"

If I rest my hand on the window I can make a black hole, a pool among the white ferns, and watch us floating there, a bubble of light: red plush, mahogany, porter moving down the aisle, white coat, black face, Jack, black hair, white teeth, new, smiling, silver hand, Silver, Silver King, Queen, pale face, pale fur, smoke, strangers on a moving screen, far away, mysterious, John Barrymore and Theda Bara on the Orient Express, and outside, silence, snow, the dark pines marching quickly past, row on row, and in the sky. . . .

"Whatcha lookin' at?"

"Nothing."

Printed in Canada